Critical Acclaim for the Thrillers of Francine Mathews

BLOWN

P9-BBT-644

"Everything you might want in a summer read: high-velocity pacing, constant surprise, beautifully realized characters, refined style, and a look at modern espionage that only an insider could write."
—*Rocky Mountain News*

"Mathews spins out the suspense and it all works beautifully." —*Globe and Mail*

"Packed with no-holds-barred action."
—*Romantic Times Bookclub* (4 stars)

"An intricately woven tale of trust and betrayal with characters so real you feel that you know them as soon as they are introduced. This story could be straight from the pages of today's newspapers and is both riveting and terrifying. The suspense builds throughout, and the writing is superb. . . . This is a real page-turner!"
—*Mystery News*

"An exciting thriller that sends shivers up your spine."
—*Rendezvous*

THE SECRET AGENT

"A romantic thriller that whisks readers from the realms of Manhattan high finance to the ski slopes of Europe, to the jungles of Southeast Asia."
—*Wall Street Journal*

"Propelling us masterfully through half a century . . . *The Secret Agent* is at once a murder mystery, a touching love story, and a lavishly atmospheric journey."
—*Snooper*

"Ambitious and complex . . . Readers who surrender . . . will feel immensely rewarded."
—*Halifax (N.S.) Chronicle-Herald*

THE CUTOUT

"[A] high-action thriller that kicks off in a lively fashion . . . Carmichael is one of the toughest female secret agents we've seen in a long time." —*USA Today*

"[Her] presentation of espionage and CIA tactics is impeccable. . . . Fans of spy thrillers should be alerted to this promising debut." —*Publishers Weekly*

"Mathews's pacing is vigorous." —*People*

"[An] unexpected twist elevates *The Cutout* above and beyond the average, page-turning espionage novel."
—*Denver Post*

"A brilliant counterterrorist tale."
—*Midwest Book Review*

"Sequel please!" —*Christian Science Monitor*

By Francine Mathews

THE CUTOUT
THE SECRET AGENT

Coming soon in hardcover:
THE ALIBI CLUB

and

The Jane Austen Mystery Series by Francine Mathews
Writing as Stephanie Barron

JANE AND THE UNPLEASANTNESS AT SCARGRAVE MANOR
JANE AND THE MAN OF THE CLOTH
JANE AND THE WANDERING EYE
JANE AND THE GENIUS OF THE PLACE
JANE AND THE STILLROOM MAID
JANE AND THE PRISONER OF WOOL HOUSE
JANE AND THE GHOSTS OF NETLEY
JANE AND HIS LORDSHIP'S LEGACY

And coming soon in hardcover:
JANE AND THE BARQUE OF FRAILTY

BLOWN

FRANCINE MATHEWS

BANTAM BOOKS

BLOWN
A Bantam Book

PUBLISHING HISTORY
Bantam hardcover edition published May 2005
Bantam mass market edition / July 2006

Published by Bantam Dell
A Division of Random House, Inc.
New York, New York

This is a work of fiction. Names, characters, places, and incidents
either are the product of the author's imagination or are used
fictitiously. Any resemblance to actual persons, living or dead,
events, or locales is entirely coincidental.

Book design by Joseph Rutt

Library of Congress Catalog Card Number: 2004046208

Bantam Books and the rooster colophon are
registered trademarks of Random House, Inc.

ISBN-13: 978-0-553-58629-9
ISBN-10: 0-553-58629-7

Printed in the United States of America
Published simultaneously in Canada

www.bantamdell.com

OPM   10 9 8 7 6 5 4 3 2 1

Dedicated to Cathy Rodgers,
who always knew there was more to life
than simply analyzing it

The world looks different through a rifle scope.

—FBI Special Agent Christopher Whitcomb, *Cold Zero*

BLOWN

part one

one

On the day she was chosen for death, Dana Enfield rose early and made coffee for her husband in the hushed November dawn. She had slept badly the previous night, pummeling her pillow while George looked in on three obligatory parties and made excuses for his wife. The people standing around in little clusters against the apricot-colored walls of Georgetown and Kalorama, drinks in their hands, had joked with the Speaker of the House about this morning, about the press buildup and the unseasonably warm weather and where exactly he intended to stand. They had wished her luck, Dana thought as she listened to the drip of the coffee and the creak of old floorboards somewhere near Mallory's bedroom that might or might not mean that George was already awake—wished her luck and a great photo op, with the mental kickback inevitable among politicians. Half of them probably had money riding on the chance she'd never finish her race.

She sniffed the aroma of fresh coffee as she poured it into George's mug, knowing she couldn't take the caffeine's dehydration this early in the day but craving it all the same. Then—almost as an afterthought—she reached for the sharp metal rod she kept on the counter and slit the fleshy pad of her forefinger. A bead of blood ballooned at her fingertip. She waited for the digital count to flash on the screen of the insulin monitor: within normal range.

Comforting, she thought, to be offered that assurance at the start of every new day. She lifted George's mug to her lips and permitted herself a single sip.

The Marine Corps Marathon is fortunate in possessing a remarkable contingent of navy and civilian volunteers. Navy active duty and reserve units as well as dedicated doctors, athletic advisors, and Red Cross members from all over the country come together to ensure that our race is one of the safest in the nation . . .

Daniel Becker had scrolled through the official marathon Web site at least twenty times in the past few weeks, committing what was essential to memory. The Marines who organized the event each year called it "The People's Race," because nobody was forced to qualify to enter. It was planned and executed with the efficiency of a military operation; hundreds of Marines in field dress lined the race course, handing off cups of water and bananas and protein bars at two-mile intervals. They played music, clapped, cheered on their buddies, and were extraordinarily courteous to the less athletic hordes who invaded the event in increasing numbers. So many weekend warriors had entered the lists over the years, in fact, that it was impossible to accept them all. A lottery system capped the field at fifteen thousand runners.

When Daniel closed his eyes at night, he could see the course imprinted on his brain like a snake formed from fire. Between seventy and a hundred thousand people would line the 26.2-mile race as it wound from the Iwo Jima Memorial—the pride of Marine Corps history—straight through Crystal City, past the Pentagon, across Key Bridge into Georgetown and down to the John F. Kennedy Center for the Performing Arts. It kicked by the Lincoln and Jefferson monuments, the black wall commemorating Vietnam, the massive dome of the Capitol building, and back again to Virginia across the Fourteenth Street Bridge. The race had been delayed two weeks this year by the terrorist kidnapping and murder of the vice president; but with Sophie Payne's body returned now to Washington and her funeral scheduled for the following morning, the Marine Corps had received the green light to run. Like thousands of others, Daniel was ready.

He left Hillsboro, West Virginia, before dawn, and drove straight east through Maryland until he reached the District border. He'd shopped a downtown army-navy surplus place for the standard Marine private's uniform and peaked cap; he was wearing his black army boots and dog tags. Rebekah had clipped and shaved his brown hair so that the scalp shone through to the level of his ears. He'd strapped a plastic armband to his right bicep with a label that read RACE STAFF in big block capitals.

At five-thirty A.M., Hains Point in East Potomac Park was still open to vehicular traffic. He drove his truck to a picnic area and killed the engine, conscious of ghosts in the early morning darkness.

Once, when Dolf was maybe seven or eight, he'd driven into the city as dusk fell and parked right about here. Put Bekah and the boy in the pickup's flatbed and tucked a blanket around them. They'd lain there, watching the bellies of the great jets soar so close to their faces in takeoff and landing that they could almost have touched the blinking lights. The scream of turbo engines was deafening, the closest thing to war Daniel could imagine. Young Dolf was exhilarated—leaping up from his blanket as though he might catch a plane's wheel and sail off into the sky. He was always desperate to go someplace else, Daniel thought. Desperate to fly.

He was sitting here now because of that boy and his clipped wings, the wild animal joy of a child's face when he believes his time is never-ending. He was here for Dolf and the world that boy had lost.

Dana thrust her left foot against the base of the Iwo Jima Memorial and leaned forward to stretch her calf muscles. She'd been training for six months, gradually building her mileage each week despite the injuries that plagued her body, aware that more than just her own pride rode on the outcome of this race. She was the Speaker's wife, after all—the highly visible second wife of George Enfield, whom pundits called the next presidential hopeful—and Washington society columns followed her every move with thinly disguised malice. She was thirty-seven years old, and the diabetes she calibrated throughout the day had become as famous as her height or the clothing designers she patronized fearlessly for every official function. Dana was, by nature, a private person, but George's gradual rise to power in Congress had forced her to submit to the press's mania for detail. She found she could talk about her disease more easily than her soul. Two years ago, she'd become a spokeswoman for the Juvenile Diabetes Foundation.

She was a blunt advocate for stem-cell research, despite the dictates of her husband's party, which regarded every form of fetal experimentation with horror and reproach. She flew in children with diabetes from all over the country and led tours of Capitol Hill. Sponsored hearings that supported research and put the kids front and center. Today she was running in a JDF T-shirt imprinted with the faces of those children. She'd won the signatures of ten thousand people across the country: Each had pledged a dollar to the JDF for every mile she managed to run.

You're absolutely nuts, George had said heatedly when she began to train six months ago. *Do you know what you'll do for your precious cause if you collapse and die of insulin shock in front of a whole platoon of Marines?*

"They have medical stations," she'd replied patiently. "I'm carrying insulin in my fanny pack. I'll eat the oranges. The protein bars. You can meet me at certain points along the race with soda pop."

In the end, he'd agreed to do it, and not just for the publicity she'd begun to attract. He'd somehow managed to steal a few hours from each weekend to stand vigil during her training runs, amusing Mallory on her scooter and offering water to Mommy while she clocked

her miles. He'd told the press he believed in and supported his wife. He rubbed liniment on her legs without a word, his fingertips oddly gentle as they traced
her hardening quadriceps. He did ask repeatedly if she
was determined to go through with it—and she understood the fear that loomed in the back of his mind. He
was fifty-three years old. He'd already lost one woman
he loved to an untimely death. He would never tell
Dana to stay home in bed at six A.M. on race day, but
he could not pretend what he did not feel.

Because parking was impossible to find that morning, even for a Congressional limousine, they'd taken
the Metro to Arlington like any other marathon couple.
The only difference in their situation, Dana thought,
was the photographers who'd tracked them from the moment they'd left their front door in Kalorama, Mallory
swinging between them. She'd hoped that Sophie
Payne's funeral would deflect attention from what some
reporters were calling *Dana Enfield's Run for Her
Life*. But Payne was last week's story; she was today's.

"Let me pin your number to your shirt," George
said quietly in her ear. "It's eight-twenty. Ten minutes
to the start."

As he stabbed a pin into her chest by mistake, four
flashbulbs went off in Dana's eyes. She wondered fleet-
ingly if any of the reporters had trained enough to
keep up with her.

Daniel lay flat on his back under the cover of some
bushes, avoiding the curious and trying to quell his
own jitters. For the past hour and a half he'd watched

a group of Marines setting up the tables and parapher-
nalia for Water Point 11 and Aid Station 7, as their
signs proclaimed them; about ten guys, as best he
could judge from his position a quarter-mile distant.
They were spinning tunes and working together like a
well-oiled machine, their jacket sleeves rolled high on
the bicep. Confident in their sense of mission, as he
had been once.

A two-mile loop of the course skirted the river here
at Hains Point, just past the Jefferson Memorial. Planes
from Reagan International buzzed the landscape every
few seconds. The air was fresh and clear: Today's crowd
would be enormous. The runners who survived to
reach Daniel's water station would already have clocked
twenty miles. Some of them would be staggering, their
Achilles tendons on the point of tearing. Others would
be walking, too exhausted to run the last six miles.
Ahead of them would be the bridge—the Fourteenth
Street Bridge, where the wind off the Potomac would
force the runners backward as they struggled toward
the finish. Those who limped past Daniel would seize
his cups of water gladly, and toss the contents down
their throats.

The first batch—called the Elite Group, the highest-
seeded one hundred fifty athletes from all over the
world—would be clipping off five-minute miles as
though the pace were no more difficult than bouncing
a tennis ball. Most of them, Daniel knew, were Afri-
cans. It was natural they could beat the pants off the
rest—they'd been running from something most of
their lives. Somewhere behind them would be the six-
minute milers, the fleet-footed aspirants to Elite glory.

They'd reach his current position in the next ten to twenty minutes. After them would come the rest of the fifteen thousand weary runners, hour after hour: The eight-minute milers. The ten-minute milers. The people whose best pace four hours out from the start would be a walk or a crawl. The Marines gave them a total of seven hours to complete a course the winner would finish in a little over two; Daniel had to be ready for the long haul.

He glanced at his watch. Straight-up ten o'clock. He'd already unloaded the plastic drums filled with water from the back of his truck. The Marines were pouring a particular brand of purified stuff that was heavily promoted on the race Web site. Daniel had about two dozen bottles of Deer Creek Springs stacked up next to his coolers. He broke the plastic sleeve on a stack of paper cups as the front-runner approached the entry to East Potomac Park just off Independence Avenue, a skinny little black guy with a skull cropped close as a pitted peach.

Daniel turned the tap on the water cooler and watched the liquid spill into the cup. It was tinged faintly brown, as though it came from rusted pipes; he thrust the paper cupful into the outstretched hand of the front-runner.

"Lookin' good!" he cheered, clapping. "Lookin' strong! You *go,* guy."

The man tipped the water to his lips, crushed the cup in his hand, and ran on. Another marathoner was right behind him, reaching for Daniel's water.

•   •   •

Dana Enfield was a ten-minute miler. She kept three things in mind as she made her way toward Water Point 4 in Georgetown. She had to keep running. She could not twist her ankle or fall over from low blood sugar. And she had to see George and Mallory.

They'd told her they'd be waiting there, at mile marker 9. An hour and a half into the race, and the day as bright as a new-minted penny. She craned her head for a glimpse of her daughter's face.

The crowd was heavier here on the narrow sidewalks, thrust back against the old brick buildings by the police lines that marked off the spectators from the swollen river of runners trundling down M Street. For an anxious moment she thought she'd missed them, but then somebody called out *"Dana!"* and she saw George's black hair above his suede jacket, Mallory hoisted on his shoulders. Her daughter was waving a pennant with *JDF* printed on it in blood red letters, and her mouth was open in a thrilled shriek. *Her mom. Her mom was running in the race!*

Dana's throat tightened and she drew a deliberate breath, waving to the two people she loved most. The crowd carried her past. George was trotting through the spectators, bumping them with his elbows and Mallory's feet as they dangled from his shoulders, his eyes fixed on her face. Somewhere he'd lost the photographers. She couldn't tell from his expression whether she looked fine—or as though she was going to collapse.

"Aid Station five's at Rock Creek," he shouted, "if you need it. Two miles down! See you at the Reflecting Pool!"

She nodded, waved again, and then he was behind

her, slipping back like a stone in a rushing stream. The Reflecting Pool was mile marker 14 or 15—she couldn't recall—but it meant she'd be more than halfway. She wanted to push on—wanted to pick up her pace if possible—but she was aware of a singing sensation in her brain as though her entire body was about to lift off the pavement. A warning bell clanged in her mind. *Too much insulin*. It usually took her this way, with a giddy abandon that could end in shock. She should have eaten the orange at mile marker 6, but she hadn't wanted it then. Now she was past the Marines with their bananas.

She slowed her steps slightly and fumbled in her fanny pack for a protein bar and juice pack. Glad, for once, that George wasn't watching.

Four hours into the race, Daniel had lost count of the cups he'd poured and passed to runners of every description: women of fifty shuffling toward the finish; young guys with buff shoulders and sharp-prowed noses glistening with sweat; couples running together; aging men stumbling through their last course. Hains Point was the informal finish line for many of them who could manage twenty miles but no farther. After a bit of food and a visit to the aid station, some of them packed it in. Others sat for a bit on the grassy spaces of the park, which in Daniel's opinion had to be a mistake. Once you sat down on a marathon, you weren't likely to start running again.

At first he'd tried to be selective about which runners he handed his cups. He wanted to get the Marines who were competing in their tight shorts and singlets—and the foreigners and the coloreds and anybody who looked like they might be Jewish. But after a while, the pack was so thick he couldn't stop to judge individual faces. He was the first man in uniform any of them saw, and they expected him to be reaching toward them with water. Their hands were out long before they'd lumbered up to his position. The beauty of the seamless repetitive motion caught him in its rhythm: pour and hand; pour and hand; pour, pour, pour and hand. Some of the runners spat out the water as soon as it hit their tongues, crushing the cups in their fists and tossing them to the ground; but Daniel didn't mind.

And then, nearly four hours after the race's start, he saw a face he recognized.

A white rime of sweat had dried on her flushed cheeks, so that they were mottled as frosted strawberries. She was lean as a Thoroughbred and her long legs were shaking slightly as they moved toward him; a few strands of her dark hair, pulled back in a tight ponytail, dangled by her ear. *Dana Enfield. The Speaker's wife. Couldn't miss her face, it was plastered all over the newspapers and magazines, taking money from honest people's purses and giving it to doctors so's the abortion rate could rise and keep more of the Devil's Spawn alive. 'Fore you know it they'll be breeding babies for their stem cells and killing them at birth. A real factory operation for the Zoggites in power.*

She was looking at him, too, her dark eyes filled with something that might be pain. He held out a cup.

"Is there an aid station?" she gasped, "somewhere around here?"

He pointed toward the Marines who were working the crowd farther down the road.

"Thanks," she said.

And drank his dose to the dregs.

two

The beauty of that Sunday morning—the unseasonable blue of the arcing sky, the crisp breeze tugging at the few remaining leaves—was lost on Caroline Carmichael. There are no windows in the vaults of the CIA's New Headquarters Building, no view but computer screens and cubicle partitions and the unremitting whiteness of the walls. The fluorescent lights sang to themselves somewhere high over her head, beyond the register of human sound, and a screen saver wove through its monotony of variation. Otherwise the Counterterrorism Center was quiet and almost empty. Only her branch chief, Cuddy Wilmot, was there to witness her act of defiance, and he did so from the safety of his office doorway, leaning wordlessly against the jamb. She was cleaning out her desk.

It had been more than ten years since Caroline had received her security clearance, the badge with the bar code that admitted her to the CIA's compounds and covert installations, the months of training in weapons and tradecraft and raw survival that most intelligence analysts never used. She was moving slowly this morning, like a woman who hadn't slept in days, shifting the piles of useless paper into the brown paper burn bags with her left hand. Her right arm was wrapped in a sling. Seven days earlier she'd been shot in the shoulder while the vice president of the United States died a brutal death. Tomorrow she would attend the woman's funeral. And then—and then *what*, exactly? She had no answer for the question of how to live the rest of her life. It was enough to burn the evidence she'd accumulated thus far.

"You'll have to come back for your exit interviews," Cuddy told her. "There are papers to sign. Statements. Dare will want to see you." *Dare* being Darien Atwood, Director of Central Intelligence, Grand Poobah of the nation's spooks. *Exit interviews. Vows of silence.* They would take her badge. Caroline shrugged dismissively, and remembered too late that it was painful.

What was Cuddy feeling, exactly? Regret? Helplessness? Abandonment? He was standing over her as she sat cross-legged on the industrial carpet in her jeans, no makeup on and her blond hair tumbled over her forehead. They'd met this way before, in the off-hours of a hundred Sundays wasted in the secure vacuum of the Tempest-tested vault. They'd shared sleepless nights of hunting the terrorist hydra, a beast struck down in one place only to rise in another. They were the U.S. government's acknowledged authorities on a group called 30 April, neo-Nazi killers who'd kidnapped and murdered the vice president in Germany two weeks before. But she and Cuddy had been operating on partial information for years. Deliberately deceived by the one man they'd never thought to question—their boss.

Caroline understood now exactly how she'd been used, and how she'd allowed it to happen. Thirty April had become her obsession, and like all consuming desires, this one had blinded her. She and Cuddy were the ideal pawns: eager for justice, hungry for revenge, dedicated and single-minded with time to burn. Neither of them had any family to speak of. Their hobbies were long dead. But they had each other and that perfect understanding that springs up sometimes between inhabitants of the covert world. *A world gone black,* Caroline thought now, *where the only friend you trust is the one who remains a stranger.*

They'd been endlessly useful to their boss, Scottie Sorensen, the CIA's subtle Chief of Counterterrorism. Two personable, intelligent people in their late thirties who could render the most complex organizational diagram into policymaker's English. Scottie had backed them up and supported them to the hilt and unleashed them on the truth with a pocketful of lies. Cuddy looked prepared to continue telling those lies as long as necessary; Caroline had typed her resignation and e-mailed it to the chief an hour ago.

Cuddy was on duty today, in the pressed khakis and Oxford cloth shirt of a man who might be summoned at any moment to the White House Situation Room. The fact that he could continue to slave for a boss who'd wasted more than two years of his life was disturbing to Caroline; but then, Scottie Sorensen had not planted Cuddy smack in the middle of 30 April. Scottie had saved that plum—that honor—for Caroline's husband, Eric, the guy he'd loved like a son and thrown to the wolves without a backward glance.

Eric is dead, he'd told Caroline nearly three years ago when a jet went down off the coast of Turkey; *30 April blew up his plane.* That much was true, of course—only Eric hadn't been on MedAir 901. He'd been busy crafting a legend: a perfect backstopped identity for an undercover operation so secret only Scottie knew it existed. Eric had become a terrorist killer in the employ of Mlan Krucevic, head of the 30 April Organization, while Scottie ruthlessly buried him in the minds of the people he'd known and loved. Nobody—not Dare, not Cuddy, not the budget wonks who funded covert ops—had suspected Eric's survival. Not even Caroline, his widow.

For two and a half years, the yearning for vengeance got Caroline up in the morning and kept her from bed at night. When she learned her husband was still alive—and had actually helped kidnap the vice president of the United States—it was Eric she accused of betrayal, not Scottie. Eric, after all, had walked away from a woman and a marriage and a life; Eric had handed her a living death. Sent out to find him—to find Vice President Sophie Payne—Caroline had wavered between hatred and a desire to hurt him the way she'd been hurting for years.

Now she knew it was Scottie, not Eric, who'd pulled all their strings.

Our boy got out in time, Scottie said as she walked off Air Force Two behind Sophie Payne's casket. *He's 30 April's last man standing and you're never to speak his name out loud again, hear? Blow the whistle on me and I'll have you up in front of a Congressional investigation so fast your head will spin, lady. Believe that.*

"I've already talked to Dare," she told Cuddy now. "There's nothing left to say. She has everything Eric could give her about 30 April's networks worldwide. She knows all there is to know about Scottie. She won't fire him, Cuddy. He's too dangerous."

He glanced down at the document in his hands, as though it were a script. "And you won't work here as long as he does."

"Would you?"

Of course he would. Despite the fact that Eric was his best friend.

"This is your career, Caroline. Christ—it's your *life*. What're you going to do out there alone?"

A glimpse in her mind suddenly of water fragile as blue glass, palm fronds ruffled by a breeze. The beach was empty. Only she and the sun were on it. She said nothing, and went back to trashing her files.

three

He'd changed into jeans and a hunting jacket once he got back to the truck, tossing the fatigues in a Dumpster full of marathon trash. It was a seventeen-minute drive through the late afternoon traffic to Adams-Morgan, where he stopped only long enough to send a fax. He ate the lunch Bekah had packed for him while he drove north, through the populous suburbs of Prince George's County across the Maryland border. At the edge of Baltimore he picked up the interstate and turned southwest, toward Hillsboro. It all took maybe an hour. 5:33 by his digital watch.

No one had questioned him. Nobody had thought his solitary water station looked strange among the boisterous Marines. Nobody followed him home. Daniel Becker took the endurance of his luck as a Sign. The Leader stood at his right hand.

At Harpers Ferry, he eased the truck onto the verge of the road above the massive confluence of two rivers and pulled out his cell phone. Rebekah would want to know he was okay.

A horn blared as a huge sport utility vehicle—Japanese, Daniel noticed—shouldered past his pickup.

A woman with a blond head of hair solid as a military helmet commanded the wheel. She had four kids in the back and they rode in their raised seats like royalty borne on a palanquin. *Bitch*, Daniel thought wearily. *Mindin' my own bizness while you take over the entire highway with your foreign car costs more'n my whole trailer. You and your kids'll be the first bodies on the bonfire, I'll tell you what.*

He almost reached for the M16 he kept behind the driver's seat, but then Rebekah picked up and he caught her voice like the lifeline it'd always been. "Hey, girl," he said.

"Daniel."

"First errand's done. Couple more to go."

"All right."

"Need any milk?"

"I'll see you at home."

How long had it been, he wondered as she hung up, since his wife had told him she loved him? Not since Dolf was put in the ground. He stabbed at the phone's buttons and looked around for the bitch in the SUV. Gone.

Daniel pulled out into the stream of traffic. He'd dump the truck in the lot behind Lanier's package store and pick up the bike. Just in case his calculations were wrong, and somebody *had* been watching after all.

four

The rumors of widespread illness began three hours after the marathon was officially over, and the broad hill on the Virginia side of the Potomac where the race ended was bare of everything by that time except protein-bar wrappers and empty electrolyte bottles and a space blanket or two, crumpled and dancing in the rising November breeze. Darkness fell early that day; a front had moved in from the west and rain threatened. By dinnertime the Marines had dismantled their water stations and checkpoints and loaded them into military transport trucks. Nothing of the race was left but bad news.

The initial reports were anecdotal: nausea and vomiting among a disparate group of marathoners. There were twenty-six cases in the nation's capital . . . there were forty-five . . . there were eighty-three. But who wouldn't puke after running more than twenty-six miles? The newscasters downplayed the stories; one doctor suggested a flare-up of salmonella. Then the winner of the men's race—a twenty-year-old Zairian named Felix Nguza, already in New York for a flight out of the country—turned up in a midtown emergency room prostrate with diarrhea. George Enfield caught a glimpse of the guy's face, beaded with sweat, on the evening news.

Dana had finished the race in four hours and sixteen minutes, though she'd been forced to stop twice at aid stations to have her insulin level checked. George had found her three times during the day: in Georgetown, at the Reflecting Pool, and finally at the chute reserved for late finishers in Arlington. He'd been waiting to wrap her in the shining thermal blanket Mallory thought was fit for a futuristic princess; and he'd been struck, as he did so, at how strong Dana felt. He'd expected her to fall to the ground once she crossed the finish line. She'd been laughing, instead.

The pledges she'd gathered from all across the country would bring $262,000 to the Juvenile Diabetes Foundation. They'd celebrated at home with a long hot bath and take-out Thai. Mallory stayed up late, eating noodles and drinking her first champagne. As he carried his daughter upstairs at eight-thirty, she'd whispered drowsily in his ear, "I'm going to beat the world someday, just like Mommy."

Dana started vomiting while he read bedtime stories to their daughter. Forty-three minutes later, when she slipped into unconsciousness, an ambulance arrived to take her to Sibley Hospital.

Caroline had no intention of answering the door when the bell rang at ten minutes past ten that night. She'd been ambushed by the press at least eight times since Tuesday, with requests for exclusive interviews and talk show appearances and photo ops. Because she was a woman who'd entered a foreign terrorist compound completely alone, she was a media sensation. President Jack Bigelow had called her a hero—he badly needed to find one—and there was the pitiful fact of her wounded shoulder, the interesting effect of the sling.

A few print journalists had camped on her front steps for a while, until her persistent refusal to talk to anybody about what she'd seen in Sarajevo discouraged them. Her face had appeared as a tiny inset above the vice president's photograph on the cover of *Time* and *Newsweek,* but everything those magazines printed about her was completely sanitized and came from the CIA's Public Information Office. Cuddy Wilmot had offered to put her up for a few days, just until the funeral was over, and Dare Atwood had told her to get a room under a false name at the Tysons Marriott; but Caroline knew that if she didn't go home immediately, she never would. The fugitive impulse—*shut the door on that past, that forsaken master bedroom, those bottles of wine stacked willy-nilly in hope of a party*—was staggering.

Caroline was afraid to talk to anybody—afraid that if the words started coming they'd never stop until she'd spilled her guts and screwed them all, Dare and the Agency and the husband who wasn't lying cold in his grave in Arlington. How to keep going? How to pretend she was the same person she'd been two weeks ago? How to tidy up the bits of the past and throw them on some fire, like the burn bags full of useless paper she'd sent to the Agency's incinerator this morning? Should she sell the town house she'd bought with Eric, get rid of its tidy front lawn with the boxwood hedge, its gleaming black door, the knocker in the shape of a dolphin she hadn't been able to resist?

Instead, she lay on her sofa in a pair of old pajamas and ate potato chips straight out of the bag for dinner.

She was, if the truth were told, in a smoldering depression. Depression because the weight of failure and bitterness pressed down on her mind like a cinder block hurtling from the sky. Smoldering, because the flames of her outrage were banked now, waiting for the spark to flare and consume the man she hated. *Scottie Sorensen*. Who'd hijacked her past and gagged her future. Who'd made sure Eric could never come home again.

So when the bell rang a second time, it took her a minute to react. A fist pounded on her front door and a voice shouted *"Carrie."* It was possible she knew that voice, but she'd been washing the chips down with a venerable Mourvedre and her senses were a tad clouded. She glanced at the window light to the left of the door and saw shapes looming. Men.

"Jesus fucking Christ," she muttered to the empty bottle. Where *was* that beach she'd glimpsed this morning, that tropic emptiness? She wanted only to slip out of her clothes and walk forward through the sand.

Instead, she padded listlessly to the door.

• • •

"This letter came in about an hour ago." Cuddy spoke in a strained voice as he perched on the edge of the chair he always used at Caroline and Eric's. They'd watched the pilot of *Twin Peaks* in this room. The first episodes of *Seinfeld*. Cuddy preferred beer to wine and he never touched Eric's Scotch. There was a reserve about Cuddy—a careful holding back, even among his best friends—that Caroline found irritating.

"Steve Price here"—Cuddy nodded to the *Washington Post* reporter who was studying her pajamas and sling wordlessly from the other end of the sofa—"contacted the FBI. They pulled in Shephard. Shephard called me."

Tom Shephard was the FBI's legal attaché for Central Europe. He and Caroline had met over a bomb crater in Berlin a few weeks ago, and after the frenzied hunt for 30 April through half a dozen countries, Tom had flown back with her and the vice president's body in Air Force Two.

Tom was someone Caroline refused to think about in any depth right now because he only confused her. She was Eric's wife and Eric was miraculously alive, so why did she feel this absurd desire to lean into Tom and rest? He was comforting and safe, too attractive at the wrong time, a man at loose ends with hours to kill. So why hadn't he called her during the past endless week?

She'd heard he was hiding out in a Dupont Circle hotel, waiting for Payne's funeral and the Bureau's decision about his future. Tom looked pretty much the same as always: tousled salt-and-pepper hair, craggy face, hands shoved in the pockets of his khaki raincoat.

He was roaming the room as though Caroline weren't there, his eyes straying from the books on her shelves to the photographs on her tables. *Looking for Eric,* she thought bitterly. He wouldn't find him. What pictures she'd kept were locked in a bedroom drawer. Or the sealed vault of her mind.

She glanced down at the sheets of paper the three men had brought her. "Faxed?"

"From an Internet café in Adams-Morgan," Shephard said tersely. "Right to the *Post* newsroom. Whoever pushed the button is long gone."

To the press slaves of the Beast System:
Thirty April is everywhere, even when you least ex-
pect us. Today we delivered 150 gallons of water
poisoned with ricin to a random group of competi-
tors in the Marine Corps Marathon—

"Thirty April?" she managed. "Cuddy, 30 April is *dead.*"

"That's what we thought," he said gently. "Keep reading."

—4-ounce cups of water were handed to runners
at Hains Point over a period of 5 hours. All are
thus assured of a painful and lingering death.

"We're supposed to believe they're operating in the U.S.?" she demanded. "Since *when?* Do we have any data to support that?"

"No suggestion I've found." Cuddy shook his head slightly. "No networks we've identified. Keep reading."

*This is only the first in a wave of attacks mounted
against the Jew World Order. We, the loyal followers of 30 April, dedicate ourselves to avenging our
martyred brethren, not least among them the Leader
himself, Mlan Krucevic, struck down by the criminals who rule in the name of the American people.*

Caroline snorted derisively.

*Death to Jack Bigelow & the corrupt maggots who
keep him in power. Death to the whore who betrayed
the Leader to his enemies. Death to the liberals and
Jews who have infiltrated the United States government and handed it over to the filth of the world.
Remember Waco. Remember Ruby Ridge and the
murder of the patriot Tim McVeigh.*
      The End Times are coming. Prepare.

She looked up with a frown. "Do we take this seriously?"

"Caroline—" Cuddy jabbed at the bridge of his
glasses. "Three hundred and sixty-four people so far
have reported to area hospitals. All of them marathoners. All of them vomiting. If this letter's true, the count
is going to rise."

"But do we know it's *ricin*?" Shephard threw himself into a chair. "What if this is just—"

"A hoax?" suggested the *Post* reporter. "A little bit
of food poisoning washed down on a Sunday morning? What better way to spread panic?"

"On the eve of Sophie Payne's funeral," Caroline
mused. "What are the symptoms, Cud?"

"Severe dehydration. Gastric sickness. That's about all we've seen so far."

"There *is* no clinical test for ricin poisoning," Shephard reminded them tiredly. "You just have to wait it out. See how and when people die."

"I know that."

"But I don't," Price said unexpectedly. "Since I was good enough to call in the government and hand over the original of that letter, maybe the government could help me out?"

Caroline was studying the fax. "It's not classified information. Ricin's the chemical residue left over in castor bean mash, which is produced all over the Midwest for the castor oil we use in motors and industrial products. Ricin's easy enough to make if you can get your hands on a gas chromatograph—which is available in any high school chemistry lab—and cheap as hell. Am I right, Tom, in thinking the Bureau's been worried about something like this happening for years?"

"Damn straight," he replied, "though we've been thinking in terms of aerosolized hits—a crop duster unleashed on a city, for instance. Most of our models are for airborne toxins. I doubt we counted on people lining up to drink them."

Price drew out a notebook and pen. "What does ricin do in the human body?"

"It gets into your cells and prevents them from making the proteins they need," Shephard said baldly. "Absent those proteins, cells die, and eventually so do you. If this letter's accurate, and the ricin was dissolved in water, it'd cause internal bleeding throughout the digestive tract."

"But that could be treated, right?" Price looked up from his notes.

"Treated," Shephard agreed. "Rarely survived. Depends how much ricin each person got."

"But the water must've tasted bad. Wouldn't most people spit it out?"

"The mouth's a sponge. The toxin's absorbed by skin tissues. You can die just from getting the powder on your hands. In the best case, we'll see bloody diarrhea and vomiting. If the victim lives at least five days, he or she will probably survive the attack."

"—And in the worst case?"

"Liver, spleen, and kidney failure, followed by death. Within forty-eight hours."

"Jesus," Caroline muttered. "Fifteen thousand people run that race."

The men around her were silent.

"So why have you come to me?" she demanded. "For names and phone numbers of 30 April here in the States? Cuddy just told you, Tom: We don't have any. The CIA doesn't operate on U.S. soil. That's the Bureau's jurisdiction."

"And you quit the Agency this morning," Shephard returned brutally. "I heard. Congratulations."

"We want you to pack a bag." Cuddy's voice was, if possible, even more strained than at the beginning of his visit. "Dare Atwood has ordered federal protection for you, Carrie. If this letter's true—if 30 April *is* operating in America—then you're a target."

"Death to the whore who betrayed the Leader," Steve Price murmured. "That can only mean one person."

"Bullshit." Caroline handed the faxed sheets back to the *Post* reporter. "I'm not going into hiding because of some kook with a fax machine."

"This time," Shephard said as he rose from his chair, "you've got no choice."

five

George Enfield lifted the sleeping Mallory from his lap and placed her carefully in the arms of her young nanny. "Take her back to the waiting room, Marya," he said. "I don't want her here when Dana goes."

The nanny nodded once but said nothing. Marya had witnessed more than a few untimely deaths in her native Estonia. She merely dropped a kiss on the slumbering child's head and carried her around the screening curtain that divided Dana's part of the emergency room. George's eyes followed them a trifle absently; then his gaze strayed back to the motionless figure on the gurney. Dana had lost consciousness again. It was as though she'd clung to the world as long as Mallory did, wanting every last second she could have with her daughter.

Her face was gaunt, her eyes unmoving beneath the still lids; for an instant he was afraid that she'd left him already—that she'd chosen that moment of Mallory's departure to skitter away herself, without the pain of good-bye. He sank down on his knees by the side of the bed and reached through the metal railing for her hand. The fingers were chilled and unresponsive. Something between a groan and a sob tore from his throat.

"What is it?" he'd demanded of the supervising physician as she wheeled his wife through the crowd of people in Sibley's ER. "Her diabetes? Dehydration? *What?*"

"She ran the Marine Corps?" the doctor asked grimly. "We're seeing a flood of people who did. Something was tainted. We don't know what. Just hold on and we'll try to stabilize her gastric system. I'm afraid I can't give you a private room, Mr. Speaker—"

All around him, in pairs and groups and lonely solitude, were men and women of every age and ethnic background, doubled up in pain. George stopped counting at sixty-three. Had all these people run the marathon? He began to grasp the extent of the problem, began to be terribly afraid. The doctors would not—or could not—tell him what was wrong with his wife. He started calling every contact he could think of—people at the FDA, Dana's personal physician, his Chief of Staff simply for comfort—at nine-thirty on a Sunday evening.

There was a brief moment when Dana gave him some hope, after the violence of the vomiting and the exhausting bouts of diarrhea—a period when the morphine had taken hold, and her tortured entrails were blessedly quiet. She'd stared at the ceiling, her fingers locked in his. "I want to talk to Steve," she said.

"Steve Price?"

A nod. "I want to tell him. What I saw."

The Enfields had known Steve Price for nearly ten years, since the journalist had traded the editorship of his family newspaper for an investigative reporter's job at the *Washington Post*. But why Dana wanted to talk to Steve, of all people—rather than her best friend or her sister or even himself—baffled George.

"Please," she said faintly. "Get him now."

He called the cell phone number he found in his Palm Pilot and caught Price on the second ring.

"Shit," the journalist muttered when George told him where he was. "I was afraid of this. I've called your house four times. You know it's ricin?"

George hadn't known. He told Price to get his ass to the hospital and hung up shouting for Dana's doctor. Demanding an antidote—any kind of antidote—for a poison that'd never had one.

Price spared George the unwanted words of commiseration. He leaned over the gurney to kiss Dana's cheek, oblivious to the odor of blood and vomit that rose from her failing body.

"Hell of a race, girl," he said. "Unbelievable. You rock."

She smiled crookedly at him and closed her eyes. "I want you to take down what I have to say. I want it to get to the right people."

He pulled out a tape recorder. "Shoot."

"I remember where things went wrong," she said. "Mile twenty. Hains Point."

George saw Price's expression change, saw the brows draw down and the lines around the mouth harden. There was something about Hains Point—something Price already knew. "You're sure? What do you remember?"

"I was feeling like crap—I'd taken a shot in my thigh, but I was afraid I was going to faint. I asked the first Marine I saw for help."

"And?"

"He wasn't with the others at the aid station. He gave me water. It tasted weird—sort of muddy or metallic—but I figured that was just me. That my levels were out of whack. I drank it anyway."

"All of it?"

"All of it."

A faint sound, almost a whimper, from high in Price's throat. George turned away from them. *She asked for help and the bastard poisoned her.*

"What did he look like, Dana?"

"Older," she replied with effort. "Older than a Marine. In his thirties, maybe. White. Five foot ten. Bright blue eyes. Cammies. No music. A couple of water drums and a stack of bottles."

She paused to draw breath. Price reached for her hand and squeezed it.

"I thanked him for the cup.... But I remember: He didn't smile or wish me well. Which was odd. Everybody else did. I got my blood tested at the aid station, ate a banana and drank some juice, then ran the last few miles."

She began to pant, and with the automatic surge that had become horribly routine, George reached for a basin. Price watched as Dana retched out her guts in her husband's hands; she vomited mostly blood.

"I'm sorry, gentlemen," said a nurse at the partition, "I'm going to have to ask you to step into the hall. Mrs. Enfield needs rest."

"You'll tell them, Steve?" Dana whispered.

He blew her a kiss. "Be strong. This is just another race, Dana girl. You'll win it."

But once beyond her range of hearing he asked George, "What've these doctors told you?"

"Squat, Steve. I don't think they know what's happening. I told them it could be ricin, and they asked me not to spread panic."

"It's ricin." He handed George a sheet of paper. "Read that. I've already shown the original to the FBI. It was some kind of terrorist hit. Nobody knows how many . . ."

His voice trailed away, and he glanced over his shoulder toward Dana. "You should be with her, buddy."

"Tell me what you know. I'd rather hear the truth."

"She swallowed enough poison to kill her. If she can hold on a few more days . . . there's a chance . . ."

"Days," George burst out. "How can *anybody* take this for days? And with her condition—"

From the curtained gurney behind them came a strangled cry. Dana arched upward, convulsed with pain, her fingers scrabbling on air.

"Nurse!" George shouted. *"Nurse!"*

six

Caroline threw on her jeans and buttoned a blouse around the bandages on her shoulder and spent ten minutes tossing clothes into the suitcase she'd only recently unpacked from Europe. Thinking: *An American cell. What did we miss? How did we miss it? Jesus, this is our fault*—She kept the television on in her bedroom, without sound, reading the marquee scroll that sped across the bottom of the screen. More than four hundred people had checked into area hospitals. *They don't even know. No one's told them yet. That they haven't a chance of surviving.* The word *ricin* had not yet been mentioned in public.

Tom Shephard had left her unwillingly at the door.

"Cuddy has my cell," he'd said, one hand reaching for her good arm. "Call once you're out of here, understand? I want to know where you are."

Caroline had stepped back from the raw emotion in his eyes, shoulder burning under her cotton blouse. She was not going to become Tom Shephard's burden— another woman he had to save. She'd deceived him enough already. Tom had no idea her husband was alive.

"We'll be fine," she managed. "You've got enough on your plate tonight."

He was due back at Bureau Headquarters, the J. Edgar Hoover Building at Ninth and G, where the director would be forced to notify the President and a press conference would have to be called. She didn't envy Tom his decisions. Tell the world there'd been a ricin attack, and risk mass panic—even if the faxed letter was a hoax? Or be accused of cover-up and conspiracy once the first victim died?

It would be easier when someone died, in fact. They'd have an autopsy, then. They'd know.

Except that Caroline already knew. Thirty April's letter had come like a valentine from the grave, a dirty assignation she'd been dying to keep. The total obliteration of the neo-Nazi group had seemed too easy, even while she watched it happen; she'd learned to expect the hydra effect. Despite the cloud of misery she'd struggled through the past six days, she knew now that she'd been waiting for these words, this knock on the door. The next round. When she could atone for all her sins.

"Did you pack your gun?" Shephard had asked.

"I'm Agency, not Bureau. We don't carry guns."

"Liar," he retorted. "Call my hotel with your number. And get some sleep."

She'd watched him drive off with Steve Price in the journalist's car, aware that Shephard was somehow relieved to have a role—to have something to do besides watch a sports channel in his jockey shorts. Like her, Tom had only been waiting.

"I don't want to sleep," she told Cuddy now. "I don't want to run or hide. I want to talk to the boy."

He glanced at his watch. "Visiting hours at Bethesda Naval are long since over."

"So what? Jozsef's the best option we've got. You can flash your badge and mouth platitudes about national security. I'll smile and look sympathetic."

"Does this mean you've decided to stay?" Cuddy asked.

"I have no choice. I'm a target, remember?"

Jozsef Krucevic was the son of 30 April's leader, Mlan Krucevic, a man Caroline had helped to destroy. The boy had flown back to Washington in Air Force Two with Sophie Payne's body. For thirty-eight hours, dangerously ill, he'd hung on the fringe of the waking world. Two days ago, however, he'd sat up in bed for the first time and eaten green gelatin; Caroline had spent a few enjoyable hours with him, explaining the nature of American cartoons. Nobody had figured out where Jozsef was going to live, or with whom. It had seemed important to get through Payne's funeral before disposing of her killer's son.

Bethesda Naval was a surreal place, with its massive central tower in the Thirties Fascist style. A light at its apex distinguished the room from which James Forrestal, once a Secretary of Defense, had jumped to his death. Caroline found suicide a macabre sort of memorial for any building, particularly a hospital. She drove her Volkswagen while Cuddy called ahead to the night nurse on Jozsef's pediatric intensive care ward and told the woman that the boy's CIA handlers needed to speak with him immediately. The nurse had refused to give them access—she lacked the proper authority—at which point Cuddy called Dare Atwood at home in Georgetown and brought the DCI up to date. A personal escort—a military doctor, by the look of him—stood waiting for them at the front entrance.

"Are you getting marathon victims in your ER?" Cuddy asked as they strolled briskly in the direction of Acute Care Pediatric.

"Seventy-four Marines, at last count," the doctor said starkly.

Jozsef seemed both older and younger than his age, with his dead-white cheeks and large, hollow black eyes. Like a child out of Dickens, Caroline thought. Too knowing, consumptive, and doomed. His frail fingers plucked at the starched hospital sheet. The legs beneath were as thin and straight as two metal poles. *Jozsef.* She had carried him on her back straight out of hell.

"Hey, kiddo. You still up?"

"They had to give me my shot," he answered irritably. "They were able to replicate Father's medicine—did they tell you? He thought it was an impossible code to break. He was wrong."

"About a lot of things," Caroline said gruffly, and reached to tousle Jozsef's hair. He'd been deliberately infected by his own father with a genetically engineered strain of anthrax. "You don't look too bad. Seen any SpongeBob lately?"

He lifted one shoulder in a petulant sort of shrug, his eyes sliding toward Cuddy. He'd met Cuddy only once, and seemed to feel awkward around him. As though Cuddy were watching and judging him. As Cuddy certainly was.

"I've been reading. *This*." He gestured toward the book; a paperback of *The Golden Compass* Caroline had given him a few days before. "I cannot decide what is real and what is false in all the words. My English is good—but my brain . . ."

". . . is better. You'll get there—stick with it. Look, we're sorry to bother you so late, Jozsef, but we need to ask you some questions."

The huge dark eyes came up to her own. "You always do. That's why you saved my life, is it not? So I could tell you everything I know?"

She shook her head. "You saved mine, I think. Or we saved each other. That's what good people do."

"I am not a good person. I am a killer's son." His gaze dropped to his thin fingers again, restlessly kneading the blanket. Caroline glanced at Cuddy, who'd remained standing in the doorway, one shoulder propped against the jamb as though it were his office. His face was expressionless; he had not yet decided what he thought of the boy—what was real and what was false, amid all Jozsef's words.

Caroline drew an uncomfortable vinyl-backed chair closer to the bed. "I was hoping you could tell me how long ago your father decided on Sophie Payne. Why he chose the vice president to kidnap, I mean. Did he dislike her personally? Did he know she was coming to Berlin?"

Jozsef shrugged again. He was pissed about something beyond this unexpected visit. Bored in a hospital that was no better than a prison? Worried about what might happen next?

"They will not let me go to the funeral," he said plaintively. "It is not fair! I want to say good-bye to Lady Sophie! Can't you make them let me out?"

Cuddy shifted in the doorway, jabbed at his glasses. "Maybe they think you're not well enough."

"I am! I'm perfectly fine! I have been fine for two days! They're not letting me go on purpose—to . . . to *punish* me because my father killed her! He nearly killed me, too!"

"Jozsef." Caroline smoothed the blanket over the thin legs. "I'll talk to your doctor. Okay? I'll talk to him. I'll let him know that I'll personally take care of you and make sure you get through it. We'll see what he says, all right?"

The boy gave her a look full of such desperate hope that she suddenly understood what Santa Claus must feel like on Christmas Eve. Did a funeral matter so much? Maybe. When it was for somebody you'd failed to save.

"How long ago did Mlan decide on Mrs. Payne?"

"At least a year," he said rapidly. "He told me he had been planning for a year. Tracking her movements. Learning everything he could. *Even in her shower at the Naval Observatory*, he boasted, *she was never alone*. He knew her shoe size. Which restaurants she went to and what she ordered. He told Lady Sophie all that, the first day he took her. He liked to see people squirm. To invade their minds. She could not have escaped him, Miss Carrie. If it hadn't been Berlin, it would have been Paris."

"I can see that."

"Even in her shower," Cuddy repeated. His careful gaze drifted over Caroline. "At the Observatory. He said that?"

Jozsef nodded.

"There were people watching her at the veep's residence? People on Mlan's payroll?"

"I don't know if he paid them. But yes, he had informants. People who followed her. People she would not notice."

"Who were they?" Cuddy asked with deliberate casualness.

Jozsef laughed—a short, bitter bark. "My father never told me those things. He was not a fool."

"No," Caroline agreed. "He was not a fool."

She studied the boy's face for an instant, seeing the brutal shadows beneath the eyes, the sharpness of the facial bones. "Were there others? Outside Lady Sophie's house? In her office, for instance?"

"I do not know! My father got his information in secret ways, Miss Carrie. He got messages over the Internet. On his computer. He did not show those things to me."

"We know there was a laptop," she said, "that always traveled with him. Thirty April's database. Would the names be there?"

Cuddy shook his head once, involuntarily.

"Some things were never written down at all." Jozsef tapped his skull with a weary finger. "He kept them in his brain. And they died with him."

"Jozsef—we think it's possible there are 30 April people operating here. In Washington. We need to find them before they do a lot of damage. Are you sure there isn't a name you remember? An American friend, maybe, of your father's?"

"You want me to betray his friends?" Jozsef sighed, his eyelids drooping. "I've told you everything I know."

"Will you think about it? And let me know if you remember anything else?"

"If you keep your promise—and talk to the doctor."

"I will."

"Then we'll discuss it at the funeral. I'm tired now. I will see you tomorrow." The eyes flashed open, dark and brilliant. "Do not forget your promise, Miss Carrie!"

"I don't like that kid," Cuddy said tensely as they walked toward Caroline's car. "He's evil inside."

"He's twelve years old, entirely alone in a foreign country, and everyone he knows has just died a violent death. Give him a break!"

"He's manipulative, calculating, and ruthless," Cuddy argued. "I don't trust him farther than I can see him."

"His life's completely beyond his control. It always has been. I feel for the little kid."

"He's not so little. Are you really going to take him to Payne's funeral?"

They had stopped at the nurses' station and paged the doctor in charge of Jozsef's medical team. Caroline had required exactly seven minutes of the man's time before she'd won his consent to an outing.

"It's a small enough thing to ask."

"He wants to go too badly," Cuddy said. "Have you asked yourself *why*?"

"He loved Sophie. They were a team, in those last few days. They got each other through. And then—and then she was dumped alone in a mine shaft and he couldn't save her. But I'll tell you something, Cuddy: It was Jozsef who brought that whole encampment down on his father's head. It was that little lad who decided Mlan had to be stopped. That means something, to me. He's *not* evil inside."

If Cuddy disagreed, he didn't show it. "We should tell Shephard about the Observatory. He'll want to get somebody on it."

"Use my cell." Caroline fumbled for it in her purse, her left hand on the wheel. "There's no point in heading to the Bureau right now. Even if they let us in—damage control is not our job. Let's visit Dare."

"At this hour?"

"She'll be up. She'll be dressed and working three phones. Trying to salvage what she can."

"But will she want to see us?"

"She'll have to." Caroline paused at the intersection with Old Georgetown Road, debating whether to head back to the Beltway or drive straight down toward Dupont Circle and the DCI's home. At this hour of the night, the snarled main arteries of the capital were relatively empty. "You realize, Cud—if Jozsef doesn't know who these people are—and everyone else in 30 April's European organization is dead—there's only one person left. Only one person who can help us."

"Eric," he said.

seven

Eric Carmichael sat on the edge of the porcelain tub, his eyes on a digital clock. The hair dye took six minutes to work; he'd been waiting for three and a half. The skin of his fingers was turning brown and the smell of peroxide was sharp in his nostrils; he was thankful for these things, uncompromisingly real. They reassured him that he was alive.

He had lost too much blood in the past week, and his memory of some days was hazy at best. He knew he'd pawned his watch somewhere between Budapest and Berlin—it was gone from his wrist, and he doubted it'd been stolen. Krucevic had always kept them short of cash, and he had no credit card in a name he could use. He'd pawned the watch, then, probably in some shop near the Budapest West train station, the day he'd walked away from Caroline toward a certain death.

He'd been trying to save Sophie Payne but he'd gone across Europe in the wrong direction. By the time he'd realized Mlan Krucevic was not in Berlin, the vice president and Krucevic were both dead, along with every terrorist operative he'd known for the past two years. He alone had survived. The whole world would be hunting him down.

What time was it, when he stood at last in the shadows of the loading dock in Berlin? One A.M.? Two? He'd been cautious and alert. Moved as silently as a cat up the exterior staircase to the security door, through the darkened complex, past reception to the sealed lab. And then the silent rush of air as the knife blade plunged toward him through the darkness, fueled by hatred. He'd sensed the stroke at the last second and dove sideways—but the sharp steel bit into his neck, a savage arc from the base of his ear to his collarbone. With the instinct of the Green Beret he'd once been—the man trained to kill in darkness or light—he'd ignored the knife and reached for the wrists, dashing them brutally against the laboratory's doors. There was a cry of pain—the clenched fingers released—the weapon clattered to the floor.

He thought maybe he'd lifted the woman—for his attacker was a woman, he was certain of that—high in the air and flung her like a dressmaker's dummy into the opposite wall. He wasn't sure. He only knew that when he finally flipped on a light and stared down at the body at his feet, her neck was broken.

Her name was Greta Oppenheimer. One of 30 April's loyal slaves. She'd used a laboratory scalpel to stab him; it lay, blade broken, near her lifeless fingers.

Why had she crouched in the office that night? Had she known he was coming?

A spatter of blood fell on Greta's chest. Eric looked down, then, and saw the stream of it trickling from his neck.

• • •

"Are you all right?"

"Yeah. Out in a minute."

He rinsed his head under the bathtub spigot, careful to keep the flow of stained water from striking his wound. He hardly knew how he'd made it to Mahmoud Sharif's apartment. The Palestinian lived with his German wife in Berlin's working-class district of Prenzlauerberg. He'd pounded on Sharif's door in the middle of the night, scaring the two boys out of their wits. Dagmar had been certain it was the German police, come to haul Mahmoud away on yet another terrorism charge. The Palestinian had crept toward the door with a semiautomatic in his hands. He'd thrown back the lock only when he saw blood seeping across his floor.

Sharif had sealed Eric's gaping neck wound with plastic cement. Ugly, but efficient; a German hospital was out of the question. He'd bear the scar for the rest of his days.

He toweled his hair with both hands and studied his reflection in the mirror. His blond hair had disappeared, and with it, his blue eyes; he'd inserted brown lenses. It wasn't a perfect transformation—he was still the same age and size—but it might get him out of Europe.

He settled a pair of wire-rimmed spectacles on his nose and stepped into the hall.

Mahmoud surveyed him critically. "I was followed tonight," the Palestinian said.

"Who?"

"BKA."

The Bundeskriminalamt—the German equivalent
of the FBI. They might be surveilling Mahmoud out
of habit—he'd once built bombs for Hizballah—or
they might be looking for Eric. "Did you lose them?"

Mahmoud shook his head. "I was only coming home.
A normal end to a normal day. Why should I arouse
suspicion? But there is a man loitering in the street. He
smokes far too many expensive Turkish cigarettes for a
punk with no job."

The sound of a child's high-pitched voice, insistent
and tremulous, drifted from the kitchen. Mahmoud's
elder boy, Moammar, demanding something from his
mother. With reflexive Muslim courtesy, Mahmoud had
not asked Eric to leave his home and spare his children
the possible horrors of their father's arrest. Eric was
Sharif's guest. He would die defending him if necessary.

Eric had offered as much eight years ago when
Sharif was a penniless carpenter in love with a German
girl from Hamburg. As chief of the CIA's base there,
he'd recruited Sharif, trained and instructed and molded
him to betray the Hizballah cell that had planted him
in Germany. Sharif had fed the CIA vital information
for nearly four years, and when his cover was blown—
when he was burned, in the parlance of espionage—
Eric had saved his life and Dagmar's. The two men
were blood brothers. In a world rife with enemies, some
named and some unknown, such things were precious.

"The BKA was all over 30 April," Mahmoud told
him apologetically. "They'll have found that lab. The
corpse with the broken neck."

And who but a 30 April terrorist would have access to such a lab? Eric thought. *They'll have samples of my blood on the floor. My DNA.*

"I'll leave tonight," he said.

"There's no need. We can hide you for weeks. Move you, if necessary, among our friends, until the hunt dies down."

Caroline's face rose with painful clarity in Eric's mind. "I don't have weeks," he replied. "I leave tonight."

Mahmoud nodded, his relief so intense it bordered on shame. "I will take you down to the garage, fold you into the trunk of the BMW, and Dagmar will drive off with the kids as though we've had a fight. She'll go to her sister's—after she drops you somewhere convenient, of course."

Somewhere convenient. Where exactly would that be, for a man hunted the length of Europe? But he merely nodded, and held out his hand. "Thank you, Mahmoud."

"I settle a debt, only. Too long unpaid." He grasped Eric's palm.

When Mahmoud had gone, Eric moved quietly into the Palestinian's bedroom and drew a small screwdriver from his pocket. It was essential that he remove every trace of himself from Sharif's apartment.

Behind the collection of Italian wool trousers and the sweeping black cloak Dagmar favored was a small wood panel. Screwed into the plasterboard wall, it covered a hole between closet and bathroom: a plumber's trap, a clean-out. The builder had designed it for easy access to the workings of Sharif's shower, but Eric had found another use for it. In all the years of his under-cover operation with 30 April, his bugout kit had lived in Sharif's wall.

The bugout kit was every clandestine agent's hope for survival. When your cover was blown and the whole world wanted you dead, the bugout kit just might save your ass. In Eric's case it held a false iden-tity: a British passport in the name of Nigel Benning; a Visa card and driver's license belonging to the same man. Five thousand dollars in cash. A gun. Enough damaging evidence to send Sharif to prison for years.

He stared at the photograph of Nigel Benning: dark brown hair, brown eyes, a pair of wire-rimmed specta-cles. Himself, in disguise. That and a token would get him a ride on the U-Bahn. The passport was too dan-gerous to use.

It was a stolen blank he'd bought years ago on the street in Prague. The serial number might already be listed in the world's immigration databases. If Mahmoud was right—if the BKA was hunting a 30 April survivor—every border would be watched. Every passport studied.

He stuffed the contents of the bugout kit in his jacket and carefully screwed the wooden panel back onto Sharif's wall.

eight

It was Tom Shephard's job to tell Al Tomlinson, the FBI director, that the Marine Corps Marathon had been hit by a terrorist. While Tomlinson called the White House, Tom got in touch with the Marine colonel who'd spent more than a year planning the race, and broke the bad news. Stannis Morrow wasn't sleeping—he'd been following the reports of mass illness with growing dread—and thirty minutes later he faxed Tom his computerized registration list of the fifteen thousand people who'd run that day. The FBI was calling each of them now, one by one.

Shephard demanded the names and service records of every Marine who'd worked the Hains Point water and aid stations—just in case the anonymous letter wasn't joking. Then he asked Colonel Morrow to send the twelve men to the J. Edgar Hoover Building immediately.

With shuddering speed the machinery slid into place. There was a protocol for chem-bio attacks, established months before in the event of such a strike against Washington. An army of medical and law enforcement personnel fanned out across the city. District police took up stations along the marathon route. Hospitals called in extra staff and braced for the flood of worried runners with vague symptoms and imperfect memories of what they'd ingested where. Remaining supplies of fruit and bottled water intended for race-time distribution, along with twelve tons of garbage collected along the route, were seized and trucked to the Bureau's Laboratory Division, where every scrap would be tested for ricin or other contaminants. And Tom Shephard held a press conference.

"Tonight the Federal Bureau of Investigation, at the direction of the President of the United States, is forced to declare a national emergency," he said bluntly into the microphone set up at 10:53 P.M. in the Headquarters auditorium. The briefing would be broadcast simultaneously on all the major television channels, preempting the eleven o'clock news, and might take out Leno and Letterman if questions ran long enough. *Shephard in the nation's living rooms,* he thought acidly. *A real stand-up comic.*

"The FBI has received information tonight claiming responsibility for the poisoning of an undetermined number of participants in the Marine Corps Marathon with the castor bean derivative, ricin." Beyond the halogen bulbs flooding his eyes Tom could glimpse the shadowy figures of the reporters and cameramen, one hundred sixty-two at last count, but even this crowd didn't begin to fill the auditorium and he was reminded incongruously of his high school drama club days, the dress rehearsals in a darkened house, audience reaction impossible to judge. "The ricin may have been

ingested in water distributed by rogue operators unaffiliated with the Marine Corps. The attack is believed
to have been the work of a person or group of persons loosely associated with a European terrorist group
known as 30 April Organization, acting on U.S. soil,
and may have occurred around mile twenty of the race
course in the neighborhood of Hains Point. Anyone
who observed suspicious activity at that location or
elsewhere during the race is urged to come forward,
and those race participants who may be experiencing
gastric discomfort should report immediately to medical facilities. A hotline has been set up . . ."

The questions were predictable and the answers
were few. *No, we haven't identified the terrorists involved. We have no estimate of the number of casualties
but it is likely to run in the hundreds. There is no cure
for ricin poisoning. We have no reason to believe that
30 April's leader Mlan Krucevic survived last week's attack on his compound outside Sarajevo* . . .

The chief problem, Tom thought as he stepped
down from the podium with a description of ricin's
chemical structure in his hand and the press still clam-
oring for information, was that they hadn't a single
fucking lead to follow. Caroline had called from her car
and urged him to check out Payne's Naval Observatory
staff—but the FBI had already reviewed the personnel
files and clearances of everybody employed by the vice
president, from the moment she'd been kidnapped
two weeks before. They'd found nothing suspicious.
All five of Payne's employees looked clean as a whistle.

*Ricin is composed of two hemagglutinins and two
toxins, RCL III and RCL IV; these are dimers roughly*

66,000 daltons in molecular weight...the B chain of polypeptides binds to cell surface glycoproteins...the A chain acts on the ribosomal subunit...inhibits protein synthesis...leads to cell death. Basic structure is similar to botulinum toxin, cholera toxin, diphtheria toxin, tetanus toxin...

In other words, he thought savagely, you rot out your guts and then you die.

"Tom?"

He glanced toward the door. Steve Price, the *Post* reporter, flashing his badge at the conference room guard. "You missed the show," Tom said.

"No choice. I got a call from George Enfield."

"The Speaker?"

"His wife's dying of ricin poisoning."

"Jesus," Tom muttered.

Price swung toward him, an athletic figure in a plaid shirt and down vest. He looked like a war correspondent: craggy face, unkempt hair, and functional clothes, hot on the trail of a major story. The Front was down there somewhere on the street.

"Dana remembered a guy at Hains Point," he told Tom. "Handing out water. It tallies with the letter."

"What'd she tell you?"

"I taped it." He lifted his recorder tantalizingly in the air. "She asked me to get it to people who could use it. I figured that meant you."

Sibley Hospital sits off Massachusetts Avenue, in a section of Washington known as Spring Valley, where the homes and the trees are a century old and antiques

stores vie for commerce with gourmet food shops. Unlike most urban hospitals, Sibley, the preserve of the
well-heeled and the genteel, is usually immune to violence. Tonight, however, Tom Shephard was forced to
abandon his rental car three blocks from the emergency
room entrance. A thicket of vehicles cut off access: private cars, television vans, and three ambulances desperately fighting to reach the main doors. It was four
minutes past midnight, and busy as noon.

"This is all because of the marathon?" demanded
the forensic artist standing beside him. *"Fuck."*

Casey Marlowe had his IdentiKit under his arm. It
was a baseline collection of facial features he could
plug into a suspect sketch and refine as his witness suggested. If, Tom thought, the witness was still alive.
They shouldered their way through the throng of people at the hospital doors.

Tom forced himself to look into the victims' faces:
this red-haired woman, no more than thirty, whose
brow was blistered with sweat and whose eyelids were
closing, supported by a man who was lover or brother
or husband—his mouth twisted with anxiety and fear.
This kid of nineteen, in a Georgetown University sweatshirt, whose mother was struggling to keep him upright as he staggered forward. The couple who were
helping each other walk to the door. The guy in his
sixties who'd sunk down with his back against the hospital's outer wall. He was vomiting blood.

At least sixty people stood on the chilly pavement in
front of Sibley, and more filled the waiting room beyond the doors.

"The hospital is closed!" a voice rang out at the

head of the line. Tom craned to find the source—a figure in blue scrubs, squat and grim-faced, who leaned
through the half-open door. "The emergency room is
full."

A groan went up from the crowd. "Who ever heard
of a hospital *closing*?" one voice shouted furiously. "My
daughter's been poisoned! She needs an IV feed, not a
cot in a gym, God damn it!"

"City fire regulations prevent us accepting even one
more patient," the man in scrubs said brutally. "I repeat, *the hospital is closed*. If you require medical care,
and you ran the Marine Corps Marathon today, we
suggest you report to one of these four medical relief
centers being set up in area schools. Volunteer doctors
are standing by to help. If your emergency care is un-
related to the marathon, return home and call a private physician."

A roar of protest rose from the wavering knot of
people as the man in scrubs waded into their midst,
a sheaf of papers held high. Tom grabbed one and
scanned the printed lines. The closest medical station
was at American University, a few blocks away. The
woman beside him was weeping from frustration.

"Hey, Shep," Casey Marlowe said. "Ever seen a war
zone? Best advice I can give you: *Keep moving*. This is
going to get ugly."

Tom fumbled in his pocket for his FBI badge. He
held it high and surged forward.

Dana Enfield was adrift in uneasy dreams. She had lost
Mallory in the marathon crowd, but the little girl's

voice followed her relentlessly, high-pitched above the roar of the spectators. *Mommy! Mommy! Don't leave me! Mommy!*

Dana knew, with a surge of panic, that George had let go of her daughter's hand. He was running through the tight ranks of people lining the race course, yelling something she couldn't hear. What was he telling her? What was he trying to say? Was she in insulin shock? She tried to stop running—tried to fight against the current of the racers sweeping her forward—and failed. George slipped backward. She reached for him, panic surging—*Where was Mallory?* And then she saw The Man. Standing stock-still in the middle of the oddly deserted road, a cup of water in his outstretched hand.

"Dana," George murmured in her ear. "*Dana.* Sweetheart, can you hear me?"

She forced her eyelids open. Her lips were thick and parched, the animal smell of blood in her nostrils. She tried to speak. No sound came.

"Honey, these men are from the FBI. They'd like to talk to you. Steve sent them."

Her memory returned then: She was sick. The race was over. Every fiber of her body screamed with pain and the blur of faces—how many faces?—swam above her.

"Mallory," she croaked.

"She's home with Marya," George soothed. "Sleeping." He reached for a cup of chipped ice, tipped a few fragments onto her tongue. She closed her eyes again and savored the cool and perfect presence of this one thing. For an instant she remembered the brilliance of snow. She'd skied last winter in Utah.

"Dana."

She brought George into focus: dark hair graying at the temples, lined face, worried eyes. Too worried.

"Am . . . I going to die?"

"The FBI wants to talk to you. Will you try, honey? Can you try?"

She managed to nod. One of the blurred faces swam closer. The other stayed near the door, watchful and silent.

"Mrs. Enfield, I'm Casey Marlowe," said the voice at her elbow. She strained to see him, but the face ballooned sickly and she squeezed her eyes shut. "You remembered a man who gave you water at Hains Point. You thought it might have been tainted. Can you describe this man for me?"

She swallowed hard and groped for George. He slipped another piece of ice between her lips. "I'm so sorry," she said, "that I did this to you."

"You did nothing, sweetheart. Except run your heart out. Do you remember the man?"

The Man. Of course she remembered.

"Can you tell me what he looked like, Mrs. Enfield?"

The face had a sketch pad and pencil now.

Dana gathered all the life that remained to her, and tried.

nine

"Ever been to the DCI's house?" Cuddy asked as Caroline negotiated the narrow cobbled streets of Georgetown.

"Once. Years ago. She had a party when she became division chief." Caroline spotted a single empty space among the cars lining O Street and pulled the Volkswagen neatly into it. "She came to my wedding. And to Eric's funeral."

Cuddy unbuckled his seat belt. "Doesn't mean she's going to like your idea."

"No. But she'll listen to it."

The ancient maple trees lining the brick sidewalk had thrust their roots well under the paving, heaving the surface as efficiently as a family of moles. Caroline stepped carefully over the curb and glanced up at Dare's house. A classic three-story Federal with black shutters and a historic plaque; lights burned behind the curtained windows to the left of the door. A few dead leaves skittered down the street; from the corner of her eye, she caught sight of a man slouching along the sidewalk with a duffel over his back. *Homeless,* she thought. *Vietnam vet.* And mounted the three marble steps, waiting for the bellow of Dare's dog from within.

The bark came right on cue as she lifted the door knocker, followed by a brisk patter of high heels. Dare would be fully dressed, although it was nearly midnight. She'd been on her way to the Agency when they called.

"Caroline," the DCI said as she swung wide the door. "Cuddy. Come in, won't you? Don't mind Alistair— he's a big lap puppy."

The Airedale was as tall as Dare's thigh; he grinned at them hugely and thrust his nose into Caroline's palm. The distinctive terrier smell of wet lambs' wool rose comfortingly from his coat. She followed the DCI down the hall's checkerboard of black and white marble and into the sage green living room.

Daniel had parked his motorcycle three blocks away on O Street, near the entrance gates of Georgetown University, where the welter of locked student bicycles and secondhand cars offered useful cover. He'd stored his rifle in a duffel bag he'd strapped to the motorcycle's rear, and it was easy now to sling it over his shoulder and head toward the lights of Wisconsin Avenue. He knew exactly where he was going. He'd cased the place before. He intended to take his time getting there, and make certain he wasn't being followed.

He'd done his recon well. He'd followed the DCI's chauffeur-driven navy blue Town Car on his motorcycle several times over the past two weeks, from the CIA's back entrance to this street in the heart of Georgetown. Once, the Town Car had led him to the gates of the White House and he'd been tempted, there and then, to weave through the concrete security pylons and straight up to the guardhouse, shooting as he went; but Daniel was no hothead. He was too smart to throw away his chance at glory in the End Times with some kickass assault on the Zoggite Seat of Power. He'd cut past the Town Car as it turned off Pennsylvania. And kept going toward Georgetown and the door that he knew was left unguarded.

Darien Atwood's house sat halfway between Thirty-sixth and Thirty-fifth Streets. It had no garage, but a narrow brick walk fronted by an arched door separated the house from its neighbor. The path led around the side of the old structure to the walled garden behind. It had taken Daniel only minutes to learn that the lock was just a simple Colonial latch.

"You're telling me there's a 30 April cell in Washington?"

"We think so. With at least one member in the vice president's residence," Caroline said.

She and Cuddy were seated uncomfortably on a camelback sofa. The living room ran the length of the row house, with an area for dining set out in front of a pair of French doors. Beyond these lay the walled garden, a well of darkness Caroline kept at her back. Her eyes stayed fixed on the DCI.

Dare Atwood turned restlessly before the fire. She was a tall, angular woman with iron gray hair and a face as lined as crumpled tissue paper. Tonight, in deference to Sunday, she'd worn gray flannel trousers instead of correct executive suiting; a cashmere sweater gripped her throat. "Why didn't we get this information out of Budapest?"

It was her oblique reference to Eric Carmichael, and the CD-ROM full of data he'd downloaded from 30 April's computer. Terrorist networks and financial backing worldwide. Names, dates, and places of hits ample enough to roll up cells in half a dozen European countries. Nothing that suggested a terrorist presence in the United States.

"We don't know," Cuddy answered. "Maybe because Eric never had it."

"—Or deliberately held it back." The DCI's cool gray eyes flicked remorselessly over Caroline's face. "This could be his bargaining chip. The most essential piece of the puzzle. The one piece he knew we'd need."

"Maybe," Cuddy agreed cautiously. "Or maybe he never knew there were 30 April cells in the U.S. Maybe that truth died with Krucevic. We can't say."

"Tell that to the President," Dare retorted bitterly. "Hundreds of people are showing up at hospitals, all of them poisoned, eight days after he declared victory on 30 April. He looks clueless. Worse—he looks weak. We'll be the first people Jack Bigelow blames, of course. This is our blunder. The hit we didn't see coming. Even though we've got no jurisdiction in this country—"

"What if we tried to find him?" Caroline interrupted.

"Eric?" The DCI stopped pacing, hands on her hips. "Are you *nuts*? Do you think I want to see Eric Carmichael's face *anywhere* this side of hell, Caroline, with the vice president's blood on his hands?"

"He could help. He may know something."

Dare laughed harshly. "Too late. It's absolutely out of the question. Eric screwed the deadliest terror organization on the face of the earth—*and* the President of the United States. I'm not going to let him screw me, too."

Daniel was lying on his stomach as he'd been taught to do by the army overlords who'd driven him like a steer through that Bosnian winter, years ago. His fingers were steady on the M16's barrel as he focused his telescopic sight. He hardly needed it, here in the November garden, motionless beneath the bare twigs of a dogwood tree. He was only thirty feet away from the three people talking around the fire.

He could smell the wet clay of the Potomac riverbank, the sickly sweetness of decaying leaves. Woodsmoke from the chimney of this three-hundred-year-old house. It was strange, how often he'd found himself outside in the dark like this—watching the perfect life of another human being unfold before his eyes. The richness of the silk damask on that sofa, copper red; the black and tan dog sprawled with its muzzle reaching toward Atwood's feet. The younger blond woman, thin and tense as she gestured with her hands. The faded pattern of the Oriental rug and the dark gleam of mahogany throwing back the flames. Order. Beauty. And the chaos he alone could bring.

He fixed her head in the crosshairs, and fired.

ten

It was not the first time he had wandered one of the world's great cities without a place to call home. As he hoisted himself out of the trunk of Dagmar's sedan and kissed her on both cheeks, the two solemn little boys watching from the backseat, Eric had already decided where he would go. The Mitte District of Berlin—where Sharif's wife had bolted with him to an underground parking garage—was too chic, a decade after unification, for flophouse hotels. Dossing in one of the parks would get him arrested. He'd double back toward the Bahnhof Friedrichstrasse, the gloomy old train station that had once been the main portal to East Germany, and catch one of the all-night elevateds to the western part of town. There he could wait for the first fast train of the morning. Frankfurt, maybe. Munich. Even Paris was only fourteen hours away.

His blood quickened at the thought of Paris. Border security might ask for his passport as he approached the edge of France—but in unified Europe, they usually did not. Somehow he felt he could be safe in Paris. It was a city 30 April had never hurt.

He mounted the concrete steps leading out of the

garage into the chill drizzle of a persistent rain, and glanced casually in both directions as he reached the street. It was dark and empty of life. Better to run surveillance detection regardless, he thought. Sharif had been followed.

He turned right, allowing himself a few seconds to get his bearings, locate this street corner on the map of Berlin he carried in his mind, and drop into one of the pretimed and perfectly cased routes he'd perfected over months of wandering black in the German capital. Surveillance detection was a simple technique, though hard to master: A man walking a route he knew at a briskly maintained pace would always outstrip his more tentative followers, and the distance between them would lengthen inexorably as the agent covered more known ground. Eventually he could enter The Gap— the brief period of time when he would actually be out of sight of his pursuers—and get his real business done. Service a dead drop. Leave film in a letter box. Hand off a document in a brush pass with an apparent stranger. Or simply vanish. Without the surveillance team ever realizing he'd known they were there.

Tonight, Eric intended The Gap to fall squarely near one of the entrances to the Friedrichstrasse train station. But at the corner of Friedrichstrasse and Unter den Linden, as he waited for a light with the rain beading his black leather jacket, he felt rather than saw the black Mercedes slide alongside him. Nosing at the curb as two men got out.

They aren't on foot, he thought, *and they came out of nowhere.*

And then the automatic pistol in his ribs. The hands, firm and insistent, gripping his arms. They thrust him headfirst into the backseat without a word.

It was Scottie Sorensen's habit to rise before five-thirty, an hour of darkness in the fall of the year, but on this night he had no intention of sleeping. He sat in his oak-paneled library with a glass of vintage rum close at hand, and listened to the news bulletins on public radio. By the time Cuddy called from the DCI's house in Georgetown at 1:13 A.M., Scottie was already tearing down Langley Pike alone.

He'd left his wife sprawled facedown in the king-size bed, her slim brown arms flung out like an angel's and her fan of blond hair lying like a discarded wig on the pillow. Now that he was nearly sixty, insomnia spiked Scottie's sleep at least four times a week—and he would wake, mind churning, to creep through the vast spaces of the house, a shadow amid other shadows. How many surreptitious entries had he made, over the long spiral of years? All the Soviet consulates in remote corners of the world, plundered by night through a faulty window or a coded lock whose secrets he'd bought with his faultless charm; the voice-activated transmitters stashed in such ordinary objects as ashtrays and chair legs and even, once, the stuffed heart of a child's teddy bear. All the rooms of women, too, with marriages and secrets to betray—some of them seduced for the greater good of America, others for the greater good of Scottie Sorensen.

Spying had been his proxy for deeper motives: the desire to penetrate, to thieve, to take something for nothing. Now that he was lapped in his final posting, the morbidity of Headquarters, insomnia was his passport to memory. His dark kingdom.

Lola never even knew at what hour he left her bed on these midnight excursions. Would she, he wondered, really care?

She was his third wife and the current source of his wealth: a twenty-six-year-old studio executive's daughter born and bred in L.A. She'd married Scottie two years before, after a whirlwind romance in which he'd managed to figure as James Bond, Sean Connery, and the daddy she'd always yearned to please. They met during a period of uncharacteristic earnestness on Lola's part: an internship on Capitol Hill wangled by her father, who'd contributed heavily to the last Republican campaign. She was twenty-three then, blond and sinuous and fresh as a newly opened daisy. Scottie had noticed her during one of his routine pilgrimages to the Senate Intelligence Committee; he'd invited her for drinks. Beguiled her with delicious allusions to episodes of daring and danger. Fucked her senseless, later that month, on Bermuda's pink sand.

With little in the way of education and nothing in the nature of history, she'd lapped up his legend like a series pilot. They were married in London, where his two little granddaughters lived, and spent their honeymoon among the breweries and golf courses of Scotland.

Even then Lola had been growing bored—her notion of a honeymoon being to rent out the entire city of

Cannes and fly in her three hundred closest friends—
but she'd put up with his tiresomeness rather bravely.
She had the prospect of furnishing the Great Falls
house, bought with her father's money, awaiting her
at home.

It had been a riotous two years, Scottie thought as
he flashed his badge at the security police officer man-
ning the Agency's back gate, but he knew Lola was
restless. She'd expected more glamour: sudden trips to
Europe and Asia on private Agency planes; exclusive
Washington parties where his odor of power and her
long legs were noted and envied; invitations to the
White House; perhaps even a thigh holster. He'd suggested they might be posted abroad—to Greece, maybe,
or London. She'd been agog with fantasy.

And now, because Eric Carmichael was alive, Scottie
would probably be fired.

He composed the cable he'd come here to send
while he was still crossing the empty parking lot.

IMMEDIATE BERLIN BUDAPEST WARSAW
PRAGUE PARIS LONDON ISTANBUL SECRET/
NOFORN/WNINTEL HEADQUARTERS 3455

1. C/CTC ADVISES THAT CASE OFFICER
   MICHAEL O'SHAUGHNESSY ALIAS NIGEL
   BENNING DECLARED DEAD APRIL 1997
   IS ALIVE AND MEMBER OF 30 APRIL
   TERRORIST GROUP. HE IS BELIEVED
   TO HAVE SURVIVED RECENT RAID ON
   SARAJEVO HEADQUARTERS.

2. INTERPOL CURRENTLY SEEKING
   O'SHAUGHNESSY/BENNING IN
   KIDNAPPING AND MURDER OF U.S. VICE
   PRESIDENT. O'SHAUGHNESSY/BENNING
   ALSO WANTED BY FBI. HEADQUARTERS
   REQUESTS ALL CONTROLLED TERRORIST
   ASSETS IN EUROPE BE TASKED FOR
   INFORMATION LEADING TO
   O'SHAUGHNESSY/BENNING'S ARREST.

3. O'SHAUGHNESSY/BENNING BELIEVED
   ARMED AND DANGEROUS. ALL PERSONAL
   CONTACT AND/OR AID TO FUGITIVE WILL
   BE CONSTRUED AS CRIMINAL. PHYSICAL
   DESCRIPTION TO FOLLOW.

O'Shaughnessy was Eric's official cover name within the CIA; Nigel Benning was the alias Scottie alone had known Eric used. It was unfortunate to have to sacrifice him so ruthlessly—but Scottie could not imagine Lola settling happily into retirement at his side, content to dig among the marigolds while he perfected his golf game. She was far more likely to skip town for good, her bank account in tow. He would have to arrange his future differently. While it was still his to arrange.

eleven

"Where is she?" Tom Shephard demanded as he stepped through the front door. The narrow Georgetown house was crowded with people, as though Dare Atwood had decided to throw an impromptu shindig in the middle of the night. Only the klieg lights focused on the body and the wash of blood seeping into the Oriental carpet suggested that something had gone terribly wrong.

"Over there," Cuddy answered. "With the dog."

Caroline was crouched beside a black and tan terrier, her left hand rhythmically smoothing the animal's springy coat. Shephard could see her lips move. Muttering sweet nothings to soothe the dog—or herself? He stepped carefully around a white-coated crime scene tech and edged past one of the Bureau's ballistics experts, who was having a heated argument with a uniformed D.C. cop. *Jurisdiction,* Shephard thought. The issue rarely arose in the District's all-too-frequent murders. But Cuddy had possessed the presence of mind to call Shephard's cell in the first few minutes after he dialed 911. Shephard hadn't waited for authorization to dispatch a team from the FBI's Laboratory Division.

Dare was a government official. Her murder fell automatically under the Bureau's aegis.

"Hey," he said.

Caroline and the dog both looked up. One of them had been crying. He wanted to fall on his knees and wrap his arms around her so she'd never stare straight into the eyes of death again, but they were in the middle of a crime scene and half of D.C.'s forensic experts were stepping over Caroline, and Tom was not the sort of man to wear his heart on his sleeve. He hunkered down beside her and kept his hands to himself.

There was blood all over Caroline's white blouse. The dog's? Or Dare Atwood's?

"Allie needs a vet, Tom," she said. "His paws are bleeding. He tried to charge through the French doors when the gun went off."

"Can it wait?"

She shook her head. "Dare would want us to . . . to take care of him. Alistair was her baby." Her eyes filled again and she looked quickly down at the long snout resting in her lap. The Airedale gave a whiffling sigh.

Tom rose, then glanced at the French doors. One of the panes was shattered—from the bullet, he supposed—and the dog had done its best to claw his way through the rest. Beyond, in the small walled garden, a team of forensic people was combing the damp ground. Searching for anything—footprints, the impression of an elbow, a broken twig, a clutch of fibers snared on some bark—that might lead to the killer.

He turned back to the DCI's body. A middle-aged man was closing her eyes; he'd already sponged the blood from her shattered forehead. The medical examiner, Shephard guessed. He introduced himself.

"It's pretty straightforward." The doctor was already packing up his instruments. "She was assassinated in her own living room in front of witnesses. I'll have the bullet for you by morning. But I'm thinking it came from a high-powered automatic rifle. The skull cracked like an eggshell."

"Military issue?"

"Could be."

"Doc—would you have a minute to look at the dog? It's nothing major—some cuts and glass—but he's bleeding..."

"I'm not a vet," the man said curtly, "but under the circumstances—"

"Thanks."

Avoiding the sight of the black plastic bag being zipped over Dare Atwood's iron gray hair, Shephard focused on Cuddy. "So what happened?"

"Caroline and I were sitting on the sofa—"

"—with your backs to these windows?"

Cuddy nodded. "Dare was standing in front of the fire. All of a sudden the glass shattered and she fell over. Dead. Half her forehead shot away. I don't think she knew what hit her."

"And?"

"Caroline dropped immediately beside Dare. Screaming her name. The dog went nuts. I took cover behind the sofa."

"Brave of you to admit."

"I thought it made sense," Cuddy rejoined wryly.

"I grabbed Carrie by the ankle and hauled her over to me. There was nothing she could do for Dare."

"No," Shephard agreed. "And then?"

"I heard the guy pounding past the side of the house. Toward the street. I ran to the front door and tried to catch some glimpse of him—"

"Also brave."

Cuddy shrugged impatiently. "It was a calculated hit. He only fired once. I figured he was more interested in getting away than getting me."

"See anything?"

"Just the guy's back. He was running toward Wisconsin. Dodged right into Thirty-fourth Street as I opened the door."

"Did he still have the gun?"

"He had a duffel slung over his shoulder. The gun may have been in there."

"I saw a guy with a duffel," Caroline said abruptly. "When we arrived tonight. He was walking toward us down O Street. Slouching along. I thought he was homeless. Caucasian. Clean-shaven. Under six feet— about Cuddy's height—with a wool cap fitting close to his skull. Harsh features."

"You saw all that in the dark?" Tom glanced at his wristwatch. One-thirty in the morning. "What time was this?"

"After midnight," she said defensively. "That's partly why I noticed him. He was the only other person on the sidewalk. And he passed under a streetlight while I watched. I *saw* him, Tom."

"Does he look like this?" Tom pulled a folded

paper from his pocket and flashed it in front of her eyes.

She drew a shuddering breath and nodded once. "Where did you get that?"

"Dana Enfield."

"The Speaker's wife?"

"She was poisoned at the marathon today. I don't think she'll last the night. But she gave us this."

Caroline studied the forensic sketch. It showed the world a fighter: square-jawed, pugnacious, with a sharp beak of a nose under a peaked military cap. "He was a Marine?"

"Dressed like one. The sketch doesn't square with the list of personnel at Hains Point we got from the Corps. I've seen those guys. Seven of the twelve are black, to start with, and the rest are barely twenty."

"So . . . you think this . . . shooting tonight"—Cuddy glanced uncomfortably at Dare's corpse, which was being lifted onto a gurney—"is linked to the ricin attack?"

"Death to Jack Bigelow and the corrupt maggots who keep him in power," Tom quoted. "Yeah, I think it's linked."

"He was supposed to kill me," Caroline muttered. Her cheeks were wet and she was still stroking Alistair's fur. "Not Dare, me. She should be alive right now. If we hadn't bothered her tonight—"

"She'd have died regardless," Cuddy interrupted brutally. "We didn't lead that man here, Caroline. This was all part of a plan. He knew where to hide and where to aim. He cased the house."

"Question is," Shephard added, "how many others are on his list?"

His cell phone bleated; they waited while he took the call.

"Al Tomlinson," he mouthed over the receiver. "My director. We're wanted in the Oval Office ASAP."

twelve

BERLIN, 5:23 A.M.

The black Mercedes had taken Eric to what he guessed was a safe house on the northern outskirts of the city. Blinds drawn down over the windows, furniture as gray as the city morgue's, two couches and a coffee table with ashtray conveniently provided. He was certain that the large mirror on the dividing wall was designed for purposes of observation, and that a camera and a tape recorder would be playing behind it. Eric never smoked except for cover, and he did not accept the cigarettes they offered. The two men had refused to identify themselves, and this was unusual in his experience of German police. They took his backpack and removed its contents to another room he was not permitted to enter.

He felt a curious mixture of despair and relief: relief that the long hunt of years was over, despair at the impossibility of escape. Once, he thought of Caroline: alone somewhere in Washington, waiting for Payne's funeral. He refused to think of her again.

Do you know why we've brought you here? one of the men asked. He was short and aggressive in posture, with the bland Bavarian looks of a dairy farmer. Eric mentally labeled him Klaus.

"I don't speak German," he said, firmly British, "and I'll thank you to explain this outrage fully—if not to me, then to my consulate. I'm a U.K. subject and a fellow member of the EC and we don't take kindly to having our rights abused."

Klaus drew back his arm and smashed his fist into Eric's nose. Pain seared through his head and he felt the warm wetness of blood on his lip.

No, he decided as he reeled backward, *not the police.*

The second man was an ascetic-looking type with deeply set eyes whom Eric had christened Ernst. He handed Eric a handful of tissues and clapped a hand on his shoulder sympathetically. "If that is how you choose to play the game, my friend," he murmured in English, "so be it. There's no hurry. We have all night."

You're aware of the bombing of the Brandenburg Gate, two weeks ago?

"How could I not be? A *dreadful* tragedy—dreadful."

He held on to the British accent for the first five hours of interrogation and beating. Klaus, he decided, was a fairly stupid man, but he had once studied boxing with a master. He seemed to know the internal position of each of Eric's major organs, and how to target them with punishing force. Ernst confined his contact to offerings of towels and water. Ernst alone asked the questions.

*We're looking for the maker of the bomb. We think
we've found him. A man by the name of Mahmoud
Sharif. He's Hizballah, a dangerous man. You could do
a lot for yourself by helping us.*

He told them he had no idea what they were talking
about. He'd never heard of Sharif in his life.

*You stayed with him all last week. You're his friend.
You're not Hizballah but maybe you're IRA or an arms
dealer or something else, Nigel, we really don't care. We
figure you've got your own business to conduct and we're
sorry to be keeping you tied up like this, but we'd like to
know what happened to Sharif.*

"I told you. I don't know Sharif."

*He did a bunk not five minutes after his wife left the
apartment tonight. Disappeared completely. We thought
we were following* him *when we tailed Dagmar's car,
but lo and behold, you* popped out of her sister's garage
like a jack-in-the-box and we knew we'd been snookered. Did you do it on purpose, Nigel? The old bait and
switch?*

"Who's Dagmar?"

Ernst held him this time while Klaus punched him
repeatedly in the stomach; Eric vomited and then
blessedly blacked out.

*We want Sharif, Nigel. People died at the Branden-
burg. Innocent people. And a lot of us lost our jobs.*

The voice was Ernst's and although it came from a
great distance away it percolated through his groggy
brain. *A lot of us lost our jobs.* The aftermath of the
Payne kidnapping. The right-wing chancellor's suicide.
The Social Democrats in power again. New brooms
making clean sweeps of government ministries.

"Where was I supposed to be this week?" he demanded vaguely.

"A little corner in Prenzlauerberg named Knaacke-strasse, Nigel. Good old Communist working-class neighborhood. Perfect for that sodomite Sharif and the whore he calls his wife. You know Sharif. Wires home appliances with plastique. Televisions—stereo systems—any type of electronic article. Where is Sharif, Nigel? What hole has he gone down this time?"

They weren't police and they weren't even official, he realized with a blaze of understanding. They knew nothing about Eric Carmichael. Nothing about 30 April beyond the newspaper headlines.

"I don't know what you're talking about."

Two hours later, his accent was faltering and his senses were consumed by a universal pain, one that jarred his attempt to reason so thoroughly that he concentrated on the effort as though it were a pinpoint of light piercing the darkness. Waking, after a dream. Caroline's taut form as she rappelled off the helicopter skid at the Farm, her hair blown into her eyes.

"Does this Sharif bloke live here in Berlin, then?" he asked thickly.

Ernst was losing his patience. "You were in his wife's car. Probably in the trunk. You walked out of her sister's garage and we followed you. We followed Dagmar, too. She gave you up quite easily, I might add. Probably because she had the children with her. People are extraordinarily frightened of Klaus."

"I don't know why. He's such a little fuck."

The fist in his right ear, this time; his head ringing. Eric began to laugh, a weak and gurgling sound that brought the blood welling to his teeth. Three of them felt broken and his face was a raw pulp, but the humor of the situation overwhelmed him. "You bloody git!" he whispered. "Don't you know when a girl's telling a tale and leading you down the garden path? Oh, Lord—what Monika will say when she hears!"

"Cut the crap," Klaus snarled, "and tell us where to find Sharif."

"*Monika,* darling, is Dagmar's sister. She lives in an apartment building in the Mitte District with her husband, a traveling salesman for Siemens."

He was almost babbling in his giddy delight, almost telling them what they wanted to know. Klaus raised his fist again: Ernst held him back.

"We followed you there."

"Then you also know she's a luscious little piece. Too lonely for words. Very correct German husband, very tedious for a girl like Monika. I was staying with her while her man was on the road. Her sister—who I gather is somehow connected to this Sharif fellow you're hunting—claimed I was staying with *her.* Since you asked. Family feeling, and all that. Thinking fast on her feet. Protecting Monika's honor. Not a bit of truth in the whole bloody yarn. You've been right well snookered, I'll tell you that."

The door to the adjoining room opened and a young woman—blond, coiffed, as neat as a flight attendant for Lufthansa—appeared. She tossed Nigel Benning's alias passport on the table without a word; Ernst picked it up and flipped through the pages. Eric knew what he would find: an entry stamp for Poland. An exit stamp for Hungary.

"What are you doing in Germany, Nigel?"

"Just passing through, really." He closed his eyes, a tide of weakness tugging him into the shallows. "A hiking tour all on my own. Tony Bloody Blair did for my job six months back, so I put London behind me and set off for the Continent. A good pair of shoes, a good backpack, and the world's your oyster. Budapest last month, Poland before that. I'm working my way home to the white cliffs of Dover now, if you must know, and after this unfortunate experience I'm liable to hasten my trip."

"Come on." Ernst was speaking German now and he seized Klaus's elbow. "We're wasting our time. We should have nabbed the wife."

"Want him dead?"

A fractional pause, as the brains of the operation considered his alternatives.

Then Eric was lifted, wobbly as an old mattress, and dragged out of the room.

thirteen

Adele Bigelow raised her head from the pillow. A light shone from the master bedroom's walk-in closet, and the glare hurt her eyes. She felt blindly for the wristwatch resting on her discarded book and saw that it was the middle of the night. Jack had never bothered to come to bed. Like a bell sounding in deep water, memory returned sharply. *Chemical attack. Hundreds dying. A riot in the streets of Spring Valley.*

"Jack?" she called as she threw back the covers. "Honey?"

The closet door swung slowly open and there he was, backlit against the vivid light: an aging man with a powerful frame, stooped over the golf magazine cupped in his hands. He was sitting on the bench he used to pull on cowboy boots. His body was curved like a question mark, something in its lines too defeated and weary, and Adele thought, *Oh, Sophie. Why did you have to die?*

She had liked the vice president. Liked the easy humor and intelligence the woman mustered through five months of grueling campaigning after the nomination was secured, liked the raw emotion that surged beneath the carefully controlled surface. They were different people, of course—Adele hated the White House limelight, loathed politics, and survived by effacing herself completely in public—but at least Sophie had been a woman she could trust. She had no agenda beyond the work meted out to her in the Old Executive Office Building; no rivalry with the First Lady she nurtured in back halls. They were both mothers of sons—had that, at least, in common—and both tried to shield Jack Bigelow from the savagery of the press or his own Cabinet. Now Sophie was gone.

Jack might stand before the microphones and declare that the United States would never be held hostage by terrorist thugs; he could celebrate the courage of Sophie Payne or Caroline Carmichael and pose while he handed out medals—but there was still the annoying American tendency to need *somebody* to blame. It was all too possible, Adele knew, that Sophie's murder would scuttle Jack's second term—and as much as she longed to retire to Montana, four years in the White House would never be enough for her husband.

"Didn't mean to wake you," he said now. "Got a meeting in a couple of minutes."

He could have waited in his office or any one of the sitting rooms that ran the length of the private part of the residence; but he'd retreated to the bedroom closet. *Poor Jack.*

"A meeting at this hour of the night?"

"Dare Atwood's been killed."

She sank back against the pillows, listening to the surge in her own heartbeat, the brutal words. Darien Atwood, dead. She hardly knew the DCI—the Iron

Maiden look had always intimidated her—but then
she remembered a dinner at the woman's house, before they were voted into power: old bricks and glossy
black shutters in Georgetown. The musty smell of
boxwood.

"How?"

"Shot in her own living room. Sniper."

"And are you next?" she demanded querulously.
"Are they killing all of us, one by one?"

"*Addy*. You know I'm well protected."

"I know nothing about it," she whispered.

Jack glanced away. The glossy magazine slipped
from his knees to the closet floor, a sprawl of neatly
clad men chipping as though their lives depended on
it. "I'll bring you coffee. Seven-thirty. You've got the
hairdresser at nine."

She rolled away from him, her back to the door.
The least she could do was stay awake. And listen for
gunfire in the distance.

It was Shephard who buttoned Caroline's brown wool
bomber jacket over her blouse to hide the bloodstains,
his hands gentle on her wounded shoulder. Cuddy
was busy discussing Alastair, the dog, with one of the
cops—trying to convince the man that the Airedale
didn't belong in the D.C. pound, that Cuddy would
be happy to take charge of Allie until Dare's next of
kin arrived. Tom could feel something inside Caroline
collapse as they stood alone on the floodlit brick walk-
way that led to the street. Her chin sank to her chest

and her frame seemed to buckle. He folded her close, his heart wildly beating.

"I'm sorry," he muttered, his mouth in her hair. "I'm so sorry." When what he wanted to say was, *I love you. Jesus Christ I love you Carrie and you could've died tonight*—

She released him abruptly and swept her hand over her eyes. "Fuck," she said tiredly. "I'm so bad at death. The fucking unfairness of it all."

"Fairness," he echoed. "It could have been you tonight, you realize that? He could have shattered your head in the split second after he shot Dare's."

"I wish he had."

"Don't say that." He shook her slightly, agonized and furious at once. "Do you know what it feels like? To care this much about a woman with a death wish?"

"Tom—" She stared past him, a goaded look on her face. "I don't *want* you to feel. I don't want to be responsible for anybody else's heart."

"Why? Because your husband was killed three years ago, Carrie? My wife died, too."

"It's not the same." She laughed harshly. "Christ, is it *not* the same."

"Because Jen wasn't a terrorist martyr? Bullshit. *Bullshit*." He spun away from her, trench coat flapping. It was stupid of him to force the issue this way, two o'clock in the morning and Dare's blood still drying on her clothes, but he couldn't help it. "You can't go into the grave with them, you know. You've got to keep living."

Her lips parted as though she might tell him to calm down or go fuck himself, but instead all she said was, "We've got to get to the White House. Will you drive?"

He glanced back and saw Cuddy emerging from the door, the dog with bandaged paws on a short lead. "I've got Caroline," he called in his most efficient voice, no hint of high drama in his words. "You bring her car, okay?"

And to Caroline, carefully impersonal as he opened her passenger door: "I don't know *how* we explain the mutt to White House Security."

The group of people assembled outside the Oval Office had dispensed with chitchat. All were too busy composing briefing points in their heads to even glance at each other. Al Tomlinson was head of the FBI; he'd worn a blue blazer and tie for the occasion. Matthew Finch, the President's Chief of Staff and oldest friend, was in a bulky sweater and corduroys. Cory Rinehart, who'd been Dare's deputy for six months and would probably be forced to take over the intelligence community helm until Bigelow could appoint a successor, had worn a dark gray suit, as though he fully expected to move seamlessly from the White House to Payne's funeral at Arlington. Nobody liked Rinehart at Langley, but he'd risen through the hierarchy on a steady cocktail of politics, ambition, and ass-kissing. Caroline felt decidedly outclassed in this group, still wearing the jeans she'd thrown on earlier that evening and a lipstick she'd managed to scrounge from her purse. Her bomber jacket masked the bloodstains on her blouse, and nobody'd urged her to take it off and stay awhile. But then, she was only here as an interested observer and unwilling target of homegrown terrorists, whenever anybody chose to remember that fact. She was a *referent*—refer-AUNT, with heavy emphasis on the final syllable—as they persisted in saying out at the Agency. An authority to whom the room could defer whenever conversation lagged.

Tom and Cuddy were muttering to one another in lowered tones, Tom scowling and Cuddy fingering the bridge of his glasses. He'd left the Airedale sound asleep on the backseat of Caroline's car with the Secret Service to check on him. Tom had mastered his unruly emotions during the brief ride down Pennsylvania Avenue, saying nothing until he asked for Caroline's badge at the White House gate; and maybe he'd never force her to face the truth again. Maybe she could go on pretending that his whole heart wasn't in his eyes when he looked at her. That she didn't yearn for the comfort of his hands. Shephard was nothing like Eric Carmichael. He'd never desert her without a word, send her alone into death, make her knees weak and her skin burn at the touch of his fingertip. He would simply take care of her for the rest of her life. The idea was overwhelming; it felt like sleep at the end of an insomniac year. *And they call this betrayal?*

She was fighting the impulse to cross the hallway and blurt out the truth—tell him everything he didn't know about Eric and the past few weeks in a headlong apology and confession that would ensure Tom Shephard never looked at her again—but at that moment the President walked swiftly down the corridor toward them and she was forced to pay attention.

Bigelow, she saw to her surprise, was also wearing jeans.

"Good evening, Mr. President," the group chorused dutifully, although it should have been *good morning*; only Matthew Finch stepped forward and reached a hand to Bigelow's shoulder. They all waited until the two men walked toward the President's desk before following them through the door.

There was a small conference table here and a larger one in the Cabinet room adjoining, but Finch had taken a wing chair and Tomlinson another, so the rest disposed themselves in comfort. Bigelow kicked his chair back and put his boots up on the shining surface of the desk. *He's not really relaxed,* Caroline thought with the reflexive habit of the leadership analyst. *He's just going through the motions, and hoping it helps. Does he own that desk? Or does it pass, like the room, to his successor?*

"Well, Matt? What've we got?"

"Eight hundred thirty-six people checked into hospitals at last count," Finch replied with a glance at his notes, "and Director Atwood murdered at home."

"I know that," Bigelow retorted impatiently. "Let's not waste time kicking the barn door closed on the horse's ass. I'm angry as hell about poor Dare—liked and respected her. She did a damn fine job over in McLean and we're all the poorer for her loss."

Cory Rinehart opened his mouth to say something in acknowledgment, but Bigelow's attention was already elsewhere.

"We're not sitting here at two A.M. to weep for the

DCI. We've got a nutcase on the loose. I want to know what we're going to do about it. Al?"

The FBI director edged forward on his chair and clasped his hands soulfully between his knees. "We think this is a well-planned and executed campaign of revenge for the destruction of 30 April in Europe."

"You seriously think anybody survived that raid last week?"

"It seems clear somebody did. The letter to the *Washington Post*—"

Bigelow dismissed Al Tomlinson with a glare. "Barn door," he said. "Horse's ass. Ms. Carmichael— you witnessed the raid on 30 April. Think anybody survived it?"

"Just me, sir. And Jozsef Krucevic."

"No boy in a hospital bed is spiking the nation's punch bowl with chem-bio agents. So who is?"

Cory Rinehart shifted restively in his chair, and despite her misery and exhaustion and the lives she'd failed to save, Caroline felt the ghost of a smile pricking her lips. Rinehart might be Acting Director, but she—Caroline—was the Referent. Life and soul of the President's party.

"According to one of our sources, 30 April had agents in place in Mrs. Payne's household well before the kidnapping," Caroline told Jack Bigelow. "Presumably they're still active, sir. That suggests a Washington-area cell with links to 30 April abroad."

"Americans?"

She glanced sidelong at Tom Shephard. "That's correct."

"Just sitting tight over there, off Mass Ave? Waiting

for Sophie Payne's replacement to move into the Observatory?" He thrust his feet to the floor and stood up restlessly. Took a turn before the window. It was floodlit at night; the rose garden outside looked for all the world like the exercise ground of a maximum-security prison.

"Why the hell didn't you mention an American cell before, Ms. Carmichael?"

"We only learned of it tonight, sir."

"It's also a matter of jurisdiction, Mr. President," Cuddy Wilmot added. "The CIA does not operate—"

"—against American citizens on American soil," Bigelow intoned wearily. "I *know*. But are these kooks who came from abroad? Are they Central European neo-Nazis embedded in our home turf, waiting for a reason to kick some American ass?"

"No," Shephard said.

Bigelow stared at him. "*You*. You're the Bureau guy. One who was in Berlin. Brought Soph's body back. Right?"

"Right."

"Tom Shephard is currently acting as chief of our 30 April Task Force," Tomlinson supplied helpfully. "Before he went to Berlin, he was Deputy Chief of Domestic Terrorism."

"Good enough," the President said dryly. "So what kind of terrorist kills their own, Tom? Answer me that. What kind of guy knowingly takes out nearly a thousand Americans just like himself, entirely at random, for the fucking hell of it?"

"Timothy McVeigh," Shephard said quietly. "Who blew up the Alfred P. Murrah Building in Oklahoma

City a few years back. Our ricin killer mentioned him in his first letter to the press—and his second. We received this half an hour ago, sir."

He handed a piece of paper to Jack Bigelow. Caroline already knew the words by heart.

> *Thirty April has struck a blow for justice with the execution of Darien Atwood for her numberless crimes against the American people. True Citizens throughout this great land need no longer cringe beneath the jackboot of government spies who harass and terrorize our every move. Jack Bigelow's puppet is dead. Timothy McVeigh is avenged. More of the Zoggite minions are scheduled for the firing squad in coming days. Now is the hour to take to the streets. The Leader is gone but the Faithful will achieve his vision. The End Times are at hand.*

Bigelow glanced up. "What kind of crap is this?"

"It's the calling card of the American patriot movement, Mr. President, which some people estimate at nearly twenty million strong."

"Patriot movement? What the hell is that?"

Shephard's weathered face was virtually expressionless, but Caroline alone knew he had no patience for the ignorance of these people he served, these people he'd warned, who hadn't bothered to listen until voters were dying by the hundreds in the streets of Washington. Tom's anger ran deep and straight to his gut, and when he chose he could lash out with a ferocity that was frightening; but Caroline saw that at this critical moment his emotions were coiled tight as the safety on an automatic. The conversation was important to Tom. He would not waste his best opportunity in years to focus the President's attention.

"The patriot movement—the True Citizens, they call themselves—believe that this nation will be destroyed in a final apocalyptic race war pitting White Christians against everybody else," he said carefully. "They call it the *End Times,* and they hold training camps all over the country designed to equip their faithful to survive. Flip a True Citizen on his back, and you'll find a 30 April sympathizer, sir. They're fellow travelers."

Bigelow frowned. "Are you talking about militia groups?"

"Partly. The average True Citizen is white, male, in his mid-thirties, single, and highly skilled; he hates gun control first and foremost and everyone who's different from himself in descending order after that. The militia movement recruits heavily among that population. But I'm also talking about people like William Pierce—a former physics professor from West Virginia. Highly educated, charismatic, and an ardent worshipper of Adolf Hitler."

Bigelow raised a quizzical eyebrow. "Never heard of him."

"No. Pierce founded the National Alliance, a neo-Nazi group that worked and played on his three-hundred-and-fifty-acre compound outside Hillsboro. He broadcast hate radio there and ran his White Supremacist record label, Resistance Records. He also wrote *The Turner Diaries.*"

"Now *that* I recognize. Banned book, right?"

"In a manner of speaking." Al Tomlinson shifted

uncomfortably. "It's an underground novel about the final race war in America. Required reading now at Quantico for our trainees. Pierce blows up Bureau Headquarters in the book—and a copy was found in McVeigh's car. He got the recipe for his fertilizer and fuel oil bomb from it. *The Turner Diaries* has inspired a lot of violence, Mr. President, over the past few years. Particularly against blacks and Jews."

"And you think it gave our ricin boy ideas?"

"Possibly," Tom Shephard said. "If not Pierce's book, then certainly the movement he represents. True Citizens believe the U.S. government is a bunch of puppets whose strings are pulled by Jews and foreigners. That most elected politicians operate in violation of the Constitution, which True Citizens say gives every one of us the right to flout laws we don't like. True Citizens refuse to pay federal taxes. They hate programs that foster diversity and tolerance—like public schools—and usually keep their kids at home, where they can be taught to think as narrowly as their parents. They're often aligned with fundamentalist Christian churches that regard non-Christians as the devil's spawn. True Citizens are an armed resistance operation quietly spreading through the heart of America. You and I, Mr. President, are the kind of people it's their duty to kill."

Bigelow might have dismissed all this as the loose screed of AM radio, but the rapt attention of those listening around the room stilled any impulse to quip. He turned to the FBI director. "The Bureau is watching these jokers, I suppose?"

"As much as we can, without violating their civil rights. The Domestic Terrorism unit was ginned up as a direct result of Oklahoma City. It handles roughly a thousand cases a year—"

"But somewhere along the line," Shephard interrupted, "the American public decided McVeigh was a maverick and a wacko who represented only *himself*. A lone operator. Whereas McVeigh's just the tip of the iceberg, Mr. President. And we refuse to see it."

"Why?" Bigelow asked simply.

"Some people would say that this *whitewash* of the terrorists in our own backyard is due to the fact that the Radical Right is a vocal part of *your party*, sir. A fringe part, of course. Most of them don't even vote. However—"

A pregnant silence fell; Shephard was on dangerous ground here, and knew it. He'd achieve nothing if the President threw him out of the Oval Office.

"Go on," Bigelow said.

"As Americans, we'd all like to believe our enemies are *outside*. Aliens with names we can't pronounce. *Illegals*. Even the words we use to describe them are designed to distance. It's *them*, not *us*. We're united against terror, aren't we? Victims, not thugs. We don't want to believe the bomb will come from the guy two blocks down the street we've known all our lives."

Bigelow threw himself into his desk chair and stared ruminatively at Caroline's sling. "What I never understood," he muttered, "was how he could kill all those children. In the day-care center. Which he must've known was there, right?"

He was talking, she realized, about McVeigh.

"There's a photograph," she said slowly, "that I saw once and have never forgotten. Two little boys dressed in wool jackets and short pants—like the kind John-John wore to JFK's funeral. They've got those bony knees and thick shoes and the older boy has his arm around the younger one. He's trying to comfort him. Because they're walking, alone, toward the door of the showers at Auschwitz."

She paused. The room was very still. Tom was watching her as though determined to mount a rescue.

"You look at that picture and know they were pulled away from their parents just minutes before. You can see that the older boy is trying hard to be brave. For his little brother. He's taking care of him. That image has come to mean everything about the Holocaust to me—the murder of innocence. The evil implicit in that walk from daylight into shadow. But also the love. The love between two people in the face of unspeakable horror."

She cleared her throat. "What I'm trying to say, Mr. President, is that you can kill anyone—even a frightened little boy and his brother—if you no longer see them as human. McVeigh did it. Our guy with the ricin and the gun did it. I believe he's going to do it again."

fourteen

Daniel turned off the motorcycle's headlamp as he cruised slowly down Paddock Road and swung into Dressage Lane. The development was named Tara, as though the echo of Vivien Leigh in a white tulle ball gown might elevate the moderate-income housing to breathless elegance. Barely fifteen years old, Tara had once been a Virginia horse farm. All the streets were wistfully named for aspects of stables that had little to do with the D.C. suburbs. On this sharply chilly night in November the town houses—some clapboard, some brick, all vaguely Colonial—were silent and slumbering. Most were ablaze in white exterior lights that picked out their blank windows and concrete stoops.

The Carmichael place sat at the endpoint of a cul-de-sac. It was narrow and high, the living areas built over the garage, with a raised set of steps leading to the front door. A dense mat of zoysia grass, dun-colored now, stretched from sidewalk to juniper foundation plantings. Daniel had noticed that the house was frankly anonymous the first time he cased the place a few days before. No plastic play structures fading in the rain, no wreath on the dark green door. No garden, and not a hand tool misplaced. She probably paid a bunch of Hispanics, he thought, to cut her grass each week. She'd pay 'em to have her kids for her, if she could.

Unlike the rest of Dressage Lane, the house was dark inside and out. He circled the cul-de-sac, rode slowly back up the street, and killed his engine at the intersection with Paddock Road. No sense in alerting the woman he was there by gunning the bike in her driveway. He couldn't quite figure Caroline Carmichael: smart enough to kill the Leader, but stupid enough to be listed in the phone book. No security system on her house. She must actually believe she was *safe*. Un-important. Despite the floating pack of press people who showed up during daylight hours.

Or maybe, he thought suddenly, she wanted to be killed. Wanted this kind of penance for the war she'd waged.

He shifted his duffel over his shoulder and trudged back up the street, keeping his booted feet on the grass to muffle his approach. He'd expected at least the pale blue glow of the television screen flickering from a window. He'd hunkered enough in these bushes during the previous three days to know how she was living. The bags of chips on the coffee table. The bot-tle of wine at the ready. Lying on her sofa like trailer trash in her sweatpants and bedroom slippers. He could understand that—the woman *had* to be haunted by the blood she'd shed. She'd meddled in things that didn't concern her—and the Leader had died for her sins. Cut down by the Beast System he'd sworn, like Daniel, to overthrow.

Because it was an end unit, a nice swath of lawn

wrapped the far side of the house. He dropped the duffel in the shadows and quietly unzipped it. The M16 was a matte black; it did not even gleam in the neighbors' lights. He'd learned to use it years before, during a harsh winter's tour in Bosnia.

He'd joined the Army Reserve when the cost of farming and the taxes on the Hillsboro land strained his budget past breaking point. *It's only one weekend a month, Bekah,* he'd told his wife as he signed the papers, *and maybe the Feds'll look more kindly on me once I've served my time.*

Four months after basic training, he'd been deployed to Bosnia to keep the Dayton Peace Accord.

It was a Sign, he thought now: a Purpose preordained by the mystery of the Lord's ways. He was lost among the ranks of the Fifth Corps and the Old Ironsides Division, twenty thousand strong, and he had no idea why he was expected to tramp through the cold ten thousand miles from home in the dead of winter. Dolf was four years old. Daniel sent a letter back to Bekah signed *Your tax dollars at work, Sweetheart,* and spent Christmas Eve on night patrol, terrified he'd trigger a land mine.

Instead, he'd encountered the Leader: Mlan Krucevic, a desperate and brilliant fugitive, charged with crimes against humanity by the Tribunal at The Hague. Krucevic and his men scattered Daniel's patrol and took him captive. In the dark hours before morning, the two of them began to talk. Or rather, Krucevic talked. Daniel listened.

Remembering that face now—the uncompromising cruelty of the mouth, the clear dark eyes and crushing intelligence—bitterness surged through Daniel. *He had been robbed*. First of his son—his Dolf—and now of the man he'd worshipped like a god. Anger surged upward and his grip tightened on the duffel bag. He'd intended to simply shoot Caroline Carmichael in the head while she stared drunkenly at the television screen, but he could see now that that kind of death would never satisfy him. He needed to feel her pain—needed her to beg for mercy on her bleeding knees—needed to see the terror in her face as she died.

He lifted the gun in one hand and drew a knife from his boot with the other. He didn't care if the entire U.S. government was hunting him right now for Dare Atwood's murder—he'd force open the back door and take the woman while she slept. The Leader's vengeance was singing in his veins.

fifteen

Wally Aronson's apartment in Berlin's Scheunen-viertel sat on the top floor of a converted nineteenth-century mansion, one that had survived two world wars with only minor reconstruction. It was a largish place, particularly for a man whose wife and kids had departed the previous month for Maryland: a high-ceilinged living room filled with antiques gathered in postings to Moscow and Budapest; equally antique plumbing; a couple of deserted bedrooms that echoed when his polished shoes clicked down the parquet-covered corridor. The CIA's station chief in Berlin was a major player—a linchpin in the delicate business of liaison with German intelligence—and he merited the kind of expansive accommodation State Department officers coveted. But Wally was unusual in choosing to live in the Scheunenviertel, the old Jewish Quarter of Berlin, rather than the expat ghetto of leafy Charlotten-burg. He liked the food he found in the Quarter—it reminded him sometimes of Queens—and he liked the feel of the old walls leaning toward one another across the narrow streets. Only the black swastikas sprayed on the nearby synagogue had the power to trouble him.

He rose early by embassy standards and walked out in search of the morning papers, German- and English-language both. He bought fresh soft doughnuts and steaming Turkish coffee and consumed them while he read the papers. The loneliness Brenda had left behind felt less weighty then, as he sniffed the *Berlinerluft*— the light, soft air that was the pride of the city, but which Wally always thought smelled dampeningly of the soft brown coal burned throughout Central Europe. He could imagine himself the spy with a thousand faces, haunting the no-man's-land of the Cold War as le Carré had done. He was a good case officer— Caroline Carmichael had said once that Wally was born to hold somebody's hand in a rundown bar and pay them for the privilege—and he'd risen fast through the covert world. Wally was spare, short, and kindly-faced with a graying goatee and a waspish sense of humor. His father had been a successful salesman. Which in fact was what Wally had become: a dealer in souls and morals. *Your secrets for our dreams. Your hopes for solid cash. With a cyanide pill on the side.*

Chief of Station—COS, as it was known among Agency people—was primarily a managerial role. Wally sat in on embassy meetings and trained up the kids fresh off the Farm and reviewed cables before they were sent home, chafing all the while at the ops he no longer got to run. He was not so far removed from the street, however, that he'd lost his tradecraft. And so, even before he had a chance to turn around, he felt the man following him back from the newsstand this morning. Wally, Caroline once remarked, had eyes in his ass.

He was intrigued by the surveillance. Was it his old friends the Russians? The North Koreans, perhaps, operating in Berlin? A training run for the German service, which had picked him out like a familiar landmark, Wally the Chief of Scheunenviertel? He strolled casually past the entrance to his apartment building, sipping his coffee, and dropped into one of his surveillance detection routes.

It was possible, of course, that a more sinister construction could be placed on this watcher. It was barely a week since Sophie Payne's body had been recovered; her funeral would take place back home in a matter of hours. Thirty April might be blasted to smithereens by his good friend Caroline, but revenge was ripe for the taking. It'd be a terrorist coup to snuff the CIA's man in Berlin; Berlin was 30 April's backyard. He made a play of dropping one of his newspapers and, as he bent to retrieve it, glanced casually back the way he'd come.

The paving was empty.

Vaguely irritated—disappointed, if the truth were known—he wandered on for a few hundred more yards. Checking, surreptitiously, to see if the tail had reappeared. By this time he'd left the Scheunenviertel behind—had crossed the Spree near Mon Bijou Park—had the buildings of Humboldt University looming before him. He glanced back.

Nothing.

He turned into a side street and began to walk home.

When he reached the elegant old building on Sophienstrasse, his footsteps slowed. A man was slumped on the marble steps leading to the entry. His watcher. Wally was sure of it.

"That's ballsy," he muttered. "Wouldn't want to tire you out with a long walk, friend. What can I do for you?"

The man raised his head. His face was a mass of bruises, the blood still fresh and the features raw and swollen. His hair was incongruously brown. But Wally had never forgotten the look in those eyes—like a wolf too wild to be taken.

"*Eric,*" he said.

sixteen

She'd been called into the Agency in the middle of the night many times, but it was always unnerving to see the vast parking lots empty under rank upon rank of brilliant lights. The electrified barbed wire that surrounded the compound was less obvious in daylight, and the SPOs—the security police officers who manned the gates—walked right up to the car window to stare intently at her badge and face before waving her through.

She and Cuddy would do what they could in the last few hours before Sophie Payne's funeral. There might be some clue Cuddy had overlooked in the disc full of data Eric had sent out of Budapest—or a name lost in the thousands of pages of 30 April files. A link between the neo-Nazi group and somebody here at home—an academic conference where two men had met, a stint in a jail cell where two killers joined forces.

"I'll get out a tasking cable to Berlin," Caroline was saying as she and Cuddy swung into the Counterterrorism Center at 3:14 A.M. "Wally may have some assets left he can query—"

She stopped short, staring at the silver-haired man

seated in her cubicle. He had a pile of her files—the ones she'd yet to destroy—before him on the desk and was systematically going through them, half-glasses resting on his nose, red pen poised.

"Berlin has already been tasked," he said, holding out a copy of a cable. "They have all they need to wrap up this investigation."

Caroline took the sheet of paper.

C/CTC ADVISES THAT CASE OFFICER MICHAEL O'SHAUGHNESSY/NIGEL BENNING DECLARED DEAD APRIL 1997 IS ALIVE AND MEMBER OF 30 APRIL TERRORIST GROUP...

"You burned him," she said hollowly. "Cuddy—he's blown Eric sky high. There's no cover left."

Cuddy took the copy of the cable and scanned it rapidly. The core of Caroline's body had deadened, as though all function of heart and bone had suddenly shut down. There was no way back. No help to be found.

"Pity you tossed so much in the incinerator, my dear," Scottie said easily. "These files are sadly incomplete. That will look *very bad* when the Inspector General investigates what you knew, and when. Rather as though you had something to hide."

"Get out of my desk," she said with effort. "Please."

Scottie laughed and swiveled in her chair. "I received your letter of resignation, Carrie. It saved me the trouble of firing you. But I must say I'm rather surprised to see you here. I'd have thought you'd borrow a page from Eric's book—and turn up dead."

"That's not funny," Cuddy said sternly, as though Scottie were a little boy with a bad sense of humor. "You know Dare Atwood has been murdered. Why weren't you at the White House?"

"I had documents of my own to incinerate," Scottie replied comfortably. "Sad about Dare. Who'll take the dog, I wonder? We all know who'll take her office. I must make my obeisance to Rinehart sometime this morning."

Caroline was holding the shreds of her temper in both hands. Cross Scottie now, and she'd lose her final slim hope of bringing Eric home safe and alive. "I'm withdrawing that resignation. I'm here to help."

"I'm afraid that's impossible," Scottie replied. "I've already informed the Inspector General's office of your decision, and added my own Memorandum to the Record detailing Eric's survival. I'm sure there will be quite an extensive investigation, Carrie. Of how you managed to cover up this sordid mess for so long."

"You know I knew nothing about it! Dare—"

Dare was dead, and any truth she might have believed had died with her. The only other person who understood how Eric had been used—how Caroline had been deceived—was Cuddy Wilmot. And he was easy enough to destroy.

"Under the circumstances," Scottie said dryly, "I cannot possibly allow you access to classified information. Your clearances are completely compromised."

"You wouldn't dare do this." Somehow she managed to keep her voice level. "I know enough to end your career, Scottie. Enough to ruin everything you've worked for."

"But it would be simply your word against mine. And I'll make very sure your word is dirt." Scottie reached for his phone. "I'll call the SPOs now. They'll escort you to your car."

"You realize you're prejudicing this entire investigation? That Eric is the only possible lead we've got to the 30 April cell in D.C.? You *need* Eric, Scottie. He's the one person who can save your ass."

He gazed at her pityingly. "You don't really think he'd bother, Caroline, after all we've been through? Having burned my bridges with Eric, as it were, I had no choice but to burn *him*."

"Scottie," she lashed out, "people are dying out there. *Innocent* people. They're dying because of *you*. The evil you've done for your own amusement. You *owe* it to Eric—to everybody in this institution—to try to put things right. To find this killer before he does further damage."

A buzzer sounded at the entrance to the vault; Scottie rose briskly from Caroline's desk. "I have no intention of supporting this investigation. I want it to spin out as long as possible, Carrie. I want the Bureau to make their usual hash of it and I want the media to come calling. While the bodies fall and the nation screams in panic, our jobs are the most secure they're ever likely to be. The President will be forced to admit just how much he needs us."

"Good God," Cuddy said blankly. "You don't mean that, Scottie. You've spent your life—"

Their chief reached for a cardboard box sitting at his feet. It held a jumble of items: a cup full of pens, a framed photograph of William Webster shaking

Caroline's hand; an award for merit she'd earned five years ago. He handed the box to Cuddy.

"That'll be the SPOs buzzing. Walk Caroline to the car, will you, Wilmot? And decide on the way whether you want to leave with her. It's a decision you shouldn't make lightly."

seventeen

Daniel had crept from his own bedroom in the black heart of night often enough to know that the quality of silence in a sleeping house is different from an empty one. There were the times he'd lain awake and the times he'd wanted to be sure that Dolf was blissful and unaware in his own small room; times later, when Dolf was in the ground, that he'd sprawled on the boy's sterile bed and cursed Bekah for washing the sheets. He craved the scent of his son like another man craved drink or sex, and sometimes he huddled in the boy's closet, just to breathe in the elusive memory of him. It took Daniel only three seconds in Caroline Carmichael's pitch-black room to know she wasn't there.

As the realization came, he was passing in front of her full-length mirror, and the sudden unexpected reflection of his own shoulder, his head beneath the tight wool cap, startled him so much that he swung around and smashed at the figure staring back at him. The hard metal haft of his M16 slammed straight through the plasterboard wall and the mirror shivered into a hundred pieces, glancing off his face like the most vicious of kisses. He stood panting, engulfed by disappointment.

After that it was enough to pull the covers from her bed and hurl a lamp to the floor before he turned and fled down the narrow stairs to the side window he'd cut open. He tossed the rifle through the opening and slid one leg out onto the grass. Thinking: *Where the fuck is that bitch I come all this way to kill her maybe she knew maybe she knew I was coming and ran Jesus H. Christ I've got to find the girl there's no time left I—*

He stood still, balancing on one leg, aware suddenly of the flashlight's beam edging around the back of the house, a small perfect orb of light that bled an elliptical trail like a comet's. Bobbing. Shifting. A man searching with a flashlight for a burglar who might just be there.

Daniel sank like a stone into the narrow space between the house's outer wall and the juniper trailing sharp fingers across his cheek. A neighbor'd heard or seen him. How many trackers were there? One? Five? He disregarded the M16 lying blatantly on the frost-tipped lawn. The comet was bobbing closer, and he could hear the man's breathing now. Footsteps. The light circled the gun.

If the guy turned and sprinted back around the house toward whatever vehicle had brought him, or if he reached for a radio and called in backup, it would all be over. Daniel was cut off from his motorcycle and his road home, his road forward. He teetered slightly on his haunches but with the luck that sustained him, the cop—a uniformed patrol officer on the night shift,

Daniel could see his stubble in the flashlight's beam—
was bending forward, a handkerchief in one hand.
Reaching for the M16.

Daniel sprang.

He landed heavily on the man's shoulders, pitching
him forward so that his chin butted painfully against
the ground. The cop gave a grunt of surprise but
Daniel's left hand was over his mouth by that time and
the knife was curving around the front of the throat,
nicking at the flesh as the man's head strained against
him. He smelled cigarette smoke and shampoo and
the tang of fear, then the knife slashed confidently
through the jugular and the windpipe and the head
was just a latex mask dangling from his hands.

The body slumped forward and blood spurted over
the frozen grass. Daniel wiped his knife on the cop's
jacket and dragged the M16 from beneath his hip.
With a burst of static the man's radio went off and
Daniel jumped as though he'd been shot. His hands
were shaking and slick with blood. He'd have to toss
his gloves somewhere. But first, he had to get to the
bike.

eighteen

Wally hoisted Eric to his feet. "You're dead. Aren't you? *Dead?*"

"Nearly three years." His broken lips were painful to look at. He swayed where he stood. "I can tell you everything, Wally, but I can't make it much farther."

"Come inside. There's an elevator."

He helped him negotiate the steps and the heavy door, noticing the grimace of pain when he touched Eric's ribs. Broken, probably. Once Eric had taught Wally how to march three days without food, how to creep silently over an enemy and throttle him without a sound, how to lie in ambush and avoid forward-looking infrared. Wally had tried to be worthy, to live up to Eric's toughness and physical courage, to win a word of praise from this man he and his buddies regarded with awe. They'd vied for the right to buy Eric a beer at the Farm's bar. And now here he was, slumped like a bum on Wally's doorstep. Both of them middle-aged.

When he'd heard of Eric's death in that bombed plane, Wally had left his station's vault at a run and taken shelter for half an hour in the embassy's men's room. Swallowing the pain that hardened his throat and attempting to believe that a man like Eric could be gone. Dead like anyone else.

"Who beat you up?"

"Don't know."

He thrust back the ancient lift's iron grille and steered Eric inside. Pushed the button for number four and waited for the elevator to ascend. Eric sagged against the cage, his eyes closed. "Thanks, Wally."

"You weren't on MedAir 901. When it went down."

"No."

"Caroline—"

"Knows now. She didn't until last week."

"—When she came to Berlin chasing Sophie Payne," Wally said. Remembering the feeling he'd had that Caroline was holding something back—that he was denied access to the ops in her mind. *Fuck. This is fucking going to get me fired.* "Who else knows?"

"Scottie," Eric said vaguely, and clutched at the elevator's bronze bars as the cage lurched to a stop.

Wally sighed inwardly with relief. If Scottie Sorensen had brought Eric back to life, everybody else could go to hell.

nineteen

"I'll resign." Cuddy strode beside Caroline and the security police officers toward the parking lot. The SPOs said nothing, but they held her elbows as though she were a prisoner who might break for daylight.

"No. You need to be here."

"And work for *him*? Caroline—" Cuddy stopped, too aware of the presence of outsiders. "I'll call you at your hotel tomorrow. We'll discuss this."

"But you'll go back inside now. You'll tell Scottie you'll stay. Understand? You have to, Cuddy. Otherwise we're all screwed."

He understood in those few syllables what she expected. Not blind loyalty to the institution or the martyrdom of leaving by her side, but a far crueler sentence: She was asking him to turn traitor. To double back against the only family he could name.

As they walked briskly toward her car she added, "And get that disc."

The one Eric had sent out of Budapest last week, Cuddy thought; the single shred of proof he'd actually been working for the good guys.

"What are you going to do?" he asked her.

"Call Shephard. And volunteer."

Tom's voice, when she reached his cell phone, was like a lifeline unreeling through the predawn darkness. She clung to the careless confidence of that voice, the thoughtless strength, without allowing herself to consider why he was so necessary right now.

"Did you know your house's silent alarm went off an hour ago?" he demanded.

"No."

The fiber-optic system Eric had installed while the house was under construction was undetectable to the naked eye. Threaded through the frame of the building itself, and monitored remotely by a crack government security contractor. She'd never had to use it. *Until tonight*.

"Ricin Boy?"

"There's a dead cop lying in your backyard, Caroline. He's stripped to his underwear and his head's nearly cut off. You realize what this means? He found you. He *found* you."

"Just like he found Dare," she said bitterly. "Now he's got a police uniform he can use. We've got to warn the Secret Service detail working Payne's funeral."

"Already done. Where are you?"

She was driving toward Chain Bridge, under the canopy of oak trees arching down to the Potomac River, where the rapids furled white against the concrete supports. Nearly four A.M., and no sign of morning on the horizon. Sophie Payne's funeral in approximately

six hours. She was due to pick up Jozsef at Bethesda
Naval soon.

"Where should I be?"

"On your way downtown. Carl Rogers—he's head
of White House Security—wants you at a briefing.
Before this show gets started at Arlington."

"What time?"

"Soon as you can. Carrie—he could have murdered
you in your bed." Tom sounded strained to the breaking point, and she remembered the intensity of that
drive to the White House, the emotion that had kept
her firmly on her side of the car, terrified of what might
happen if she touched him. "Once Payne's funeral is
done, you need to get out of this city. Have you heard
anything about Atwood's request for federal protection?"

"Ain't gonna happen, Tom." She swallowed hard,
concentrating on the steep upgrade to Arizona Avenue.
"I was just fired."

"What?"

How to explain? Tom believed Eric was dead. He
thought she was a widow. He knew nothing of the
many ways she'd deceived him. But he'd hear the truth
in a matter of hours—or one version of it. Dare was gone
and nobody with clout was left to help her. Scottie's
next move would be an international manhunt for Eric.
It was a brilliant plan: Divert the public's attention from
Ricin Boy, and win a knighthood from Jack Bigelow
for his pains.

"Fired? Are they *nuts*? You're the only person in
Langley who knows her ass from a hole in the ground!"

"We'd better talk, Tom."

"I'll meet you at the Bureau in twenty minutes."

When a whistling Scottie Sorensen swung out of the office at four-thirty A.M., bound for the DCI's corridor and his meeting with Cory Rinehart, Cuddy Wilmot decided to smoke his first cigarette in nearly two years.

The darkness was still heavy as he fumbled for a match in the chill morning air of the courtyard that linked New Headquarters and Old. It was filled with daylilies in the summer; marble statues of an indeterminate modernist type; a plaque or two commemorating something already forgotten. Ducks, in spring weather, paddling in the fountains. The Agency—buildings, memories, people—felt like his whole life; but tonight it was all simply smoke and ash.

He'd watched Caroline's taillights disappear through the back gate and then he'd walked directly back to CTC and informed his chief he was backing him up the whole way. It was then Scottie had asked for Eric's CD-ROM. Cuddy had taken it from his desk and watched while Scottie snapped it neatly in four and tossed the shards in his burn bag.

Cuddy inhaled greedily and watched the end of his cigarette flare like hope in the darkness. What was the nature of loyalty, after all? Was it dedication to country . . . to the safety of a bunch of people who didn't even realize they were targets . . . to an idea he'd once had of justice or integrity? Was it blind adherence to a chain of command—or did it come down to a few people you knew and loved, the few people who'd watched you bleed?

In the end there was nothing but the ear you gave to that inner voice, the one that refused to steer you wrong. He was listening now, had been listening for hours, and with his blood singing the old familiar nicotine chant, he felt clearheaded and unequivocal. He pulled out his cell phone.

It was the easiest kind of electronic transmission to intercept, but Cuddy trusted this palm-sized bit of circuitry more right now than all the lines running in and out of Scottie Sorensen's Counterterrorism Center.

"Steve Price?" he asked as the *Post* journalist picked up. "It's Cuddy Wilmot out at the CIA. There's a piece of the 30 April story I think you need to know."

twenty

The harassed doctor who had been working for more than twenty sleepless hours arrived at the room where Dana Enfield lay and paused in the doorway. Two other gurneys had been moved into the space, holding a man of fifty and his son of twenty-three, lying side by side. Chuck and David Yearsley. For six months they'd trained for the Marine Corps Marathon and they'd finished the race together. Kay Wallace guessed it would be their last.

The Speaker of the House, as the doctor could not help but think of him, sat motionless by his wife's bed. Perhaps, Kay thought, he had finally dozed off. Or perhaps Dana was already dead. She had known people to sit like that for an hour before summoning a physician. Only the doctor had the power to make death real.

She checked the Yearsleys' vitals, then forced herself to walk forward. At the sound of her step George Enfield turned his head. The strangeness of coming face-to-face with someone famous—of seeing in the flesh a man known only by television—swept over her. She could not help smiling foolishly, despite the exhaustion of the hard hours and the hopeless chaos of the waiting room four stories below. He was holding his wife's hand.

"How is she?" Kay asked.

"Maybe you can tell me that."

She bent over Dana's fevered body and listened to her heart with a stethoscope. The beat was irregular and weak. She checked the chart and noted that insulin was being fed into the woman's veins along with a solution of sugars; a perfectly balanced continuous stream of fluids. Dana's levels had been checked the previous hour. She'd been given morphine for pain and acetaminophen in an effort to bring down her spiking temperature. "Any vomiting lately?"

He shook his head. "There's nothing left inside."

Kay gently palpated Dana's abdomen. It was stretched taut over the rib cage, but the feel of the major organs troubled her. They were distended with fluid; Kay guessed it was probably blood. Dana's gut was slowly dying. And there was nothing Kay could do.

"How many people are there?" Enfield asked.

She knew instantly what he was asking. "One hundred thirty-two in this facility," Kay said, "and some seven hundred others in places around the city."

"Has anyone died yet?"

She studied his lined face, seeing the anguish behind the famous façade, then shook her head. "No one has died here. I don't know about the rest."

"Then maybe we're wrong. I mean, it's early days yet. It *could* be ricin—but even if it is, maybe the dose wasn't strong enough to kill. Maybe the worst of it's over, you know?"

"Maybe."

Like the others on staff and all the volunteers who'd shown up to help, she'd read the case histories the Centers for Disease Control were sending out electronically to every hospital in the nation. The most brutal story was that of Georgi Markov, an exiled Bulgarian journalist. An assassin had stabbed Markov with the tip of an umbrella while he stood in a queue for a London bus. The umbrella tip injected a tiny metal sphere holding an infinitesimal amount of ricin—estimated, Kay recalled, at 0.28 mm^3—into Markov's leg. The journalist had died three days later of severe gastroenteritis. Murdered by a fellow commuter.

Every person who'd drunk ricin-laced water at the marathon, the young doctor suspected, had ingested a hundred to a thousand times more poison than Markov.

Enfield's eyes strayed back to his wife. "What do you think? About Dana? Has she improved at all?"

Kay's throat tightened. This was the part she hated most about medicine: the desperate need for hope. They all wanted it in these rooms tonight—some reason to believe. To hang on. The mothers and husbands and best friends looked at her with such pain and hope in their eyes—asking her to reassure them. To pretend that she could save the people they loved. The weight of it was killing her.

"While there's life, there's hope," she stuttered, her hands clenched in her pockets; and when she smiled at George this time, there was nothing foolish in her eyes.

twenty-one

Eric lay sprawled on the bed that had once belonged to Wally's son, a dish towel pressed to his left cheekbone. Wally had filled the towel with crushed ice and fed him four ibuprofen tablets with some bottled water; he'd found an old stretch bandage in a cupboard and wound it with unexpected tenderness around Eric's cracked ribs. The purple bruising on his abdomen made Wally grin savagely, but he listened without comment to what Eric told him. If he had his own thoughts about the healing wound on Eric's neck or the possible use his old friend had made of the past three years, he did not offer them up for consideration. He was already late for work and he'd recovered enough from his initial shock to say frankly, "No, buddy, I don't think I *want* to know what you've been doing while you've been dead. From the look of you, it isn't healthy to know. Sit tight and stare at the ceiling for a while. I'll be back at lunch."

As he lay with his eyes fixed on the room's pale shadows, listening to the creak and stir of the old building and the unknown lives around him, Eric considered Ernst and Klaus. They should have put a bullet in his brain. Instead, they'd dumped him in an alley near Tegel Airport. Ernst had pocketed the five thousand dollars he'd found in Eric's money belt and Klaus had kept the fake passport. Eric had nothing now. His bug-out kit was shit.

When his screaming frame hit the concrete sidewalk near dawn he'd hunched himself into a doorway and sat, for an hour or longer, while the cold hardened his bruised muscles. When sunlight crept into the doorway he began to walk, forcing his battered mind to concentrate. To find someone. A friend who could help. *Wally.*

He'd made no contact with the CIA for the past three years, but he'd kept tabs on the stations operating in every city 30 April called home. He knew Wally Aronson was COS, Berlin. He'd tailed Wally only once—to find out where he lived. Wally'd never noticed him.

Until this morning.

I've got to get home, he'd said. *I haven't a cent or a document I can use, Wally, and I'm wanted by everybody under the sun. I need an exfiltration. Talk to Caroline. Or Cuddy Wilmot. Go as high as Dare Atwood, if you have to. But don't go through Scottie.*

"Don't go through Scottie," Wally had repeated, a strangeness in his eyes. "Why not?"

Eric shook his head.

"Do you know what you're asking?"

"For absolution," Eric had said bluntly, and would say no more.

•   •   •

Wally got the news about Dare Atwood's murder as soon as he walked through the embassy door. It was Mrs. Saunders who told him—the station's acid-tongued, scarlet-lipped career secretary, who arrived before any of the case officers each day. He'd tossed her a "Morning, Gladys" with deliberate cheerfulness before he noticed that she'd been crying. Her mask of makeup was blotched with tears and her eyes were brilliant behind her glasses.

"What's wrong?"

"Just in," she muttered, handing him a cable. "And this one. *Not* that I believe it."

The first transmission had gone out from Washington only an hour before—the middle of the night on the East Coast, Wally noted.

IMMEDIATE NOFORN NOCONTRACT
CONFIDENTIAL HQS ADVISES DIRECTOR
SHOT AND KILLED BY UNKNOWN ASSAILANT
00:15 HOURS THIS MORNING ACTING DCI
RINEHART IN CHARGE. DETAILS TO FOLLOW
AS AVAIL. RINEHART.

He stared blankly at Gladys Saunders.

"Read the next one," the secretary ordered. "*Not*, as I say, that I believe it."

... CTC ADVISES THAT CASE OFFICER
MICHAEL O'SHAUGHNESSY/NIGEL BENNING
DECLARED DEAD APRIL 1997 IS ALIVE AND
MEMBER OF 30 APRIL TERRORIST GROUP ...

Wally sank down into the nearest chair. "What the hell—?"

"That's Carmichael's pseudo. You remember," she prompted. "*Eric* Carmichael. Married to that woman who was here TDY last week over the 30 April business. He died in MedAir 901, Wally. There's a star with his name on it in the Headquarters atrium. So why in God's name are they telling us this bullshit?"

"I don't know," he murmured, his eyes scanning the rest of the cable rapidly. *Don't go through Scottie.* Because Scottie knew the truth? Because the CTC chief's APB was already winging its way to Berlin?

Wally's body went sharply cold, then hot. "This went out to the FBI. Interpol. Which means German liaison will have it in a matter of hours. *Gladys—*"

Any other day, Mrs. Saunders would have scowled at the use of her given name. This morning she never registered the abuse.

"Where's the report we got from the BKA—the woman with the broken neck at the 30 April front company on Kurfürstendamm?" Wally demanded.

"It was a lab. Not a front company." She handed him the report.

As he'd thought: two different blood groups retrieved at the murder scene. One, the victim's. The other—Eric's? Who had a slice cut out of his neck and a body so battered he could barely stand?

Go as high as Dare Atwood, if you have to. Only Dare Atwood was dead.

Wally felt the first faint stirring of an inner glee—an operative's exultation—that would eventually overwhelm and subdue all his acquired managerial caution and his sharp sense of present trouble. *Here was a problem and a mystery.* Enemies with the faces of friends. His first rogue op in nearly eight years.

Trying hard to suppress a look of roguish joy, he said, "Get me Cuddy Wilmot on the secure line."

And closed his office door. He needed to think.

twenty-two

"Do you run?" Caroline asked as Tom fast-forwarded for the hundredth time through the marathon footage he'd culled from local news networks. On the screen, lean women in neoprene tights dashed through the starting line in a fluid knot, their smiles ebullient. His gaze slid past them, searching for Ricin Boy somewhere in the crowd. Like trying to pick out a single shadow from the hundred cast on a beach.

"I ran *this* marathon once."

And that quickly, the stuffy darkened room in the bowels of the J. Edgar Hoover Building disappeared and he could feel the springy mud bank of the C&O Canal. Flowing away beneath the soles of his feet, endless as a cinema reel, empty and blessedly riddled with birdsong. The towpath had always been there, through the years of high school and the infrequent visits during college, through the early happiness of his doomed marriage, the hopeful apprenticeship in the Northern Virginia office. The C&O Canal stretched unimpeded across the District border with its mile markers and its occasional bridges arching overhead, its scattered outbuildings from the lost days of barge-borne commerce.

During that final year of Jen's illness, he'd willed himself to train for the Marine Corps Marathon. He'd taken the towpath each weekend for increasingly arduous runs, the miles mounting as the months passed. Ten miles. Thirteen. Sixteen. Twenty. He had logged his records of endurance each week as Jen slipped closer to death, the chemotherapy sapping her strength, the radiation mangling her chestnut hair.

Caroline shifted restlessly and a scent he could not name drifted faintly to his nostrils. She smelled clear and green, somehow—like skin freshly showered—and the awareness of his own funk of coffee and sweat and used clothes depressed him suddenly. He was so tired. And desperate for a lead.

"There's nothing here," he told her bitterly, turning from the screen. "There's nothing *anywhere*. I've dragged a dozen people out of their beds in the middle of the night to monitor Internet chat rooms—the favorite place for neo-Nazi bullshit and pissing contests, all the good ol' boys getting their rocks off preaching violence and bloodshed from the safety of their computers—but nobody's *talking* tonight, Caroline, nobody's congratulating himself for a kick-ass strike against the Beast System. The American Patriots are lying low, and who can blame them? Shit, it's nearly five A.M. and these people believe in good clean living. They know how important it is to get their sleep."

"What else?" she asked bluntly.

"I've got people at every field office in the country checking incident files for hotheads who've threatened to blow our house down. I've got airports and border checkpoints staring up the ass of every thirty-something guy with a crew cut. I've got Laboratory Division study-ing the ballistics of the bullet that took out Dare. And I've got fuck-all, Caroline. I've got *shit*. I'm just sitting here waiting for the next blow to fall."

"What about Payne's staff?"

"Your *agents in place*? Your *American cell*?" He snorted bleakly. "Didn't want to bust up your party back there in the White House, girl, but you're dream-ing."

"Jozsef—"

"Jozsef's a kid who needs a place to belong. He'd tell you anything you wanted to hear."

"But it makes sense that Krucevic—"

"All *right*," he said too loudly, his anger breaking the surface. "*All right*. You want to read up on Payne's people? Be my guest. Their personnel files are all on that desk. Extensive security clearances and background checks vetted by the Bureau's best. Half the staff has worked there for years—before Payne even took office. The others she hired herself, when her husband the senator was still alive. I'm going to get more coffee."

He thrust himself out of his chair, snapping off the useless news footage, and left the conference room without waiting for her reply.

It wasn't Caroline's fault. She was just trying to help. But the futility of this search for one needle in the nation's haystack was driving him mad. He kept seeing faces: the faces of the dying at Sibley Hospital. For no other reason than a sick man's pleasure. He was certain that 30 April had nothing to do with Ricin Boy, however much the creep might mention the ter-rorist group in anonymous letters. Tom knew a True

Citizen when he heard one. In this matter of home-grown violence, Caroline could be no help at all. She'd only get herself killed.

Worst of all, he felt responsible. Guilty. For having failed. For years he'd been warning his bosses that Ricin Boy was coming, and when they couldn't be bothered to listen he'd simply left the country. The people at Sibley were dying because he'd given up.

Stupidity, he thought. *Complacence. The unwillingness to believe in the fact of evil when it bears a familiar face. We've done this to ourselves.*

Caroline resisted the impulse to go after Shephard. She understood what the investigation cost him—not just the exhaustion and the unavoidable responsibility, but the frustration and the rampant desire to control what was happening. They were so much alike: intensely focused, analytic, driven people who could not stand the fact of evil or the destruction it caused. Both of them hated to witness pain. Funny, then, that they had such an ability to nourish it in themselves.

The first time she'd seen Tom, standing amid the rubble of the Brandenburg Gate, she'd mistaken him for a mourner. He'd lost his wife to breast cancer a few years before, and she'd sensed instantly that he brought that pain to every crime scene he visited. The clipped speech and brusque impatience were merely Shephard's protective cover, ways of disguising how deep this wave of terror had gone. For Tom, the loss of each marathon runner—the pitiful end of the cop in her backyard—was personal. He didn't have to tell her. They were two of a kind. Maybe that was why she yearned toward him, toward the arms that had held her outside Dare's house a few hours ago: She craved someone who understood and accepted her weakness as well as her strength.

Except that Tom had no idea who she really was. He had fallen in love with a fraud. She'd been lying to him ever since they'd met: about 30 April, about Eric, about her own divided loyalties. She'd allowed him to believe she was *single,* for Chrissake. All to protect Eric—who probably didn't give a shit if she was alive. She'd ruthlessly sacrificed a good man's feelings for the sake of one who'd deceived and betrayed her at every turn. She should be shot by a firing squad at dawn.

And if she could have all the lies back, unspoken— would she change a thing?

She closed her eyes in the stillness of the abandoned office, the FBI files untouched. That quickly Eric's presence filled her mind; he was never very far from the center of it. Eric, whom she still loved, would always love, no matter how pointless her ache of longing might be. Where had he gone, the night he'd walked away from her down a darkening Budapest street? Scottie would say he'd deliberately abandoned her to save his own skin. But Caroline had blown too many of Scottie's lies, and she knew Eric had left her for only one purpose: to try to save Sophie Payne.

He'd sent Caroline to Sarajevo and had probably gone himself to Berlin. He'd urged her to call in backup support through the embassy, but he'd walked toward the heart of evil alone. That was like Eric. He'd never tell her to hide from the hunters, as Shephard had. He'd never wrap her in cotton wool or bare every last thought of his secret soul. But as she sat in the quiet office an hour before dawn, six thousand miles from Berlin, she could feel Eric breathing. The deep, unspoken cord that had always bound them was the only thing keeping him alive.

With a sigh she came back to the room, the pre-dawn darkness, the monumental problem in front of her. She reached for the personnel files.

Not even in your shower at the Naval Observatory were you alone, Mlan Krucevic had told his hostage; and Sophie Payne had showered, it seemed, under the eyes of Norman Wilhelm, chauffeur; Candace O'Brien, personal appointments secretary; Conchita Rodriguez, general maid; Nancy Williams, housekeeper; and Rosco Finn, chef.

Payne had lived in the Naval Observatory—a classic Victorian white-framed beauty set back on wide, treed lawns off Embassy Row on Massachusetts Avenue—for nearly two years. It was an enormous house for a single woman with one son away most of the year at Yale, but she'd taken to the place like a duck to water. Redecorated discreetly. Borrowed art for temporary exhibits. Thrown parties on the wide covered porches and in the breezy dining room.

She'd inherited the housekeeper and maid, Caroline saw, and both had been working for the vice president's residence during two previous administrations. The chef, Rosco Finn, she'd brought over from her home in Georgetown.

Rosco looked like a pleasant guy in his mid-forties. Raised in upstate New York; educated in a smattering of kitchens and then at the Culinary Institute of

America; a sojourn in San Francisco afterward; personal chef on a yacht cruising the Mediterranean for two years before being hired by Payne. *The Mediterranean.* He could have met anybody there—in the balmy, luxurious moorings of Ibiza and Portofino. Even a terrorist.

She glanced through the testimonials culled from FBI interviews: Rosco's high school teachers; some friends from Rochester; the executive chef in San Francisco; the yacht owner. All of them benignly bland, remarkably free of incident. They praised his soulful way with fish and insisted he had never been arrested for speeding or the possession of illegal substances. None of them gave her the slightest sense of who Rosco exactly *was*.

Candace O'Brien was more of a close personal friend than a secretary, it seemed; she'd graduated, like Sophie, from Smith College. O'Brien was the ex-wife of a university professor who'd spent most of his teaching career at Georgetown; the two women had struck up an acquaintance at some alumni function. When Payne's husband died suddenly of cancer and she decided to finish out his Senate term, she'd hired O'Brien—newly divorced—to keep her appointments. A family face among the bewildering array of staff.

Caroline studied the woman's résumé. Art history at Smith; a classic nice girl's major in the early 1960s. Marriage to a boy from Brown. One daughter. A stint abroad while her husband had taught at the University of Leipzig, in 1990.

Caroline frowned. Mlan Krucevic had taught at the University of Leipzig in 1990. Had O'Brien met him there? Would she or her husband ever have come in contact with a molecular biologist? She leafed back through the file: no mention of what subject Dr. O'Brien taught at Georgetown. She would have to find out.

And then there was Norm Wilhelm. Mrs. Payne's chauffeur.

The testimonials this time, she noticed, were from neighbors who'd known him all his life in a small town in West Virginia. The police chief. The local minister. Norm's boss at the trucking company, who'd contracted with him for years as a driver. And three people from an organization called Joseph's Table—a charitable group for the homeless operating along the Fourteenth Street corridor in Washington, D.C.

Joseph's Table? Had Sophie Payne found her personal driver lying on a heating grate in front of Capitol Hill?

It would be like her, Caroline thought with a pang. Payne was the kind of woman who probably hadn't been able to look away from the bundles of overcoats sprawled along the city streets every rainy winter. She'd have tried to practice the politics she preached. Tried to make a difference in at least one life.

And Wilhelm's file bore out her faith: not a single incident that might arouse suspicion. Norm Wilhelm seemed to have been devoted to Sophie Payne during the final months of her Senate term and the two years at the Observatory.

She turned to the last page of the file. Wilhelm's next of kin was listed there: a woman named Rebekah Becker, of Charleston, West Virginia. Caroline wrote the name beneath the O'Briens' and Rosco Finn's. If

Tom refused to take the American cell seriously, she had that much more freedom to search.

"We got this footage from your security people," Tom told her as he dimmed the lights and adjusted the image on the monitor. "I want you to take a good look at the guy. And then keep your eyes peeled every time you're unprotected on the street."

She should have expected pictures. Eric's fiber optics would have sent them directly to the security firm's monitors. She was looking at her own house, the staircase a pool of black and the figure vaulting up it a sickly glowing green. Infrared images of Ricin Boy. If it weren't for Cuddy and Tom, she'd have been dreaming in her bed when he came with his knife.

"That's an M16," she said coolly. "Think he's ex-military?"

"Could be. Or haunts gun shows like the rest of his Patriot friends."

She watched as he smashed her full-length mirror. "Angry."

"Do you recognize him?" Tom was attempting a similar calm, a lid firmly clamped on his earlier anger.

"He looks like that sketch of yours. Like the guy I glimpsed on Dare's street. But there's not much to distinguish. On infrared, he's a heat source begging to be tracked. Nothing else."

"I've got people working on the film," Tom said abruptly. "What I'm asking, Caroline, is whether he could be this guy—O'Shaughnessy. Benning. Whatever his name is. Thirty April's last man standing."

"What do you mean?"

"Your boss sent this over half an hour ago." He tossed a sheet of paper toward her; she scanned it swiftly; her chest constricted, the breath failing to come. Eric's vitals; his photograph as Benning; and worst of all: a still shot from Sophie Payne's kidnapping. The photo captured Eric lifting a stretcher bearing the vice president into the belly of 30 April's chopper.

Eric the terrorist.

"Is Benning our Ricin Boy?"

"No," she answered. "How many people have seen this?"

"The entire law enforcement world, probably. Did you know him?"

"I knew him."

"You did? The whole time we were working the Payne kidnapping? You *knew* there was an Agency guy inside 30 April? And you never told me?"

She would not look at the confusion and hurt on his face. "Why do you think I resigned?"

"You said you were fired!"

"Sometimes it's a little of both."

"My God—I begin to see why!" He thrust himself away from his chair and stood staring down at her in disbelief. "Caroline—who *is* this guy?"

"My husband," she said.

twenty-three

"George," she said clearly sometime before dawn, "don't marry a bubblehead. *Mallory*."

He leaned closer, stroking her cheek. It was hot, and dry as a withered leaf. "She'll be here soon. Another few hours."

Dana shook her head. "No sympathetic idiots. No *rebound*, you hear? Take some time."

"Shhhhh." He went on stroking her face, feeling the hard bone beneath the skin like the bedrock of a familiar country. Her eyes were cloudy, the irises indistinct and muddy.

"She needs someone who can answer her questions. Someone with a brain. Who knows—"

"She needs *you*," he insisted, his vision swimming. "You."

Dana smiled faintly and her eyes slid closed. She did not speak again.

When she died at three minutes past six that Monday morning, she was looking at something beyond George's shoulder, beyond the acoustic tile of the emergency room's ceiling, an ecstatic vision fueled by her failing liver and the morphine the doctors had pumped liberally into her veins. She gripped his hand, the long thin fingers loose as pickup sticks, her lips parted.

He said urgently, "*Dana*. Dana, I'm here. Darling—" but he might as well have been background static to the music in her head. She did not look at him. Her frame lifted slightly from the pillow, straining against life—and then he felt her slacken. That quickly, sense bled from her eyes.

He continued to sit in the silence she'd left, waiting for a breath that never came. If he called the nurse now and allowed someone to see her, they would say she was dead—and it would be true, then, it would be all over, his life gone without hope in the time it took to drape a sheet. They would wheel her away. There would be forms to sign.

He sat in the silence, praying for the wretched day to begin with fresh coffee steaming on his bedside table, the drumbeat of Dana's shower from the next room.

He put his left hand to his eyes. His right still held hers.

part two

MONDAY, NOVEMBER 22

twenty-four

It was a beautiful day for national mourning.

Sharp, crisp autumn weather, Monday the twenty-second of November. All but the pin oak leaves had long since fallen in decay, and the sharp branches of bare trees reached toward the monuments on the opposite bank of the Potomac. Thousands of people lined the cavalcade's route from the National Cathedral to Arlington National Cemetery. In their hands they held pictures of Sophie Payne, and the pale pink roses she'd reportedly loved.

Caroline Carmichael was able to see it all, panoramic as a Hollywood back lot, from her jump seat in the White House limo.

She sat between Matthew Finch, Jack Bigelow's Chief of Staff, and Jozsef Krucevic. If word of her firing—her appalling disgrace—had reached the Situation Room in the early hours of the morning, nobody had seen fit to boot her from the funeral cavalcade. Maybe it was too late to rearrange the seating, or maybe she had Finch to thank for the privilege; he was an independent thinker and she guessed he'd not yet condemned her.

"You'll be seated in the row directly behind the President and Mrs. Bigelow," he was saying now, "with Jozsef next to you. If a camera focuses on your face, just gaze at the casket. Or the President."

"I'd prefer to stand."

"That's a risk. You'll be more of a target."

He was still operating on the first script he'd been handed, then—the one in which she was a hero, not a criminal, the wife of a terrorist.

"The consignment of the body could take half an hour, including the President's speech, and in your condition—" Finch's gaze wandered to Caroline's right shoulder, bandaged under her plain dark suit. She'd left the sling at home.

"I'll stand," she repeated. "I want a good view."

"Carrie," he said gently, "FBI plainclothes and Secret Service people are crawling all over Arlington. Let them do their job."

They don't know who to look for, she thought. *I just might.*

Jack Bigelow had considered a horse-drawn cortege for Sophie's casket. He could have walked with her son the length of Pennsylvania Avenue, his familiar face somber above a black wool coat. But Sophie had been only a vice president, after all, and the obvious parallel to John F. Kennedy's assassination might be considered excessive. Not that Bigelow was afraid to borrow the trappings of national myth: far from it. Sophie's murder in the fullness of her political career was the stuff of tragedy. Unlike Jack Kennedy, however, Bigelow's running mate had died far from home, at the hands of terrorists. Her death was a national embarrassment. Already he was being held to blame.

The Speaker of the House had announced his wife's death from ricin poisoning at a press conference that morning. George Enfield had vowed in a voice shaking with emotion to launch a full Congressional investigation into what he was calling "the administration's massive intelligence failure." The statement was followed by a police sketch of the ricin killer mounted on every screen in America.

Bigelow fingered his tie in the back of the limo and glanced sidelong at his wife. Adele looked elegant and composed, her hair swept off her high forehead; but he knew the lines of strain around her mouth. Had she slept at all?

"Thirty April?" she'd repeated blankly when he'd gisted his two A.M. meeting for her over early coffee. "I thought we wiped them all out."

"We *did*," Jack muttered. "But this is some kind of copycat thing. Probably just a lone nut. They'll get him, sweetheart. This is nothing we haven't lived with before."

But Adele, with thirty-one years' experience of her husband, had known he was lying to her. One man had promised to see Jack dead. She was gazing out of the limousine window, her fingers clenched tightly in her lap, no doubt calculating which of the hundreds of faces slipping past intended to pull the trigger.

• • •

The sleek black cars crossed Memorial Bridge and slid through the cemetery's gates. Serene on its hill, the white-pillared Custis-Lee mansion rose up before them. The chauffeur in charge of Caroline's limo moved without hesitation through the vast park of gravestones, the broad avenues twisting sinuously upward; but then Norm Wilhelm, Payne's personal driver, would have practiced the route before this high-profile performance. Caroline had sized Wilhelm up as she'd entered the car, her mental checklist drawn from his FBI background file. He was forty-three years old, with trim brown hair and unsmiling eyes. It was possible, Caroline thought, that he felt the pervasive sadness that overwhelmed her whenever she passed through the iron portals of Arlington.

Eric's gravestone was here, one more blunt white square of granite lost in the swollen ranks. The grave itself was empty, of course, but Caroline would never forget that misty day in early May nearly three years before, the sound of taps haunting the air. The smell of nitrogen rising from the fertilized lawns. She had nearly swooned from the pain of that hole in the ground, the inexplicable descent of widowhood.

"What is this place?"

Jozsef, his eyes wide in a painfully pallid face, was studying the rows of glittering white headstones. The manicured hillside looked nothing, Caroline thought, like the mass graves or simple wooden crosses of Bosnia. He might be forgiven for failing to connect it to the funeral service just completed at the cathedral. The most he'd seen of Washington, D.C., was the interior of the naval hospital.

"It's the most hallowed burial ground in America," Matthew Finch said briskly. "Four million tourists a year visit it."

"This is where we'll leave Mrs. Payne," Caroline added.

She felt, rather than saw, Norman Wilhelm glance at his rearview mirror and wondered what he made of the conversation. Whether he held her responsible— held Jozsef responsible—for his employer's death. But when she looked at him directly his profile was steady, his hands tranquil on the wheel. *How odd*, she thought, *that all of us must follow her casket together.*

"It's a place for kings." Jozsef's eyes were fixed on the view. "She ought to sleep here, Lady Sophie. With flowers on her grave."

He looked down at his empty hands and a shadow passed over his features. He was thinking, Caroline realized, that he should have brought a bouquet—but did not know how to begin to ask for one. She was suddenly angry at herself for having failed the boy, for having been so consumed by her own anxiety that she had neglected his feelings. But she'd scarcely slept in the two hours after her disastrous parting from Tom Shephard. Forgetting the flowers was the least of her problems.

Shephard had nearly thrown her bodily from the FBI building at five-thirty that morning. *I can't trust you, Caroline. You know what that means? I can't even talk to you anymore.*

She closed her eyes sharply at the memory of Shephard's face, furious and ugly. Shephard's voice, like a slap across the mouth. He believed she'd deliberately used him. As indeed she had. Tom had shut her firmly out of his heart and mind—and it was only now that she stood on the far side of the closed door that she understood how much she'd relied on his caustic humor, his quick intelligence, his unshakable conviction of her worth. Tom's contempt hurt. She was lonelier than she'd been in weeks—since the first hour she'd understood that Eric was alive, and had lied to her for years.

Eric. Where was he now?

The loneliness intensified, deepened, became a pit as dark and broad as a grave.

The limo pulled to a stop on Memorial Drive, above the amphitheater where Jack Bigelow intended to make his remarks to several hundred chosen guests. Caroline watched as the vice president's casket was carried by six uniformed men past monuments honoring the crew of the *Challenger* space shuttle and the Iran hostage rescue mission; already the dead woman had entered the public domain of grief. Matthew Finch's door was opened by a Secret Service agent and the Chief of Staff stepped out, turning to assist Caroline. She felt for the walkie-talkie she'd placed in her suit pocket, then reached for Jozsef's hand.

The boy's doctors had permitted him to attend the funeral provided an ambulance stood by. Jozsef was weak enough to require Caroline's support simply to reach his place in the amphitheater. At the moment, however, he seemed oblivious to their arrival. He was staring at a solid bit of fur three inches long: a rabbit's foot. With a pang, Caroline understood how precious the good luck charm was to the boy. Sophie Payne had been clutching it when she died.

"Do you think . . . ?" Jozsef glanced up at Caroline. "Instead of flowers?"

"I think it's perfect," she assured him gently. "Exactly what Mrs. Payne would want to remember you by."

The world's great had turned out in force: The new chancellor of Germany had flown in as a mark of penance for the safe haven his country had granted 30 April; so, too, had Jack Bigelow's closest ally, Tony Blair. The Speaker of the House, the Senate Minority Whip, and the president of Yale—where Sophie Payne's son was a sophomore—were seated together in close conversation. Caroline picked out a leading man and his current wife, dressed in their very best Armani mourning; the French and Spanish ambassadors; a National League pitcher; a famous model.

She saw Jozsef safely seated in his designated row behind the First Lady, Matthew Finch at his side, then edged her way to the amphitheater's top level and positioned herself near a stone pillar. The Secret Service detail working the funeral was familiar with her face and her role as Jozsef's babysitter; if they knew she was already persona non grata in Washington, they didn't betray it. Carl Rogers, chief of White House Security, had given her the transmitter that morning. He was middle-aged and gray-haired, with an athletic body and a web of laugh lines creasing his face. Rogers no doubt wanted her wired so he could track her at all times. Overnight, she'd turned from friend to suspect.

"Good to go?" he asked easily.

She adjusted the microphone clipped to her blouse and said quietly, "Nobody, but nobody, gets in to see the Wizard. No way, no how."

He smiled at that, and flicked one finger at her in salute. As he strolled away she watched him work the upper fringe of the crowd, his eyes wary.

Was Ricin Boy lost somewhere in the sea of faces, quietly waiting?

Three stories of scaffolding built by the media giants rose from the amphitheater's far wall, directly opposite the Memorial Drive entrance; klieg lights and technical equipment sprouted from the steel poles. Along with the news anchors established there, the Secret Service would be using the advantages of height and closed-circuit screens to monitor the crowd below. Each agent had Ricin Boy's sketch in his pocket. And a description of the stolen police uniform the killer might be wearing. Security was beyond tight; but Caroline knew her enemy was no fool. *Where would he hit? When?* She began deliberately to study the crowd: watching, thinking.

Sophie Payne's Episcopal priest, a woman with a sleek head of red hair and lacquered fingernails, led the mourners in passages from Scripture and the Book of Common Prayer. Her words rang out across the stillness of the chill November morning.

Behold, I shew you a mystery; We shall not all sleep, but we shall all be changed.

Peter Payne, Sophie's orphaned son, strode toward the casket with a fixed expression. He had Sophie's dark hair and his dead father's strong chin; and indeed, the past few days had changed him utterly, Caroline thought, so that he might never sleep again. What had the minister been thinking when she chose those words? Of a child reared by parents more dedicated to public office than to him? He placed a sealed envelope on his mother's coffin and turned abruptly away. Two hundred fifty million people were denied a shot of his grief.

Adele Bigelow laid a fan of pale pink roses on Sophie's bier. The First Lady's right hand lingered for a few seconds, at about the level of the dead woman's heart; then she made her stately way back to the gallery of seats. Jack Bigelow followed. With bowed head, he lowered himself to the kneeler carefully arranged to position him well above the casket, so that he could pay homage without disappearing from camera view. His eyes met Caroline's for an instant, then moved on, withholding all recognition. She no longer existed for the President of the United States.

It was nearly her turn to approach the casket—to say good-bye to this woman she'd completely failed. She waited for the line of Cabinet members and dignitaries to thin. Jozsef stood taut beside her, his fingers gripping the soiled white rabbit's foot. She reached for his hand.

They walked stiffly forward, too aware of the lights and the crowd and the filming cameras, the boy clutching his good luck charm, until the kneeler rose in front of them and they could fall gratefully at its feet. Caroline shuddered to think what was being said about them even then by the smoothly practiced talking heads: *And there's the CIA agent who found Mrs. Payne too late, and the son of the terrorist who kidnapped her. Allegations released this morning suggest that Caroline Carmichael knew more than she admitted about 30 April, and inside sources say that the CIA fired her only last night as a result . . .*

With a shaking hand, Jozsef placed the rabbit's foot next to the fan of roses. Tears streamed down his cheeks; his lips moved in words Caroline could not understand. She bowed her head and tried to find a few of her own. Some way to beg forgiveness for failure.

"Miss Carrie? Miss *Carrie!*"

A hoarse whisper, the words laced with desperation. She glanced at the boy and saw that his eyes were agonized in his white face, his lips blue. He was going to faint.

She put her good left arm around his shoulders and helped him upright. He leaned against her heavily, stumbling. She ignored the empty seats and led him toward the amphitheater's exit aisle, aware that she was disturbing the symmetry of the televised moment. Beside her, Jozsef retched convulsively.

"Mad Dog to Code Central," she muttered into her microphone. "We need an ambulance, *over.*"

"Roger that," a distorted voice replied.

Jozsef bent double, hands clutching his stomach, and vomited all over her shoes.

She waited, one hand smoothing his thin back, until the gasping stopped. They were almost free of the crowds. A few more steps might do it, so that the boy didn't have to be taken on a stretcher from the graveside ceremony and focus all the media attention once more on himself.

"What's going on?" asked a quiet voice at her elbow.

Carl Rogers.

"He needs help," she told the security chief. "The ambulance."

He lifted Jozsef in his arms and strode swiftly toward Memorial Drive. Caroline followed.

Quiet fell like a closing-night curtain beyond the amphitheater's walls. Here, the air was broken only by the staccato bursts of amplified speech and a sudden rush of applause as President Bigelow stood before the podium. He was supposed to close the ceremony now with his eulogy. The moment of greatest peril, though he would be standing behind the bulletproof screen.

Caroline glanced over her shoulder, sharply uneasy, her view of the amphitheater blocked. She couldn't believe Ricin Boy would miss this kind of show. It was too perfect. Too available.

She halted, undecided.

The ambulance sat thirty feet ahead: large-bodied and square, its lights flashing silently. At the sight of them, the passenger door opened and a female EMT stepped to the curb.

Rogers called out, "Hey. We need your help. The kid's sick."

It was Caroline who noticed the gray car.

It was nondescript and rather old, idling slowly to a stop in front of the ambulance. Chrysler maybe, or

Chevrolet. The back window slid open a few inches and a narrow cylinder—the shaft of a gun—snaked through it. Before Caroline could draw breath to shout, it fired.

With a startled expression the EMT catapulted to the ground.

Rogers swore aloud and dropped to one knee, Jozsef huddled in the circle of his body. He'd been trained to protect and it was what he did instinctively, even as he struggled to reach his weapon. Caroline heard him grunt as a bullet plowed into his right arm. She began to run, shouting into her microphone, "Mayday on Memorial Drive! Mayday on Memorial Drive! Armed gunman firing!"

She had no idea what she intended to do—hurl herself in front of Jozsef, maybe. She had no gun, and her wounded arm would never aim right anyway. Rogers had raised his left hand. The gray car's back window shattered like spring ice on a pond and the driver—a *woman,* Caroline saw clearly, wearing an Arlington police officer's uniform—pulled out onto Memorial Drive with a screech of tires. A parting shot sang directly over Caroline's head as she crouched at Carl Rogers's side.

"You're hit," she said.

"I'm all right, God damn it." His teeth were clenched on the pain. "It's just a flesh wound. But that *girl*—"

The ambulance driver had vaulted out of the cab and was bent over the fallen EMT, searching for vital signs.

Jozsef had made no sound—no cry for help or scream

of terror—and for an instant Caroline was afraid he was dead. She reached for him. He'd passed out cold.

"Get the limo driver," Rogers gasped. "Wilhelm. He can take the boy back to Bethesda Naval. But you stay, Caroline. Understand? You *stay*."

Of course, she thought heavily. *I'm the one who walked out just in time for a murder. I'm the one they'll blame.*

A world away in Berlin, Germany, Eric Carmichael thrust himself out of sleep. The sound of a door closing: quiet as the cocking of a gun.

He sat up and stared wildly around, no idea where he was, reaching automatically for the weapon he no longer carried as the door to the hallway swung open.

Wally. The bureaucrat's face, gentle and mournful as a priest's.

He remembered, then. Sophienstrasse and the shadows beneath the high ceiling. He tried to stand but the bandages tight around his rib cage brought the pain to his lips.

Wally, walking slowly toward him, hands outstretched in a plea for calm. And behind him, Ernst and Klaus, with their guns trained on his head.

twenty-five

As he crossed the Potomac and headed north into Maryland, Norman Wilhelm allowed himself one swift glance into the backseat of the limousine. The boy lay sleeping quietly. The rescue squad had offered him a blanket and Wilhelm had accepted it with his usual economy of speech, anxious to get away from the cemetery as quickly as possible. Now that he'd left Virginia he felt easier, as though in crossing the river he'd burned a greater bridge in his mind.

He had submitted no resignation but he knew, now, that he would never work in the capital again. He had enjoyed the six years in Sophie Payne's employment—first as the driver of a senator's wife, on those sporadic occasions when her husband's popularity demanded the protection of an ostentatious car and unofficial bodyguard; and later, through the funeral rites following the senator's death from cancer, and Mrs. Payne's campaign to succeed him. They had been, he reflected, the most important years of his life.

He had met Sophie in a soup kitchen off Adams-Morgan on a frigid morning in January: she the politician's spouse embarked on a high-profile bit of do-gooding; he the drunk who'd rolled in off a heating grate for a cup of hot soup. He could not remember now why she had looked at him, or why he'd managed to make eye contact with the tiny figure in the vintage Chanel suit; he only knew that he went back for soup a second time, and that she took the trouble to talk to him. A few gentle questions, piercing in their accuracy. He had warmed to conversation as though it were heat from a flame. Maybe because the truth was easier to tell to a complete stranger.

He'd talked about driving his own rig for a national transport line. About the years he'd spent roaming the country with complete freedom and a wide-open future. And then about the loss of brakes on the downslope of Interstate 70, coming into Salt Lake, the stink of burning rubber and the panic of being unable to slow the eighteen-wheeler on the icy road, the runaway truck ramp too far to reach, the twelve cars in the lane ahead.

He'd injured twenty people that afternoon and lost his license to drive. Lost his savings in lawsuits and his reputation as a trucker. Lost his livelihood and his future. At the age of thirty-five lost his reason to hope.

Sophie Payne had finished serving soup and smiled her thanks to the charity executives who'd steered her through the ordeal. She shook hands with a varied cast of homeless as she made her exit, pressing her business card into Norm Wilhelm's palm with the strict instruction that he must call her the following day.

He had shoved the card in his pocket, his face burning, and roamed the streets for a week and a half before he found the courage to pick up a pay phone. He could admit now that Sophie Payne had saved his life.

When she'd been named Jack Bigelow's running mate two years before, he thought he'd be replaced with a driver from the White House pool—somebody trained by the Secret Service and accustomed to shepherding the VIPs of politics through the minefield of the people they served. But Mrs. Payne had demanded he stay, and had seen that he got the security training he needed.

The next six months are going to be weird enough, Norm, without losing the best friend I've got. Don't tell me you're leaving. You can't, understand?

She had trusted him, he thought with a painful constriction of the throat; trusted him as the one familiar, constant face at the end of the day. The man who would never ask invasive questions. The man who was content to respond whenever she called and get her safely where she needed to go. He'd always picked up her favorite takeout—Thai soft-shell crabs—and dropped off her dry cleaning. He'd ferried her from tennis dates with Alan Greenspan to cocktail parties on California Street and unmentionable assignations with the married politician she'd briefly enjoyed. He knew what her public profile cost her and how lonely she was. He'd watched the age lines mounting in her face, the endless demands of position and responsibility that eroded her personal life. Sophie lived by herself in the huge house assigned to her at the Naval Observatory, missing her Georgetown garden—and the time she'd once had to cultivate it—intensely. Only the two of them truly understood how much of a hostage she'd become. Even before the kidnapping.

The newspapers said the terrorists had locked her in the trunk of a car. When he'd first heard the details— the story was all over the media, impossible to avoid— he had felt the sort of horrified fascination he'd experienced in flipping through a lesbian porn magazine at a newsstand. The details were too lurid, so impossible to accept in relation to the blunt, birdlike woman he'd worshipped for years that he'd wanted to puke—and yet was unable to tear his eyes away. Sophie Payne, bound and gagged in the trunk of a car. Violated. Diseased. Choking on her own blood. He could not get the images out of his mind.

And so that glance into the backseat, the quick look at the boy who wandered in drugged and peaceful sleep. The ambulance driver had shot him full of tranquilizers for the trip to Bethesda, as though he actually cared how the kid arrived. The son of a murderer! The reason Mrs. Payne was dead! For an instant, Norm considered stopping the car and stuffing the kid in his own trunk. It would do the little shit some good to understand what terror was really like.

But instead he slowed his foot on the accelerator and slid smoothly into the right-hand lane. The exit for Bethesda loomed ahead, the curve of the highway lapping a belt of ancient trees, a few scattered highrises visible through their dark trunks.

He had to be careful now. He had a job to do. He only wished it might repay half his debt to Sophie Payne.

•   •   •

They had told him they'd be waiting in the Linden
Hill parking lot, just off the Beltway ramp; and so he
turned right as he'd been instructed and took the
gradual incline of the side street at a cautious twenty-
five miles per hour. It was important, he knew, that the
car attract as little attention as possible; but somebody
would surely notice a limousine on a Monday afternoon in a residential neighborhood.

*Nobody'll think twice about a shiny black car in that
high-class suburb,* Rebekah had told him stubbornly. *If
you just keep your shirt on, everything'll go smooth as pie.*

Most of the linden leaves lay in deep brown piles
against the curb. It was only lunchtime now, but the
early November light was turning milky as weak tea.
Norm shivered, his eyes searching the street ahead.
Where was she? Where was the car? Had they been
caught after all?

He never thought of Rebekah without wanting to
save her. For Rebekah he had betrayed Sophie Payne's
trust and his own sanity repeatedly over the past year.
He did not believe the things she insisted were true,
the worldwide conspiracies and sellouts, the hateful
screed of Daniel's warped mind; but for her, Norm
had committed crimes his own conscience would never
forgive. He had told Daniel what he knew because the
information might keep Rebekah safe.

Norm Wilhelm had been raised to believe that blood
was thicker than water, and even after the kidnapping—
even after Sophie Payne's horrible public death and his
own knowledge of exactly how he'd contributed to

it—he'd had no choice but to go on helping Daniel. Rebekah was his kid sister, the only relative left, the sole tie to his West Virginia childhood. He understood nothing about her life and very little about the man who held her in such thrall—had held her like a slave since she was seventeen. *Daniel Becker.* Norm's childhood friend. Rebekah's husband. The dangerous and deadly true believer.

It was Daniel he glimpsed first, sitting in the driver's seat of his battered white pickup. They must have ditched the gray K-car, then, Norm thought with relief. Daniel's sharp-featured face with its hook nose looked too placid for a guy who'd just fled the scene of a murder. Norm hoped it was Daniel who'd pulled the trigger and snuffed out the EMT's life, that Rebekah had been driving, and not the other way around. It had come to this: After months of fear and threats and the unrelenting loss of everything Norm Wilhelm valued, he was reduced to hoping his sister was just an accessory to murder.

The truck's passenger door opened a crack and Rebekah slid to the leaf-strewn sidewalk, her face expressionless as she stared at Norm's approaching car. She wore no makeup. Her hair, the mouse brown shot through with gray, was pulled dully back behind her ears in a ragged ponytail. Her jeans were torn and her sweatshirt was the same one she'd had on last Christmas, bulky and sexless. She might have been thirteen or forty-five for all her clothes said about her. The deep lines running from her nose to the corners of her mouth, however, told their own story. Those, and the flat gray listless eyes. She had gone into the grave with her son, Norm thought; she had no intention of coming out anytime soon.

He pulled up behind her truck and killed the engine. She had her hand on his door before he had time to undo his seat belt.

"Is he okay?" she demanded.

"Guess so. They gave him something so's he'd sleep."

She dived for the limo's rear door and hauled it open. "You're late, you know that?"

"Wasn't easy to get through Arlington after what you pulled. There're cars all over, press and cops and whatnot."

"We had to shoot that girl. Otherwise, he'd have been sent back in the ambulance." She shoved an arm under Jozsef's shoulders and lifted his frail form. The boy's mouth fell open, his arm lolled, but he slept on. "Anybody follow you?"

Norm shook his head. That was one thing he could be certain of: He'd had enough security training to detect hostile surveillance.

"Good. You go with Daniel now."

Her husband was standing there suddenly, his deep blue eyes fixed unblinkingly on Norm. Daniel had one hand on the frame of the driver's door and his right foot resting on the running board. "Shove over."

"What?" Norm glanced at Rebekah. "I thought I was coming with you-all."

"Plans've changed. I'm driving." Daniel forced him back into the limo and slid behind the wheel. Before

Norm could object, he had turned the key in the ignition and thrown the car into reverse.

Norm tried to get a last glimpse of Bekah as they were leaving, but she wasn't looking at him. She was too busy lifting the sleeping boy into the back of the truck, a terrible maternity in her face.

twenty-six

She picked out the tail as her car dove into Spout Run, heading south toward Tysons Corner: a navy blue Chevrolet as broad and blunt as a Third World road-block, two guys in shades holding down the front seat. They'd been able to blend with the hordes of traffic exiting the National Cemetery for a while, and she'd been too lost in her own thoughts to bother checking for surveillance; but here, on the single-lane ramp winding past a woodland stream, there was nowhere for an unmarked government car to hide. Just a lemon-colored Beetle perched like a bird of passage between Caroline and the Feds as she sped uphill, thinking: *They want me to know they're here. They're hoping I'll be terrified, and talk.*

It didn't matter, really, whether they were FBI or Secret Service. Carl Rogers's deputy, a guy with the improbable name of DiMaggio, had questioned her for an hour and a half before allowing her to leave Arlington. Jozsef and Jack Bigelow and most of the funeral guests were long gone by that time; just Caroline and the human shields and the people hired to pick up discarded paper programs remained.

Why did you walk out of the amphitheater, Caroline? Did you receive a signal of any kind? Did you recognize the woman who drove the shooter's car? The FBI hadn't charged her with a crime—what could they possibly charge her with?—but of course she was someone to follow. Someone to watch.

She ignored the turnoff for Chain Bridge Road, as though she just might be going somewhere else—Dulles Airport, maybe, to catch a jet out of the country—and then, at the last minute, veered sharply to the right.

The tail jammed on his brakes with a suddenness that brought the car behind him screeching to a halt, fist on the horn. Caroline glanced in her rearview mirror, a smile flickering over her face; the driver behind her was swearing viciously as he made the turn. These weren't the "Gs," then—the Bureau's top watchers, the only ones who could keep up with the CIA's operatives head-to-head on the street. They'd wanted her to know she was under surveillance, and she'd just explained that she'd gotten the message. Now the real games could begin.

Cuddy was waiting for her in the lobby of the Tysons Marriott when Caroline pushed through the hotel's doors that afternoon. She nearly looked right past him: He had the essential spook's ability to blend in with the crowd, brown head bent over a magazine, elbows resting on his khaki knees. Swathed in the carefully neutral upholstery of a national chain, he managed to suggest a computer programmer or an accountant or a man who floundered pathetically in sales, and none of the dozen people wandering through the public space of the hotel gave him a second glance. Eric had a similar quality, she remembered, something he and Cuddy shared regardless of their differences. They were the mutant drifters, always overlooked, always at the edge of the frame. That kind of tradecraft was a gift— more Moneypenny than Bond.

Caroline glanced deliberately at him, face expressionless, and the look he returned was bored and impersonal. Screaming *no contact*. Cuddy knew, then, she'd been marked.

She walked past, making for the bank of elevators. Five people were waiting in the alcove—three men and a teenaged girl staring sullenly at her shoes while her mother whispered urgently in her ear. If the Feds had tailed her to Tysons, Caroline thought, they'd probably already deployed people in the lobby. One or all of these men, waiting silently to accompany her to her room. Her hotel phone would be bugged. She swayed slightly as she stood before the blinking lights that signaled the descending steel cage, and tried to quell a finger of panic. *I'm trapped.* Her purse was dangling from her clasped hands, her suit jacket slung over it. *How can I be trapped already?*

Cuddy eased into place beside her. He was holding a section of the *Washington Post,* the newsprint folded in quarters, whistling slightly under his breath. Completely abstracted. Lost in his own world.

The bell clanged; the doors opened; all seven of them squeezed on. The trap closed. Began to rise upward.

"Could you hit twelve, please?" Caroline asked no

one in particular. Her voice was steady and low. One of the silent men stabbed the button.

"Nine for me." Cuddy was standing uncomfortably close to her at the very back of the elevator car. She resisted the impulse to lean against him.

The mother and daughter got off at eight. None of the three men moved.

Cuddy raised his head as the ninth floor approached, his hand with the newspaper sliding easily down to brush against Caroline's leg. Her fingers reached for his. The newspaper slipped deliberately under her draped suit jacket, wedged between the cloth of the coat and the leather of her purse. She clutched it with her fingernails as he nodded vaguely at her companions and swung off the car, a creased section of the *Post* still clutched in his hand.

The three watchers tried not to make eye contact with Caroline or each other. She studied their profiles in turn, trying to memorize the features. One was Eurasian—Filipino and Spanish, perhaps—with jet-black hair and broad cheekbones. A powerful figure, broad-shouldered, not above middle height. The second had the loose-limbed grace of a cricket player, a sharp prow of a nose, fair hair that would not stay where it was combed. His hands rode easily in his pockets and, as Caroline's eyes roamed over his face, he glanced at her quickly and smiled. She smiled back.

The third man wore an inexpensive suit of a polyester blend; his tie was perfunctory; his brown hair cut without the slightest imagination. His fingers, like the features of his face, were square and thick, the eyes he refused to fix on Caroline were of a muddy brown.

He was the obvious choice—everything about him suggested a government functionary just one step removed from security guard—but Caroline's instincts screamed otherwise.

The elevator doors opened on twelve and they all pressed back against the walls to let her leave first. She walked quickly away, head down and card-key in her hand. At the threshold of Room 1223, she jammed it into the door's slot, aware of the measured footsteps behind her. They would not follow her into her room— but she was determined they should see her enter it. She thrust open the door calmly and slammed it shut as they passed.

Cuddy's newspaper carefully hid a flat plastic bag the size of a sandwich. Stuffed within were a few square inches of plastic and something that resembled a dead animal. She lifted them wordlessly, her spirits rising. A prosthetic chin, a pair of cheekbones, a pert little turned-up nose. The dead animal was a head of auburn hair. On a scrap of paper tucked inside the bag a few words were written. *Back parking lot, 15 minutes.* Cuddy had just given her freedom.

"Scottie'll have your ass in a sling," she said as he turned the wheel easily and drove toward the parking lot's exit. Cuddy handled his small Japanese car with the precision and speed of an F-16 pilot; she tightened her seat belt.

"I wasn't followed."

Of course Cuddy had checked for surveillance. He knew how Scottie's mind worked. If the CTC chief kept Cuddy employed, it was purely to track where he led.

"I didn't pay my bill," she attempted.

"I'll take care of it. They've got your imprint, right?"

"And most of my luggage." She closed her eyes and leaned her red head against the leather seat.

She'd found the Eurasian on the point of quitting his room as she walked out her door, Cuddy's disguise hidden in her gym bag. Beneath the pert nose and the red wig she'd placed her laptop and Walther TPK, wrapped in a change of underwear. She took the elevator to the fitness center, and though the Eurasian went along for the ride and slipped a cell phone from his pocket as she left, he made no attempt to follow her onto the aerobic machines. She hadn't used them.

The women's locker room was empty. In a cubicle, she'd straddled a toilet and quickly applied the latex facial features Cuddy had given her. These were the pride and joy of OTS—the Office of Technical Services—whose masters could change a Caucasian woman to a turbaned Sikh in a matter of minutes. The techniques had been learned at the feet of Hollywood's king of special effects, and the latex pieces were so well crafted as to be indistinguishable from skin.

In a matter of seconds her oval, narrow features became catlike and vaguely Slavic. The auburn wig, bobbed at the chin, turned her into a coquette. She was several inches shorter and light-years more relaxed in running shoes and loose-fitting yoga pants. Nobody—not even FBI surveillance—would connect her with the woman who'd crossed the Marriott lobby a quarter-hour before. She sailed out the front door without turning a head.

"Thanks, Cud," she said brusquely. "How in God's name did you know I needed you?"

"I heard what happened at the funeral. Is Carl Rogers okay?"

"He'll live. At least Jozsef's safe."

"Don't you think it's a *little* weird," he demanded as he breezed through a yellow light and headed toward the river, "that the kid pulled you out of that funeral at exactly the moment our shooter drove by? Doesn't that make you *think* at all?"

"He was sick, Cuddy. He puked all over my shoes."

"I *told* you. He wanted to go to Arlington too much. He *pulled* something, Caroline. It didn't work—but the timing's there. Too fucking good, if you ask me. Did anybody question him? FBI? Secret Service?"

"They sent him back to the hospital," she retorted tiredly. "I'm the one they wanted to screw to the wall."

He laughed. "Yeah. *Your* timing, by the way, left a shitload to be desired."

Was he right? Had Jozsef staged that white face, that choking vomit and the terrible helpless weight dragging on her arm? Did he know exactly who his father had recruited to kill?

Cuddy glanced at her. "Shephard was spitting nails. All that security and his guys missed the car. Missed the gun. Missed the uniformed woman cop in the unmarked car. Hell, they probably waved her right through multiple checkpoints. He'll be lucky if he has a job tomorrow."

She could imagine Shephard's face: impatient, strained from lack of sleep, furious at himself and the wanton killing he should somehow have prevented. She wanted to find him, wanted to say that he was *not responsible,* not for this. Nobody was guilty but Ricin Boy himself and the woman who'd driven his car. But Tom turned his back on her and walked away without a word. He didn't have time for Caroline and her half-truths, her protective gaps that left people dead on the ground. "You talked to him?" she asked Cuddy.

"He called to tell me that as far as he was concerned, you were completely compromised and off-limits. End of story." Cuddy downshifted and careened onto the bridge. He did not look at Caroline to see how she took the news.

I can't trust you, Caroline. You know what that means? I can't even talk to you anymore.

"The Detail asked for my contact information," she managed. "Burning out of the hotel immediately after I gave it to them might not have been the best idea."

"Eric's been arrested," he said quietly. "That's why I came for you. You can't sit twiddling your thumbs in a climate-controlled box while Scottie runs a backhoe over your life."

"Oh, *Jesus,*" she burst out. "Do you have a gun I could just put to my head right now, Cud? Do you? Because I can't take much more of this. You know?"

"Don't flip out on me, Caroline. *Please.*"

"Sure. Fine. Who the *fuck* arrested him? FBI? Interpol?"

"The BKA. He's in Germany."

"Germany! Why the hell is he still in *Germany?*

That's the last place on earth he should be. *Christ*—of all the *stupid . . .*" She slapped the armrest in frustration. "It's like the man wants to die, Cud. *Stupid, stupid*—"

"You're flipping out, Caroline."

"I think I'm allowed."

Cuddy did not argue. A red light changed to green. Somewhere on this Monday afternoon people were working at desks and thinking about simple things like what to have for dinner. What time was it in Germany? Five or six hours ahead of D.C.? Evening, anyway. Eric being systematically interrogated in a concrete-floored cell.

At the thought of him—trapped, alone, desperate— she was filled with a fear and longing for him sharper than she had ever known. *Eric. My love. Fight them. I'm fighting, too.*

"What happened?" she demanded. "How'd the Germans find him?"

"Your old friend Wally turned him in," Cuddy said.

She stared at him, aghast.

"Don't look like that," he muttered. "I *told* Wally to do it."

He took her straight into Washington at two-thirty in the afternoon, when the traffic was at something like an ebb. He drove her to a small apartment off MacArthur Boulevard just past Reservoir Road, with a galley kitchen and a racing bike suspended from the triangular space beneath the staircase. A bachelor's pad, one bedroom and two baths with a home officecum-den and a pullout couch for unexpected guests. The living room was square and sparsely furnished but you could climb through the front window with your coffee mug in the morning and stand on the roof of the bay window below. The place took up the top two floors of a hundred-year-old row house facing the canal.

He had talked while he drove, in a voice so low she had to strain to catch the words, a voice that compelled her to listen.

"Eric alone and hunted the length of Europe is exactly what Scottie wants, Caroline. Eric alone is an invitation to murder, you understand what I'm saying?"

"But—"

"Think of the headline. *Terrorist Gunned Down in Standoff with Berlin Police*. Or Madrid. Or Istanbul. You can't tell me the FBI hasn't issued orders to shoot to kill. That's Scottie's dream scenario. The one he's always had in his pocket."

Cuddy hadn't looked at her much as he ricocheted along the riverbank toward Georgetown. The car hugged the wide curves of the Potomac at a speed that was nowhere near legal.

"With Eric dead, finally dead, there's nobody to screw Scottie's perfect little world. We can't give him that one, Carrie. We can't let our Great White Chief walk away clean. We've got to fight."

"By shutting Eric in a hole?" she shot back bitterly. "Where the fuck are we, anyway?"

Cuddy had pulled up next to a leafless cherry tree drooping over a cracked curb. A pink flamingo stabbed the mulch near a set of entry stairs.

"Steve Price's house."

"The reporter?" She was incredulous. "I don't even *know* him."

"Exactly. So Ricin Boy'll never think to look for you here."

He had thought of everything, it seemed. A change of clothes for the woman she'd become—black mini, stiletto heels, a set of breasts far more impressive than her own. As she stood with her small black shoulder bag in the center of the empty living room, he delivered his whole script in rapid-fire staccato. Al Capone with words of one syllable.

"Wear the clothes and the Look when you go out. *Wear* them, Mad Dog. I want Caroline Carmichael to disappear from the face of the earth, you understand?"

"What if the Bureau gets nervous?"

"I'll tell Shephard you're heading to Hank's for some R and R. Leave the number where you can be reached on Long Island. Then have Hank screen your calls."

She considered this; it might work. Hank was her great-uncle, the man who'd raised her from the age of twelve. Hank would die for her, if only she'd ask.

"And don't call me at work," Cuddy warned. "If you need to meet, have Price get in touch. He can contact me without looking suspicious."

Caroline glanced despairingly around the unfamiliar apartment. "The poor sucker can't realize the danger he's in. What he's taken on by helping me."

"He's well paid."

"By whom?"

"You, Carrie." For the first time that day Cuddy smiled. "There's a quid pro quo involved. You get a room that's clean; Price gets your story. And *God*, does he want it. Just decide which one to tell him. Personally, I'd use the power of the press for all it's worth."

"I should find another hotel. I could register as Miss—Miss whoever I am." She shook the latex mask at him.

"Jennifer Lacey." He handed her a wallet. Driver's license, Visa card, passport—all in the Look's name.

"Raphael just *gave* you this stuff?" Raphael was the legendary head of OTS. "What lie did you tell him?"

"—That I'd recruited the wife of a terrorist," he said indifferently.

"You're mounting an op!"

"Damn straight."

She studied his face; as usual, the steady brown eyes gave nothing away, but by this time she could almost read Cuddy's mind. "CTC is your cover job. Scottie's your target. I'm your girl on the street and Eric's the bit of business you're using to distract the audience. What exactly do you want me to do, Cud?"

"Stay alive. And work your leads. I can't, sitting under Scottie's nose."

Her leads. The names of five staffers in the Payne household and a twelve-year-old boy who might or might not be poison.

"You can start with this."

He was dangling a CD-ROM in a plastic case.

"You managed to save Eric's disc?"

"No. Scottie ordered me to hand it over and I

watched while he destroyed it. But he didn't think to ask if I'd made copies."

Of course Cuddy had made copies.

"You took classified information out of the building, Cud."

"With Dare dead and the original destroyed, there's no record we ever got Eric's information. I think we can use it to undermine Scottie without admitting this disc ever reached the CIA."

"And what about Eric? What happens to Eric?"

"The BKA has charged him with murder." Cuddy pocketed her keys; apparently even her Jetta was to be confiscated. To be parked at Dulles while some blond double flew to JFK, if Caroline knew Cuddy. "His blood and prints are all over a stiff they found at the Berlin lab. We'll extradite him, of course."

"That could take months."

"Not this time. The Germans are falling over themselves to look helpful. They want the credit for nabbing Sophie Payne's kidnapper, and the public's thanks for returning our terrorist to crucify. I'd give it three days before he's home."

"Three *days*? Cuddy—that's not enough *time*. Not enough to—"

"Pin Scottie to the floor with a scalpel? We'll manage it. We've got more friends than Scottie does."

She sat down abruptly on her suitcase, all the hopeless misery suddenly overwhelming her. *Three days*. She would lose him for good this time.

"It's not all bad, you know," Cuddy said awkwardly. "Eric's under twenty-four-hour armed guard and he's guaranteed a ticket home. He's got a chance to tell his story in federal court with the entire country watching. He's got a *chance*, Carrie."

Instead of a bullet in the brain.

She had to agree it was something.

twenty-seven

"What have you got for me, Kaylie?" Shephard demanded.

He was standing just inside the yellow tape that separated a ghoulish band of spectators from the abandoned black limousine Norm Wilhelm had driven through Arlington National Cemetery that morning. Wilhelm was still sitting in the driver's seat, hands in his lap and a slack expression of contentment on his middle-aged face; most of his brains were spattered over the armor-plated door.

"Hair samples and some mucous," Kaylie Marks answered briskly. She was a slight woman in aqua hospital scrubs; the bones of her face were prominent as a horse's. Kaylie had spent nearly a decade in the Bureau's Laboratory Division and was in charge of the forensic team dispatched to this deserted spot on the vast asphalt parking lot of White Flint Mall, after a bunch of suburban skateboarders had bolted in terror from the sight of Norm Wilhelm's blasted cranium.

The first police response had come at three-fifteen; it had taken another forty-five minutes to connect a random chauffeur's murder with Jozsef Krucevic. His doctors had phoned the Secret Service, asking when the boy would be returned to Bethesda Naval. It was the first hint anybody had that Jozsef had vanished.

And he didn't walk away, Tom thought, *leaving this mess behind him. The kid was in no state to walk.*

"I took the samples from the backseat and head-rest." Kaylie held up a plastic bag for Tom's inspection. "Kid was sedated, right? That'd explain the drool. And he was under a blanket?"

Tom nodded.

"We found some wool fibers. We can compare this stuff with whatever data Bethesda Naval might have—but DNA sampling will take time, you know."

"Any blood?"

"Nothing major in the back," she said cautiously. Major blood didn't need explanation; it was all over the front seat. "Just spatters we'll probably find are from the driver. And *this.*"

She dangled a second bag with a single hair in front of Tom's nose. He strained his eyes to see it; brown and long: Jozsef's was black and short.

"Probably a woman's," Kaylie added. "Snagged on the headrest."

"Back or front?"

"Back."

"But Jozsef was alone—"

She frowned. "Way I see it, sir, is either she sat in the seat after the boy was taken from the car—unlikely, since his samples weren't disturbed—or she bent over to lift him out."

"And her hair swung forward and caught," Tom

said approvingly. "A woman drove the shooter at Arlington. Did this one kill Wilhelm?"

"Not from behind. The shot to the chauffeur's head was probably fired by a right-handed person sitting in the front passenger seat." Kaylie set down the evidence bags and moved swiftly around to the right-hand door. Tom followed her. "He or she placed the muzzle flat against the temple and pulled the trigger. The powder burns are almost circular. And another thing—the bullet passed right through Wilhelm's brain and exited over his left ear. We found it buried in the inner plating of the driver's door."

"M16? Like Dare Atwood?"

"No way." She shook her head regretfully; like all the old hands of Laboratory Division, she relished a consistent investigation. "The bullet's a thirty-two caliber. Handgun. Beyond that, I can't tell you much. There are fourteen thousand kinds of ammunition manufactured in the United States, and none of it's traceable."

"But this slug may match the bullet that killed the EMT on Memorial Drive. Any long brown hair in the limo's front seat?"

"None."

It made sense, Tom thought: The woman had driven the gray Chrysler K-car through Arlington National Cemetery while someone—Ricin Boy?—fired out the back window; then she'd taken Jozsef from the rear of the limo while her partner finished off Wilhelm. But how had the hit gone down? There was no sign of a struggle—no damage to the car or its driver. It was almost as though Wilhelm had been expecting to lose his passenger ... as though he'd driven here to White Flint Mall, a bare few miles north of Bethesda Naval Hospital, on purpose to meet his killers ...

Tom straightened and stepped back from the bloodied limo door, his exhausted mind suddenly racing. *Wilhelm had known his killers.* He'd deliberately stopped to hand off the boy. Caroline's voice—Caroline's stubborn insistence spiraled through Tom's ragged thoughts: *Thirty April had agents in place inside the Naval Observatory.* Wilhelm? Or one of his friends?

"Thanks." Tom turned abruptly away from Kaylie Marks. He had to get back to Headquarters; he needed to pull those background files.

"Sir!" the forensic technician called after him. "*Sir!* There's one more thing!"

He stopped short. "Well?"

With the air of an art dealer unveiling a particularly choice piece, Kaylie held up a small square card between her fingertips.

"Prints," she said. "A nearly perfect set of somebody's right hand. We found them on the underside of the back door handle."

For the first time in nearly a year, Rebekah felt the singing, light-headed joy of the Lord's presence as she plunged the truck through the ruts of the unpaved road. She was buoyed by it, this return of the Savior and the enfolding love that steadied her hands as she gripped the steering wheel. When He had struck down her Dolf in His terrible mercy and carried him off to Glory at His right hand, she had not understood His infinite wisdom or the plan that lay so clearly marked out before her. She had turned her back on the Lamb. She had wailed in the desert against the hardness of this misery, this brutal, wrenching loss that cut the living heart from her body. She had sunk deep into the abyss of her grief, had wanted self-murder, wanted the pain of torn flesh and violence, as though in bleeding herself she might understand what her boy had endured before the end.

She had sinned, again and again, in the treachery of her disbelief. He had tested her will and her allegiance and she had failed every test. But the Lord had returned, to show Bekah just how much His love could stand; this time, she was ready. She could lift up her face and welcome Him with open arms, because He had seen fit to give her a second child, washed new in His blood.

The Savior was riding shotgun at this moment beside her while the sleeping boy wedged behind her seat moaned in drugged dreams. His Divine Love governed Bekah's every move, and she knew now, with the certainty of this singing joy, that no one had seen them. No one would follow. They had delivered the boy from his enemies, and they would protect and rear him against the final assault of the End Times.

"...*washed new in the blood of the Lamb,*" she muttered aloud. *"Washed new in the blood of the Lamb."* She would fix Dolf's favorite meal—ham and potato salad and baked beans—and this boy, this Son of the Leader sacrificed to His Enemies, would eat and be glad.

Ahead, in the dirt pullout beside the switchback

that led toward the farm, a motorcycle was waiting. *Daniel.* When he caught sight of the truck, he stepped out into the road, his arms waving. A slight figure in his old field jacket and wool cap, his sharp-featured face neither welcoming nor touched with Glory. Bekah frowned, her fingers white on the wheel. What was he doing here? It wasn't part of the plan. But she must Trust in His Goodness. Must shut her mind to the voice of the Devil, the voice of Reason, which was as nothing to the sword of Faith.

She pulled over behind the bike.

"Well?" she asked as she rolled down the window.

"Get out, girl."

"But, *Daniel*—"

"Take the bike home. I'll call you from the road."

His strong blunt hand was on the doorframe and she saw what he meant to do—how he meant to take the boy for himself and head out into the night with his bloodshot eyes and his face lined with weariness from the long hard servitude under the Lord—and all her agony welled up inside her. The singing light-headed joy melted into desolation. *My God, my God, why hast Thou forsaken me?*

"Come on, now," he snapped, "I ain't got all day."

"What about the boy?" she whispered. "He needs dinner."

Daniel glanced into the back. "Don't know which end is up, looks like. You go on home. I'll be in touch."

She jumped from the truck's running board to the ground. He brushed past her, not a word or a look of comfort. There was blood on his field jacket, she could

see it now, and the smell of sweat rose from his unclean skin. How long since he'd sat down in his own
house? How many days? She'd lost count.

"Where's Norm gone?"

He didn't answer. The truck door slammed.

"Daniel—I asked you where my brother is!" she
shouted over the sound of the ignition.

He lifted his hand in salute, broad flat fingers swerv-
ing out from his forehead like he'd been taught by the
Zoggite masters. She pounded once on the hood of
the truck but he surged forward, arms roving over the
steering wheel, and that quickly she was alone. Dust in
her nostrils. Darkness falling. And the first spattering
of harsh rain.

twenty-eight

Wally Aronson eyed the dark-haired man lounging on the opposite side of the conference table and compiled a mental dossier. *Ernst Haller, thirty-nine years old, born and educated Heidelberg, grandfather a Luftwaffe pilot World War II shot down over British Channel, grandmother killed in bombing of Dresden. Despises Americans. Christian Democrat by birth, BKA by training, reputed fascist by inclination. Boss already fired at last week's government ouster; our boy Ernst has little or no future in the present climate. He badly needs a victory.*

"I'd like to extend the thanks of the entire U.S. government, Herr Haller, for your resourceful and dedicated pursuit of a man I can only describe as one of the most dangerous, violent, and sought-after criminals of the past decade," Wally said handsomely in the German that was mother's milk to him.

It was probable Haller had a similar mental dossier on Wally and knew exactly how many members of his extended family had died at Dachau sixty years before, which might account for the nostrils pinched as though sniffing the acrid air of the ovens; but the BKA's finest smiled swiftly and bowed his head, an angel submitting to benediction, basking for this instant in the ardent gratitude of the last foolish superpower on earth.

"It was simply a matter of solid police work," Ernst replied in English, a false politeness designed to demonstrate his immunity to all American blandishment. "And, naturally, the cooperation of *yourself,* Herr Aronson. But for your phone call—"

Wally waved a hand distractedly, as though to say *Just doing my job,* when in reality it was unheard-of for the U.S. embassy to throw away one of their own without first summoning the FBI, and any self-respecting federal policeman should have known as much and smelled a rat—"We have a number of details to discuss, I'm afraid."

"Jurisdiction," Haller suggested delicately.

"Well—*yes.* I realize you badly want this man up before one of your federal judges on a charge of murder, and I completely understand the desire to see justice done—I mean, that *poor woman* with her neck broken, lying like so much trash on the floor of the terrorist lab—I suppose there's no question she'd entered it legitimately? She must have had *access,* I mean? Possibly . . . a member of the terrorist cell herself?"

"A receptionist," Haller said primly. "Most respectable. It is unlikely she had the slightest inkling of the true nature of the company's operations."

"No. Surely not," Wally mourned. "Although the hour at which the alleged murder took place was, I understand, somewhat unusual for a receptionist? The middle of the night, I think your medical examiner said was the time of death—?"

Haller shrugged. "Murder is still murder, no matter what hour of the day it occurs."

"Of course. I merely wished to suggest that this loss, however regrettable, came nearly a week after the kidnapping of our vice president. That crime—and Mrs. Payne's subsequent death—might be considered to outweigh or supersede, purely in *prosecutorial terms*, of course, the unfortunate death of this...receptionist."

"Meaning...?"

"That I have been authorized to formally request the extradition to the United States of...Nigel Benning, Michael O'Shaughnessy, whatever he calls himself... as soon as humanly possible. You *understand*, Herr Haller," he added appealingly. "The American public needs some kind of resolution. A sense of closure. A culprit for the enormity visited upon Mrs. Payne. They need to see justice done."

Haller steepled his hands. "You want the man delivered to the airport tarmac at five o'clock in the morning so that a chartered plane may depart without the notice of the enraged German populace, which blames this terrorist for the recent destruction of a piece of historic Berlin?"

"Exactly," Wally returned affably. "The United States government understands you wish to earn full publicity value from this arrest. The President is willing to offer his official thanks to the new chancellor. Your own name will be highly praised in letters of appreciation to your department head for the efficiency of your entire operation. But we want the man returned."

"That is not what *your boss* has told me." Haller's

eyes gleamed with wicked amusement from the opposite side of the table, and abruptly Wally sat back in his seat, as though momentarily puzzled.

"My boss?" he repeated. "I'm afraid I *have* no superior in Berlin. You're speaking to the top of the food chain, Ernst."

"No, no, no," Haller returned softly. "I refer to your agency's counterterrorism chief. Your...Mr. Sorensen. He telephoned me only this afternoon. But a few hours ago."

"I see." Wally trailed his pen indolently over the notepad in front of him as though the information were unimportant.

"It is Mr. Sorensen's ardent wish—and the wish of your entire organization, as he so forcefully assures me—that this man should be tried and sentenced in the German courts." Haller's bland gray eyes stared innocently at Wally. "Now will you tell me, Herr Aronson, exactly what kind of game you are playing?"

Eric lay on the thin mattress that covered the concrete slab jutting from his prison wall. The room was roughly six feet wide by ten feet deep, and in addition to the bed held a toilet bolted to the floor. He had been stowed in the twenty-four-hour-lockdown section, where the most dangerous men were kept; his wrists and ankles were shackled. Unlike a regular cell, which admitted light and air through the bars of its cage, this one had a solid steel door. A square foot of grille served as the only window on the cell block corridor.

The prison sat in the eastern sector of Berlin on the

outskirts of Prenzlauerberg: It had once served as a madhouse under the Communist regime. Communist East Germany did not admit that criminals existed— merely perversions of a mental or philosophic nature that could be ascribed to unrepentant capitalist mania. Unification had returned the madhouse to its proper usage, and West German funds had spiffed up the paint and the drains. The steel box still reeked of urine and fear.

In his solitary confinement, Eric had leisure to see that his predecessors in lockdown had whiled away the hours by scratching graffiti into the steel with the links of their chains. It was painstaking work; and all with an end to the most banal of expressions. *Sternheim sucks dog cock.* He closed his eyes. He had a lot to think about.

Did you kill that woman? Wally had asked as he paced the length of the interrogation room, his hands in his pockets and his balding head shining with the discomfort of his situation.

"She came at me with a scalpel." He'd pointed to the ragged wound in his neck. "Nearly cut my fucking head off."

"Are there any others? Thirty April survivors?"

"I don't know. None I've found."

He had wanted to scream in agony at the man. *Why did you do it, Wally? Why did you turn me in?* but there would be microphones embedded in the walls, and surveillance cameras. Any kind of real communication was impossible. Wally was playing a part. He hadn't looked Eric in the eye since the moment he'd returned to Sophienstrasse with the federal police in his pocket.

Wally knew the answer to every question he'd asked; they had rehearsed this, in the high-ceilinged room with the gray shadows, while Wally rolled tape around Eric's ribs. Something was going on—Eric could smell deception like a dog scented heat—but whatever it was, Wally wasn't telling.

"You'll be provided with a German lawyer," the station chief had offered at parting. "And you can expect a U.S. debrief team. I'd tell them everything you know. It's your best hope, Mr. O'Shaughnessy, regardless of whether you're tried in this country or extradited."

Everything you know. Which of the stories was Wally expecting? The cover lies—or the truth? There was very little to choose between them—Eric had lived his cover too well. There was the child he'd shot in Bratislava. The break-ins and kidnappings all over Europe. The murders he'd witnessed and failed to stop. The voice of conscience he'd strangled in his sleep.

He'd called that life a necessary compromise. If he'd showed squeamishness—hesitated even once to carry out 30 April's orders—he'd have died long ago. And he wanted to live, wanted to baby the trust he'd earned until the moment he could betray 30 April from within. For years, he and Scottie Sorensen had agreed: *It is impossible to penetrate a terrorist group and destroy it without becoming a terrorist yourself.* But the American public refused to understand this brutal truth. On the one hand, they demanded perfect human intelligence of coming threats. On the other, they screamed at the CIA's habit of buying information from known killers. Scottie's methods would never have stood up to Capitol Hill's scrutiny; he was *dirtying his hands.* And so he and Eric had agreed to complete deniability. Complete operational silence.

Why had it all mattered more than anything else in life? Eric could no longer remember. Because Scottie had chosen him? Because a plane blew up and friends of his died? Whatever it was—this passion that had killed every raw feeling in his soul—it was over now. He just wanted to go home.

With a screech of metal, the bolts on his door were thrown back. He rolled to an upright position, his eyes narrowed at the dazzling flood of light.

Wally stood there, a guard at his elbow. The station chief held a pad of paper casually toward Eric. Scrawled on it in black marker were the words *Cell's bugged*.

"Good evening, O'Shaughnessy," Wally said. "I've come for a chat. We've got exactly fifteen minutes."

twenty-nine

Steve Price was used to working on very little sleep. He had covered two wars and three national elections for the *Washington Post* during the nearly fifteen years he'd worked in the capital, and since his divorce seven years earlier he'd earned the reputation of a hard partyer. He'd been known to arrive at his cubicle in the National section of the vast newsroom before dawn, still wearing black tie and reeking of Scotch-laced cigarette smoke; but his personal life rarely affected his prose. He might be one of the most sought-after dinner guests among Georgetown's league of ambitious hostesses—he might be privileged to call no fewer than seventeen senators by their first names and to flyfish with three Cabinet members—but Steve was a pro. He would answer his cell phone in the middle of an orgasm, if necessary, and be on the scene of a story twelve minutes later, smelling faintly of semen and already composing his lede. He could write through a missile attack and required no editing.

His managers at the *Post* were terrified he'd be seduced away from the political fold with a foreign correspondence offer from the *New York Times*; as a result,

Steve was paid the earth and given his choice of Paris or Moscow. So far he'd refused both. Nobody was sure why he preferred to remain in Washington, but nobody bothered to ask too many questions. Steve was entitled to his secrets. His employers were simply glad he stayed.

By four o'clock that afternoon he'd filed four stories, two of which had already gone up on the Internet edition as breaking news; all four would appear under his byline—though one of them was shared—in Tuesday morning's paper. *Dana Enright, Speaker's Wife, Dead at 37* was one; it recounted the midnight scene at Sibley Hospital and the fact that the ailing marathoner had provided the FBI with the killer's composite currently being broadcast all over the country. A companion piece updated the appalling statistics of the latest ricin victims, fifty-three dead and seven hundred ninety-eight in critical condition; it was accompanied by a heartrending photograph of a mother holding her son that some people were already calling "the Terrorist Pietà." *Director of Central Intelligence Assassinated in Georgetown Home* included interviews with the medical examiner and the FBI's Tom Shephard, and suggested vaguely that Dare Atwood's killer might well be a former military sniper. Finally, Price's favorite piece: *Administration Flounders in Face of New Crisis.* Every journalist alive dealt to a certain extent in schadenfreude—the ghoulish appreciation of another person's misery—and Steve was no exception. He enjoyed making Jack Bigelow squirm.

Even Jonathan Wills, the *Post*'s hard-bitten managing editor, would agree that Steve Price had done his bit for the glory of the rag during the past sleepless two days; so that when the reporter yawned prodigiously and kicked his chair away from his desk, announcing to the journalistic world in general that *Fuck I'm tired I'm going home to get drunk and screw,* nobody argued. Some wondered who he was planning to fuck, exactly, and others started a furtive betting pool on likely candidates; but none of them attempted to teach him his job. If Price wanted to walk away and miss the breaking shit in the war going on down there in the rush hour Monday streets, the mounting deaths and the panic among policymakers and housewives alike, so be it. They could all write circles around Steve Price anyway.

As he swung out of the newsroom, he was thinking how pissed they'd all be when they saw his exclusive interview with Caroline Carmichael the next morning. He intended to e-mail this crowning glory to Jonathan Wills in a few hours. But Wills called him back before he reached the escalator. Ricin Boy's latest fax had just come across the wire, announcing to the world the rescue of 30 April's anointed one. Jozsef Krucevic had vanished.

Spavač, Caroline read, and clicked in frustration on the icon that led nowhere.

She had found three of these Croatian file names buried in the data Eric had sent home on his pirated computer disc. *Spavač, Alat,* and *Šaka.* Someone—Cuddy?—had translated the words as *Sleeper, Tool,* and *Fist.* Each had the symbol of a folder next to its name, and each listed between thirty-five and forty kilobytes of information stored. But when she tried to open them, she got a completely blank screen.

Encrypted, she thought, *or the data failed to transfer when Cuddy copied the disc.* He would have suspected encryption and put one of CTC's techies onto the problem. Or would he? Cuddy had been wary of the secret of Eric's operation leaking throughout the Counterterrorism Center. Maybe he'd been afraid of asking for help—or had simply given up on these. He'd already gone through most of Eric's intelligence in the week since Caroline had returned home.

She could follow her branch chief's trail by the havoc he'd wreaked in 30 April's interests worldwide. Five front companies in the Netherlands, Germany, and Slovakia had already seen their assets seized by Interpol; a network of embedded operatives in Poland had been arrested four days before. Krucevic's primary financial backers—a charismatic Catholic politician in the south of France and the head of a private relief organization operating throughout North Africa—had resigned abruptly from their posts. Both were facing criminal investigations. The FBI had formally requested the freezing of nearly one hundred million euros held in Swiss banks. It had been a good week for counterterrorism—until Ricin Boy struck.

Sleeper, Tool, and *Fist.* What did they mean? Bits of undigested data that Eric had copied by mistake? Names of genetically engineered bugs that 30 April had intended to unleash upon the world? Operational tags for hits that had never taken place—murders, kidnappings, bomb sites yet to explode?

But to Caroline, they sounded like names.

A rattle of keys in the front door's bolts brought her head up swiftly. She clicked out of the CD and closed the laptop's cover. From her position on the living room floor—back pressed against Steve Price's dark blue sofa—she had a perfect view of the entryway. Her snub-nosed Walther TPK was already leveled at the door.

"Caroline!" Price's head curved around the jamb and he shot her a smile. "Guess what? That kid you saved just broke out of jail."

She gleaned two things immediately from the reporter's glib account of Jozsef's disappearance: Norm Wilhelm hadn't fought his killer—indeed, he seemed to have gone placidly to his death by prearranged appointment—and Jozsef's kidnapping might just be Eric's salvation. With the boy missing, Eric was the last hope the government had of learning where the next terrorist blow would fall.

Her gut instincts were right: Jozsef had told the truth. One of Sophie Payne's trusted staffers knew 30 April intimately.

Beneath her sick worry for the boy, Caroline's mind leaped with hope. *Tom Shephard would finally understand*. He would know that she and Jozsef hadn't steered him wrong. His quick wits would travel from the place of execution to the heart of West Virginia, and to the spider's web of connections Norm Wilhelm had left behind. Within hours, Tom would jump on the next of kin. It was a waste of time for her to head in the same direction. Instead, she made Steve Price repeat every detail he knew, spent a few moments in careful thought, then called Dr. Bill Lewis at Bethesda Naval Hospital.

Lewis was the head of Jozsef's medical team. It was he who'd released the boy into Caroline's safekeeping only that morning; he wouldn't hesitate to talk to her.

"Do we log telephone calls from patients' rooms?" he repeated blankly after she commiserated about Jozsef's apparent kidnapping. "Sure we do. You wouldn't believe the places some people call. Tibet. New South Wales. We've got to be able to pin them for charges."

He put an administrator on the problem and buzzed Caroline's cell phone a bare twelve minutes later. Jozsef had made only one call during his week-long stay: two hours after Dare Atwood's murder the previous morning. The number was local.

"We have tracing capability at the *Post*," Price told her. "But why do you want to know? You think the kid *arranged* to be picked up at White Flint Mall?"

"It's a possibility," Caroline said heavily. "His timing—pulling me out of the funeral just as a drive-by shooting occurred—was far too perfect. Yeah, I think he made contact."

"I'll get the name and address," the reporter returned, as though raising her bet in poker, "if you'll give me the story first. *Your* story. No bullshit, just the straight poop. Deal?"

She hesitated only a second. "Deal."

thirty

"Carmichael's been arrested *already*?" Cory Rinehart frowned. "I'm surprised. The BKA is usually less... resourceful."

"Wally Aronson turned his old friend in," Scottie replied dryly; he planned on kicking Wally the length of Europe for having done so. "Apparently Eric showed up on his doorstep begging for help."

Rinehart glanced up from the cable he was reading. He'd had the good taste to remain in his own office down the hall from the DCI's, which he'd rather ostentatiously locked before such witnesses as Dare Atwood's weeping secretary and the Deputy Director for Operations, pending the arrival of Dare's next of kin. *A daughter,* he'd told Scottie disbelievingly. *Lives somewhere in Miami. I didn't know Dare was ever married.*

"This thug sought out our COS Berlin?" he demanded now. "That's interesting. Very." Rinehart ran one of his small and rather delicate hands over his beautifully trimmed black hair. He was a spare man, compact and athletic, his clothes almost obsessively pressed; a former navy pilot, Scottie remembered. A tactical thinker trained to take out the incoming. Appearances mattered to Cory Rinehart; even his shoes were expensive and perfect.

"I've been thinking about this whole goddamn rigmarole. The idea that Atwood was running Carmichael alone—it doesn't make sense. I can't find a trace of any financial arrangements in her records. No suggestion that the two of them even communicated."

The late DCI's office door might be locked, Scottie reflected approvingly, but Rinehart had already used his key. "You think it's possible . . . Wally Aronson was involved?"

"Not with Headquarters sanction," Rinehart said quickly. "But if Carmichael knew him well enough to find his doorstep . . . it does suggest . . ."

". . . a rogue operator," Scottie finished. "Yes, I see your point. You want Aronson recalled?"

"That's a job for the DDO." *The Deputy Director for Operations.* In this case, Hal Rickler, spymaster to the nation's spooks and one more person who'd demand admittance to Scottie's dangerous circle of conspiracy. He could not have it.

Scottie sighed. "Remember who you are, Cory. *Acting Director.* You don't have to explain a single one of your decisions to anybody now but the President."

The casual reference to Jack Bigelow served as a reminder of exactly how delicate a business they were tossing like a football around the room.

"Will the BKA let us talk to him?" Rinehart demanded abruptly.

"Wally?"

"Carmichael."

Scottie shrugged, uncertain how this might serve his ends. "It's early days yet. We're still negotiating jurisdiction. The Germans want to try him on murder charges. I think we ought to let them."

"Are you out of your fucking mind?" Rinehart demanded softly. "If the connection to the Agency's Berlin station came up ... the CIA would be held accountable for the destruction of half of downtown Berlin and the murder of Sophie Payne. We are *not* going to let that happen."

"If you say so." Scottie's eyes were hooded. "What alternative would you suggest?"

"Extradite the bastard as soon as possible. Film his arrival in handcuffs on every major news channel nationwide. Hand the President a terrorist he can prosecute— and say fuck-all about where he came from."

"But Eric will talk. On every major news channel." Scottie eased back in his chair as though the prospect of his enemy babbling in a sort of political reality show held no terrors for him. "He'll embarrass not only the CIA but the entire Administration. Jack Bigelow won't thank you for that, Cory. He certainly won't *appoint* you to fill Dare's shoes on a permanent basis."

"I never hoped for that," Rinehart said.

Liar, Scottie retorted silently. *You've wanted this job since you picked up your badge from Security thirteen years ago. I know your kind. I've recruited better men than you.*

But when he spoke it was in a measured tone entirely free of the rancor flooding his veins.

"Aronson reports that Eric's been roughed up.

Somebody worked him over with a cleaver. It'd be a gift if he never survived his holding cell."

Rinehart's eyes—a clear and remorseless blue— betrayed no shock. "Could that be arranged?"

Was it possible, Scottie wondered with a vague uneasiness, that the A/DCI was willing to hand him so simple an avenue to power? Would Rinehart submit to lifelong blackmail, purely for a snatch at Dare Atwood's private suite?

"Why don't you send me to Berlin, Cory?" he suggested gently. "We need eyes on the ground. I know the key people at the BKA—and I can get access to Eric without leaving a trail."

A smile flickered briefly over Cory Rinehart's face. "Eric was one of *yours,* wasn't he? Almost a son, people used to say."

"I have two daughters. They're all grown up now."

Rinehart reached for a personnel file and hoisted it meaningfully. "I've been reading up on Carmichael. He was quite a CO. You gave him his last three postings, I think. Plums, all of them, Scottie. Strange that he'd betray you so completely. And you in the dark the whole time."

The drift of the conversation was clear. If Wally Aronson's friendship for the doomed man was suspect, then Scottie's was career ending.

Very well, he thought with distaste. *You scratch my back, Cory, and I'll scratch out your eyes.*

He rose. "Have you told Bigelow we've got Eric?"

"Yes. And also that you fired his wife." Rinehart's gaze locked with Scottie's. "The President wasn't happy about that. She's his perfect hero."

"And more compromised than anybody in the building."

"Except yourself."

Scottie raised one eyebrow. "Are you requesting my resignation, sir?"

"Not yet." Rinehart dropped Eric's folder back on his desk. "I want to see how you solve our problem in Berlin. Why don't you leave tonight, Scottie?"

thirty-one

Josie O'Halloran lifted two twenty-five-pound bags of ice from the flatbed of Mike's truck and carried the slippery weight, frigid against her breasts, into the service entrance of the store. Rainwater had pooled on the concrete floor and the glitter of a fish scale winked from the rusted drain at her feet, but the November chill flooding through the two narrow rooms cut the stench like a knife. The odor this afternoon was a stew of seawater and diesel fumes and good fresh fish, reminding Josie of the Boston docks and her father's trawler heading for dawn on the Georges Bank. Forty-five years ago, maybe fifty, when she'd been a kid with dirty knees and corduroy pants her mother deplored. A different lifetime; and what would her mother think now if she saw Josie's hardened hands, encased in plastic gloves as transparent as a proctologist's, shoving the ice around the chars' gills? *Waste of a good education,* she'd say bitterly. *For this we sent you to Manhattanville?*

But her mother was dead eighteen years and Josie had learned in her refined Catholic women's college exactly what it meant to be a child of the working class, a girl who got A's but still smelled of the docks, no debutante with an MRS degree, Josie O'Halloran. The boys from Holy Cross and Villanova and Georgetown had figured it out, too: One look at her broad Irish face and red hair and blunt hands and they'd moved on to what Josie called the Kennedy Irish— the kind whose money and dark good looks made up for an entry stamp at Ellis Island. She'd left Manhattanville without the requisite diamond ring or the postgraduate tour of Europe but with the highest marks in her class. *Josie,* Sister Regina Mary had said a month before graduation, *there is a gentleman I'd like you to meet. You're a good girl and a hard worker and I think it just possible he might offer you employment.*

"That's all of it, Jo," Mike sang out from the open doorway. "Need anything else?"

"Nothin' you can give me, sweetheart." His young cheeks were flushed above the demonic goatee and for an instant she wanted to pinch them lovingly. Instead, she smiled and waved him back into his belching truck, wondering at what point men had become her sons and not her lovers. She was fifty-eight years old, she'd never lost her figure, she kept her hair styled and dyed; but maybe it was the men who'd changed, slipping back like a point in a riverbank her current had left behind forever. She saw most of them now as little boys, never much older than the two grandsons whose picture she kept on the ledge near the lobster tank, grinning out at her with all the wit and malice of the devil's own.

She sighed and looked over Mike's delivery: fresh bluepoints and Wellfleets, although who would buy them on a Monday was questionable—oysters on the half were a weekend commodity. Harpooned swordfish steaks, always a good seller. Your Dover sole. Your catfish and farm-raised salmon for the types who liked fish but refused to pay steak prices. Wild king fillets. Chesapeake Bay blue crab. Sea scallops and the tiny succulent rock shrimp that were never frozen before they arrived at O'Halloran's Seafood, the kind Scottie Sorensen liked to buy.

The bell over the door jangled and Josie hurriedly reached for her heavy rubber apron. Sasha, her counter girl, had called in sick for the eighth time this month. "Just a sec," she shouted. "I'll be right with you."

He was standing there when she appeared as though she'd conjured him, silver head bent toward the chilled glass of the lobster tank, completely absorbed by the antennae probing the slick surface. Scottie in his Bond Street raincoat. The one man she could never see as just a little boy.

He came almost weekly, but the sight of him still had the power to shift her heart up a gear. *He might offer you employment,* Sister Regina had said; and so he had. Employment in Beirut as his personal secretary, the job other women had drawn blood to win. Beirut in the mid-sixties, its last golden hours of pleasure before Eden's fall, Beirut of the secret gardens and the ripe blushing fruit and the sex on the couches in the middle of the day. She had been Scottie's secretary, his confidante, his bodyguard and muse. Occasional bedfellow. All-purpose dinner partner when cover required it. Chief shopper for whatever wife was currently in power. She had served Scottie Sorensen in a number of ways over the past thirty years and knew exactly what was essential: the things he wanted and the ways he got them. Even how he preferred his bluefish cooked.

"Hello, Jo," he said without turning around. "How're you keeping?"

"Well enough. And you?"

She did not have to ask whether the work was interesting. She listened to the radio and watched her TV. A man with a gun had killed the Director last night and nobody could say where he'd got to. She had never been one to beg for privileged information. He'd tell her soon enough.

"You realize," he said casually, "that three of these monsters are eating a fourth alive."

She couldn't see the lethal drama played out in the tank—his head was blocking her view—but she'd caught the scene often enough. One lobster on its back, skinny legs flailing, while the others tore at its entrails.

"I flew those in from Bar Harbor on Saturday," she said calmly. "Does the Latest like lobster?"

The Latest was what she'd always called Scottie's wife; it had been too tiring to keep track of all their names.

"Loves it," he replied, "but not tonight, Jo. I'm flying to Berlin in a few hours."

"So you didn't come to buy fish."

His eyes met hers. "Are you alone?"

"Completely."

"Then take off your apron and sit down. I have a job for you to do."

thirty-two

When the buzzer sounded at the door of the vault, Raphael waited coolly for one of his acolytes to press the security release button. He remained on his barstool before the drafting table, his fine-boned left hand working with the metal stylus under the magnifying lens. No visitor was worth disturbing his concentration. It was essential that the pattern of wear on the forged Burmese chop replicate the hidden flaws deliberately placed on the original document by the immigration authorities in Rangoon. Raphael was legendary for his ability to ignore everything that was not essential to his trade.

Cuddy Wilmot, with whom Raphael had worked for the past three years on delicate and unspeakable business, was standing a few feet away from him. He felt the air change behind his back but did not glance in Cuddy's direction.

Raphael was the Master. He resembled a charcoal figure touched out on canvas by the hand of Leonardo: the lithe curve of his form, the sweeping arc of his golden head. Only the wings, furled in silence, were missing.

He set down the stylus and pushed aside the lens. Flexed his fingers and sighed. Then he turned at last and looked at the man waiting quietly in the doorway.

Cuddy dipped his bespectacled face slightly; in supplication, Raphael liked to think. "Raphael. Would you have time to speak to me?"

He reviewed his mental log. Nearly ten hours of painstaking work lay ahead of him; the fact that it was late on a Monday was irrelevant. There was the voice-activated microphone his subordinates had embedded in the frame of a personal photograph the President would present to a Middle Eastern dictator, bound to be hung in the man's office: The quality of the disguised wood grain would have to be checked by Raphael alone before it was delivered to the White House that night. The infrared landing lights for the unmarked airstrip in the Andes should be tested. The tiny camera he was supposed to plant in a female case officer's lipstick was still waiting on a shelf, and the woman was due to fly out to Paris in three days. None of the objets d'art produced by the Office of Technical Services left Raphael's shop without his personal approval. In less than seven years, he had gained an empire.

"Give me half an hour," he said. And thus terminated Wilmot's audience.

The Office of Technical Services had been known for years as "Q branch," but it was gradually acquiring another name: Raphael's Chapel. Most of the people who benefited from his perfection had no idea where he'd come from, or even if he had a last name. Raphael preferred it that way. He wore only black, as though prepared at any moment for clandestine escape. His tow-colored hair reached to his shoulders and was tied back efficiently with narrow black ribbon. In another man the look would be effeminate; in Raphael, it suggested he came from a vanished century—the eighteenth, perhaps—and could kill with a rapier's touch.

It was unclear where he lived. When the others who worked for him arrived each morning, he was already there; when they left, he remained behind to close the vault. It was rumored that he drove an antique green Lotus of a model not seen since Steve McQueen's salad days; but the assertion had never been proved. Some members of OTS argued that the picture of Raphael doing anything other than flying under his own wing power was completely absurd.

He had been born in North Dakota thirty-six years before and named Pete Petersen. At the time of his hiring by Andrew Nunez, the OTS chief, he was on his way to prison. What fell in between—the transformation of a North Dakota boy to a Prince of Darkness—only Raphael and Nunez understood. He never spoke of the past to anyone. He knew deception for what it was: the highest form of survival.

Nunez was on the verge of retirement when he discovered Raphael in the Metro section of the Sunday *New York Times*. A young man of extraordinary beauty, photographed in handcuffs in the midst of a Princeton University lecture hall. The previous year, Pete Petersen had decided he was tired of his inconsequential life and had set about creating a new one. At the age of

twenty-eight, he had crafted what clandestine operatives would call a legend: a fully fleshed-out alternative
existence, complete with an assumed name and birth
certificate, which suggested he was eighteen years old.

He had called himself Raphael Alighieri, after two
heroes of the Renaissance; described himself as home-
schooled in Switzerland by a philosophy professor from
Rome and his sculptress wife, both long dead; and given
himself an orphaned adolescence wandering the world.
He submitted a portfolio of charcoal sketches and a set
of test scores well above the Princeton mean. Princeton admired the artistry, approved his SATs, and offered financial aid to the impoverished boy with no
visible means of support.

It was only when a former acquaintance from Bis-
marck spotted him at a football game that the imposture
was exposed.

He was charged with theft by deception and sentenced to a year's penal servitude.

In Nunez's eyes, as he scanned the *Times* article,
Raphael had just written a near-perfect application for
the CIA.

During forty years of service, Andy Nunez had made
OTS what it was: the premier technical innovator of
Agency Ops, the heart of forgery and deceit, green
room to the Greatest Show on Earth. When he joined
the CIA in the early sixties, the Office of Technical
Services did not exist. It was called something else and
it employed a coterie of accomplished artists and drafts-
men, many of whom regarded themselves as unionized

labor working in the equivalent of the government printing office. What they carved, etched, engraved, and printed was criminal when viewed from the perspective of their adversaries: foreign currency, foreign passports, foreign birth certificates, and letters of recommendation, not to mention the myriad entry and exit visas from places technically immured behind the Iron Curtain.

Andy Nunez began his career by learning how to open mail without leaving a trace. How to detect and replicate the pitfalls and deliberate traps embedded in visa stamps from mainland China. How to mix foreign inks and reweave paper fibers to ward off the bloodhounds of forgery. Nunez progressed to working exfiltration from Beijing to Hong Kong, to managing defectors and disinformation during the Vietnam War. He replicated Vietcong diaries filled with false intelligence and made sure they found their damaging way back home—although he knew not a word or character of Vietnamese. He flew in more prop planes to more airstrips in the heart of the jungle than any man should be able to survive. He was best known, however, for the creation of elaborate disguises culled from the techniques of Hollywood special effects, whose innovators he befriended and admired.

Under Nunez's direction, Raphael Alighieri came into a kingdom. The old man passed on every secret and skill he possessed to the young Prince of Darkness. When he retired, it was with the knowledge that OTS was in the hands of the angels.

• • •

Raphael was waiting for Cuddy when he reappeared exactly twenty-five minutes later in the OTS conference room. He had a narrow black laptop open on the shining surface of the table.

"This is a very close hold," Cuddy cautioned, and handed him a DVD.

Raphael slid the disc into his laptop without comment.

The footage was brief: perhaps thirty-five seconds of Sophie Payne's last public appearance. She stood on the podium in Berlin's Pariser Platz in front of the new American embassy while the Brandenburg Gate exploded.

The screen flickered, went blank, and then resumed with a shot of a stretcher being raised into the belly of a medical chopper.

"Is that Payne on the gurney?" Raphael asked with a quickening of interest.

"Forget the gurney. Look at the man on the inside, working the winch."

Raphael's eyes narrowed. Then he sat back in his swivel chair, a pen delicately tapping his elegant lip. "Eric Carmichael. I worked with him only once. Disciplined and not unintelligent. He's supposed to be dead."

"That's the problem."

The Prince of Darkness sighed and closed his eyes. The air of the conference room was suddenly charged with an energy that was almost sexual. "Tell me."

"Scottie put Eric under deep cover with 30 April two and a half years ago. When Payne came back in a coffin, Scottie burned him. Eric's under arrest in Berlin and his wife's just been fired."

"How thorough." The voice was acid. "Federal police, or local?"

"BKA."

Cuddy had learned a good deal about Raphael during several tense seconds the previous year, when they'd crouched together in a pit behind a roll of barbed wire waiting for a terrorist asset to cross through the teeth of an Israeli border patrol. The guy had been shot in the back by his own people before he reached the ditch, and it was Raphael who wormed through the barbed wire and hauled the bleeding man to safety. The next three hours were ones of screaming tension and near death, an exquisite shell game that had not succeeded in saving the asset's life. He was a child of Hamas, nineteen years old, and he'd died in the trunk of an embassy car.

Scottie Sorensen blamed Raphael. It was Raphael who'd planned the botched exfiltration and provided the necessary documents and facial camouflage. Scottie had accused Raphael of selling secrets to the enemy for favors that were probably homosexual. Raphael had submitted to polygraphs, hour after hour in various outbuildings in Virginia. Whatever was concluded about the nature of his libido was irrelevant; he had sold nothing to anybody. The dead agent had been blown within Hamas for the previous two months; the organization had merely been waiting for the perfect moment to kill him.

"Scottie just stopped by and rifled my drawers,"

Raphael told Cuddy casually. "About an hour before you showed up. I let one of the Girls deal with him."

The Girls were Betty and Alice, fifty-something women who'd trained under Andy Nunez and whose deceptive skills were prized above rubies. Raphael loathed Scottie and refused to perform the slightest miracle on his behalf.

He lifted a set of earphones to his head and murmured into a microphone.

"Yo," said a disembodied voice.

"Betty, sweet, what did the Prick want this afternoon?"

"Cover docs for an op in Berlin."

"His own?"

"A woman's. She's traveling NOC."

NOC: nonofficial cover, unaffiliated with government. The woman would be posing as an academic, then, or a businesswoman.

"Think he's flying in his latest lay?" Raphael asked.

The voice snorted. "Not by the look of her picture."

"Was it on file?"

"He brought it with him."

"A private contractor, then. How *delicious*. I'd like a list," Raphael said abruptly, "of everything he took. Also the woman's photograph. The Prick has no idea you're here?" he demanded of Cuddy.

"None. He sent me home to pack."

"You've been fired, too?"

Cuddy shook his head. "I'm on my way to Berlin. Eleven-thirty tonight. Scottie and I are supposed to explain the truth to Eric."

"The Prick said nothing about this woman?"

"Nothing at all. She could be a polygrapher."

"I would be astonished if she were. Thanks, Betts."

He shoved the headset down around his neck and stared into the middle distance for a few seconds. "Eric. *Berlin*. You want me to pull a Houdini? Get him out of the chains and the locked box before he drowns?"

"Better than that." Cuddy's voice dropped, as though Betty or Alice might still be listening. "I want you to end his life for good this time."

There was an instant's silence. Then the Prince of Darkness stretched and flexed his fingers, a cat unsheathing claws. "Only if I can screw Scottie in the process," he bargained softly.

"Why bother, otherwise?"

Raphael smiled. "Go home and pack, Cuddy. I'll be at Dulles to kiss you good-bye."

thirty-three

Cy Phillips had spent his weekday afternoons on the battered stool behind the counter of Sunny's Truck Stop Delite for more years than he could remember. The big rigs that rumbled through Wheeling, West Virginia, on their way to the rest of the continent— chuffing off one mammoth interstate before diving into another—had always fascinated Cy, even when he was a boy growing up under Eisenhower, long before the octopus-tentacle roads had reached out to strangle his quiet town in noise and exhaust. He had a picture of himself in overalls, standing proudly on the step of his grandpappy's cab, back when such rigs were called tractors. Grandpappy's was bright red with an eagle taking wing across the hood; its sloping fenders reminded Cy of the curving hips of the bombers his dad had flown in the war. The colors of that photograph, his gap-toothed smile and Dennis the Menace grin, were bleached and almost indiscernible now, and his heart no longer beat faster when an eighteen-wheeler pulled into the asphalt lot beyond the door. He was sixty-one years old and the smell of fry-cookers and cigarette smoke was permanently embedded in his clothes and hair. He spent hours staring at the screen of a minuscule black-and-white television set he kept plugged in near the register.

Only three people were sitting in Sunny's when Daniel Becker walked in out of the rain at seven o'clock that evening. This was unusual, because most of the haulers who made Wheeling their first stop on a transcontinental run had a fondness in their stomachs for Sunny's. Cy's cooking was old-fashioned and comforting. Beef pot pie and meat loaf with mashed potatoes and gravy. Deep-batter-fried chicken. Lemon meringue and chocolate silk pie. Sunny's prided itself on its pie. It offered thirteen varieties on any given day. Some of the truckers rolling in from the west at five A.M. ate nothing but pie and coffee for breakfast, and it was Sunny's they thought of during the long downhill run off the Appalachians. Maybe the empty seats around the curved counter could be chalked up to the new industry regulations the government had imposed— telling the most seasoned of drivers when and how they could break their runs. Or maybe it was Monday night football: haulers pushing through to Ohio so they could pull off at eight o'clock and catch at least part of the game in their sleeping lofts.

Regardless, Cy had already sent his Maureen out to fill Tab Lowar's cup a third time with coffee and Minnie and Mort Jacobs were plowing steadily through their pies. Tab was flirting with Maureen outrageously—he had an eye for a pretty girl, and despite the fact she'd never quite lost the fat from the third kid, she had a nice head of hair on her and a good pair of pipes. Cy

had already turned back to the news broadcast when
the rusting bell over the door jangled.

Daniel didn't speak to the boy during the first part of
their drive. The kid was still groggy and confused by
the sensation of the pickup truck wallowing through the
rutted back roads of Hillsboro. Daniel was feeling
groggy himself; the long two days of sleeplessness and
tension—the chemical surge of death in his blood—
had finally taken their toll. His eyes were red-rimmed
and he had a permanent hack in his throat. There was
a pain between his shoulder blades that felt like a
slowly tightening wire, but the luck had held so far—
the luck had held. He had to seize the singing current
of this luck, the Leader sitting at his elbow, and drive
on. He had to stay alert. He drummed his fingers restlessly on the steering wheel, and hummed a tuneless
tune.

He had wound deliberately through the rolling farmland and isolated hillsides, familiar from endless days
of childhood boredom, and stopped only once before
the highway junction in Wheeling, just as the rainy
dusk came down. The small plot of ground where he
pulled up outside Charleston was shabby and painful in its ordinariness, the plastic nosegays from a convenience store stabbed into the damp sod. ADOLF H.
BECKER, the carved letters read, 1990–1998. He had
stopped to whisper his love over this muddy hump in
the ground not because he needed to remember the

reasons for vengeance but because the boy in the backseat was ungrateful, and this failure troubled him.

"Who are you?" Jozsef had asked suddenly in a clear and undrugged voice from just behind his left ear. "Where are you taking me?"

He had tried to tell him, then, about his dedication to the Leader and the greatness of the Army the Leader's Son was destined to rally—about the Glory of the End Times and the power of a blow struck against the Devil's Spawn—but the boy had stared at him blankly from fathomless black eyes. Daniel had no idea whether Jozsef understood what he was saying. Some kind of intelligence moved in that fragile head, of this Daniel was certain, and the boy's mastery of English seemed broad enough. But no comprehension—no joy at the liberation—came through the boy's expression. Daniel almost thought he saw fear in Jozsef's face.

"Why did you take me?" Jozsef repeated.

"We delivered you from that nest of godless Zoggites they call the Federal Government because we knew your daddy woulda sooner died than seen you paraded for the cameras at that Jew whore's funeral," Daniel shot back. "Seems to me you ought to be down on your knees thanking us, boy, for everything we done. That place was crawling with police and federal agents. We *all* coulda been killed."

"Like the woman you shot in the ambulance."

Daniel did not reply.

"What happened to my driver?"

It was a natural question—but at the memory of Norm, at the raw terror that flickered briefly from his brother-in-law's kindly eyes as Daniel pressed the .32's muzzle against his skull, a small fire blazed in Daniel's brain. Norm had died a soldier's death. A patriot's sacrifice. Daniel had merely been the Instrument.

"What we did, we did for your father," he told the Accuser in the backseat. "I can tell you one thing, boy: He'd have shot you himself rather than seen the fool you made, sitting up there next to the President."

When he stopped at Sunny's Truck Stop Delite, it was in the hope that this faceless parking space off the thundering highway would temporarily shield him, absorb him as it did all the hapless wanderers in need of coffee and a warm meal. Jozsef had said nothing directly to him in the past half hour, but from the pallor of the boy's face Daniel guessed he was hungry. The last bite he'd taken himself was from a packet of five-year-old military rations, desiccated and foul-tasting, just before dawn. More than twelve hours ago.

He would have liked to be able to trust Jozsef, but that was impossible. The boy had no faith, no gratitude for what Daniel had risked to save him. Daniel could hardly walk him into the truck stop, where anybody at all might hear what the boy had to say, so he left Jozsef bound and gagged in the pickup's cab while he fetched the grub.

He stopped short just inside the heavy glass door, the bell still jangling, and glanced around the restaurant. Three people finishing up, a waitress with a good bit of flesh on her bones, the old man behind the counter.

"Evenin'," he said curtly. "I'd like some food to go."

The old guy handed him a menu without even glancing at his face, eyes fixed on the television in front of him. "What is this world coming to?" he asked of nobody in particular. "Those police in Washington just *sleeping*? All those folks sick and dying, and now this joker's snatched some kid. Makes you sick, dudn't it?"

Daniel's fingers felt like wood as he opened the menu and the typeface—luridly orange—wavered before his eyes. He could feel the dull thud of anger surge in his blood—*Who is this fucker dumb as a stump with a gut big as Christmas to talk so loud about what he don't understand? Sweet Jesus the trials I been through and all for the love of You*—

"Fried chicken's good," the man suggested helpfully, eyes still on the screen.

"Cy, them two want a slice each to go," the waitress chirped as she bounced up to the register with a twenty-dollar bill flapping between her long crimson fingernails. "They said as how I could keep the change. Man oh man, is that an evil-lookin' sonofabitch or what?"

They were staring at the television screen, mouths open and avid, and in that instant Daniel understood. He dropped the menu to the floor and reached for the gun cradled in his shoulder holster, drawing it so quietly and so swiftly that by the time Cy and his waitress glanced up, directly into the face of the killer they'd just imprinted on their brains, there was only a second's fraction of appalled recognition before he let both of them have it full in the chest.

After that it was like shooting trout in a barrel to round up the other three.

He took the twenty bucks from the fat girl's hand and a whole cherry pie he found in the refrigerated case.

thirty-four

Candace O'Brien had lived since her divorce in that leafy section of town that falls somewhere between the eastern half of Georgetown and the western edge of Dupont Circle and that is called, depending upon the taste of the resident, by either name. It is bounded to the north by Embassy Row; but Candace had turned her back on Massachusetts Avenue tonight. She had no desire to walk anywhere in the direction of the Naval Observatory, the white-porched and turreted confection that had briefly been Sophie Payne's home. Candace had passed some very pleasant and hectic months in the mellow paneled library that served as her office, with its gentle view of sloping lawns and distant traffic. But she'd quit her job as Sophie Payne's appointments secretary the day the news broke that the vice president had been murdered. She had already collected her few things from her borrowed desk.

The great house would be floodlit tonight like the crime scene it was; she did not wish to see it again.

She was killing time this evening, walking despite the wet night and the fall of darkness, her solitude drawing her to the end-of-workday bustle on Connecticut

Avenue. She considered browsing among the new offerings at her favorite bookshop or searching for a fast
and dirty dinner at the local gourmet caterer. But she
had no appetite, and fictional escapes couldn't help
her. So she wandered aimlessly, her face damp and her
hands plunged into her pockets, avoiding the gaze of
passersby with that perfect fixation on the middle distance that is an art among urban dwellers.

For days Candace had been gripped by indecision.
Should she remain here in Washington, where life was
extinct? It was the town she'd always chosen for other
people's reasons—first Gerry, who'd set her up as an
academic's wife in those long-ago years of the 1970s—
and then Sophie, who'd become her friend despite her
best efforts to remain at a careful distance, and whose
consuming life of constant exposure and glittering
celebrity had seemed, for a while, like Candace's own.
As keeper of the social books, she'd walked in spirit
with Sophie to those state dinners, those cocktail parties on P Street, those meetings with Italian prime min-
isters and heads of international agencies. But Sophie
was dead. All the elegant clothes she had amassed in
private fittings with Candace's help hung like cast skins
in her darkened closet. Poor Peter, Sophie's son, had
not known what to do with all those clothes; he'd asked
Candace for help, but she turned him over to Conchita
the maid; she'd refused to watch while they packed the
boxes for homeless shelters.

She ought to go away—find a house in a remote
corner or establish herself on a prolonged vacation in
the south of France. Such things sounded reasonable
for women as lonely as herself who attempted, among

the pages of Anita Brookner, to conduct lives of meaning; but Candace could not summon their kind of resignation. She was waiting for the conclusion of the disaster. She had been waiting ever since the day Sophie disappeared from Berlin.

I was told to call you if I needed help.

Jozsef's words over the telephone line in the wee hours of the morning had seemed, for all their youth and faintness, like the voice of Judgment.

They're letting me go to the funeral. Will you be there, Mrs. O'Brien?

Candace had lied and said she'd look for him— would introduce herself—but she'd been unable to face the high Episcopal rites in the National Cathedral, the words of tribute and sadness that could never encompass Sophie Payne's life. She'd been unable to look this son of Mlan Krucevic in the eye. Instead, she'd sat at home while all the hours of mourning and interment sped away. Only twenty-three minutes ago did she learn that the boy had never made it back to his hospital bed.

Had she failed him as completely as she'd failed Sophie?

Candace saw now with surprise that her footsteps had carried her in a great circle, past the Phillips Collection and the Metro stops and the diagonal thrust of New Hampshire Avenue. She turned reluctantly down her own brief block and reached for the keys she kept in her pocket.

There was someone waiting in the rain at the top of her town house steps—an absurd figure in high heels, with overly protuberant breasts, a mop of auburn hair swinging pertly around the chin. *Obvious,* she thought wearily. *Screaming her sex from the rooftops. Can men really be so stupid?*

The woman would be the latest acquisition of the attorney who owned the town house's ground floor. Candace braced herself to slide past as the visitor stabbed aggressively at the front buzzer; but to her surprise, the figure turned to study her intently as she approached.

In sudden apprehension, her breath caught in her throat, Candace kept walking down the street.

"Something happened in Leipzig," Caroline muttered in frustration. "Something that gave 30 April a hold over her."

For the past hour, she'd paced the floor of Price's living room spilling her guts while he worked his magic. By six o'clock that evening, he had enough copy to fill the front page of the *Washington Post*—and a name to go with the phone number Jozsef had dialed at two o'clock Monday morning.

Candace O'Brien. The dead vice president's friend and appointments secretary.

Caroline was tracking a whisper and a doubt now through a labyrinth of years, searching for the moment when Candace O'Brien turned traitor. She'd made considerable progress, mostly because she'd seized whatever help Steve Price offered: calls to Georgetown University and off-the-record access to Gerry O'Brien's professional files; unofficial soundings of the social elite who'd observed Candace in action under Sophie Payne; an after-hours chat with the chairwoman of a local

Smith College alumnae group, where Candace was respected but not well known. *Never well known.* The woman was visible and invisible at once: a surface calm hiding a turbulent depth.

"You're convinced it wasn't just a social call?" Price asked. "You really think this broad's tied to Jozsef Krucevic?"

"Social calls don't happen at two A.M."

"He's a kid. Maybe he couldn't sleep."

"Then he'd have rung the nurse down the hall," Caroline retorted. "Come on, Steve! The kid's never set foot in the U.S.—and he has this woman's number memorized? His father gave it to him. Made sure he could recite it down to the last digit. It was Jozsef's safety net. In case Mlan couldn't be there to help him."

"Sounds far-fetched to me. Maybe the kid dialed a random number and came up with Candace."

"Nothing about 30 April is random," Caroline countered tersely. "Ask Norm Wilhelm." She went back to scrolling through Eric's bootlegged files.

There was a time when Candace O'Brien and Mlan Krucevic—Jozsef's father—lived within a mile of each other. Leipzig, Germany, 1990 to 1991. Gerry O'Brien had served as a visiting professor of molecular biology to this distinguished institution of the fallen German Democratic Republic, only ten months removed from its status as a satellite Soviet power and falling over itself to embrace the capitalist intelligentsia.

Mlan Krucevic was a holdover of the past: a Yugoslav scientist, brilliant, to be sure, and good enough for the

Communist era, but possibly eclipsed by the dazzle from the West. Gerry O'Brien emerged from Price's hurried notes as a likeable fellow: charming, less introverted than one might imagine of a laboratory researcher, glad to undertake the role of academic ambassador in this Brave New World.

Krucevic, Caroline decided, would have gravitated to Gerry and his wife. They represented what he most coveted: superpower status, an easy assumption of world dominion, and the despicably egalitarian approach to culture and education Krucevic despised. He would have learned from the O'Briens, cultivated their interest, used them in any way possible. And then, without warning, the connection was severed.

In March of 1991, Gerry O'Brien and his wife returned home to Georgetown. A year and two months before the end of their funded stint in Leipzig, Krucevic had abruptly disappeared.

"The breakup of Yugoslavia," Caroline muttered, scanning her laptop's screen. "The beginning of war between the Serbs and the Croatians. Mlan heads home and takes command of a bunch of guerrillas. Two years later he's running a prison camp in Bosnia. By the end of the decade he's indicted for war crimes, and 30 April is born."

"The O'Briens left when he did?" Price asked.

"Six weeks later."

"Maybe it was an affair," he suggested in the voice of experience. "Candace and the lady-killer. Mlan carved a wide swath among the women, didn't he? Husband finds out, decides to run home, and divorces her . . . a bare eight months later. You notice the dates?"

Caroline had noticed the dates. A decree granted by the District of Columbia in November 1991.

"So she did it for love?" she murmured skeptically.

"Violence can be very seductive. It's a power thing."

"If you say so. Who got the kid?"

"Jozsef? He'd have been a toddler in '91."

Caroline shook her head. "Krucevic was still married then, and Jozsef was with his mother. I'm talking about the O'Brien girl—a daughter. Fifteen when they lived in Germany. I don't see any custody provisions here."

Price frowned. "Nobody I've talked to has mentioned her. She can't have lived with Candace for *years*. And besides—she'd be all grown up now."

"Yes," Caroline mused thoughtfully, "if she survived. I think we should visit Ms. O'Brien, don't you?"

thirty-five

Julie Cohen had been in the FBI's Charleston, West Virginia, field office for ten months now. It wasn't her first choice—she'd have liked San Francisco or Chicago—but she was only two years out of Quantico and options were limited. She'd been raised in the heart of Boston, a New Englander to the bone, and her roots were obvious in the flatness of her vowels. The Charleston locals called her a Yankee, and their tone was rarely friendly. There was a gulf looming at Julie's feet that had as much to do with geography and culture as it did with law enforcement. Another woman might have treated the place with scorn. Julie was intelligent enough to recognize she had a good deal to learn.

This stormy Monday evening, for example, she'd have been utterly lost among the twisting roads surrounding Hillsboro if it weren't for her boss, Stan Heyduk, directing her quietly from the passenger seat. It was a beautiful landscape, if you liked wilderness and farmland punctuated by mine shafts and the occasional gurgling stream, but in Julie's eyes the rolling countryside was riddled with malice. She'd researched the region well before she reported for duty in Charleston last January. William Pierce's three-hundred-acre compound and neo-Nazi radio station were here in Hillsboro, and she knew enough about Pierce to make her skin crawl. In his novel *The Turner Diaries* he had proclaimed that the bodies of Jews like herself should be heaped on bonfires on every street corner in America. She had a disturbing suspicion that the woman she was about to meet was one of Pierce's fellow travelers. There was the name she'd chosen to give her son, for instance. Adolf Hitler Becker.

The isolation of the countryside, the rainswept darkness cut by her own frail headlights, oppressed Julie's spirits as much as the knowledge of the distasteful duty that lay before her. She'd been brought along because a female agent was considered helpful in dealing with women. Julie was the last person to defer to male strength, but she was glad tonight for Heyduk and the guy in the Camry's backseat who'd appeared suddenly by helicopter only half an hour ago—a Stanford Business grad named Jason Bovian who was not much older than herself. Bovian was on Tom Shephard's 30 April Task Force at Headquarters, which meant Rebekah Becker had something to do with the ricin attack. He was eager and unafraid, his seat belt off and his head leaning over the front seat, eyes fixed intently on the road ahead. Bovian had reason to want this woman: Thirty-six hours after the start of the Marine Corps Marathon, four hundred fourteen people had now died. Nearly as many looked like they would never recover.

Julie shuddered involuntarily at the thought of the pictures she'd seen—wasted faces staring uncomprehendingly at the camera lens like refugees from a bewildering war. Everybody in the car tonight felt the same sense of urgency; it circulated like exhaust. They were all terrified of what Ricin Boy might do while they were driving.

Julie had briefed Bovian competently enough with the information she'd culled from state databases. Norm Wilhelm's next of kin, Rebekah Becker, no longer lived at the address he'd given in Charleston, and the new residents could offer no forwarding address. Becker's name was not listed in telephone directories. Julie had tried to summon the woman's vitals through motor vehicle registrations or tax rolls: She'd found absolutely no trace of Rebekah's existence. No Becker children were enrolled in state schools; no public utility accounts were paid by Becker checks. Julie tried credit reports and discovered that Rebekah Becker—or Rebekah Wilhelm, as she must once have been—had never borrowed money or held a credit card. She had never signed a mortgage. In all the most obvious ways of modern life, Rebekah Becker did not exist.

When Julie turned to criminal records, however, she unearthed a gold mine.

Rebekah W. Becker was listed as the mother of an eight-year-old boy who'd been accidentally shot to death by a state trooper thirteen months before. The child had been a passenger in a pickup pulled over for lack of registration. The driver—a man named

Lanier Hodge—had opened fire on the trooper as he approached the truck. The police officer had been wounded in the left shoulder and the pickup sped off, igniting a high-speed cross-country chase that ended tragically in a hail of bullets. It was Hodge's girlfriend who identified the bodies and sent the Charleston police to the Becker family compound a few hours later.

The Hillsboro address was in the criminal report. So was the name of Rebekah's husband, Daniel Becker, and the fact that he was an old army buddy of Lanier Hodge's. Hodge had taken the boy, Dolf, to a shooting range that afternoon for target practice. He'd been in tax revolt against the U.S. government and had refused to pay for his truck's registration.

It was the first hint the FBI got of Ricin Boy's name.

Daniel Becker. Private, First Class, U.S. Army, posted overseas in Bosnia-Herzegovina 1995. Held ten days by Croatian guerrilla forces and judged to be suffering resultant trauma by army doctors. Refused consideration for Special Forces. Honorably discharged 1998.

It was Tom Shephard, Bovian's boss, who'd discovered that last nugget of information. He'd also learned, from anecdotal reports, that Becker was a rare hand with a gun. He'd come into the army knowing how to shoot with an accuracy that was attributed to his West Virginia boyhood. What his commanding officers remembered, however, was how much Daniel Becker liked hitting his targets. It was a source of pride. One of the few in his sorry life.

• • •

Tom was miles away from the car winding through the back roads of Hillsboro, standing over the body of a middle-aged man lying on the wet asphalt outside Sunny's Truck Stop Delite. Gray-haired, staring wide-eyed at the sky, a ribbon of scarlet threading from his punctured chest and his high-crowned trucker's hat lying where it had fallen a few feet away. Five more corpses lay inside the blood-spattered restaurant, but it was this man who most interested Tom. He was the last one killed, Shephard thought, and that meant he was a point of departure that must be studied and understood.

Tom crouched low, his eyes running the length of the rain-soaked corpse. From the man's wallet he'd already learned the victim was Buford Sayles and that he drove eighteen-wheelers for Rac Transport. A thirty-one-year veteran of the road, bound for Ohio and then North Dakota. Parked next to the body was a beat-up old pickup with the keys still dangling in the ignition and a blanket Tom recognized in the rear of the cab. *Jozsef's blanket.* There were prints all over the interior of the truck and the Bureau forensic people were lifting them now.

It was possible Sayles had witnessed the carnage inside Sunny's and been shot for his pains. Possible the trucker had chased after Ricin Boy and tried to save the child confined in the backseat. Except for one thing. Buford Sayles's eighteen-wheeler was gone. Tom had taken down the description and the registration given out by Rac Transport and thought he knew who was driving the big rig now.

He rose and turned back toward Sunny's, his gut clenching sickly on the smell of blood. Two of the dead were Sayles's age; the women were younger, maybe in their mid-thirties; and the final victim just a kid—twenty-three if he was a day. News reports—sensational and magnified by the killings' possible terrorist link—had lured a silent crowd to the edge of the police barricade despite the rain. One of them was the waitress's father. Tom would have to talk to him soon.

What to say? *Your daughter was smashed like a bug on this guy's windshield, tossed out like a piece of trash for no reason. I'm sorry. Sorry for her kids.* He would manage something better, of course, but he could not drown out the fury that was building inside him, or the words of bigotry and violence threading through his brain.

> *. . . I applaud this man's courage and only wish my family duties did not prevent me from riding out right now to join him . . . Four hundred dead in Washington is four hundred less of the vermin we'll have to kill later to cleanse this nation . . . I wish he'd hit New York and Chicago and Los Angeles, too, maybe then all the fucking non-whites who've ruined this country would go back to the holes they crawled out of . . . If God had wanted those runners to survive he'd have given them the strength to do it. Burn in hell I say . . . Darien*

Atwood's got the welcome mat out for all you Jew assholes on the ash heap...

Those postings and hundreds of others like them, some anonymous and some attributed to nicknames or handles of nauseating swagger, all vicious, filled the chat rooms of neo-Nazi Web sites the FBI had followed all day. Ricin Boy had a growing host of fans in America's heartland, all waiting for his next move like children agog at exploits of Robin Hood. But none of them—not www.aryannations.org or www. posse-comitatus.org or www. americannaziparty.com or any of the thousands of white supremacist Web sites Tom's Domestic Terrorism unit monitored—dropped a hint as to where the next blow would fall.

Somewhere down the highway, Tom thought savagely, *beyond the next pool of blood.*

He did not understand a world where the murder of a young mother was cause for high-five congratulations.

In the backseat of Julie Cohen's car, Jason Bovian leafed through the Becker file. In the thirteen months since her son's death, Rebekah Becker had attempted suicide three times. Twice with pills, once with a knife she'd used to hack at her wrists. Medical records were privileged information, but the local hospital, concerned about Becker's mental state, had alerted West Virginia's department of human services and requested outreach. Assessment attempts proved unsuccessful.

Representatives of the department had twice driven up to the Becker house. Twice they'd been threatened with a gun.

Bovian frowned. The woman could kill herself and welcome provided he learned three things: Was her hair brown? Were her prints on the back door handle of Norm Wilhelm's limo? And had she driven the gray K-car in a cop's uniform while her husband fired at a defenseless paramedic that morning?

He glanced up as Julie eased the Camry to a stop. There it was in the headlights: a dripping steel cattle guard and security gate in front of a double-wide trailer mounted on cinder blocks, a clearing beyond maybe fifty feet square. A stockade fence twice as high as a man, razor wire spooled along the upper edge. A set of muddy tire tracks leading to the side of the house. There was a utility shed, and a snowmobile on a disengaged trailer; a child's wading pool, cracked at one side; a dispirited plastic play structure that had once been orange. Several winters had weathered it to peach.

Bovian waited for the inevitable bark of a dog but none came. From the appearance of the Becker household, he should expect the steel gate facing them to be wired. The search warrant he'd brought was useless—unless Rebekah Becker herself opened the trailer to them.

She walked slowly down the driveway in her baggy old sweatshirt as though it were perfectly normal to find strangers at the end of the road. She carried a flash-light because it was dark and raining and she could not help remembering the other time, nine o'clock on an October night when her boy should've been safe in his own bed. She'd known, even as Daniel took the long walk from the trailer door to the police car pulled up in front of the barrier, that the news was bad. She'd known her Dolf was gone. *Killed by them sumbitches in the government who refuse to let honest folks live in peace.* She rolled her arms in the stretchy cotton fabric of the sweatshirt and plodded forward, thinking of her son's face in the Charleston morgue. *Oh Sweet Jesus. What did I ever do wrong in this life to deserve pain like that?* It gnawed at her guts like a tapeworm.

No police car this time, just a cute little silver com-pact with West Virginia plates. A girl and two men get-ting out, all of them in suits. *Suits.* The girl ought to be home makin' dinner for her man. *What are the suits doing in the driveway? Is it Daniel, Dearest Jesus? Is he caught already, him and that boy without his dinner?* For an instant Rebekah wished she'd just stayed in the house and pretended nobody was home. But Daniel had told her to act normal if anybody came. He didn't want people getting suspicious.

"Mrs. Becker?" the girl called. She had dark hair cut to her chin and nice brown eyes. A real cute little thing. What she wanted with going door-to-door Rebekah did not know.

"Who's asking?" she demanded.

"I'm Julie Cohen, FBI." The girl reached into her raincoat and Rebekah flinched. But it was no gun—

just a badge she was handing through the iron grille of the front gate.

Rebekah didn't take it. She just stood there, frozen as stone, with her hands rolled in the sweatshirt. *Sweet Jesus. FBI. And the Leader's boy taken off in a truck to God knows where. Daniel—*

But Daniel had left hours ago. She was on her own.

"What you want?"

"Are you Rebekah Becker?"

"Maybe I am, maybe I ain't."

The FBI woman stuffed her badge back in her pocket. *Snake that she is, with her cute haircut and her foreign car. Nothing but a Federal.*

This time one of the men stepped forward, nice-enough looking, with his clipped hair and blue eyes, another plastic badge in his hand. Rebekah didn't bother to look at it. Meant nothing to her. The calling card of the Devil.

"Stan Heyduk, FBI—and this is Special Agent Jason Bovian," he said, his voice curt. "We're looking for Mrs. Becker. Her brother, Norman Wilhelm, was found dead this afternoon."

The world tipped sideways, reeled like a drunken man, and Rebekah reached involuntarily for the steel gate, her worn hands gripping the top bar. *Daniel. You wouldn't. Not Norm. Not my Norm.*

"Dead?" she repeated stiffly. "How, dead?"

"He was shot in the head."

"What kind of shit you tellin' me? Norm's not dead."

"I'm afraid he is, Ms.—"

Daniel. Daniel, Daniel—how could you? A bullet in his head. Just like Dolf. Poor Norm, who'd never hurt nobody, who didn't even see it was a crime to work for that Jew Whore what the Zoggites put in power.

"Are you Mr. Wilhelm's sister Rebekah?" the FBI man persisted.

Oh, Norm. Now there's none of us Wilhelms left.

She nodded once, her face set in granite. No tears. This is what it meant to live in the End Times: Survival came from the decisions you made. Daniel had done what he had to; he was a soldier, for God's sake. He'd known Norm would blab everything that'd happened once the kid turned up missing. He'd known he owed absolute secrecy to the Leader, until the Overthrow triumphed. This terrible sacrifice. Her brother.

"Mrs. Becker. We need you to come into the Charleston field office to discuss the disposition of the body. And to answer a few questions."

"What kind of questions?"

The girl held up her hands placatingly. "When you last saw your brother, for instance."

Seven hours ago. Christ Almighty.

"It's just the usual procedure in a death of this kind, Mrs. Becker. We're all terribly sorry for your loss."

"Cohen," Rebekah said suddenly. "That's a Jewish name, isn't it?"

"Would you come with us now?" the girl asked. "Or would you prefer to talk inside?"

Rebekah stared at the Federal—at her unlined face, the pale lipstick so perfectly applied to her firm mouth.

Jewish. No wonder she ain't at home like a respectable woman. Doing Satan's work at the dinner hour.

"Is your husband here, Mrs. Becker?"

With a blaze of understanding Rebekah saw it all, then: *The FBI was lying to her. Daniel would never hurt Norm.* They'd tried to use her sorrow to get her to break. To betray her man.

But she was tougher than that. She knew what she had to do. She'd known ever since Daniel left her standing by the abandoned bike at the side of the road. She, too, was a soldier of the End Times.

A tide of rage surged upward from Bekah's shoes—rage mingled with a hideous joy. This time she'd seen through their lies and obscenities first. This time, there'd be no body waiting on the morgue's cold slab for her to identify.

She released her hold on the steel gate.

"You'd better come in," she told them all. "I'll answer your questions right now."

Tom Shephard took the call forty-three minutes later on his way to the Alleghenies. He swore aloud for a full two minutes, Bovian's eager face suspended before his eyes. Then he turned the rental car around and headed back toward Charleston.

Later, when the team sent out from Bureau Headquarters picked through the debris and reconstructed the crime, they came to the conclusion Rebekah had been wearing the belt of explosives throughout the conversation at her front gate. But she'd bided her time until the Devil's Spawn who'd come to deceive her were standing in the trailer's small kitchen, which smelled faintly of fried pork and baked beans. She'd gathered them all in a tight knot near the kitchen table before she pulled the cord and blew herself and the trailer straight to Jesus.

part three

thirty-six

"Mommy! Mommy!"

The wail from the makeshift bed on Dana's chaise woke George Enfield at three minutes before six o'clock that Tuesday morning. Mallory, in the grip of a night terror, arms flailing among the down pillows. The child was reaching for someone who would never hold her again, for the perfect childhood swallowed in a yawning pit. It had been the same the night before: She would not sleep alone in her room, and her dreams were restless. He thrust himself out of bed and took three steps to the little girl's side, lifted her by the shoulders, soothed her awake. *Sshhhhhh. You're okay. You're okay.* Which of course was the biggest lie.

Mallory's tiger eyes—more his than Dana's—fluttered open and she stared at him, unseeing for an instant. Then memory lurched back and her expression flattened; she turned her face into his pajamas, buried it there, as though if she shut out this day she could recapture the one she'd been dreaming. Dana striding like a racehorse down M Street, maybe? Dana tall and elegant in one of her spangled evening gowns? Yesterday he'd stood for a full eight minutes in the scented darkness of his wife's closet, breathing in the last of her.

He smoothed Mallory's hair and said nothing, both of them bleached in the faint light of early morning. *Another day,* he thought, *pretending to go on.*

He had done this before—mourned a wife dead too soon. Mary Alice Carver she'd been, a Chicago banker's daughter, mangled in the wreckage of a commuter plane off Sea Island, Georgia, twenty years ago. In the blackest depths of his sleepless nights he asked himself why he was cursed with this tendency to lose the people he loved most. Was it God's way of evening the score? He'd grown up a fortunate son, privileged and sheltered, groomed for public office. He'd been either too young or too old for the major wars, sailed through college and law school, was undefeated in his bids for political seats. But here, in the heart of his home, where he'd kept the only thing that really mattered— here, he was as cursed as Job.

His grip tightened on Mallory's thin shoulders and she curled into his embrace, half asleep again. He could not replace Dana. But he could devote himself to the child she'd left behind.

He laid her tenderly back down against the pillows and brushed his hand across her forehead. She had another bit of hell lying in wait for her: the funeral, scheduled for Friday. Her first taste of public violation. Of reporters scavenging among the bones of her grief.

George stared out at the tulip tree rising beyond the window, its branches etched against the brightening sky. *Another day without her.* The first time—in the hours after Mary Alice's death—he'd vowed to show nothing. He was a public figure, after all. He had to instill confidence and bear up despite adversity; it was important for his constituency to see. *Strength*. George Enfield had strength. A quality people needed to believe in.

This time he didn't care if the networks caught his fury in full frame, if his voice broke in the microphone and his careful politician's mien shattered like a bludgeoned mirror. Dana had died for the most vicious of reasons. A random victim of the politics of hate. The world he'd polished like an apple, the bright shining lies of government he'd supported and upheld, had failed her.

He left his sleeping daughter and trudged down the stairs to retrieve the morning paper.

On the front page, he found Steve Price's profile of Caroline Carmichael.

"Where is she?" he demanded when he'd been put through to the Oval Office. "Where is this bitch you've set up as a hero? She's been canned and left town and nobody can tell me how to find her. Not even *Price* will pick up his damn phone."

Bigelow was an old hand at managing the violent and the enraged. "George," he soothed. "My deepest sympathy. You've lost the world in Dana, I know. Your pain and grief must be terrible. How's that beautiful little girl o' yours?"

"Fine," Enfield said abruptly. "Devastated, naturally. But—"

"Hope you got our flowers. Adele sends her love. Our thoughts are with you."

"Yes. Thank you. What I wanted to—"

"We'll be with you Friday, of course, at the National Cathedral. I've suggested we hold a general memorial service one day soon, for all the people hurt by this vicious lunatic. I spent part of yesterday on the Mall, you know, in one of the medical tents. Blows your mind, buddy. People dyin' in agony, and for no possible reason they or I can understand. But you know that better than anyone. Shit, I'm preachin' to the converted."

"Have you seen the *Post*, Mr. President?"

A fractional pause. "Yes, siree. Wouldn't be a mornin' without the daily dose o' dirt those folks shovel on my plate."

"I plan to ask for a formal Congressional investigation of the intelligence-gathering process leading up to the Marine Corps Marathon." George said it bluntly.

"If you've read the paper, you know we've got a suspected terrorist sittin' in jail right now in Germany."

"I don't live in Germany. Neither did my wife," George retorted scathingly. "I don't *care* what happened there last week. I want to know what's going on right now, right in my own backyard. The questions Steve Price raises—complicity and cover-up at the highest levels—are too serious to ignore. People are dying, Jack. *Dana died*."

"Searching for someone to blame, George?" Bigelow inquired kindly. "Don't think it'll help. Makes you feel better in the short term, but it just pisses people off in the end. Tragedy's tragedy because it comes without warning. Otherwise we'd give it a different name."

"Like politics?"

Bigelow laughed, ignoring the bitterness in George's voice. "Glad you haven't lost your sense of humor. Kiss that little girl for me, now."

He hung up before George could ask again where Caroline Carmichael had gone.

thirty-seven

When the sun rose faint and acid that Tuesday morning, Caroline was already sipping coffee in Steve Price's Boxster, which was exactly the kind of fast car she expected the reporter to drive. They were just outside of Frederick, Maryland, and heading for the Cumberland Gap; Caroline was concentrating on getting the hot restorative liquid in her mouth without melting her latex.

She'd traded Jennifer Lacey's regulation short black skirt and high heels for a pair of close-fitting black Lycra pants and a black cashmere sweater; she could move and breathe in these without having to think about them. In deference to Raphael's Chapel, however, she had submitted to the chest prosthesis. She'd secretly always wanted to know what it felt like to have large breasts, and now she knew: as though she'd strapped on armor. Raphael's artwork might not stop bullets— but Caroline was willing to bet it would thwart a knife.

"Awake yet?" Price asked.

"No." He'd insisted she get some sleep last night— the first real sleep she'd had in forty-eight hours—and it was like heroin to an addict in withdrawal: She could not get enough. "How much longer do we have?"

His eyes flicked down at the dashboard clock. "Another hour, maybe. We'll stop for food before then."

They were on their way toward a place called Rochester: a small town buried in western Pennsylvania. A map lay open on Caroline's knees. The coffee was intended to help her follow it.

She'd said nothing of this strange collaboration with Price to Cuddy when he'd called her cell phone from Dulles last night. He hadn't had time to chat.

I'm in the men's room, he'd said, *and I'm on my way to Berlin. I'll call when I can.*

"You're going to see Eric? Oh, God, Cuddy . . ."

What she'd wanted to say was *Save him, save him,* but fear and longing overwhelmed her. She wanted to drop everything—the secrecy and the hunt and the urgent need to find Jozsef—and run to Eric's prison cell. The thought that Cuddy would be with him in a matter of hours made her heart leap. Maybe the Agency could work a deal.

"Who sent you?"

"Scottie. He's already on the plane."

Hope died. "Then how in *hell* are you going to—"

"I've got to go, Caroline."

"*Sleeper, Tool,* and *Fist,* Cud," she urged before he could hang up. "Ask Eric what they mean."

She thought they were on the trail of one of the three now, but it was equally possible she'd thrown Steve Price into a wild-goose chase. The journalist did not seem to mind. The fact that she'd gone black in her own city and was practically a fugitive from the law did not disturb him. He told her he could scent a great story. Waiting for them somewhere in Rochester, Pennsylvania.

They'd found the place through Gerry O'Brien, Candace's ex-husband, when the woman's apartment remained persistently dark and neither telephone calls nor repeated buzzing of the front door produced a response.

"My wife never travels," O'Brien had said gently when they tracked him to the small house he owned not far from his university research laboratory. Caroline noted the refusal to speak of Candace as part of the past, the solitary trappings of the man's minute sitting room that suggested he'd never progressed further than the decree of divorce issued nearly ten years before. "She is a retiring sort of person, despite her very public job. And I do not think she would dine out with friends on the night of her employer's funeral . . . She loved Sophie Payne."

They had presented themselves as old acquaintances, which was immediately unsuccessful because the professor clearly knew his ex-wife's habits and could not place a Jennifer Lacey nearly twenty years Candace's junior. Steve Price he understood instantly.

"You're the *Post* reporter, aren't you?" There was a glint in his mild blue eyes. "I don't think Candace would wish to speak with you. Oh, no, I do *not*."

He was on the verge of showing them the door when Caroline glimpsed the antique engraving of the Berlin Reichstag, perfect and serene as it had only been in the years before the bombings of World War II, and had said involuntarily, "Did you find that in Leipzig?"

O'Brien had stared at her with renewed interest. "Yes. Do you know Germany?"

"A little. You lived there for several years, I think?"

He shook his head. "Not long enough."

"You returned before your teaching stint was through," Caroline persisted, "because of Mlan Krucevic."

After the briefest pause, O'Brien said, "Who are you, really?"

"Please forgive me when I say that I cannot tell you, Professor."

"Is Candace in trouble?"

"I think she may be in danger."

"Because of that man," he concluded. "Krucevic. And his killing of her boss. Yes, I see. Perhaps you had better sit down."

He told them, without much urging and with very little sense of tragedy, of how disaster had overcome his life.

There was the foreignness of Leipzig, its unexpected elements: an expanse of concrete housing built by the Soviets; the old university buildings falling into decay; the mix of weary economy and desperate striving; the glamour of the West. *Their* glamour—his and Candace's and their daughter Adrienne's—which drew the academic community of the former East Germany more than an offer of free bananas or luxury handbags or uninhibited travel could ever have done. In 1990, the O'Brien family walked abroad in Leipzig's ancient reconstructed streets as the living embodiment of American privilege, and they paid dearly for that fact.

"I believe that Candace had certain plans," Gerry O'Brien said judiciously as he gazed down the long tunnel of memory. "She is not a woman of considerable resources, you understand—*inner* resources, I would mean, such as might sustain a person in solitude—and when she realized we were destined for Europe she imagined a far different kind of life. She had notions of superb food and charming atmosphere, of trips to the countryside in search of antiques. Of her daughter thriving in a cultured world. Of a better time, perhaps, than we'd had at home."

He did not explain what had impoverished their style of living in Georgetown, leaving aside that failure out of habit; but Caroline could imagine it well enough. Gerry in his laboratory, Candace struggling to be the perfect academic wife without the slightest talent for it. The lavishness and the elegance of these discreet Georgetown blocks impossible to imitate on an academic's salary. And Adrienne—who was Adrienne? A teenager. Torn from her native city during the most tumultuous years: high school.

"Candace found Leipzig uncongenial," O'Brien murmured. "She fell into a kind of depression. I believe I noticed it only when it was too late."

"And your daughter?"

The biologist said nothing, studying Caroline's face. Then he said, "I wish I knew for certain who you are."

Her eyes flicked to Steve Price's; she shook her

head slightly. "Would it help if I told you that I am not an enemy of yours?"

"But possibly of my wife's?"

"She has not been your wife for almost ten years," Caroline pointed out brutally.

"That makes very little difference when it is a question of loyalty."

True, she thought with a sharp memory of Eric. *What do I think I have to teach this man?*

"What happened?" Price asked.

"I failed her," O'Brien said simply. "I blame myself for that."

The reporter shifted in his chair. "A lot of marriages fail. It's not always a question of fault."

"Not always. But in my case? Decidedly. I had lost the art of *seeing,* you understand. When it was most critical."

"What did you fail to see?" Caroline asked.

"How unhappy I had made my family by my inattention. I enjoyed Leipzig, you know. Enjoyed the whole moveable feast. But my family was miserable."

"And that's where Mlan came in?"

O'Brien shrugged. "We met Mlan at the usual faculty parties. There was the advantage that he spoke English extremely well. Candace had no German. I do not know when he first began to worm his way into the heart of my home; I only know the result."

He fell silent, an expression of doubt flickering over his face; the old worry, again: that he might say too much.

Caroline leaned toward him in appeal. "Professor, I've spent most of the past decade tracking 30 April.

I know more about them, probably, than anyone else in the world. Nothing you can say will shock me. Nothing will surprise me very much. Did Mlan seduce your wife?"

"Candace?" O'Brien smiled bitterly. "That man would never have looked *twice* at Candace. It was Adrienne he wanted. It was our daughter he destroyed."

Price was checking his messages now as he drove toward the Pennsylvania border, and Caroline's coffee was gone. He tossed the small phone into her lap and said, "Whole world's looking for you, missy. And they've all read my piece this morning with their Grape-Nuts. Good thing you got out of town. There's talk of testimony on Capitol Hill."

She did not answer him. They were passing through the highway interchange for Wheeling, West Virginia, and she was thinking desperately of Shephard: Six people in Wheeling had been gunned down over their dinners yesterday, and the evening news buzzed with the sensational headlines that the FBI had bungled an arrest—and three agents had been blown to bits because of it. Details were closely held and she was hoping against hope that Shephard hadn't been standing in that trailer in Hillsboro. But where else *would* he have been standing? It was the obvious choice. The white-shoe Fed's logical conclusion. She'd jumped to it herself—and gone in the opposite direction.

I should have called him, she thought, *even if he'd blasted me to hell and back. I should have called and said good-bye. Oh, Tom—*

He had offered her something like trust all those weeks ago in Berlin, and she'd abused it unmercifully. He was honest and up-front, the kind of guy who defined that elusive word *integrity*. She'd valued his belief in her, the warmth she was terrified to call love. And failing in Tom's eyes had shamed her.

The desire to win him back—to be somebody Shephard could talk to and rely on—was one part of her compulsion to track down 30 April. She needed desperately to redeem herself. To make good, if it could be done. But old lies and Ricin Boy and a bomb in a West Virginia trailer had changed all that. She'd probably never hear Tom's voice again.

You could call Bureau Headquarters, she thought. *Get somebody in Domestic Terrorism and ask for the victims' names. Say you're calling from Hank's, in Long Island . . .*

But Steve Price brought her thoughts sharply back to the Porsche and the road, stilled her hand as it reached for the cell phone in her purse.

"Weird, isn't it, to think of that girl and the big bad terrorist?" Price said conversationally. "Fucking Mommy and Daddy with her rebellion while she does the criminal genius on the side. Freud would have a field day."

It was a sordid little story Gerry O'Brien had poured out last night: how his daughter, a slight creature with enormous dark eyes behind her thick glasses and the frail, floating fingers of a poet, had fallen in love with science and destiny. She had a gift for research, Adrienne—something of her father's native brilliance, although Gerry O'Brien simply called it intelligence when he spoke of himself. The girl had been mesmerized by

Krucevic: by his message of genetic determination, of racial purity, of the refinement of the human strain to eradicate all that was mediocre. It was an old message—old as the campaigns to Sterilize the Unfit that had swept through the West at the turn of the last century, wizened as the Nazi dream—but to Adrienne it was a revelation. Genes determined eye color, femur length, the description of an earlobe; why was it incomprehensible that they should determine intelligence as well?

"She fell under his thrall," O'Brien had said, as though the girl had been taken body and soul into the realm of the Undead. "She could talk of nothing else. How her career path was formed. The search for what she called the Intelligence Gene. I thought it was all science. I didn't understand he'd taken her until the baby began to show."

It was all comprehensible then: the sudden abandonment as Mlan returned to Yugoslavia and his own private war; the O'Briens' hasty return to the United States; the disappearance of Adrienne from the divorce decree. By that time, O'Brien explained, she was living in a home for unwed mothers and had declared herself a ward of the state. She refused to recognize Candace and Gerry as her parents.

"But why the divorce?" Steve Price had asked quietly. "What did this mess have to do with the two of you?"

"I can see you're not a parent," the professor said simply. "If you were, that is a question you would never have to ask."

They were driving now toward the Allegheny Mountains and Rochester, Pennsylvania, because in the last few seconds before showing them the door Gerry O'Brien had given them Adrienne's address.

"She never gave up the child for adoption," he told them. "I understand it was a boy. She lives in seclusion, in a sort of house attached to a laboratory; the recipient, I believe, of a MacArthur Fellowship. I suppose I ought to be proud. She has accomplished so much—"

"How did you get her address," Caroline interrupted, "if she cut all ties to you?"

"My wife. She had it from Krucevic." The mild blue eyes met Caroline's bleakly. "I learned only a few months ago that the two of them had corresponded for years. I may add that it was one of the greatest shocks of my life."

thirty-eight

Tom Shephard was only a few exits away from Caroline Carmichael as she swept past in Price's fast car; but he was in no mood for spies or journalists and it was a good thing they missed each other. He'd spent the better part of the previous night watching Kaylie Marks pick body parts out of the blasted trailer with tweezers and trash bags while Julie Cohen's husband, David, stood bent-backed under the klieg lights. Clutching his stomach as though it would not stop cramping. The stench of burnt flesh and sodden charred wood and plastique everywhere. Television vans filming the carnage. Demands for Tom to comment.

He'd called in roadblocks all over the state and ordered surveillance at the Pennsylvania and Ohio borders, repeating the stolen Rac Transport truck's vitals to every law enforcement body he could reach. He was convinced Daniel Becker had not been in the trailer when it blew sky-high; convinced it was Becker who'd shot up six people in Wheeling that same night. Kaylie Marks had told him the markings on the bullet taken from Norm Wilhelm's limo door matched the one that had killed the medical technician at Arlington;

it remained to be seen if the same gun had killed all the others.

Just before three o'clock in the morning, Tom left the ravaged clearing that had once been the heart of a farm, kicking at stray pieces of play structure all the way to the flattened security fence. It was clear by then that Rebekah Becker had detonated the bomb, that Julie and Stan had been with her, and that Jason Bovian had been right behind them. Shephard had only known the kid a few days, but he'd liked him. Bovian was bright and dedicated; he had the endearing habit of bringing Tom the entire Hundred-Acre Wood whenever he asked for a twig.

All those years in school, he thought now, remembering the kid's Stanford MBA. *His parents taking out loans. Proud of him. Shit.*

The parents lived on Staten Island; it was impossible for Tom to make the visit himself, walk up the pathetic concrete path to the storm door and wait while the sleep-fuddled father adjusted his glasses. Tom had called the head of the New York field office at home and told him to break the news. Then he'd slept for two hours in his car, setting the alarm on his sports watch. Waking every fifteen minutes in case one of the roadblocks had found the fucking bastard.

The call came at 5:34 A.M.

The truck was parked on a Cambridge, Ohio, backstreet, shit out of luck and empty.

Tom threw his car into gear and raced for the state line.

• • •

"So how'd the sonofabitch roar past all our people?" he demanded as he stood in the light rain two hours later. "How'd he drive this sucker till it was bone-dry and nobody—*nobody*—pulled him over?"

"They'd have gotten a gun in the mouth if they had," his companion answered laconically. "Stands to reason he slipped through the net. Doesn't take more'n an hour to get here from Wheeling, where the truck was stolen. By the time you got the word and the heat out, guy was long gone."

Mackie Sterne was a captain in the Cambridge police force, a twenty-year veteran of the streets and a man who clearly had nothing but contempt for the federal agent who stood before him now. "You want us to take evidence outta the cab? Send it straight to the Bureau? Happy to help."

Tom shook his head. "I've already asked for a forensic team. I'm impounding the vehicle. Leave your yellow tape and a uniformed officer to guard it and I'll guarantee we'll take it off your hands in under two hours."

"Doesn't solve your problem," Sterne pointed out shrewdly. "Problem being, which way to head next. You got any idea where this creep with the sick kid has gone?"

"Mackie, have any vehicles—car, motorcycle, ATV, baby carriage—been reported missing in Cambridge during the past eight hours?"

"Thought of that," the policeman replied with satisfaction. "Figured the truck was ripped off around dinnertime yesterday, gave it maybe two hours to hit Cambridge what with hugging the back roads, and started checking missing car reports as of eight P.M. last night. There're only two. A little old lady's low-mileage Buick, which she discovered gone at the crack of dawn. Turns out she'd left it parked in front of the house with the keys inside and the motor running and one of her neighbors very kindly moved the car up the drive and into the woman's garage. End of story. Second car was reported twenty minutes later—snatched from the opposite end of town from where we're standing, by the way. Found that one completely stripped and abandoned in the Wal-Mart parking lot."

So maybe Ricin Boy hadn't stolen a car. Tom didn't have to ask if any bodies had turned up with a single bullet to the brain; Sterne would've told him. He glanced around the quiet block of warehouses—all of them fronted with loading docks—where the killer he now thought of as Daniel Becker had chosen to abandon his Rac Transport. The district was perfect cover for a stray eighteen-wheeler. Tom was surprised anybody had noticed it.

He didn't walk, Shephard thought furiously, *dragging the sick kid behind him. Is there a railroad track nearby? A freight they could have jumped?*

He began to pace down the alley, scanning the buildings on either side.

"We've searched those warehouses," Sterne said impatiently.

Eight or nine o'clock at night. He knows the roads are watched. Maybe he's even seen a roadblock. Or heard some kind of bulletin on the truck's radio. Dark. Rain coming down. Jozsef on his last legs. Where would he go? When all the world knows his face?

At this hour—just after eight A.M.—the loading
docks were finally coming to life, metal doors rocket-
ing skyward and the first delivery van looming at the
far end of the alley. A belch of smoke from a diesel exhaust pipe, somehow more pungent and acrid in the
rain. Beyond it, nearly two blocks distant and behind a
vacant lot that separated the warehouses from a busy
freeway, a bus was heaving its cumbersome way into a
turn.

"There's nothing down here," Sterne insisted. "We
need to go back to the station and check the computers."

"That's it," Tom said. He'd stopped short, his eyes
narrowed. "That's it, Mackie. Our boy's gone Greyhound."

It was important to get to Pittsburgh because there
was somebody Daniel knew near that city, somebody
he could call if things got tough, but he refused to
take the bus directly toward Pennsylvania because that
meant a route through Wheeling again and Wheeling
was a bad place for Daniel now. He'd kept the radio
humming during that wretched hour and forty minutes of coaxing the big truck along roads never made
for it, heading by sense and luck toward the farthest
point his gas would take him. Buying more was out of
the question.

He'd had a lot of plans for what he'd do once the
boy was riding shotgun—circle back toward Washington and pick off the head of the FBI at his house in
Potomac, which Daniel had already cased; or drop

some ricin in the D.C. water supply off Reservoir Road. Send a few more faxes claiming responsibility. There was even the plan for explosives in the Metro system, which he'd intended to detonate on an Orange line train while it traveled under the river from Foggy Bottom to Rosslyn; he figured it would be the toughest place to stage a rescue and casualties would be nice and high. Sunny's Truck Stop Delite had changed all that. Daniel knew now that his picture was circulating, and he was spooked. It was Christmas Eve 1995 all over again, and a party with guns was waiting in the trees.

Near Cambridge he knew he was rolling on fumes and he was about to tell the boy they'd have to hoof it when the bulletin came across the dash. *Explosion in remote West Virginia trailer, casualties uncertain, FBI involved, possible suicide bomber.* He'd known. Known instantly. He'd taught Bekah how to pack the plastique in the makeshift belt, how to set the circuit and keep it broken until the last second. They'd practiced belting trees they didn't need on the farm, an old Army Ranger trick, circle the trunk and detonate from a safe distance. Bekah's sorry eyes, the deep rifts running from nostril to chin, the pain cut into her wrists over and over—all flashed before his vision like a stigmata and he cried out, unconscious of the boy beside him, a knife gone straight into the gut.

After that he didn't care about the truck or exactly where they landed. He was hurting, and the edges of his mind had curled where the exhaustion etched them like acid. When the engine sputtered and died he grabbed the boy by the shoulder and shoved him hard down the alleyway, straight toward the neon bus station sign. Consigning Bekah to her Maker. They'd taught him about this in Basic, how it was hard to lose a buddy in the field, somebody you'd trusted with your back. *Dolf, son,* his thoughts raged. *Your mama's coming. I'll be along soon.*

He'd told Jozsef he'd shoot him dead if he put a hair out of line and then sent him straight up to the Greyhound window with some of the last cash Daniel had. Enough to buy two tickets to Erie, heading north first to Cleveland and then east along the lake. Four, maybe five hours, the bus pulling out at nine-fifteen, and enough change to send the boy a second time to the fast-food counter with an order for hot dogs and soda. Daniel ate the tasteless food standing outside the bus station in the cloudless dark, his body shoved up against the building's brick wall and his eyes constantly moving. Night patrol. He'd done it a hundred times. Only this time he had the Son of the Leader by his side. Jozsef shivering like a stray dog, food untouched, hands clenched in his pockets.

"I don't think you really knew my father," he said once, in a voice so low Daniel barely heard it. "If you did, you'd have managed this better. You're making it up as you go along, aren't you? Papa always said that was the first sign of panic."

thirty-nine

It was Josie's job to handle the details of her operations, and after nearly twelve years in semiretirement, calling her own shots, she'd grown to expect complete autonomy in the field. It was annoying, then, to have Scottie acting like she was a three-year-old. Telling her where and when to set up, what the constraints might be. As though she couldn't research the situation for herself, case the area, analyze the opportunities. *This jerk has him jumping,* she thought as she deplaned in Frankfurt and re-embarked for the short hop to Berlin. *A serious threat to national security,* he'd said. *Pack your bags, Josie.*

She'd gone about it like the professional she was. Called her daughter and told her to cover for her at the fish store. Called Mike and cut her deliveries in half. *But Mom,* Sheila had protested, *you can't just take a vacation at the drop of a hat. You've got to plan for these things. It's Thanksgiving week. We expected you Thursday.*

Josie pleaded doctor's orders and overwork and the sudden need for a holiday in the sun. By ten that evening she was sitting at the Lufthansa gate with the tickets and passport Scottie had given her, a passable photo and name. Mary Devlin. Fair, fat, and fifty. With the separate components of a Steyr rifle worth nearly three thousand dollars in her checked baggage.

Some women worried about their jewelry when they traveled; Josie worried about her scope. She'd wrapped it carefully as a baby in her pashmina scarves.

At the last minute, almost as an afterthought, she'd tossed the bleached-out photograph of Patrick in her suitcase and shut the lid firmly on his grin. Patrick was always with her on these jobs, his chipped front tooth hovering somewhere beyond her peripheral vision. Patrick the Second-Story Man, Patrick the charming drinker, Patrick who could dance her off her feet and make her feel more gorgeous than Miss America. He'd worked for years cracking safes and burgling embassies for the CIA; hence the nickname. They were all Second-Story Men, the guys who could climb like cats into any room, no matter how secure or how high off the ground. Like Patrick, they'd grown up in the Boston mafia or the Chicago mob or somewhere off the Vegas strip and were trying to earn the gratitude of the Feds when they weren't selling guns or whiskey. Bill Harvey, their ostensible superior, used to let the FBI know when one of his boys was traveling official; nobody arrested a Second-Story Man.

Josie had met Patrick on one of his flying visits to Bogotá, back when it was still a glamorous Latin town and Scottie was cooling his heels there before a stint in Embassy Athens. Patrick had recognized the last trace of her Southie accent, knew immediately everything she'd tried to hide for years, and loved her for it. No Georgetown or Holy Cross stuck-up, he.

Patrick taught her how to pick locks and how to hide contraband and how to smuggle her best friend across any border. Taught her how to bug a phone and clean a rifle, how to nail her five-shot groupings from three hundred meters, how to uncap a beer with her teeth. He left her pregnant, unmarried, and thirty years old on the night of his last job, when the Second-Story Man was shot off a window ledge and fell forty feet to his death.

If I cannot be safe, Patrick me darling, she thought as her plane took off from Frankfurt, *then for Chrissake let me be brave.*

She ignored the fancy place where Scottie was staying and checked into one of the no-longer-fashionable small hotels in the western half of the city, just off Ku'damm. It was possibly a three-star, probably a two, and the bathroom was smaller than Lufthansa's. No minibar, the mattress nearly on the floor, a nice down quilt in the German fashion. She'd been to Berlin only once before, and though the jet lag was fuddling her brain she forced herself to take a long hot shower and then study her city map over coffee. She could sleep when her work was done.

There were maybe ten prisons strung out around the inner suburbs and districts of Berlin, two of them juvenile detention centers, one specifically for women. She concentrated on finding the other seven, ignoring those that did not tally with Scottie's instructions. It was a small place, unofficial, near the St.-Elisabeth Stift—a medical clinic. A scattering of buildings around an inner courtyard off Eberswalderstrasse. Scottie had suggested she rent a room in a building next door or get access to a stairwell—as though stairwells had windows—and wait for the armored van with the prisoner to return from its daily jaunt. Josie had other ideas. There was the clinic, for crying out loud—and why couldn't she, Mary Devlin, have a relative waiting inside? *I'll get over there in an hour,* she thought as she leaned back against the inadequate bedstead and stared thoughtfully at the leaden Berlin sky. *But now I'm going to nap a little.*

We aren't as young as we used to be, Patrick, and that's a fact.

It's no use, Cuddy thought wearily as he waited for the next question to fall in the room's thickening silence. *He'll never leave me alone with Eric, and I've got no way of reaching him. I might as well have stayed in Langley.*

He had gone to Dulles at the appointed hour and waited in a bar for Raphael. Contact had come in the form of a drink sent to his table by a leggy blonde, who smiled at him cheerily from the corner. He'd nearly choked on the Scotch as he read the note on the back of her business card—*Bambi Trixx, Room 419, Hotel Adlon, Berlin*—and had adjusted his glasses twice before he believed it. *Raphael in drag.* He wore a chamois-colored suede skirt and a black leather jacket. His platinum hair was entirely his own, loose and curled in a smooth bob. The angelic features transmuted perfectly, the makeup applied by an artist's hand. Unlike Cuddy, Bambi traveled first-class, sipping champagne over the Atlantic. Cuddy had no idea where Raphael was now, but thought it was a good bet that Room 419, the Adlon, was one of the best suites in the house.

Sleeper. Tool. Fist. Like Caroline, Cuddy had seen the empty folders with the Croatian names, and like her he'd translated them for himself. How to ask Eric what they meant in this room with the wolf at the door?

They had landed in Berlin at noon local time. Wally Aronson was waiting for them in a khaki trench coat, looking for all the world like a collaborator out of *Casablanca*. November in that part of Germany was wet and harsh, and the vaguely sinister outline of mustard-colored cranes suited the atmosphere. More than a decade after unification, but construction pits still yawned throughout the city. The prevalence of skeletal buildings made the burned-out hulk of the Brandenburg Gate, destroyed by 30 April two weeks before, almost easier to bear.

Scottie carried himself like a spymaster of old that morning. He barked orders and refused lunch and did not stop at the Adlon, where Wally had reserved rooms, demanding to be taken immediately to Eric. *You would think,* Cuddy commented inwardly, *that he'd missed his wayward child. Eric—his prodigal.* Scottie's air was one of bewildered sorrow, a man grievously betrayed.

He was lounging now in his chair as though overcome with boredom or perhaps the effects of jet lag, long legs outstretched idly in their perfect British suiting. A few imperious words to his German goons, Ernst and Klaus, had succeeded in winning the suspect's temporary removal from solitary confinement to a CIA safe house, though Eric still wore shackles on his legs and wrists. The safe house was in the Grunewald, west of Berlin, down a cobbled lane hard by the lakes and forest that made the area a sporting mecca for city residents; but nobody within the tidy cottage was enjoying the view. The curtains were drawn.

It was the obvious course. Any BKA interrogation room would be penetrated, and Scottie could never allow Eric's confession to be recorded. He'd promised Ernst something—a public trial in a German court?—in exchange for exclusive debriefing rights; and the German agent had insisted he come along for the ride. Scottie and Ernst in the hunting grounds of the vanished Hohenzollerns, two survivors of a century of blood sport.

Once at the door of the safe house, however, Scottie had nodded to Wally Aronson and the station chief had taken the BKA agent gently by the arm. Preventing him from following Scottie and Eric over the threshold. Ernst was smoking quietly outside now while Wally chatted in his amiable, nonsensical way; two prison guards wandered about the grounds, fingering the guns concealed in their pockets and blowing on chapped fingers.

"You fucking piece of shit." Eric said it quietly. "I went through hell for you, Scottie. I'd have died for you if you'd asked. And you sold me out. You know how stupid I feel? How unbelievably fucking *stupid*?

You were like a father to me. Only I wasn't your son—
I was just somebody you could use."

"Here's the deal," Scottie mused to no one in par-
ticular. "Dare's been murdered by one of your friends,
Eric, and Rinehart's taken over as DCI. Remember
Rinehart? No? A nice young man. Obsessed with power.
He'll do whatever I tell him to keep it."

"I don't give a flying fuck who's running the CIA,
Scottie. Who's running you?"

"I've told Rinehart that Dare single-handedly shoved
you deep into 30 April and successfully destroyed the
evidence before her untimely death. Rinehart wants you
brought to book. In the U.S. That's what the President
has ordered, too. If you don't get the death penalty
for Sophie Payne's murder, Eric, you'll spend the rest
of your life in jail."

Eric grinned. All his teeth bared. The white cut
through the mass of bruises was painful to look at.
"I'll be tried first, before a jury of my peers. Or a panel
of German judges here in Berlin. I'll tell them the
truth about your brutal little games, Scottie."

"Which will get you exactly nothing." Scottie's gaze
was still fixed on the curtained window, as though his
eyes somehow saw the lake through it. "You and I
used to play poker, Eric. Don't you remember? Don't
you *remember* how I'd call your bluff, over and over
again, and you'd come up short? I can read your death
in your eyes. You've got dogs in that hand right now.
Threes and sevens. *I'm holding aces, asshole.* Rinehart's
my ace. Jack Bigelow's my ace. The *American people,*
who are scared shitless and running for any hole they
can hide in, are my aces. They want a terrorist's head

and I'm in a position to give it to them. I'll be crowned king of the universe before I'm done."

"Cuddy knows the truth," Eric said steadily. But he did not look at him, and Cuddy felt his face flush with shame. "Caroline knows."

"Caroline's out on the street. The FBI's tailing her under suspicion of collusion with her killer husband. Cuddy is working for me—and the day he stops is the day I turn him over to the law, burned from head to toe."

Eric's eyes drifted toward Cuddy, found his face where it leaned wearily against his hand. Cuddy managed to shake his head slightly, once. A profession of faith. Eric's expression remained impassive. The wound in his neck resembled a garrote.

"Did you come to Berlin to gloat?"

The CTC chief sighed with impatience. "I came to offer you a deal. The best I can do. The *only* thing I can do. With Rinehart's okay."

"What deal?"

"Your confession—your promise to enter a guilty plea—and your willingness to work with us, Eric. In exchange for twenty years to life. No trial, no risk of the death penalty. You've heard of turning state's evidence, right? Thirty April's rapidly making a charnel house of the District and we need whatever facts you store in that animal brain."

With sudden violence Eric thrust himself out of his chair. "*Guilty* plea?" he spat out, his manacled hands clanking against the conference table. "Guilty of *what*? Protecting your ass?"

Scottie stood up and reached for his suit jacket. "I'll

tell Ernst you're not cooperating. He can take you back to your cell."

With his fingertips, Eric lifted the edge of the table and tossed it at Scottie. It flipped once, and though Scottie stepped instinctively backward, one of the metal legs caught his cheek high on the bone, cutting instantly to blood.

"Wilmot," Scottie said calmly as he drew a gun and pointed it steadily at Eric, "get the prison guards. This boy's beyond saving."

forty

"You can't be serious," Brett Foster said flatly. He raised his pen from the yellow legal pad he used for notes. "*Resign?* You won the last election with sixty-three percent of the vote, George. That's a *mandate.* You're Speaker of the House."

"I've lost Dana," George Enfield shot back bitterly, "and I've got absolutely no interest in politics right now. I want to spend more time with Mallory. She's all I've got left."

The two men were sitting alone in the Speaker's inner office, a beautiful and spacious old room with deep crown moldings and twelve-foot-high windows. The drapes were a strong Federal blue velvet and the desk was Biedermeier; Dana had helped to choose both. Around the walls were photographs from nearly two decades in public office: George shaking hands with two previous presidents; George fly-fishing the Rappahannock; George standing tall on the deck of an aircraft carrier. Dana, gorgeous as a catwalk model, at the last inaugural ball.

"Look," Foster urged, "we're in recess. Through the Christmas holidays. You don't have to hang around here and you don't have to make any snap decisions. Go home to Memphis. Take some time to think and to heal. But for God's sake, don't make any announcements you'll regret. It's way too soon, George."

He liked Brett Foster—the forty-year-old had been his Chief of Staff for nearly three years now, and he had not reached the pinnacle of a Capitol Hill career by dumb fucking luck, so George usually trusted his instincts and followed his advice. Except when everything in his being counseled otherwise. Like today.

"I'm flying with Dana's ashes to Massachusetts after the funeral Friday," he replied. "She wanted them scattered in Nantucket Sound." *The part of her life that came before me, before Mallory, before the public scrutiny she frankly hated. Oh, God—why didn't I let her live her life while we still had time?* "That means we've got a lot to do in the next three days. I want you to call a staff meeting for nine-thirty and a press conference for ten A.M."

"Dana wouldn't have wanted you to give up," Foster insisted urgently.

"And I didn't want her to die," Enfield retorted. "So we're even, aren't we?"

Candace O'Brien watched the press conference from the foot of her bed a few minutes before she checked out of the hotel. She was mesmerized by George Enfield's face. She saw in it the traces of her own guilt and grief at Sophie Payne's murder. *He understands,* she thought. *He's just like me.*

She had never returned to Dupont Circle the previous night. Instead, she had walked swiftly past her
own home and cut down the alley to the detached
garage where she kept her car. She'd driven into the
darkness without a notion of where she was heading,
knowing only that she had to leave this place—this
place where she was hunted. She'd briefly considered
the small Eastern Shore town of St. Michael's, which
had felt like a haven the only other time she'd been
there; but she could not quite remember the way and
was too rattled to find a map in her sterile glove com-
partment. She'd thought of Adrienne, with the sick
feeling of inadequacy that always attended the memory
of her daughter; and in the end she'd driven in circles
for two hours, roaming the Beltway. A few minutes
after eleven P.M. she pulled up to a traveler's hotel outside Silver Spring and accepted it by default.

She'd hoped the morning would bring calm and
decision. Enough strength to return to her home or
leave the country forever. But the newspaper was lying
outside her room and she could not ignore the photographs of dead runners, the paeans to Dana Enfield.
The long investigative profile of Caroline Carmichael's
treacherous role in the terrorist drama. Candace read
it avidly, turning the pages with impatient flicks of the
hand.

It was strange to feel that she knew more about
these events than those writing the story. That she had
the full fabric, while they randomly wove threads. She
turned on CNN in the hope an update would be available and caught her first glimpse of George Enfield's
face.

"...*calling back the members of the House Intelligence Committee to conduct a full-scale investigation into the failure of our intelligence agencies to anticipate 30 April's threat against American interests...expect full cooperation from the Administration, which the President himself has assured me will be the case...appalling tragedy that should never again be allowed to strike the American people...parties responsible held accountable...after which process, I will resign to take care of my daughter...*"

His daughter. Candace sat staring bleakly at the screen long after the Speaker had disappeared and the story had shifted to the Gaza Strip. *His daughter.* Disaster had struck and a young life was changed forever; but he would be there for his child, he would shepherd her through the crisis, as Candace had never done. Too weak. Too fearful of failure. And hesitating even now, when the brutal cost mounted daily.

George Enfield had shown her what she had to do. She had been longing for days to tell someone the truth.

forty-one

"So is it worth all this?" Caroline asked Steve Price as they left the gas station's convenience store with coffee cups and a map in their hands. "All this effort for a single story?"

"It's much more than a story," he replied as he slid his lanky frame into the bucket seat. "It's the power of the pen, baby. The power to shake governments and end careers. The power to ruin lives. Or make them. I love what I do because there's such purity to it." He grinned, his sharp features relaxing into boyishness. "It's just my way of playing God."

If playing God meant drawing the entire nation's attention to himself, Caroline thought wryly, Price did it better than anybody alive. He'd tossed a copy of the morning paper in her lap, and as the Porsche shot forward she studied the front page. Her face stared back: a portrait of official mourning, stolen from Arlington Cemetery. It was no accident Jozsef was pictured beside her: They were both breaking news.

"Steve." She glanced at him sidelong.

"Yeah?"

"This isn't . . . well, it isn't exactly *friendly*."

"Meaning . . . I didn't take your side? Look, Caroline, I'm happy to help you if I can—but I'm not going to feed the *Post*'s readers a simple tale of the CIA run amuck," he said shrewdly. "I need complexity. I need shades of gray. I've got to keep people reading tomorrow, and the next day, and the day after that. I've got to raise doubts and controversy and get us both on *Larry King Live*, you know what I'm saying? I've got to spin this sucker out until the furor's so high that nothing short of a presidential impeachment will answer. That's how journalism works."

"By 'sucker,' I guess you mean me. What about the truth, Steve?"

"What about it?" he shot back. His weathered face—so attractive, so genuine, Caroline thought—gave nothing away, but there was a light of humor and recklessness in his brown eyes. The Porsche was flying along the damp highway and the singing note of the tires was like a banshee in her brain. His hands were sure on the wheel—as sure as his theories, his comfort with Beltway spin.

"I've got to tell both sides of the story so objectively that nobody knows what really happened," he explained as though she were a child. "Even during Watergate the *Post* stood by that policy: We quoted Nixon as much as we quoted Deep Throat. Hell, probably more."

"Are you saying you don't believe a word I've told you?" she demanded.

He shrugged. "Yours is one version. There are probably as many lines on this thing as there are people involved."

"Then what the fuck are you doing driving this car?"

"I'm chasing the story," he sighed. "Look—maybe you're a crook and a liar and a link to terrorism worldwide. Or maybe you're a lone soldier fighting a losing battle against a bureaucracy that would rather see you die than do your job. I don't know. But I'm sure as shit not gonna let you out of my sight, girl. Understand?"

"Yes. I understand you're using me."

He snorted in derision. "And what was that last night? When you spilled your guts to the reporter? You expect me to believe you weren't using *me*?"

She said nothing. The coffee he'd bought her was hot in her hand and the window beside her was rain-streaked. Price had taken her in, tracked her leads, and driven her west with an enthusiasm that was real. The front-page slam was simply his fee for services rendered.

"Okay," she temporized, "so truth is what you make it. I can see your point—as an analyst, I look at a bunch of facts and make my own sense of them. It's my *interpretation* the policymaker reads, not just the facts themselves. But I don't string out a story to make myself indispensable, and I know evil when I see it. You don't spin 30 April for a shot at *Larry King Live*."

He reached out and squeezed her knee. "You do your job, Caroline—I'll do mine."

"Even though you're at risk, chasing this particular story?"

"I like risk. Drink your coffee before it gets cold."

She did as she was told, staring out the window at the Alleghenies.

They were simply one part of the undulating chain of serrated hills that stretched from the Carolinas to Maine and that went by many names—Adirondacks, Smokies, Appalachians. To Caroline, however, the place and its syllables evoked a more primitive time. With the flatlander's distrust of tree-clad fastnesses, she thought of *Deliverance*. Of the kind of man who would murder Dare Atwood in cold blood in the safety of her own living room, who would hand poison to thirsty runners simply because he thought they were different from himself, who revered a murderous fascist like Mlan Krucevic. *Americans just like me*. She shivered involuntarily.

Price thrust his sleek German car confidently around hairpin bends, his attention claimed by the road, and seemed to need neither her conversation nor the directions she'd offered to give him.

"What do you think of this place?" she asked suddenly. "It's starting to give me the creeps."

He shrugged. "I grew up in Mississippi. Totally different kind of country."

"You don't sound like a southerner."

A faint smile creased his engaging face. "Child, din' yer mamma ever tell you that southerners is *stupid*? Cain't set up to be a *journalist* if'n ya sound *stupid*."

"Come on," she said, laughing, "seriously. How long ago did you leave Mississippi?"

"Thirty-nine years, seven months, and fourteen days ago," he returned with swift exactitude. "The morning after my father's newspaper office was burned to the ground and he was lynched by a white mob from the tallest tree in Greenville."

"*What?*" she demanded. "I had no idea. *Steve*—"

He kept his gaze fixed on the road. "That's what they tell me. I was only three. My father was a firm believer in the rights of the Negro. The rights of the coon to stand tall beside his white masters. Oh, yeah, Daddy was a great liberal. He used the family paper to say so and his neighbors didn't like it. Word in Greenville is that Abel Price peed all over himself while they tied the knots in the rope. Jabbering how he'd reform. Nobody bothered to listen by that time; they were too drunk with power and corn whiskey."

"Jesus," Caroline whispered.

His face remained expressionless. "My mom took me to her people. I was raised in Richmond."

"Have you ever gone back?"

"Sure I've gone back. Somebody had to eat crow. Daddy left me that job. Along with a legend and a handful of ashes."

The words were cruel and sardonic; she supposed they allowed him to live with a deeper horror. "And you became a reporter."

"Without the family paper. The *Greenville Standard* had been run by Prices for almost a hundred and fifty years, but Daddy pissed that down the wind along with the contents of his bladder the night he was martyred for his cause. Have you thought of what you're going to say to this woman when we get to her place?"

An abrupt change of subject. His whole manner, Caroline thought, had altered subtly in the past half hour, the easy camaraderie fled into the hills.

She tried to recover. "I'm going to ask her to help."

Price laughed harshly and downshifted into a curve. The car had been steadily climbing, nosing its way west and north, into the heart of the Alleghenies.

"Think about it, Steve. Jozsef's been snatched by a 30 April supporter. The child Adrienne conceived in Leipzig was Mlan's; he's Jozsef's half-brother. If Ricin Boy knows that—and it's conceivable he does—she'd be the logical person to ask for help."

He did not reply.

"You think I'm ridiculous?" she pressed. "Naïve?"

"I think you're surprisingly ignorant for somebody who works intelligence."

"But if Adrienne *knew* that her mother is involved . . . under suspicion of aiding a terrorist . . . she might be able to see reason . . ."

"She despises her mother," Price retorted. "She's been entrusted with a legacy: to rear the last great Leader's Son. Children are all that's left when the father dies. The only bit of immortality he has. She'd know how important that was to Mlan."

"I'm not so sure. He was willing to kill Jozsef."

"Or give him the tools to survive." Price's eyes when they met hers were flat and alien. "Isn't that why we're out here in the middle of nowhere? To find a kid who's just snowed the entire U.S. government?"

Tom Shephard held the door of the Greyhound station open as Mackie Sterne followed him inside. Three people and a small girl of perhaps four were loitering there. The Columbus bus was due in about half an hour. The ticket window did not open until ten, and repeated phone calls to the number listed on the Plexiglas screen had produced only a recorded answering system. From the posted hours of operation, it looked as though the window might have been closed around the time Daniel Becker visited the place last night.

"What do passengers do when there's no ticket seller?" Tom demanded. "Pay their fare on the bus?"

"Can do," Sterne said. "Or there's the automated machine against the wall."

"That requires a credit card," Tom observed. "Becker's not that stupid. He won't leave a trail."

"Already did." Sterne nodded toward the truck parked three blocks away. "You'll be wanting a warrant to search the automated records."

Tom did not waste time arguing. He was studying the schedules posted on the station wall. He had never used a bus for transport—his taste having run to trains and airplanes even as a college student—and this world was foreign to him. The bus routes branched like aging veins all over the map of the United States.

"Mackie, if you were going to take this thing outta here, which way would you go?"

"Really only got but two choices," the police captain returned immediately. "East to Wheeling, west to Columbus. Those'd be the most direct routes. Doubt he'd go back to Wheeling."

Not when all of West Virginia was crawling with the Feds, Tom thought, and his wife was lying in pieces out at the old homestead.

He scrutinized the wagon wheel that was Columbus. The options there were numerous: north to Toledo, southwest to Cincinnati and the Kentucky border; or hell, he could've gone for broke and headed straight on till daylight and the Republic of California. *Not likely,* Tom thought. *Too much of a commitment. He needs to disappear.*

"What about heading north?"

"Toward the Lakes?" Mackie shrugged. "I suppose as how he might. Akron. Cleveland. Erie, Pennsylvania. All nice places to visit."

We haven't got a clue which way he's chosen, Tom thought with the weariness of despair. *He could be anywhere right now.*

"Let's call the national Greyhound office," he said with decision, "and inform them they've got a probable terrorist on board one of their buses. We'll alert all the stations in a hundred-mile radius. All the buses on probable routes. Send out a description of Becker and the boy and see what turns up."

"Do that," Mackie warned, "and you'll have a bloodbath on your hands."

"I already do," Tom replied.

forty-two

BERLIN, 2:15 P.M.

While Cuddy had stood in miserable silence on the periphery of Scottie's charmed circle that afternoon, Raphael Alighieri, Master Deceiver and Compacter with the Devil, spent two hours and twelve minutes dialing his way through a list of Berlin hotels. In passable German he asked each person who answered whether he could speak to a guest named Mary Devlin. At the first seventy-three attempts he came up short. Mary was a tough old bitch to find, and he was almost ready to believe she wasn't in Berlin at all, though the tickets Scottie had procured for his contractor had dropped her at Tegel that morning just like themselves.

Maybe she's staying with friends, he thought, *the cocksucking old ass-wipe.*

Raphael had tracked Scottie's spoor through his trusted proxies, Betty and Alice, and he knew a great deal about Mary Devlin. He had a copy of her picture and the cover job Scottie had chosen. He had the itinerary the woman had followed, landing first in Frankfurt and connecting to Berlin. Only the hotel was a blank. That and the reason Scottie had recruited her.

Mary Devlin worried Raphael. She was part of a pattern, ill-defined but recognizable, of Scottie's maverick ops—the ones he held close to his chest and kept off the Agency books as he always had, the most deadly kinds of deceptions, shared with none but their victims. Raphael was fascinated by Mary, with her broad Irish face and her coarse skin and the lank red hair that she obviously struggled to control in an elegant manner. Her photograph showed her as common as a Dublin fishwife, and as enduring.

"Get me her real name," he'd snapped at Betty when she'd reached him at the Adlon. "Get me her background, for fuck's sake. She's got to be somebody he knows. Scottie wanders, but he never wanders far off the Farm. There have *got* to be records on this woman."

Betty had hemmed and hawed and promised to resurrect Christ if he'd give her half an hour; and Raphael had gone back to his steady Germanic dialing.

On the ninety-sixth call, to a little hotel called the Kurfürstendammer Hof, the receptionist paused when he stated the name, then said: "I'll put you through."

Raphael hung up before the first buzz sounded, rubbing his hands in satisfaction. Mary Devlin, Kurfürstendammer Hof, was his for the taking. He had a compelling desire to sniff inside her drawers.

When writers of spy fiction dreamed up lethal assassins, they inevitably portrayed them as ruthless loners. Men who lived in isolated chalets in glamorous Swiss resorts, whose vast sums of blood money paid for frequent plastic surgery. Men who hid out in private coves along the Maltese coast or who moved their yachts from port to port. Men who used sex as a safety valve and who killed without remorse. Men who were damaged.

Men. Never the local fishmonger with grandsons and a numbered account. Never Josie O'Halloran of South Boston and Beirut and Manhattanville '64.

It's our little joke, Patrick me love, Josie thought as she made her deliberate way toward the St.-Elisabeth Stift on Eberswalderstrasse. *Our little joke and six million in the bank over the past twelve years. That's one thing you left me—the wit and the balls to earn my bread.*

There had been a time when Bill Harvey, who'd run the cryptanalysts of Staff D and a motley agglomeration of Second-Story Men on the side, had been called in to help with a smattering of assassinations. These were the Company's glory days, the late fifties and early sixties, when Camelot was ascendant and the dictators of left and right were so many pieces on the post–World War II chessboard, waiting to be taken. Patrice Lumumba, butcher of the Congo. Rafael Trujillo, who threw his enemies to the sharks or hung them by meat hooks in the Dominican Republic. Fidel Castro, who had the audacity to kick big business out of Cuba and alienated half the Miami mob in the process. They had all been in the CIA's sights during the Eisenhower and Kennedy Administrations, back when Khrushchev was a threat and the deadly flower of Vietnam was only half blown.

The attempts at murder were ineffectual and slapdash. Unwilling to get its hands dirty, the Agency recruited the underworld as proxy killers. All the fumbling half-assed mistakes were exposed a decade later, when Josie's Patrick was long dead and the conversations he'd held over casual barbecues, the murderous quid pro quos, seemed ludicrously naïve. Nobody had been hurt except the Great White Fathers of American Intelligence, who stood before the Church Commission with their pants puddled around their ankles. Josie was living in Athens then, buying Scottie's Number Two her extravagant Christmas and anniversary presents, hustling little Sheila to the American school each morning. She hadn't given a damn what Congress thought of assassination. It was all a question of deniability. Of getting the baddies before they got us first. She was bored by the semantics and the pussyfooting around. Sometimes a gun to the head was a blessing in disguise.

You could write your own ticket, Josie darling, Scottie had said after her retirement lunch in 1988. *Just be discreet. Use your cover. Use your tradecraft. You're an independent contractor with a lifetime of training. It works for all the old friends shoved out the door.*

She'd bought a Bushmaster first, then a Czech CZ, and most recently the Austrian Steyr, which was light and easy to manipulate in a woman's hands. She could carry it, broken down, in a capacious kilim-covered carpetbag that suited her shambling form. She was carrying that bag now, tucked next to a box of chocolates and a basket of fruit and a couple of paperbacks, as she turned into the medical clinic. Her nap had refreshed her. She was blithe as a spring chicken. It was possible she would spend a few well-earned days in Paris after the job was done. All that remained was to scout out the proper killing ground, then head back to Ku'damm for a hearty meal.

"Did I tell you the Prick tried to hit on me in the first-class bar on the flight over?" Raphael inquired as Cuddy sank into the luxurious sofa that dominated one end of the Adlon's Room 419. "God's truth. Bought me a Cosmopolitan—which naturally Bambi loves but I had to *choke* down—and ran his fingertips along my thigh while he talked of his world travels. Told me he was an executive flying in to do a deal with Siemens. Pathetic old fart. That wife of his is hardly thirty, and already he's searching for Number Four."

"No, no," Cuddy corrected as he rolled his sleeves to the elbow. His jet lag was becoming manageable now. "Bambi's good for a quick fuck in the lav, but never a candidate for Number Four. Number Four is going to bring millions. She'll have to."

"Bambi's *very* expensive," Raphael protested, hurt.

"So is Scottie."

The Prince of Darkness was back in form, black-clad and blasé as he lounged with a glass of Grey Goose. The drapes were drawn against the gray wet afternoon and a CD was playing softly; Cecilia Bartoli, Cuddy thought, singing something that sounded like Vivaldi. He caught the word *sangue* repeated with violence in her liquid throat: *blood*. Raphael's equivalent of a fight song.

Cuddy reached for a minibar beer and struggled with the bottle opener. The blood looked like being

Eric's and Cuddy's and all the good guys' and he wanted very much to get drunk.

Raphael's hair was tied at the nape this afternoon and he was wearing a pair of narrow, boxy spectacles that lent him an instant Euro cachet. He looked, Cuddy thought, positively German. Tomorrow he'd probably be French.

"Did you see him?" he asked Cuddy.

"Yes. They keep him cuffed—ankles manacled—and run two prison guards outside the door. Scottie puts the questions and Eric avoids the answers. Scottie offered twenty-to-life for a complete confession and state's evidence. Eric went for Scottie's throat."

Raphael sipped the Grey Goose, his gaze that of a twelfth-century contemplative. "So he hasn't given up."

"Not yet. Scottie's got the scratches to prove it."

"Good. Did the Prick bite back?"

"He slapped Eric's wrist and left in a huff. We're supposed to revisit the whole thing tonight—Scottie can't go home empty-handed. His future depends on polishing Rinehart's butt."

Raphael reached for a folded map of Berlin and spread it open on the coffee table. He had highlighted several roads in different Day-Glo colors: blue, pink, and yellow.

"Here's the secret cell block where our boy's being held," he said, "and here's the location of the safe house. Correct?"

"You knew that?"

"Talked to Wally. Wally's a bud from way back. Here are the three main routes one could take from the Grunewald to Eberswalderstrasse. Notice they all converge right here."

He laid one almond-shaped fingernail on an intersection where blue, pink, and yellow paths met. "At the Pankow U-Bahn station," Cuddy said. "And? Your point is?"

"This is where we'll stage our rescue." Raphael sat back and smiled triumphantly. "The prison van carrying Eric *has* to take one of these routes back to St.-Elisabeth's tomorrow. It doesn't matter which. They all debouch at the same point, a block from the hospital. That's where we'll magic him out of the van."

"How?"

Raphael reached for a graphite-colored pen lying innocently on the hotel desk next to his laptop. The music, Cuddy realized suddenly, was coming from the computer. The Vivaldi had given way to Mozart; fanciful and childlike after the bitter dregs of revenge.

"I've told Wally to visit Eric before he's taken from his cell tonight. Urge him to sign the Prick's confession. When he reaches for a pen in that safe house, give the boy *this*."

Cuddy held it before his weak eyes. An unexceptionable gray barrel, a medium blue plastic clip for securing the thing to a pocket flap. But Raphael's toys were never unexceptionable. "What's it do?"

"Click it once, you sign your name. Click it twice, it's a high-powered laser capable of cutting through steel."

Cuddy had an image of Eric confined in his rolling van, waiting for the doors to open on freedom. The pen in his cupped fingers slowly burning through metal.

"And if the truck hits a pothole?"

"He loses a finger." Raphael shrugged indolently. "He's got steady hands. Or did. The best lock-picker I've ever schooled." He reached for his vodka bottle. "Cheers."

forty-three

He was down to the fundamentals now, down to the echoing tile in the public bathroom and the humid scent of the boy's unwashed skin as he slumped against Daniel's shoulder. Down to the last hundred bucks and the dry mouth and the constant thrum of his pulse in his own ears; down to the cramped certainty of the gun lying potent against his chest. Down to the last leg of the journey.

They'd hopped the 9:40 P.M. bus to Cleveland last night, sitting way in the back as darkness and peace enfolded them. Few people talked on this graveyard run toward the Great Lakes, and the words they shared were muffled by the high-backed seats. Daniel had kept his fingers locked on the boy's wrist but it hadn't really mattered in the end; Jozsef had fallen heavily asleep, his cheeks flushed, before the bus even stopped at Akron.

That'd been a bad time for Daniel, when the buffering ranks of passengers ranged between himself and the hunting world shifted like wheat under a spring wind, some filing off, new bodies taking their places. A situation in flux was a dangerous situation: He'd felt his fingers twitch, longing to pull his gun and freeze them all to silence. The bus driver had looked hard at Daniel, the only man who'd spurned this chance to stretch his legs and use the facilities, the clock ticking close to midnight; but bus drivers were used to eccentricity and a rampant desire for privacy and he'd probably figured Daniel was unwilling to disturb the sleeping kid. When the bus at last drove on to Cleveland, his insomniac brain was jumping.

Northern Ohio at two o'clock in the morning, the Rust Belt rain harsh and without pity. The next bus to Erie would not board for four and a half hours. He'd kept Jozsef hunkered at his feet in the claustrophobic night, the two of them outside in the raw darkness, Daniel alert as a sentry with his legs straddling the boy's drooping head. Jozsef grew hotter as the night grew colder and the breath in his throat rattled painfully. He slipped in and out of dreams or fever. There'd been something about the boy being sick, Daniel remembered, and the doctors at Bethesda Naval trying hard to crack his disease; but Daniel had been certain that was behind them when he put his gun to Norm Wilhelm's head. The idea that maybe Jozsef needed medicine— needed a hospital bed and a nurse—had never struck him before. It was out of the question anyway.

All tuckered out, he told the driver as he lifted the boy onto the Erie bus. *Shame to make him travel this time of the morning.*

But now as they waited for the ride to Pittsburgh Daniel's anxiety was spiking. The boy's eyes would not stay open and his head lolled like a drunk's. Daniel kept a paper cup of tap water trained against Jozsef's lips and forced him to drink, the water dribbling down his shirt like a baby's. Ten o'clock in the morning. The next bus maybe twenty minutes away. *Jesus Christ kid don't fail me now. We got to keep goin', keep serpentining under the crossfire, if yer movin' the bullets just sing over yer head, know what I mean?* When he pulled the cup away at last, a pink ribbon of bloody spit clung to the boy's lip.

He put his arm around Jozsef, propping him up, and kept his eyes stonily on the clock. The station's ticket window had opened three minutes before, and the gray-haired black woman behind the counter fingered her dangling spectacles where they lay on her broad chest. Her lips were moving slightly and she held a piece of fax paper in her hand. A line was forming for tickets and people were shifting restlessly as the woman scanned her painful way through the text. Then she looked up sharply and studied the faces assembled before her, one by one. Leaned forward to stare into the waiting room.

Daniel's eyes met hers without intending it, a failure caused in part by the clinging weight of the sick boy and the mesmeric ticking of the clock's second hand and the exhaustion that welled like floodwater through his brain. He saw the woman's eyes widen as she looked and saw her turn hastily away, as though searching for help or a phone or a button she could push, and that quickly he'd risen to his feet and screamed, *"Don't move you hear me?"*

The cry cut the morning in half. Nothing routine, now, from the startled gape of the waiting passengers— were there ten? fifteen?—to the gun gleaming dully in his reaching hand. He could not remember whether he'd reloaded after Sunny's Truck Stop Delite. Six bullets then. Nothing since. Had he left the extra magazine in the cab of the stolen truck, all the way back through the nightmare hours of Cambridge? Or was it sitting in the duffel bag at his feet?

A toddler started to wail—red hair dangling to her shoulders, thighs sweet as sausages in her dirty white tights—and the mother, an obese young woman with acne and a pierced navel, slapped a hand over the little girl's mouth. What was the black bitch with her finger on the button fixin' to do?

"Everybody down!" Daniel barked. "Everybody down with your hands out flat on the floor where I can see 'em. *Move it*."

They fell like dominoes, heads plastered to the stained linoleum. He skirted their bodies and fired without aiming through the glass window, shattering it completely. There was a cry but he ignored it as he ran to the station entrance, throwing the bolts to lock the doors. *Nobody leaves*, he thought frantically, *nobody in or out. Choke points. Command and control.*

One of the people lying on the floor—a guy in jeans and a leather jacket with a redneck beard scraggling all the way to his belt—shifted and turned his head to stare at Daniel. His hands were thrust against the linoleum like he was doing push-ups or thinking about a spring for Daniel's neck, and that quickly Daniel pointed the gun and fired again. The man sagged and flattened.

"Anybody else moves," Daniel said calmly, "they die like Rambo there. Understand?"

A sob came from somewhere. He kicked open one

restroom door and snaked his gun inside. *Nothing.*
Nobody. He did the same to the other one. All quiet
on the Western Front. The ticket seller was lying flat
on her back, eyes on the ceiling, a can of Mace clutched
in her hand.

He knew now that he'd remembered to reload, that
the gun was potent and hot and victory just a few
hours away. He glanced at Jozsef. The kid was sprawled
on his hard plastic bench, not as dead to the world as
the two Daniel had just shot. They would wait for a
bus and driver to pull in to the terminal and then make
their getaway. He had the situation, Daniel thought,
well in hand.

"Erie," Tom Shephard told Mackie Sterne as he cut
off the call from Headquarters. "Gunshots fired in the
Greyhound terminal and hostages inside. Police in a
cordon and talk of a S.W.A.T. team. Can you find me
a helicopter, Mackie?"

"I s'pose I could," the police captain said grudg-
ingly. "Told you there'd be a bloodbath."

"That was always true," Shephard replied. "A few
bodies today instead of hundreds tomorrow. Somebody
had to make the choice."

forty-four

The styptic pencil Scottie kept in his shaving kit hurt like the devil when he pressed it against the edge of the cut. He took the pain unflinchingly, his gray eyes fixed on his reflection, hard and flat as lake ice in January. The table leg had been capped with metal and the cut was a clean one, high on the cheekbone. Without stitches it would undoubtedly scar.

He did not bother to curse Eric under his breath or hunt out a German doctor through the hotel switchboard. He merely plied the styptic pencil, watching it turn pink with blood. He did not expect Eric to break. The hatred in his face had offered no room for negotiation. Scottie would not have respected him if it had. He had never trained Eric for compromise.

We've got to try one more time, Cuddy had urged in the confines of the elevator as they parted on their separate floors. *You can't just turn your back on the only source we've got. People are dying at home, Scottie. We need what Eric knows.*

Cuddy had been careful not to plead his friend's case—not to wheedle or suggest plausible alternatives, parallel deals. He had been a model of deference and submission, Scottie thought with contempt; Cuddy would do anything he asked, and thank him for the indignity. It was unfortunate it was men like Cuddy who survived. And men like Eric who fell to the knife.

He turned the hot water faucet to a gush and soaked a washcloth. The Adlon's linens were superb. He wrung out the cushy white square and pressed it against his face. The laceration sang out wildly under his fingers. He clenched his teeth. The entire atmosphere of the Adlon—the cultivated grace, the ancient lineaments of the historic building rising like a phoenix from its Cold War ashes—was a testament to an American triumph. The defeat of Communism and the rise of capitalist democracy. Liberty and justice for all. Scottie had dedicated his life to that proposition, and the luxurious toweling he now held in his hand was confirmation of its worth.

Of course I'll try one more time, he'd muttered to Cuddy as he left him in the hall. *I'll try a dozen times if I have to. You think I'd let that bastard screw me?*

Cuddy had no reason to know that Eric's time was very short.

He left the marble-lined bath and walked to the phone. He'd forced Josie to tell him every last detail of her preparations, though he'd read the annoyance in her voice. She hated his impulse to ride her, but he'd been her boss too long and the habit of control was hard to break. She was staying in a hole-in-the-wall off Ku'damm, lying low until he called. It was, he decided, high time.

"Ms. Devlin?" the receptionist repeated coolly in his ear. "I'm sorry. Ms. Devlin has checked out."

"That's not possible."

"I'm afraid it is, sir."

"But—" He hesitated, struggling to regroup. "Is there an O'Halloran staying with you?"

He was forced to spell the name. Still he turned up nothing. The receptionist was growing impatient and he had no choice but to disconnect.

Josie had gone AWOL. A slow smile curled his lips. She was trying to teach him a lesson. By this time he ought to trust her.

Josie's flight had taken her no farther than an airport hotel in the Tegel district, but she was deeply afraid as she sat in the comfortless bar, the remains of a vodka tonic before her. Someone had entered her room at the Kurfürstendammer Hof. She'd known it immediately upon her return from casing the target.

Whoever it was had made no effort to disguise his presence. There was the fragment of paper she'd left in the doorjamb, lying unnoticed on the carpet; the three hairs she'd arranged in the wardrobe, disarranged completely; the in-room safe where she'd stored her passport standing wide open. Nothing had been taken. *A tour d'horizon*, she thought as she surveyed the sifted room. *A scenting of the enemy.* On her bed was a piece of complimentary notepaper with a few words written in neat print.

Ask Scottie what happened in Bogotá that night.

She did not have to ask which night. Three years and seven months in Bogotá had come down, in the end, to a few hours of error and loss.

Three A.M. and she'd still been up, waiting for the phone call from Patrick, for the lilt in his voice that told her he had never been more alive, for the rush of relief heady as sex. But it had not been Patrick who'd called. Scottie's voice over the wire, hard and dry. *He was blown. I'm sorry, Josie. You can fly out with the body on Friday.*

She had vomited in the plane's lavatory all the way back to Washington and watched as the casket was released to a man she'd never met, a man who looked through her and had no interest in her name; one of Patrick's relatives from Boston, maybe, she'd never been sure. Most of that spring she was lost in a daze of morning sickness and misery. Home leave, compassionate leave, baby Sheila born in August and her next posting a Headquarters one, buried in biographic files.

It had been Scottie who'd rescued her three years later. He'd demanded she accompany him to Athens and get danger pay to boot. There was no end to the miracles he'd pulled on her behalf.

Ask Scottie what happened in Bogotá that night.

Her hands had trembled at the implications of that sentence. One, because the writer knew who she really was—not Mary Devlin but Josie O'Halloran—and her cover docs were blown. Two, because if he knew all that, he probably knew why she was in Berlin. Three, because he'd hinted at something terrible in the past she'd tried to bury. And four, because a seed of doubt was inevitably sown. *Had Scottie kept something from her? Lied to her? God preserve us, killed Patrick himself?*

She ordered another vodka and drank it neat.

Her first duty was to get out of the Kurfürsten-dammer Hof; her second was probably to get out of Berlin. But for now, she was attempting to plan her next step. There was the job to consider. The past and all its wrongs to think of. Scottie, and whatever he knew.

She picked up her carpetbag and headed for the elevator.

forty-five

"Do you know anything about the sacrament of penance?" Candace O'Brien sank into one of the Speaker's conference chairs. "Have you ever submitted to it at all?"

"I'm a southern Baptist," George Enfield replied, "by policy if not conviction. In Tennessee we scream our sins out loud and the world applauds. How can I help you, Ms. O'Brien?"

"Be my priest, Mr. Speaker."

He'd agreed to see her because she'd mentioned Sophie Payne, and he vaguely remembered a factotum hovering in the vice president's background. The middle-aged woman looked like a social worker come to inspect his premises, he thought, with her knees locked primly together and her neat black purse suspended from her hands.

"Let's backtrack a little. You were Sophie Payne's social secretary, I think? We met once or twice at the residence. Are you looking for a job?"

"No. May I say first how desperately sorry I am, Mr. Speaker, for the loss of your beautiful wife?"

He ducked his head as though to avoid a blow. He

had heard similar things all day, offered apologetically or diffidently or in the timid fashion of a subordinate who fears to invade; but somehow Candace's words were more heartfelt and they pierced the wall he'd thrown up in self-defense.

"I remember her," she said, "in silk that beautifully suited her hair; and I remember her sitting before a group of your colleagues and telling them exactly why they ought to support stem-cell research. She had poise and character, Mr. Speaker, and we cannot spare either."

"Thank you," he said with difficulty. "I don't mean to rush you, but I'm afraid I have a great deal to do. If you could explain why you came, perhaps . . ."

"I saw your press conference." Deliberately, she unsnapped her purse and withdrew a single sheet of paper. "You want to find 30 April. My daughter can tell you exactly where they are and what kind of horror they're planning next. But you will have to find her quickly."

He was staring at her bleak expression rather than at what she offered. "I don't understand."

"My daughter Adrienne is one of 30 April's agents in America. I've known that for the past three years. In a foolish attempt to protect her, I've betrayed everything and everyone important in my life. Mlan Krucevic demanded information about Sophie Payne, a woman I loved and admired and who believed I was her friend. I told him all I knew, on a regular basis, because I thought it would keep him from destroying my child."

Her fingers fluttered slightly on the hasp of her bag. "You have a daughter yourself, Mr. Speaker. I hope

that some small part of you can understand why I
acted as I did."

"You gave 30 April Payne's schedule?" Enfield's
voice was harsh.

Candace nodded. "Every last detail, from the moment she took office. I told myself that nothing really
bad could happen to her—she had a crackerjack Secret Service detail, and Krucevic could never hope
to enter this country with the kind of indictment he
carried—but there was the foreign travel as well. The
less-protected exposure. From the day of the Berlin
kidnapping I've been unable to live with myself."

"Jesus *Christ*," Enfield whispered. A dull throb of
rage was mounting in his gut, shattering the careful
box he'd built around his pain. *Sophie. Dana. All those
bodies on the Mall. And this prim lump of a woman
telling him calmly how she'd done her bit for disaster.*
"You deserve to burn in hell."

"I am," she said, rising. "I will. You can send your
investigators to find me. I won't run away. I'll talk on
the record. But use what I've given you, Mr. Speaker.
I still don't have the courage."

She was gesturing toward the piece of paper. He
glanced down at it, disbelieving.

Adrienne O'Brien, it read, *39 Fern Gulch Road,
Rochester, Pennsylvania.*

"In the end that's my true sin," Candace said.
"Cowardice."

She'd been up since dawn, sitting on the stool in her
jeans and an old sweater, a glass of orange juice near at

hand. Misha was playing in an adjoining room with the blocks he loved to set out in patterns across the wide expanse of oak floor, and his music was humming softly in the background. No other sound but the rain on the tin roof and the enfolding leaves, the secret comforts of a tree house. Adrienne's attention was completely focused on the sticklike array of human DNA she had captured in electron micrographs minutes earlier; she was barely conscious of the passage of time, or the distant sound of an approaching car.

She was looking for a few specific genes that she knew must work in concert: genes that dictated the quality of human intelligence. She had been hunting her quarry for five years, and although she had isolated several likely candidates, there were gaps in the array. Adrienne was confident she would fill them; she knew the genes were out there. The human brain was formed according to the imperious logic of deoxyribonucleic acid; therefore, the limits and possibilities of the entire sea of thought must be genetically determined as well.

She glanced up from the ghostly images and reached for her juice.

It was a pleasant place to build a laboratory: isolated, shade-enshrouded, with the haunting call of owls at midnight and the scurry of hidden things in the undergrowth. She had never needed the stimulation of colleagues. Of a university campus. Not since she'd left Johns Hopkins with her doctorate three years ago, at the extraordinary age of twenty-two. Adrienne thrived on solitude and the uninterrupted world of thought; and Mlan's money—Mlan's limitless fund of gray cash from unknown sources and unquestioned motives, flooding electronically through front companies and numbered accounts—had made her world possible.

Now Mlan was dead.

She winced and thrust the thought away. She mourned him, of course—he was one of the few people in the world who could talk to her. They shared a common tongue. But Mlan had died the way he'd lived and he'd protected her to the last. No matter how many accounts the FBI froze, how many front companies Interpol unmasked, Mlan had given her the most marketable commodity of all: her career. He'd paid for the years of schooling, the internships in Switzerland, the breathlessly expensive equipment in this lab. Now she had her MacArthur Genius award. Her reputation. Her work.

If she ran out of funding she'd abandon Rochester and get a conventional researcher's job. But it would be a tug, for Misha as much as herself. Misha had never been suited to what was termed the real world.

"Mama," he called fretfully as though in answer to her thoughts, "I need turquoise. This blue is too red."

She jumped off the stool and walked swiftly across the floor he'd turned into a block mosaic, the delicate gradations of color so infinitely subtle they defied the eye's attempt to make sense of their transition. The movement of shades was like a shoal's path through a tropic sea. *Brilliant,* she thought. *So brilliant. None of them will ever know.*

They had told her when her son was four that he was a high-functioning autistic. He possessed a remarkable intelligence, certainly, but his obsessive absorption in

minute patterns, in the daily assembly of a perfectly
ordered world, was akin to a record needle caught in
a groove. Playing and replaying the same phrase of
sound. Arranging his blocks. Getting the order right.
He was adept with objects and numbers and facts, but
the world of emotion—the *human* world of love or pain
or laughter—was difficult for Misha to interpret or
understand. He could put his arms around Adrienne's
waist and squeeze them together perfunctorily; but if
he drew comfort or sustenance from the contact it was
impossible to say. *Therapy,* the experts had suggested.
Intervention. Adrienne had listened and nodded and
raged in her mind: *My son defies your petty conventions.*

She'd said nothing of it to the boy's father. She'd
told Mlan the good things: small glittering moments
that captured Misha's essence, dispatched in a variety
of e-mails around the world. If her son intended to
create and live in a closed universe only he could understand, she would give him that right. That freedom. She
despised all the categories the world could devise, except the ones she invented herself.

Where, she thought, would she go when the money
dried up? Stony Brook? CalTech? The Institute for
Advanced Studies? Falling over themselves to claim
her. No one had yet isolated "the smart genes," as she
called them; there was one team working desperately
in France and another in Japan conducting parallel research; but Adrienne was certain the map she was
drawing had only one name on it. *Hers.* She'd been
born for this. Her research would revolutionize world
culture. Not since the research of Watson and Crick

had science held such potential to redirect the course of human history.

"I'll find you turquoise," she said, and touched Misha briefly on the shoulder. He did not respond, did not look up, his entire soul focused on the small wooden chips he turned in his fingers.

When the truth breaks, she thought as she rummaged among the cans of oddments she kept stacked in the kitchen for just this purpose—*the truth that intelligence is programmed before birth like the color of your skin or your sex or the texture of your hair—the truth will change life as we know it.* Ostracize some people and elevate others. Spur genetic screening of fetuses for intellectual ability. These were the obvious consequences, of course, but she saw beyond that first wave to the far more destructive second: With the potential of genetic engineering and the will to pursue it, the possibilities were limitless. There would be selective breeding of smart-gene bearers. The systematic marketing of a race of genius. She could envision a world in which those who lacked smart genes would eventually be barred from bearing children—or eased naturally out of the reproductive process by their lack of attractive genetic material. The human race would finally control its own evolution: honing the powers of the brain in conscious ways to craft something far superior to the familiar biped animal.

It was for this that Mlan Krucevic had paid, time out of mind, until death do us part. For the right to be present at the creation. That the super race would come from a country that prided itself on individual freedom was ironic; that it would destroy those freedoms, and the government that enshrined them, was inevitable.

The car she'd heard a few moments ago was coming nearer. Aware of it suddenly, she raised her head from Misha's blocks and listened. The engine was neither tentative nor slow. The driver knew exactly where he was going and how to find her. Secretly, to herself, Adrienne smiled.

forty-six

They left him manacled even in solitary confinement. A deliberate effort to turn him into an animal, fumbling at his unshaved face and at the fly of his prison suit when he had to pee. He was a man who'd been trained in the psychology of interrogation, both as a Green Beret and a CIA case officer. He had been beaten by experts hired to break him. Had his mind probed by drugs and sadism until he'd raved. Had been confined, once, in a cement box small as a coffin for a month at a time. There had been days when he'd wished he was dead, and if offered the slightest implement of destruction would gladly have killed himself. Eric had explored his own vulnerabilities so intimately over the course of the past two decades that he knew exactly what he could not tolerate, and when it was coming.

Denied food, he turned vicious. Denied sleep, he spiraled rapidly into depression, which was far more dangerous. He had a high threshold for pain and feared physical torture less than mind-fucks. He could not endure the sight of pain inflicted on someone he loved.

Caroline, he thought. *They'll try to use Caroline to get to me.* She was the only person left in his world.

He gritted his teeth and strained once more at the chain connecting his handcuffs, although the effort was useless. *German steel,* he thought mordantly. *The best.* He had two doors out of the present situation: Succumb to Scottie's threats or fight him.

Live like you're going to die anyway and the choices get easier. *Scottie's a shit and I will not give him the satisfaction of answers to a single question. I will not. No matter how they use Caroline. It's all a game and she and I are just pieces now.*

He heard the entry door to the cell block clang open and the approaching thud of footsteps on concrete. More than one man, and no conversation among them. His skin prickled and he sat up on the cot, wrists clanking uselessly. If it was Scottie he would lunge for him and drive him screaming out of this hole with teeth marks in his neck. *This hole is mine, God damn it—*

A command in German: He was to stand away from the door. He waited, tensed to spring. But when the steel panel slid back, it was Wally he saw. Wally with the faint expression of a satyr above his good cloth coat, a diversion from the morning's trench. Wally with a small bag of peanuts in his hand.

Beware of spies bearing gifts, Eric thought. *As though I give a fuck for peanuts.*

"Eric," Wally said genially. "How're you keeping?"

Eric did not reply.

Wally stepped forward into the cell. They met in the exact center of the eight-by-five-foot room, a bare ten inches between them. Wally reached thoughtfully for a

peanut and began to crush the shells between his fingertips, the casings dry as old paper as they sifted to Eric's
floor.

"He's coming for you again," he said bluntly. "I
thought you should be prepared. He thinks if he keeps
questioning you into the night you'll reconsider your
level of cooperation. He says you're the kind of guy
who needs his sleep."

"He's wrong."

"Peanut?"

Eric shook his head tautly. The cell was wired for
sound and his image would already be broadcast to the
small screens in the main office, possibly for Scottie's
viewing pleasure, but he was angry at every one of
these people he'd loved—Wally and Cuddy and Scottie
himself, all of them possessed of Boy Scouts' names
and the morality to match. "What's in this for you,
Wally? Did he promise you another good posting? Or
just a payoff to your retirement account? Is he screw-
ing Brenda? Or one of your kids?"

A flicker in Wally's mild eyes at that: Part of Eric's
interrogation training was the mastery of fighting back;
he'd just used it on his old friend.

"Scottie likes threats," Wally answered. "I prefer to
beg. We need your help, Eric, and I'm here to ask for
it. We need your help to save innocent lives."

"The innocent die every day. People like Scottie live
forever. I want his blood and anybody who stands in
my way won't go home again. Understand?"

Wally broke open another peanut. The smooth
brown seeds slid easily between his pink lips; his jaws

worked rhythmically. "The drama's getting old," he said. "It's not the Eric I knew."

"That Eric was knifed to death."

Wally set the bag of peanuts on Eric's cot. "Do what Scottie asks. I'm telling you, it's for the best. And eat those nuts. They'll do you a world of good."

The station chief nodded once, a benevolent doctor who'd offered his spot of healing, and backed out of the cell. The waiting guard slid the door closed without a word.

Eric lifted his chained hands and swept the bag of nuts off the bed with a roar of anguish. They scattered like candy from a birthday piñata. He beat the shells to sawdust, the concrete floor of the cell thrusting back, reverberating through the flesh of his hands. The cuffs bit into his wrists and he welcomed the pain, welcomed an enemy he could face. And then, abruptly, he stopped. Hands poised in midair.

A fragment of paper with minuscule writing on it stared back at him from one of the shells.

Beware of spies bearing gifts.

He sank down and began to frantically piece together the shreds of Wally's message.

"*Sleeper, Tool,* and *Fist,*" Cuddy said as the mellow lights of the safe house glowed around them and Scottie paced indifferently across the room. "Thirty April code names. What do they mean?"

Eric frowned. "I sent you all that on a disc. The one Caroline brought home."

"Caroline brought nothing home," Scottie interrupted, "but the habit of posing as a hero. We learned about *Sleeper, Tool,* and *Fist* from . . . other sources. What can you add?"

"Do you mean to tell me you've done *nothing* about them?" Eric demanded, his voice rising. "*Christ*—I send you the key to the American cell—names, dates, operations—and you sit around diddling yourselves?"

The red ink on the polygraph printout jumped violently, a knife-peak of emotion scrawled the width of the page. Wally had slipped the rubber cap with the branching wires over Eric's finger himself before he'd been booted, along with Berlin station's polygrapher, out of the room. Scottie would allow no one but himself to interpret the truth. Only Cuddy remained.

"In the time-honored tradition of intelligence," he said now, "yes, we sat around diddling ourselves. You've said you're willing to cooperate, Eric, and though I'm surprised, I'd like you to pick up the pace. What do you *know*?"

Eric half rose from his seat. The movement was instinctively one of violence. The conference table was gone tonight; Scottie had intentionally given his victim a wide berth.

"Three years of my life were on that disc, asshole."

"Your wife's fault it never arrived, not mine." Scottie drew his gun from its holster. He leveled it at Eric's head. "*Sleeper, Tool,* and *Fist,* or I'll blow you out the back door."

The two men stared at each other. Neither moved except for the faint tremor of Scottie's hand on the butt of the gun, and for an instant Cuddy saw the willingness to die in Eric's eyes, the seductive power of refusal, and was terrified that all their planning and hope would be for nothing.

"They're the names of three network heads in the United States," Eric said. "The idea was to mount a multipronged attack against the U.S. infrastructure and demolish it from within. *Sleeper* is Adrienne O'Brien, a biologist Mlan Krucevic knew for years and left buried until now. She's the linchpin of a small group of influential people, well placed throughout the American academic and research community, who believe in better living through science and are willing to overthrow governments to achieve it. She was supposed to raise funds from like-minded members of the financial world and infiltrate the corporate and pharmaceutical nexus. Mlan communicated with her on a private basis, and much of her intelligence was never stored in his computers. He kept it locked in the safe of his own mind. Which suggests she's profoundly important."

"Bullshit," Scottie tossed off, his eye on the polygraph box. "You're making this up. For the sake of the tapes, I categorically state: *The source is fabricating.* Next?"

Tonight's conversation, like the one a few hours earlier, was being recorded, but Cuddy had been ordered to take notes. He was typing swiftly with a stylus into a palm-sized computer. "O'Brien. Any relation to Sophie Payne's staffer?"

"Daughter."

"Pure *shit,*" Scottie interpreted succinctly. "Utter

caca. Tell us who Fist is, Eric. The folks back home need a laugh."

"*Fist* is a killer by the name of Daniel Becker. Ex-soldier looking for another mission and willing to die for Mlan."

"Sniper?" Cuddy suggested.

"Could be. But not Special Forces; too wacked. Why?"

"Lucky guess," Scottie purred, "given that Dare Atwood had her head shot off. But please don't let the *facts* interrupt your narrative, Eric."

"Becker ran into 30 April in the woods a few years ago, before my time. He's a Tim McVeigh in the making: trained by the army and then thwarted in his career. Hates government in all its forms. The list of operations Mlan gave him is long. Suicide bombers dispatched to malls; the destruction of the northeast power grid and the Port of Long Beach. His job is to recruit martyrs and spread panic."

The memory of Dare Atwood's shattered skull, the glass and blood scattered over the Oriental carpet, and the dog's lacerated paws—Cuddy punched in Daniel Becker's name and thought: *He took aim over my shoulder while he crouched in the garden.*

"Fist's role is terror," Eric said quietly, "but *Tool* is a more subtle animal altogether. Mlan understood something fundamental about Americans: If we read something in the paper or see it on TV, we tend to believe it's true. We rarely question our sources, so their power is absolute."

"Tool's a journalist?" Cuddy asked quickly.

Eric's eyes flicked toward his. "He covered the war

in Bosnia and was embedded with a militia leader for a good while. Thirteen months ago he flew from D.C. to Prague and interviewed Mlan at a 30 April safe house. No cameras permitted; just a pad and pen. He printed his profile in the *Post* and probably received a Pulitzer. But Mlan's real orders weren't in the newspaper. Tool's job is to undermine public faith in government by questioning political motives and methods at every opportunity. Particularly once Fist's panic hits."

Personally, Cuddy heard himself advising Caroline, *I'd use the power of the pen for all it's worth.*

"Fucking hell," he said out loud. "You aren't talking about Steve Price?"

forty-seven

It was the look in his eyes that made her tumble to the truth: the flat, alien, inchoate hatred she hadn't glimpsed while they'd chased leads together. The hatred was direct and personal, as shocking as a flood of icy water. Caroline had seen that kind of look before: in the eyes of Mlan Krucevic. Price meant to kill her.

His right hand snaked out and tore the latex from her cheekbone. She flung her left arm over the seat, scrabbling for her purse and the Walther she'd tucked inside.

But the man beside her grabbed her wrist in the vise of his fingers and jammed on the brakes. The car screeched to a halt on the lonely mountain road.

"You think you're so goddamn tough," he was shouting. *"You think you can kill a man and call it justice."*

With her free hand she tried to open the car door. He'd locked it automatically.

And if she ran into the woods?

He'd hunt her down and leave her body for some lost hiker to find, in another decade.

Tom, she thought despairingly. Why hadn't she told him the truth about where she was? She brought her left knee up and kicked out hard at Price's groin. He grunted, took the blow, and smashed his fist into her face.

Her nose shattered. She cried out at the pain. He was bending her left wrist backward—the fingers that had reached for her gun—and the pressure was unbearable, force applied to a frail twig.

Her wrist would snap.

She hurled herself forward, her teeth sinking into his forearm; and with a guttural howl his grip relaxed.

She scrabbled for the handle, desperate to get away from him, her breath coming in tearing gasps.

His fist fell like a mallet on the bullet wound in her right shoulder.

Once, twice, three times—

There was nowhere for her to go. The agony was a cloud, blotting out all light from her brain. She struggled and saw his fist raised again.

Her shoulder exploded. She felt the shock ripple through her body.

Then nothing more.

The Greyhound bus station in Erie, Pennsylvania, sits on Route 19 between Davis and Beibel Avenues. It is neither a new nor particularly attractive building. Not far to the west is a shopping center bound by the interstate. The parking lot of the Millcreek Mall had become the FBI's staging ground for hostage rescue, a good five hundred yards across the street from Daniel Becker's fortified position. They had to assume he was armed with his sniper's rifle and scope. They had to keep a proper distance.

A rolling carnival, Tom thought as his chopper set down in the wide grass median wedged between the interstate and the shopping mall, *with a roving band of players.* Maybe an hour had passed since he'd taken the Bureau's call and heard the name of Erie, yet the parking lot was filled with vehicles and people. He picked out the field agents first, in their black bomber jackets with *FBI* emblazoned on the back; local uniformed cops and sheriffs; squad cars pulled up with lights flashing and sirens muted; law enforcement RVs; portable water tanks for the Pennsylvania National Guardsmen; paramedics in jumpsuits. Television crews. Vans with satellite dishes. Victims' Assistance reps. Public relations people. Photographers. Reporters with ring-bound notebooks and laptop computers. There would be snipers working for the Good Guys, too, taking up position in a cordon around the bus station with their walkietalkies and their tripods and their lethal slugs. Professionally trained hostage negotiators employed by the Bureau and the local police jockeying for positions at the mike. Religious chaplains of various orders, in case Daniel Becker asked to be absolved of his sins in his final moments. A S.W.A.T. team suiting up in Kevlar somewhere offstage, just in case. Hundreds of people.

And none of them was Caroline.

At the thought of her—which sprang, unbidden, into his tired mind—Shephard winced. He'd done his best to distance the woman who'd haunted him across two continents, tried not to dwell on the fact that she was walking a Long Island beach right now, happily beyond the fray, while he was single-handedly trying to keep all hell from breaking loose. He was hurt and betrayed and furious at Caroline Carmichael but he missed her acutely: missed the swift cut of her mind, her deep knowledge of the enemy. Missed her courage. She was the strongest woman he'd ever known. And the most vulnerable. Was it the combination of the two that had bewitched him?

What if there was more to her story than deliberate deceit and criminal misconduct and possible collusion with the worst terrorist group operating on U.S. soil? What if, God forbid, he'd misjudged her?

Fuck Caroline, he thought savagely. *She's married anyway.* He jumped out of the chopper.

He moved crablike in his rotor-crouch toward the edge of the lot. A clutch of bodies detached themselves from the general mass and started sprinting toward him. *Reporters. Didn't I just see these guys in Wheeling? Or was that in D.C.? I don't remember.*

"Tom Shephard," he said as the first body reached him—a woman in a black jumpsuit. "Thirty April Task Force."

"Good to see you." She extended her hand. "Lindy Asbill. Special Agent in Charge, Pittsburgh. Becker's been positively identified by local police—caught his face in a scope not ten minutes ago. He's got maybe fifteen people in there, we can't be sure, and there are reports of casualties."

"How many?"

"At least one dead in the main station area and more shots fired. We have no specifics; Becker refuses to answer the negotiator's hail."

They were walking toward the tight knot of technical equipment and figures ranged near a mobile police support unit set up opposite the bus station.

"He won't answer the hail?" Tom repeated. "Let me try."

It'd been nearly two hours since he'd killed the woman behind the ticket window and Daniel was running out of ideas. He'd hoped the bus for Pittsburgh would pull in before the news got out but no buses came, no behemoth rolled with a belch and a squeal of air brakes under the great outdoor portico behind the station. He'd been close to making it, but now the Zionist Occupation Government was closing in. *I have faith, Lord, and I am Your Instrument and if You intend to gather me up I will take the Unclean with me.*

He had forced his hostages against the plate glass windows facing the circus across the street so they could be seen and counted. He'd offered each a chance to join the Overthrow, to take the only stand with honor in the End Times, but one of the guys had hawked and spat and the fat mother of the little girl started to scream. Now they slumped, faces pressed against the glass, while he trained his scope over their heads.

I'm only one man, Lord, he thought as he swept the vehicles and enforcement personnel with that curious intimacy of the high-powered lens, *and yet see how they fear me.*

"Daniel," a voice croaked behind him. "Daniel, where are we?"

Without moving the barrel of his gun he glanced

over his shoulder and saw the boy—saw Mlan's son,
sitting up in the hard waiting-room seat. His face was
dead white against the orange plastic and his eyes
stared blankly from hollow sockets.

"Erie," he said. "Greyhound. We're not goin' any-
wheres much for a piece."

The boy surveyed the gun and the dozen terrified
souls pressed against the station window, and a furrow
of puzzlement cut his brow. "I don't feel very well."

"DANIEL BECKER!"

The amplified voice split the air of the bus station
like the trumpet of God.

"DANIEL, THIS IS TOM SHEPHARD, FBI. THIS IS THE
END OF THE LINE, DANIEL. THERE'S NO WALKING OUT
OF THAT PLACE ALIVE, BUDDY, UNLESS YOU TALK TO US
FIRST. IF YOU'VE GOT A PHONE OR CAN REACH ONE
INSIDE, I'D LIKE YOU TO CALL THIS NUMBER."

A stream of meaningless digits followed. Daniel ignored them. The megaphone paused to give him time
to react, to reach out and touch someone. Jozsef
stood up and took a hesitant step toward the window.

"I SAW YOUR PLACE IN HILLSBORO, DANIEL, OR WHAT'S
LEFT OF IT. YOU MUST BE IN CONSIDERABLE PAIN. FIRST
DOLF KILLED, NOW BEKAH. YOU CAN MAKE THE KILLING
STOP, DANIEL. YOU CAN MAKE THAT CHOICE. NOBODY
ELSE CAN."

He stared coolly down his rifle. *Motherfucking Fed
trying to get all friendly. Only one's gonna die is him.*

One of the hostages let out a sob.

"Daniel." Jozsef tugged on the seat of his pants. "I
need a doctor."

"WE'D LIKE TO SEND A MEMBER OF THE AMERICAN

RED CROSS OVER TO THE DOOR TO TALK TO YOU,
DANIEL. WE NEED TO VERIFY THE STATUS OF THE INDI-
VIDUALS PINNED DOWN INSIDE THE BUILDING. WILL
YOU TALK TO THE RED CROSS? CALL THAT NUMBER AND
LET US KNOW."

Again, the stream of digits.

"Kid," Daniel hissed, "take this and keep it trained
on the sheep." He pulled his automatic pistol from inside his jacket and handed it to the boy. Trusting him
like he'd trust Dolf to back up his daddy when times
got tough. He didn't have to ask if Jozsef knew how to
shoot. He'd been raised by the Leader, for Chrissake.

"DANIEL, WE'RE ASKING YOU TO LET THE WOMEN
AND CHILDREN GO WITH THE RED CROSS. YOU LET
THEM GO, DANIEL, AND WE'LL TAKE THAT AS A SIGN OF
GOOD FAITH. YOU LET THEM GO, AND WE'LL HAVE A
BASIS FOR TALKING TO YOU. UNDERSTAND?"

He watched a guy with slick blond hair and an ap-
prehensive expression step forward beyond the mass
of people and megaphones, waving a white flag bi-
sected by a red cross. In the crosshairs of the scope,
Daniel saw him swallow hard. *Nervous as shit,* he
thought. *Let's give him somethin' to worry about.*

"DANIEL," said the voice of God, "WE'RE SENDING
MARK TARNOW OF THE RED CROSS TO TALK TO YOU.
WE'LL HOLD OUR FIRE."

You can hold whatever the fuck you like, Daniel
thought as he chambered his round. *Why don'tcha
hold it between your knees.* He followed the chicken-
shit named Mark as he waved his silly little flag all the
way across the street. He remembered Red Cross types

from Bosnia. Always crying in their beer about atrocities and whatnot. Mourning the deaths of civilians.
The quality of the drinking water, for Pete's sake. He
hated the namby-pamby bleeding-heart liberals who
couldn't hold a gun to save their lives but could lecture a man about the Geneva Conventions until he
was ready to scream.

"DANIEL, WE'RE ASKING YOU TO CALL US NOW."

He let Mark cross Route 19 and set his foot on the
curb before he caught the dick right between the eyes.

forty-eight

Josie had chosen the Austrian Steyr because it was ideal for a woman. Empty and without its scope, it weighed only eight pounds. The cheek piece and butt plate were adjustable and could fit almost any size shooter; the stock was synthetic with an integrated bipod. It took a .223 Remington magazine of five rounds. She didn't expect to need more than one.

She was oiling the gun now, although it had been clean when she stowed it in her luggage the day before. The rhythm of preparation was important; routine calmed the nerves. And Josie's nerves were jumping.

When she'd reached beneath the low-lying mattress in the Kurfürstendammer Hof two hours ago, the touch of the heavy contour barrel lying undisturbed had sent a wave of relief crashing through her gut. The sneak thief had tracked her down and entered her room and felt among her panties, but he hadn't discovered the gun. She'd drawn it out into the light muttering a prayer of thanks to Patrick and all his saints; and then she'd sat down abruptly on the floor. A second slip of paper, wrapped around the scope. She'd read it immediately, hating him—whoever he was.

Your man was set up. He never saw it coming. Ask Scottie what he needed to hide.

It was this second note that sent her packing, sent her off on foot with the carpetbag and her suitcase in the persistent German rain, spooked to the core. Two underground trains and a taxi later she'd fetched up in Kreuzberg, on the outskirts of the old East German airport, in a dingy hotel she figured nobody could find. Except her former employer, who was hunting her now.

Nobody but a Company guy could connect Mary Devlin to Josie O'Halloran. Nobody but a Company guy would have access to all the right files and the history to make sense of them. For most people at the CIA those twilight days in Bogotá, before the drug cartels and the unaccompanied tours and the safe zones inside the embassy, were a different century. She was being hunted by someone who knew her as intimately as Scottie did; and for the life of her, Josie had no idea who it was.

If they know who I am and they know about the gun, then they know why I'm here. I'm being set up, too. Just like Patrick.

As she rubbed the oily rag, smelling comfortingly of gun ranges and certainty and .5 groupings, she asked herself one question. *Why had they telegraphed the punch?* If she was being sent out like a lamb to Scottie's slaughter, why let her know that fact? Why attempt to save her? She had lived in the black world too long to believe in the kindness of strangers.

They don't want me to reach the target, she thought suddenly, and set down the rag. *They're trying to scare me away.* This was indeed possible but the idea was also somewhat pathetic: her last attempt to put Scottie back up on his pedestal. To trust and believe in his good faith. The truth was, she was blown. She'd been offered a warning to leave before she died just like Patrick.

Sheila and the boys would be just fine. She'd taken care of them all in her will, and there was enough money to make certain they never had to worry. But Josie wasn't ready to die. She loved the small things of her existence too much: the sharp fresh smell of brine in the mornings, the cheerful sight of Mike and his delivery truck. The tinkle of the customer bell over her shop door. The possibility of a plane flight and a different adventure just around the corner.

Ask Scottie what happened in Bogotá that night.

She folded the oiled rag in neat squares and stored it in a plastic Baggie. The Steyr was beautiful, resting across the arms of the hotel room's occasional chair; she resisted the impulse to stroke it. She had a decision to make.

"You turned Caroline over to 30 April?"

Eric was staring at him, appalled, and Cuddy felt panic rise in his throat.

"I didn't know," he faltered. "The files in the disc you sent were blank. Encrypted somehow. Or designed to erase whenever the wrong person opened them. We had no idea—"

"So you *did* get the disc," Eric insisted, his face bone-white. "How many other lies have you told me tonight?"

"I'll call the FBI." Cuddy reached for his cell. "There's a guy who'll help her—"

"It's too late for that! She's been in Tool's hands for twenty-four hours! You really think she's still alive?"

"There's always a chance."

"Wait, Wilmot." Scottie stepped forward, his hand suddenly on Cuddy's wrist. "Don't make that call. Not *yet*."

"Don't fuck with me, Scottie," Eric said warningly. "I told you what you wanted to know."

"But you didn't sign your confession," he returned genially. "And I'm afraid that's more important right now than the . . . *fate* . . . of your wife."

Cuddy stared at his boss. "Are you nuts? This is Caroline we're talking about, Scottie."

He shrugged. "She's probably already dead. Whereas my future is very much at issue. The confession, Wilmot, if you please."

Eric brought his cuffed hands to his face. "I'll kill you, Scottie. With my bare hands. *Nobody uses Caroline to get to me.*"

"But, Eric," Scottie reminded him gently, "we always have. From the very beginning. Wilmot?"

Cuddy set down the cell phone and reached woodenly into his briefcase. *It's a simple thing. A way to pass him the pen. For God's sake Eric don't blow it now.*

He passed the single sheet of paper to his boss. Scottie scanned the words he knew by heart—for effect, for the theater of the thing. He might have been a masterful tragedian, Cuddy thought, had he never gone black.

" 'I, Eric Carmichael, deliberately and without the knowledge of my superiors betrayed the government and the people of the United States by voluntarily joining the terrorist organization known as 30 April, dedicating my life to the late Mlan Krucevic . . . did willingly and knowingly execute the kidnapping and murder of Sophie Payne . . . atrocities and criminal activity throughout Europe designed to undermine democratic order . . .' That seems to be about right. Sign it, Eric. The sooner you do, the sooner Wilmot makes his rescue call."

There was a pause. Eric at bay, all the hatred and pain of the past three years blazing in his eyes.

Then he shuffled backward two steps and sank into his chair.

Cuddy placed Raphael's unexceptionable pen between his aching fingers. And watched while he wrote his life away.

forty-nine

"Misha, I'm going to be busy for a while," Adrienne said as she stood in the doorway of her son's room. "I've left your snack on the table. You can listen to your music or play on the computer. I'll check on you later."

He neither looked at her nor replied, his dark head bowed intently over the notebook in his lap. It would be numbers, Adrienne thought; a logical sequence mounting into the millions. He'd been building it for days, the figures etched neatly over page after page of lined paper, a staircase in his mind that mounted to infinity.

She pulled the door gently closed and threw the bolt. Only Misha's room could be locked from the outside—and his windows, large panes that flooded the room with light, were similarly sealed. Adrienne could not allow him certain freedoms. Lost in the ordered labyrinth of thought, Misha might wander while she worked. Require outside help to find his way back. And then the perfect isolation would be broken. Questions asked. Government people tramping through the underbrush. *Her son taken from her.*

She smoothed her hair, caught back in elastic, and turned away from the silence beyond the closed door.

"I didn't expect you," she said to Steve Price as she walked into the room that served as both sitting area and laboratory. He was still standing with a hot wet towel pressed against the bite marks in his arm; the woman lay in a heap where he'd dragged her across the threshold. "I don't want this kind of thing in my house. I have a child. You shouldn't have come."

He dabbed at the ugly punctures in his forearm, scowling. "She was going to find you. I did the best I could to contain the damage."

"You led her here."

"Your father sent her here. He told her everything he knew last night."

She took a step backward, unbalanced for a second. *Daddy? He doesn't have the slightest idea where I live.*

Her professor father with the kindly, distant smile, the mind always lost in research. Her father's hand smoothing her hair.

How does he know where I am?

"Have you got any rope? Some kind of tape?" Price demanded. "She'll come around in a sec and I don't want her moving."

She didn't ask what he intended to do with the woman. She simply turned on her heel and went into her bedroom, which sat near Misha's off the back hallway. They shared the bath. That and a galley kitchen running along one side of the lab were the sum total of the house. The strapping tape lay on a shelf in her closet where she kept the necessary things she carted once a month from Rochester, twenty-nine miles down the winding mountain road. She had never used it.

She watched while Price wound the sticky plastic stuff over the woman's mouth. The blond hair was trapped in the adhesive and the skin below the smashed nose was puffed and bruised. As Price worked, the woman's eyes fluttered open and a faint sound of protest came from deep in her throat. He moved on to the wrists, pulling them behind the back and taping them tightly together so that the flesh below the bond immediately went dead white from lack of circulation.

"Someone will be looking for her," Adrienne said.

"I'm telling you, they won't." He slid the tape expertly under the woman's ankles, trussing her like a Christmas turkey. "I'm the only one who knows where she is. Her guardian angel."

"Who is she?"

He looked up, surprised, a satiric glint in his eye. He had expected her to know.

"Caroline Carmichael. The CIA agent who killed Mlan."

While Adrienne prepared the hypodermic, Price talked quickly, filling in the details of the past three days. She never watched television and she relied on her electronic sources for relevant information: the e-mails and text messages relayed from around the world. Price was one of those sources. He communicated with her once a week. Only eight days ago, it was he who'd broken the news of Mlan's murder to her.

It was the first time he'd tracked Adrienne to her lab, however, and the presumption nettled her. His presence was a threat, a bludgeoning reminder of how much he knew. How much damage he could do.

"Fist is blown," he said as she punctured the seal on the glass vial, "and he's got Jozsef with him. The two of them have left a string of bodies up and down the East Coast and the entire world is hunting them down. We have to consider them lost."

She frowned as she watched the yellow liquid swirl into the hypodermic chamber, then depressed the needle until drops spurted from the tip. "And you want to know what else is lost." It was a statement, not a question.

"I think that's vital, don't you? If we're to go on?"

The image of a sand castle sitting high on a beach came into Adrienne's mind. The waves advancing, the water licking at the base, the fragile sand eroding. *Fist and Jozsef given up.* Misha's brother. Mlan's son. But there was the castle, the towers she had built: and the tide advancing. This woman—the contents of her head—could turn back disaster.

"You *do* want to go on?"

"There is no other choice," she answered.

He had no power to touch her, Steve Price—she would never again be the soul or body of a man—but she found she could appreciate the fact that he remained calm. Adrienne was the picture of cerebral science in her white coat and latex gloves; but behind her

impassive face her mind was seething. *This woman.
Killed Mlan. Cut him down like a beast in the dirt, fed
him to the mob. This woman will destroy everything that
matters.*

"Give me her arm."

Caroline Carmichael was conscious now, her eyes
wary as they approached. She lay on the floor, the right
shoulder of her black sweater soaked with what might
be blood. *She'll soon,* Adrienne thought, *pass out again.*
She would be growing weak.

Price rolled her over without mercy onto the re-
opened wound. Again the guttural animal noises came
from behind the suffocating tape.

"You'll have to cut the sleeve off," Adrienne told
him. "There's a lab scalpel under the sterilizing lights."

He found what he needed and sawed deftly at the
cashmere. She supposed his handiness came from surviving in war zones, the natural efficiency of the foreign correspondent; but it had been years since Price
had left Washington, and she doubted he could handle
a gun. Mlan had trained Adrienne as he'd trained his
son Jozsef: to survive. She had no religion other than
science, but like Daniel Becker she lived for the End
Times. She intended to build whatever lay beyond
them.

She tied a rubber strip around the woman's bicep,
found the vein, and slid the needle in. The drug pumped
almost instantly to the heart and then to the brain.
Thiopental sodium: in high doses, a general anesthetic
that depressed the central nervous system, slowed the
heart rate, and lowered blood pressure. In smaller doses,

truth serum. Weakened by blood loss as she was, Caroline Carmichael would find it impossible to fight.

"In a few seconds she should start to talk," Adrienne told Steve Price. "And when she's done, we kill her."

fifty

"All right," Tom Shephard said as he stared across the lifeless body of Mark Tarnow, "if he won't come out, we'll have to go in and get him. How many people we got in position, Lindy?"

"Four police snipers set up in a three-sixty radius around the station ready to cover any team we can send. The Erie chief has offered his S.W.A.T. personnel, but I'm inclined to use our guys. It's a question of time."

Our guys, Tom thought, would be a full-scale HRT deployment—the FBI's Hostage Rescue Team. That meant roughly fifty snipers and attack personnel, field tents, an MD-530 Little Bird for overhead surveillance, and pilots to fly it. Remote control surveillance robots. Day guns and night guns. The potential for a standoff to spiral out of control exactly as it had at Ruby Ridge and Waco.

Shephard knew and liked at least three of the highly trained members of HRT, and there was nobody he'd rather have at his back if *he* were the one trying to walk toward Daniel Becker across five hundred yards of naked firing range. But Becker didn't care who he killed and he didn't have much to live for. He'd know the odds he was facing—know he was surrounded—know it was just a matter of time.

"He'll take everybody in that building with him," Shephard said.

"We can't know that."

"We can. And it's HRT the world will blame." He looked steadily at Lindy, at the soft blond hair and the hard blue eyes. They were roughly equal in grade and experience, he guessed, but he had the clout of Headquarters behind him.

"Are you playing politics, Tom?" she demanded. "There's a toddler in there!"

"I'm *considering* politics. Absolutely. The Bureau's already taking heat for the massacre at the Marine Corps. We've got an assassination of the country's highest intelligence official and at least six murders along the way. Becker's a dead man, Lindy. We all know that. It's just a matter of how he dies: alone or in a bloodbath. Nothing we do should contribute to the human cost."

"And you think turning this mess over to local police is going to *save* somebody?"

"I think the sooner we move, the better." His cell phone was jangling "The Star Spangled Banner." "It'll take HRT twelve hours to load gear and get over here. We don't have twelve hours. Shephard!"

Lindy opened her mouth, hesitated, shut it again.

"Shit!" Tom exploded into the phone. "Why can't Caroline fucking Carmichael stay *out* of this?"

•   •   •

Inside the bus station, blood was beginning to pool on the tiles from the corpses Daniel had left there, and Jozsef was slumped on the waiting-room bench, his cheeks flushed with fever and the automatic pistol dangling from his hand. The toddler was wailing steadily and her mother kept asking if she could use the bathroom. Daniel shook his head. "Won't be long now. Just sit tight."

The woman's face crinkled like a punctured balloon; she was crying without a sound.

Some of the men were whispering among themselves and Daniel didn't like it. He knew they were talking about things and trying to figure out whether they had the balls or the brawn to take him, but they'd seen what the M16 could do and there weren't enough heroes in the world to go up against that rifle alone.

Two of the hostages, a kid of maybe twenty and a pregnant black girl who clung to his hand, were still staring out at the body of the Red Cross weenie sprawled at the edge of the parking lot. Nobody from the other side had had the guts to brave Daniel's crossfire to retrieve the corpse. It figured, Daniel thought. No honor among thieves.

He was feeling bone-shakingly tired and he had only two spare magazines in his backpack. That and the remaining bullets in the gun meant he had just enough ammo to finish off the people in front of him and head out the door with Jozsef, gun raised. The death would be quick and he'd die knowing they hadn't taken him in this hole. He hated being trapped, cornered and gunned down like a rat in a drain; and the sick air of the bus station—diesel, urine, sweat, and fear—was sapping his ability to think. Now he'd shot their messenger, they'd know what kind of man they were dealing with. They would be coming for him soon. He intended to beat them to the punch.

He was trained enough in tracking and surveillance to know where the guns and the scopes would be. Even the roof was just another place to die.

Dolf, son, I'm coming now, he thought. And barked out the last order.

"Everybody up against those windows. Right now, you hear?"

Jozsef had slumped down in his seat, the coolness of the plastic little relief against the raging heat of his body. He had lived through the cycles of his father's disease—a genetically altered form of anthrax—often enough to know that he didn't have much conscious time left. He was trying to hold on to the thoughts that skittered through his brain, because Daniel was dangerous now; the boy could feel violence coming off the man in waves. If only his vision were not swimming, if only he could focus better on what Daniel was doing. There had been the gunfire out in the street, and the screams from those stuck in front of them like cattle; and then a strange lull. Daniel doing what passed for thinking, Jozsef decided.

He could not keep his eyes open. He wanted nothing so much as the clean hospital sheets and the quivering cubes of green Jell-O.

Everybody up against those windows.

He mentally translated the barked words and the finality in them, heard the whimpering sobs of the woman and her little girl. It was all a part of the recurring nightmare he had lived since he could walk, the guns and the bloodshed and the ideals. He was so very tired of men and guns.

But he forced himself upright from the chair, his body wavering on his feet.

Daniel had raised his rifle and leveled it at the pregnant young woman, who cringed against her boyfriend's arm. Closing her eyes on the trigger finger.

I never asked to be rescued, Jozsef thought. *But my father believed in this man. Trusted him with his life.*

Both hands on the butt to steady it before his swimming eyes, slowly and deliberately Jozsef raised the automatic pistol.

fifty-one

Cuddy Wilmot kept the BKA van in his headlights as the highway split and curled in on itself, curving north and east. He was sitting in the back of a black Ford Explorer, Scottie shuttered and silent beside him, Wally in the front seat next to the driver. As they left the suburbs behind, they plunged into Charlottenburg, the leafy and privileged quarter of western diplomats and retired cold warriors. Then the Moabit area, the embassy car crawling steadily through the traffic on Invalidenstrasse, skirting the northern edge of Berlin's Mitte District. And finally, twenty-three minutes after they'd locked the door of the safe house behind them and thrust a furious Eric Carmichael into the pit of an armored van, Wally's driver came to a stop at the intersection of Eberswalderstrasse. St.-Elisabeth's hospital and the isolation cells lay just beyond.

They had followed the pink route, Cuddy thought, on Raphael's map; but that hopeful conversation a few hours ago seemed like a scene from a 1930s movie. *Caroline is gone and everything is changed. I threw her to the wolves.*

He had tried to reach Steve Price on his cell phone—

tried to get an answer at the *Post* or the man's apartment. He'd called Caroline's cell and Uncle Hank in Long Island and he'd even called her voice mail at the CIA, which nobody had yet thought to disconnect. And in the end, because it was the only thing left to do, he'd called Tom Shephard.

Why can't Caroline fucking Carmichael stay out of this?

Tom didn't trust Caroline and he was still nursing yesterday's grudge. Up to his neck in hostages and shooters, he told Cuddy bluntly that Caroline had given her Bureau watchers the slip. She had only herself to thank if she died. Tom had other lives to save.

Cuddy didn't believe Tom's brutal pose and he spared Eric the details as they hustled him out of the safe house. "Shephard will pass on our tip to his task force," he said carefully. "That's the most we can hope for. We've got no fix on Price's location right now."

Eric's face was white and haunted, but Cuddy was sure he'd kept Raphael's pen between his cupped fingers after signing Scottie's confession. Cuddy watched the back of the van all the way from the Grunewald as though a miracle might happen, but they were a hundred yards from the end of Raphael's pink-highlighter route and the armored truck was still sealed.

The strip of traffic lights changed from red to yellow and then to green. The van eased into its left turn, taking its time. Cuddy leaned forward, and at that instant the embassy driver cried out, *"Jesus!"*

It happened in a millisecond: the bright yellow Humvee careening across two lanes of traffic, smashing the right fender of the armored van and wedging it force-fully into the curb. A leggy blonde threw open her door and stepped out onto the rain-wet street, furious and fearless, stalking right up to the armored truck's windows as she screamed her German obscenities. A lit cigarette dangled from her left hand; with her right, she tried to pound the nearest guard's face.

"Fuck," Scottie burst out. "What the *fucking* hell—"

"Try to go around," Wally told his driver calmly, and with a snort, the man hauled on the Explorer's wheel.

Cuddy's pulse was throbbing painfully. He could recognize Raphael from thirty paces, even if Scottie couldn't. *There isn't much time. Shit, Eric, get out of there—*

The armored truck's doors flew wide and Eric stood in the headlights, cuffs and manacles gone.

The embassy Explorer jammed to a halt.

Scottie scrabbled for his door handle. His other hand held his gun.

Cuddy shouted, *"Eric, run!"*

Thirty April's last man standing jumped to the ground. Over the open car door, Scottie leveled his weapon. Eric tore around the truck toward the Humvee; and at that moment, as Cuddy watched, he stuttered in midstep, his arms arching wide.

Staggering.

Falling.

Clutching at the pavement with his hands.

Pulling himself across the rain-wet asphalt with a dark flower of blood blooming through his jumpsuited back, until he collapsed suddenly with his face in the street.

Cuddy was yelling his name and running through the downpour, away from the protection of the embassy car and Scottie standing amazed with his weapon unfired in his hand, away from Wally screaming at him to *get down,* toward the leggy blonde with the terrible expression of sorrow on her face and the man lying as though dead, three yards from freedom.

fifty-two

It was the woman with the little girl who'd memorized the digits of the phone number Tom Shephard had boomed out over the megaphone, and she shouted them in an agonized voice over the screams of her terrified daughter as Daniel Becker lay on the floor, staring at the ceiling. Two of the hostages had raced to pin him down when he fell, while a third vaulted the ticket-seller's window and grabbed the phone.

Jozsef stood alone. The pistol dangled from his right hand until his nerveless fingers released and the gun clattered to the floor. He sank down onto his knees, whimpering, spent, no longer looking at the man he'd dropped with a single bullet. The slug's impact had done something to Daniel's legs; perhaps the spinal cord was severed. Blood was pooling beneath his body on the dirty linoleum floor, and his lips were moving soundlessly.

Jozsef was trembling from fever. He'd committed what his father would consider the greatest gesture of cowardice: He'd shot a man in the back without offering a fair fight. He did not regret Daniel lying on the floor. He linked his fingers together and dipped his forehead down. He wanted nothing more than to rest. The little girl wouldn't stop wailing.

The man on the phone was talking urgently now and Jozsef caught a few of the English words.

"*...shot by that kid he brought with him...ambulance...two dead here and people pretty messed up... disarmed the guy...don't shoot if they walk out...*"

With a shout somebody unlocked the main station door, and the first to leap forward were the little girl and her mother, both of them sobbing hysterically as they staggered into the flashbulbs and the surging police and the Victims' Assistance representatives and the paramedics in their brightly colored clothes. Jozsef slid slowly sideways until his cheek touched the cool linoleum; his eyes closed. In the babble of voices and noise he heard a different kind of ending. *Lady Sophie,* he thought, *why did you have to die? We were going to live together. Now there is no one. What do they do in America to boys who kill?*

Tom Shephard found him there in the empty station waiting room, barely conscious and dreaming, while the Instrument of the Lord's Vengeance mouthed the word *dishonor* as his life swiftly bled away.

"Gerry," Candace O'Brien said.

She was standing outside his office door, almost humbly waiting in the line of students who brought their questions and difficulties to him for resolution two afternoons a week.

Professor, I'm having trouble with the organic chemistry assignment.

I just don't think I deserved a C on the midterm, Professor.

That T.A. is openly sexist. He said girls don't "get" science, Professor.

Professor, where did we go wrong all those years ago? How did our beautiful child end up alone on her perilous trip down to the Underworld?

He was struck, as he gazed at the woman he persisted in thinking of as his wife, at how nakedly she carried her suffering. Candace had never been interested in hiding things. It was he who'd thought it best to send Adrienne away while she brought the child to term, as she'd insisted on doing. He who'd tried to pretend for the benefit of his peers that his daughter was spending her junior year of high school abroad. Candace had wilted under the burden of pretense. Curling inward on herself, she'd withdrawn from him more each day. Until here she stood, the most familiar of strangers.

He gestured her inside. She closed the door gently behind her but did not take the seat he offered.

"I told them everything today," she explained. "About Adrienne. Where she lives, and how. I had to tell them, Gerry, but I thought you ought to know."

"Them?" he repeated blankly. "But who are *they*?"

"The FBI."

He sank down into his desk chair, removed his glasses, rubbed at his eyes. "Oh, *God,* Candace. What were you thinking? The FBI is after her?"

"I guess. Yes."

He stared at Candace in the unfocused way of the

nearsighted. "But what has she done?—other than live in the purest way possible for the sake of her research?"

"It's more a question of what she intends to do, Gerry."

He looked away from her, his mind racing. "Could I stop them? If I tried to explain? Is there someone I could talk to?"

"But what can you explain?"

"How young she was. How intelligent, and how vulnerable."

"She's not a little girl anymore. She had the brains to choose differently. Those choices were not made by *us*."

"No," he conceded bitterly. "She made them alone. She had to."

All the unresolved quarrels of their last months of marriage blazed in the silence between them—his need to excuse every flaw in his daughter for the sake of her promise; Candace's insistence that even genius should be balanced with humanity. *Adrienne is dangerous,* she'd argued, *because her intellect is ruthless. She has no pity, Gerry. Nothing close to love.*

"There's still the boy," she said at last. The words hung in the air.

"The boy? You mean . . . Misha?"

"If Adrienne is taken into custody . . . I thought . . ."

"That we could step in? Get a second chance at parenthood?" He barked with laughter, amazed at the simplicity of her mind. "You can't redeem one life with another, Candace. There *are* no second chances. Adrienne knows that—and so do I."

•   •   •

The thiopental sodium worked almost instantly, but it wore off with equal swiftness and the process of getting answers to their urgent questions was slow. Caroline Carmichael talked without hesitation, but she offered up the contents of her mind unedited. Adrienne began with simple things: questions about CTC's structure and operational methods, how the CIA tracked Mlan for years in Europe when his face had never once been photographed. How they'd managed to find his bunker in Budapest and the last spider hole south of Sarajevo. All the words and memories boiled down to one theme: a man Caroline called Eric.

Adrienne sat while the love and hope and raw fear tumbled from the woman's dry lips, no emotion visible in her dilated eyes. For a scientist like herself to witness the degree of emotion harbored in a brain was distinctly troubling. The brain was the seat of thought. The analytic control center. A machine as precise and mapped as a computer, the data stored in neat compartments. This torrent of feeling was impossible to reconcile with a thinking organ.

"Who knows you're here?"

"Just Cuddy. He gave me to Price."

"Will Cuddy come after you?"

"Cuddy's in Berlin!"

"What have you told Cuddy?"

"To ask Eric."

"Ask Eric what?"

"About Sleeper, Tool, and Fist."

Adrienne tensed. "Where did you hear those names?"

"They're on the disc."

"What disc?"

"*Eric*'s disc."

Adrienne glanced at Price. He was frowning.

"Her laptop," he said. "It's probably still in the car."

Adrienne motioned him to the door. "Caroline, does Eric know who Sleeper, Tool, and Fist are?"

"He should. Asked him to tell Cuddy."

"Where's Eric now, Caroline?"

"In prison. In Berlin."

Adrienne stood and turned her back on the woman slumped in the chair. *The CIA is in Berlin. Interrogating the traitor. They may already know my name.* The face of her son rose in her mind. *Misha. Oh, God, Misha—*

Her veins turned to ice.

They were coming for Misha.

Adrienne ran to her son's locked door.

fifty-three

It was late that evening when he walked back into the Adlon, the lights of the glittering palace immensely comforting after the squalor of death on Eberswalderstrasse. Scottie hesitated before crossing the luxurious lobby. He wanted a shot of ice-cold vodka to settle his nerves. It had been a close-run thing.

Too close, he thought now as he decided against the public bar and moved swiftly toward the elevator. *How had he freed himself from those cuffs and chains? Who helped him? One of the prison guards?*

Cuddy's face rose in Scottie's mind, and the single phrase half caught in the kaleidoscope of moments: *Eric, run!*

Cuddy, then, in all probability. The thing would have to be investigated in the morning. This would give him an excuse to fire the bastard; Cuddy had served his purpose.

He loosened his tie as the steel cage ascended, jet lag and a curious sensation of anticlimax flooding his body. Josie, wherever she was, had come through in the end like the professional she'd always been. One instant there was a man teetering on the edge of freedom—a man with the face of Nemesis and Scottie's entire future trapped in his hands—and the next second, a discarded parcel of flesh and bone, dead on the Berlin street.

Problem solved.

He would call Rinehart immediately, regardless of the time difference.

The elevator door slid open, and he stepped decisively out into the hallway. It was remarkable how easy they had all made it for him—his devoted colleagues. There'd been Cuddy, falling to his knees beside the body, and Wally Aronson urging in a persistent undertone, "You've got to get away from here. You drew your gun and Eric's dead. The BKA isn't going to like having their terrorist prize snatched from the jaws of justice. They'll call it a CIA setup."

"I never fired the thing," he'd protested, still bemused by the velocity of what had happened.

"The shot came from somewhere to the east, but we can't risk your involvement with the police. They'll be here soon. You're too important, Scottie. Get in the car. Get out of here. I'll deal with this mess. That's my job."

He and Cuddy had been hustled into the Explorer and driven immediately south toward Pariser Platz, the anonymity of their cover names on the hotel registry. Cuddy's hands were smeared with blood where he'd touched Eric's back, and his breathing rasped audibly in the car's silence, fast and hoarse, as though he'd been running. Or weeping. He kept his face turned toward the streaming lights of the Mitte District, and

Scottie could not tell if his cheeks were damp; it was still raining.

Let Cuddy cry. Somebody ought to mourn Eric. He'd been a good man in his way, but all good men were expendable.

He thrust the key card into the electronic pad and turned the heavy brass door handle. The room beyond was pitch-black. As he groped for the light switch, he wondered irritably what had happened to his turn-down service. No soft music, no plumped pillows, no square of linen spread neatly under his complimentary slippers. The door clicked shut behind him as the room flooded with light, and he saw her.

Josie.

She was leaning in the doorway of his marble bath as though she'd been waiting for him.

Of course she'd been waiting for him.

He grinned hugely and held out his arms. "Hey, beautiful! That was a hell of a show you put on to-night. Why are you sitting in the dark? And how'd you get in here?"

She smiled back, a smile that didn't reach her eyes. "I'm a Second-Story Girl, remember?"

"Patrick taught you all his tricks, didn't he?" He strolled toward her—toward the familiar coarse-skinned face and strawberry-colored hair, the thickened middle-aged body and the stumpy calves, the clothes she persisted in buying at discount warehouses despite the fortune he'd paid her over the past dozen years. "*Josie.* My one true friend. It's been a hell of a ride, hasn't it?"

"Tell me what happened in Bogotá," she said abruptly.

He stopped short, his hand on the silk tail of his necktie. An instant's pause and he dropped it carelessly to the bed. "The night Patrick died? I've told you. Countless times. He was blown in the middle of a ticklish job and shot in the back. Killed instantly—by the bullet or the four-story drop to the street below. Why?"

"Who fired the gun, Scottie?"

She was still leaning against the bathroom doorframe, staring at him intently, and it occurred to him to wonder whether her jobs left her this way—whether the act of pulling the trigger and cutting off a man's life inevitably brought Patrick and his sins to mind. "God knows. He was climbing into the Soviet embassy. Any one of those goons could have done it. An unfortunate casualty of the Cold War."

"But they didn't, did they? I know the second-story drill. One guy on the ground, one effecting entry. Radio communications. Dead of night. The guy on the ground covers his partner's back. He pulls him out when the shit goes down. *Only you didn't pull him out,* Scottie. You shot Patrick like a coward. You left him to die. *Why?* What had he ever done to you?"

Her teeth were bared in the terrible grimace of tears and she was close to snapping, Scottie realized.

"You need a drink," he said.

"I need the truth." She raised her right hand and he understood for the first time why she'd been leaning so fixedly against the doorframe, that incongruously slack yet rigid posture: She'd been hiding her handgun. Not the Austrian Steyr she used for long-range shots, but a neat little Beretta with a silencer he'd never seen.

He stepped backward, his hands rising in a gesture of calm. "Josie. We can talk about this."

"You can talk. I'll listen."

He sank backward onto the edge of the king-size bed. "Patrick was a good man."

"So why'd you kill him, Scottie?"

Her eyes locked on his; the faded blue held no compassion, no pain or mercy. Only a frightening resolution. But charm had always worked with Josie; she was lonely as hell, the sort of woman no man looked at twice; she craved male banter, the cajoling sense of camaraderie. She craved Scottie, had slaved for him over the years despite the string of wives and lovers; she craved Scottie and had settled instead for Patrick.

"You know, Josie," he said genially, "if Patrick had a fault, it was that incredible curiosity of his. He couldn't leave things alone. Couldn't let certain dogs lie."

"He blackmailed you?"

"He blackmailed me. We won't bother discussing about what. It was all so long ago. But what could I do?" He lifted his palms, a helpless little boy.

"Send him home," she said tersely.

"Too insecure. There was the future to consider."

"Ah. The *future*. So you traded my and my daughter's and Patrick's future for your own, is that it?"

"You'd have done the same yourself," he answered reasonably. "You know how these situations work."

"Yes, Scottie. I do." She studied him thoughtfully. "A professional always thinks of Number One. Never leaves an end untied."

"Exactly. And we're both professionals. Look at the work you did out there tonight. Was that the mark of an amateur? A softy who doesn't know the ropes? Not a chance." He stood up and stepped toward her, all his affection in his face. "And it hasn't been so bad. Think of the life we've shared, Josie! I owe you everything. Thanks."

"No thanks necessary." She lowered the silenced Beretta. "I didn't do your job tonight, Scottie. I've been sitting here in the dark for the past three hours. Sometimes the truth is worth more than you can pay."

It was Cuddy who found him: Cuddy who'd come over to Scottie's room at one o'clock in the morning with his resignation typed and ready. He found the door ajar and the music softly playing, light spilling out gently into the hallway. Scottie's elegant silver head lying back on the pillows with a single neat hole in the center of his brow.

It's too bad she didn't leave her gun, Raphael said dispassionately when Cuddy ran down to Room 419 and pounded on the door. *We could have made it look like suicide. The important thing, all the same, is to get that signed confession. Do you know where he put it?*

They lifted Eric's last sacrifice from the inner pocket of Scottie's briefcase, careful to leave no prints. And left the body for the Adlon's maids to find.

fifty-four

When Adrienne had gone, shooting like an arrow toward the rooms at the rear of the house, Caroline opened her eyes. Though her right arm hurt like hell and she didn't want to think about what her nose might look like, she was no longer groggy. The effects of the thiopental sodium were wearing off. Price had gone for the laptop. Adrienne had left her alone. She would have only seconds.

Wrists and ankles bound, she thrust herself painfully to a standing position, wavering drunkenly under the last dregs of sedative. She remembered the scalpel in Price's hand, the severing of her left sleeve. There were knives somewhere. She had to find one.

...under the sterilizing lights.

She glanced wildly around. Voices from the hallway, a child's flat words, adamant but emotionless. Adrienne more urgent. Thudding footsteps.

The lab. Where was Price?

She stumbled toward the light, desperate to reach it. Saw the steel lancets and blades glinting wickedly in the heated glow. Her hands were bound behind her, the fingers wooden and bloodless; she was too clumsy.

She turned her back on the tray full of instruments, scrabbling. She would have to hold whatever she caught blade-down, pray the surface was sharp enough to slice strapping tape.

Ignoring the clutch of panic at her throat, she reached for an instrument and sliced the pad of her pinkie. The bloody scalpel slithered from her hand and clattered to the floor.

Fuck.

The sound of a car door slamming. Price and the laptop. The boy's voice rising, now, in a cry of protest; Adrienne barked an order. Caroline clutched again, uncaring whether her fingers bled. Found the handle of a lancet. Shoved it ruthlessly at her own wrists, hands straining. The upper edge of the tape, wound maybe three times around, parted slightly; she felt the tension give. *Come on.* She hacked with awkward fingers, the blade slipping, turning sideways. *Come on, come on—*

"I want you in the Jeep in three minutes," Adrienne's voice said harshly, nearer now; and Caroline thought: *I spooked her. She'll kill me before she goes.*

As the woman appeared in the doorway Caroline dropped soundlessly to the floor, gripping the knife, her body only partially screened by the lab table. The empty chair where she'd been sitting brutally obvious. The only sound from Adrienne was an indrawn breath, sharp as a gunshot; then a stillness more terrifying.

The tape at her wrists parted. She stabbed at the bond around her ankles.

Where's Adrienne's Jeep? The door to the garage? She'd seen nothing of the place; she couldn't navigate it. Price lay waiting somewhere beyond the only exit she knew. No help outside, anyway; no salvation. She was in the middle of the woods and miles from any neighbor. The keys to Price's Porsche were in his back pocket.

The panic flooded her body now, but she cut through the last of the tape and soundlessly eased her ankles apart. *Where's Adrienne?* She clutched the lancet in her left hand—the right was useless—and twisted toward the lab table. It was a solid island of wood laminate shelves, used for storing beakers and tubes, microscope slides and titrating equipment, most of it glass. Through the spacing of the shelves she could just glimpse the doorway where Adrienne had stood. It was empty.

She glanced to the left and almost fell backward.

A boy stood five feet away, staring at her curiously. "Mama," he called. "Who's the lady?"

Caroline rolled toward him across the concrete floor. Adrienne shouted *Misha* and sprang, but Caroline reached him first, her arm coming up around his neck with the scalpel poised next to the little-boy skin, the vulnerable softness below the left ear and the jugular pumping steadily beneath it.

Misha began to scream, a thin high-pitched sound like the whistling of a tea kettle. He did not struggle in her grip; instead, he seemed to collapse inward, as though everything that was vital about him shrank away from her touch. *I'm so sorry,* she thought. *So sorry.*

Adrienne had a gun trained on Caroline—brought

from whatever hole she'd sought when she disappeared through the doorway—but it was shaking in
her hand and her gaze was locked on her son.

"He can't stand it," she said, agonized. "He can't
stand to be touched! Let him go—"

"Drop the gun," Caroline said. "Drop it or he
dies."

"You wouldn't," Adrienne whispered. "He's just a
kid."

"He's Mlan's kid," she retorted brutally, "and you
know what I did to *him*."

Adrienne's eyes slid to something behind Caroline's
back—*searching for Price,* she thought—and then her
finger snaked forward and released the gun's safety.
Click. The muzzle still wavered.

"You'll kill your son with that aim," Caroline said
casually. Her ears were straining for the slightest noise
of the man who should be running through the outer
door. The steel scalpel felt warm and plastic in her
grasp.

She tightened her hold on Misha's fragile neck and
the inhuman scream shifted a notch higher. His hands
reached spasmodically toward his mother, fingers rigid.

"Drop the gun," Caroline warned.

The muzzle jerked sideways as it fired, the bullet
singing wildly. A metallic *ping!* as it ricocheted off a
steel shelf, the crash of shivered glass. Caroline threw
Misha to the floor, her mouth open in a guttural yell,
but Adrienne sank down as though wounded herself.
The gun slipped from her hand.

Caroline rocked slightly on her feet, the knife blade
glued to her sweating fingers. The bullet had buried

itself in a wall behind her, but she was shaking from adrenaline and torn nerves. *Where the fuck is Price?*

"Slide the gun across the floor," she barked hoarsely. "*Slide* it, you understand?"

Adrienne obeyed her. She swayed forward in a heap and thrust the cold steel object across the concrete.

Her right arm screaming, Caroline somehow managed to clutch the thing as it skittered past. Then she released the boy and rose, gun leveled.

He stood between the two of them, and Adrienne stretched out one hand to her son, hands clutching his elbows, frame rocking wildly. Adrienne stumbled to her feet, as though some cord that bound the boy's sanity might snap if she wasn't careful.

"Mama, who's the lady?" he muttered.

The front door banged open.

Price, Caroline thought. *Back to spin the truth.*

She wheeled, weapon raised, steeling herself for one last effort before she died.

But it was Tom Shephard who stood in the doorway, weapon hand extended, all his rage and love in his face.

epilogue

It took her two days to summon the energy to go back to the Tysons Marriott, pay her bill, and retrieve her things.

There had been duties enough in the intervening forty-eight hours. The statement she gave to Tom Shephard's guys about Steve Price and Adrienne O'Brien; the meeting with Cory Rinehart and the presentation of Eric's bootleg CD-ROM filled with the vital information Scottie Sorensen had chosen to destroy; the awkward three hours with a polygrapher while Rinehart checked and double-checked the accuracy of the story she had to tell. He'd preferred Scottie's, there was no question, but the murder of the CTC chief in Berlin and Cuddy's firm avowal of all that had led up to it, delivered in front of the Deputy Director for Operations and the staff of the Inspector General, were facts that could not be ignored by a temporary DCI hoping for permanent appointment. Rinehart caved and ordered Caroline and Cuddy to cooperate fully with the Congressional investigative panel about to be assembled by the Speaker of the House, George Enfield.

By Thanksgiving Day, however, it was clear that

nothing further would be demanded of her until Monday and that she could take the long weekend to heal. *Heal.* Her wounded arm was stiff and her heart was aching, because nothing she'd done in the past week had prevented the disaster she'd been dreading. *Eric is gone.* Cuddy had watched him die, felt his blood on his fingertips, seen the ambulance arrive with its sonic two-toned beat cutting the Berlin night. *Raphael says it was an organized hit,* he'd told her. *Probably paid for by Scottie. We'll never know.*

She stopped by Bethesda Naval and kissed Jozsef's forehead as he lay near his intravenous feed. Tom Shephard was sitting at the boy's bedside. She had been avoiding dealing with Tom for most of the past day. She could not get the image of Tom's face out of her mind—his face as it had looked in Adrienne O'Brien's laboratory. Almost inhuman. He had stood over the woman and her boy, gun raised and arm shaking with the violence of what he'd done, Steve Price dead on the driveway outside and now these two in his power. For an instant Caroline had been terrified the gun would go off and blast Misha's head to smithereens. Urgently, she'd said, "Tom. *Tom.* It's okay. I'm *okay...*" and then the rest of his team had filed into the room and the moment of terror had passed.

The rage and exhaustion were gone from Shephard's face now, but his eyes were no less haunted. When he looked at her, Caroline saw a raft of questions she had no energy to answer. He knew that Eric was gone.

She chatted instead with the boy in the hospital bed about the tradition of Thanksgiving, the origins of turkey, what it meant to be a Pilgrim—things Jozsef would rather discuss than the details of his kidnapping and the death that had found Daniel Becker on the Greyhound bus station floor. When eventually she rose to leave, she clasped the boy's hand in hers.

"I'll drop my phone number at the nurses' station, okay? In case you need somebody to talk to in the middle of the night."

He glanced up at her swiftly; the dark eyes were impossible to read. "It doesn't help," he told her. "Nobody wants to listen at two o'clock in the morning."

"I do," she replied firmly. "I'm insomniac. Call."

He grinned at her then—the first purely kidlike expression she'd seen on his face—and watched her go out the door.

Tom Shephard followed.

"He's okay." He offered it as though she needed the reassurance. "I'm sure he'll spend years in therapy once he realizes such things exist. Or maybe he'll turn to a life of crime as the best possible use of his talents and experience."

"Where does he go when the IV feed runs out?"

"With me," Tom said quietly. "I'm heading back to Berlin in about ten days."

The firmness of the words surprised her. "So soon?"

"Jozsef's got a grandmother somewhere in the former Yugoslavia. I'm trying to locate her. I think he'd be better off with family—much better off in a culture he knows. There's too much notoriety here. He needs to heal, not to walk the world under a camera lens."

"And you, Tom? What's in Berlin for you?"

"The rest of my tour. The rest of my life." His eyes did not waver from her face. "Want to come?"

She took a step back, as though the distance might buy her time.

And when she did not reply, he said with difficulty, "I heard what happened to your . . . to Eric. I'm so sorry, Carrie—for everything that's happened to you in the past month. You've been living your own kind of hell. I refused to understand that."

Her eyes blurred with tears; sympathy from Tom had the power to undo her. "I would never have lied to you for anybody else. I had no choice."

"You loved him that much?"

"I still do."

"We all need to begin again, Caroline. You, me, the boy in that bed." He nodded toward Jozsef's door. "Couldn't we do it together?"

A boy, Caroline thought achingly. *A kid I could raise and love. What Eric and I always wanted—*

But not Eric's boy. Not Eric's dream.

There was no way to tell Tom what it felt like, today, with Eric dead for good this time. How she saw the film in slow motion, over and over again, every time she closed her eyes: Eric racing toward the yellow Humvee. The staggering stride, the body crumpling to the ground. The blood pooling on wet asphalt and the shocked disbelief on Cuddy's face. She had not been there to save him. She had not even tried. She'd chased her own wild goose; she'd never even known the exact moment when Eric stopped breathing.

Looking at Tom Shephard, she searched for the right words.

"It's way too soon," she said softly.

He pulled her gently toward him. She went with a

sigh into his arms, shaky as a child after a bout of weeping, and felt the deep and abiding comfort there.

"You're such a good man, Tom, and you'd spend your life trying to make me happy. I'd fail you at every turn."

"Don't say that," he murmured.

"It's true." She listened to the steady throb of his heartbeat through the Oxford-cloth shirt. "I'd always be looking for the ghost over my shoulder. I'd always be looking for Eric."

He held her away from him, all his pain in his eyes. "I wish I'd known the fucking bastard," he said. "Maybe then I'd understand what it takes to inspire that kind of love."

"I suppose," she said slowly, "I've never wanted very much to be safe."

It was the only explanation she had. All her life, men had tried to take care of her and she had thrust them away, walking purposefully toward the one who lived like a wolf, the one who understood that danger was at the very heart of what mattered . . .

"Promise me, Carrie, that if anything ever changes for you . . . that you'll get in touch . . ."

His arms fell to his sides, and that swiftly, she was alone with her pain again.

She began to walk along the corridor. Tom fell into step beside her.

"Where will you go?" he asked.

Caroline had no idea. She'd told Rinehart she didn't want her security clearance reinstated, she didn't need her old cubby back in the Counterterrorism Center.

She was done with the CIA. She was thinking of visiting Uncle Hank on Long Island. Spending Christmas at a beach. That the image she'd held in her mind was one of sunlight and freedom—not the frigid tundra of Montauk in December—she didn't bother to mention. Her dreams had a habit of coming true in ways she'd never wanted.

In the echoing marble entryway of Bethesda Naval she found Cuddy waiting for her: Cuddy with his bland, impersonal exterior, his willingness to be overlooked, the essential masking of the spy. He took Shephard's hand and refused to notice any tension between them and made it easier, as he always had, for Caroline to say good-bye.

"I'll take you back to the Marriott," he informed her when Shephard had walked alone through the revolving doors. "Your car's still parked at Dulles."

She let him steer her toward his small Toyota without the slightest protest. Sank back in his leather seats without the need for further conversation. They'd talked about the past week enough already to need only this silence. The ride, if anything, would be too brief.

Only when he pulled the car without warning sharply off the road did she open her eyes. They weren't at the Marriott at all—weren't even on the road there. He'd driven her straight to one of the rest areas on the George Washington Parkway. It was a lonely place at this time of year. The trees were leafless and the river thundered brownly far below.

"What are you doing?"

"Quick change of plans," he replied briskly. "Raphael's

idea. He's meeting us here and I think you ought to listen to what he has to say."

"I know he tried. To help Eric. It wasn't his fault—"

"Raphael never apologizes." Cuddy thumbed his glasses. "Particularly when his plans go well. He's thought of a way for us all to turn a quick buck. Raphael's got a *vision thing*, you know? He says the future of intelligence—of security operations—is going to be private sector. He thinks we should pool our talents and form a corporation. Somewhere offshore. In the Grand Caymans, actually. Probably because Eric's numbered bank account is there—the one where Scottie deposited his pay for the past thirty months—and though it's only about three hundred grand right now, we figure you could get at least six hundred thou for the Tara town house whenever you decide to sell it. Call it a million. Enough to keep the four of us in scuba gear and suntan lotion for at least a year."

She stared at him, her tired mind moving too slowly. "You call Eric's murder a *plan gone well*?"

He shrugged. "Got him off the hook, didn't it? No trials, no prison, no life term without parole. No Scottie breathing down his neck for the rest of his life. No FBI hunting him the world over. Yeah, I think Rafe did a damn fine job. I told him from the outset that I wanted him to end Eric's life permanently this time. No paper trail, no physical evidence, no questions asked—"

She seized his lapel tightly between her fingers and dragged him across the armrest. "Cuddy—"

"It was Wally's guys who pulled the trigger," he said apologetically. "Wally's guys who sedated him with a single shot and carted him off in a rented ambulance—"

"Are you telling me Eric's *alive*, God damn you?"

For answer, he looked over her shoulder.

A classic 1967 Lotus, bottle green and shining, was pulling up behind them. Raphael's blond head was behind the wheel.

The Grand Caymans, she thought madly. *Pool our resources. A beach with nothing on it.*

The winged doors lifted. A dark-haired man in wire-rimmed glasses lunged out, ignoring the cliffs of the Potomac and the distant sound of traffic and the black-feathered rooks wheeling tragically overhead.

And ran to her.

author's note

This book owes its existence to the patient and intelligent handling of my editor at Bantam Dell Books, Kate Miciak, to whom I am more than usually indebted. Thank you, Kate, for your cogent replies to all those e-mails and your unflagging support. Both were essential.

Most authors are the sum of their recent reading, and I am no exception. Four books in particular were my constant aids and inspiration in writing this novel. On the subject of neo-Nazism in America, Daniel Levitas's *The Terrorist Next Door* is perhaps the most exhaustively researched, persuasive, and troubling volume available. Regarding tradecraft operations and Moscow Rules, I must recommend Milt Bearden and James Risen's book *The Main Enemy*, which had the power to keep me up reading late when nothing else did. And in the matter of disguise, exfiltration, and the intriguing operations of the Office of Technical Services, Antonio J. Mendez's memoir of a life-time running "Q" branch, *The Master of Disguise*, is as entertaining as it is informative. I learned about the FBI's Hostage Rescue Team from Special Agent Christopher

Whitcomb's remarkable memoir of the sniping trade, *Cold Zero*.

My thanks also go out to those members of the Central Intelligence Agency's Publications Review Board who read this book in manuscript form and cleared it for publication.

Francine Mathews
Golden, Colorado
May 2004

about the author

FRANCINE MATHEWS spent four years as an intelligence analyst at the CIA, where she trained in operations and worked briefly on the investigation into the 1988 bombing of Pan Am Flight 103. A former journalist, she lives and writes in Colorado, where she is at work on her next thriller, *The Alibi Club*.

"Mathews, a former CIA intelligence analyst, dexterously serves up strong suspense and crisp espionage maneuvers.... A riveting, wild ride right to the nail-biting conclusion!"
—*Publishers Weekly*

If you enjoyed Francine Mathews's *BLOWN*, you won't want to miss any of her acclaimed thrillers. Look for *The Cutout* and *The Secret Agent* at your favorite booksellers.

And read on for an early look at her next electrifying novel of suspense, *THE ALIBI CLUB*, coming soon in hardcover from Bantam Books.

THE ALIBI CLUB

BY

FRANCINE MATHEWS

On sale September 2006

FRANCINE MATHEWS

A NOVEL

THE ALIBI CLUB

THE ALIBI CLUB

On sale September 2006

PROLOGUE

MARCH 12, 1940

There were nine people waiting in the stuffy room that faced the aerodrome's tarmac, ten if you counted the sleeping child swaddled in a blanket in the Italian girl's arms. Three women, six men, several nationalities, and the brazen churn of propellers beyond the frosted window. Each of the waiting passengers was desperate enough to leave Oslo in the dead of night and dead of winter, so the air hummed with suppressed violence and restlessness and incipient hysteria. No one spoke.

Jacques Allier had his back to the wall nearest the door, an evening newspaper grasped in one gloved hand, the other thrust in his pocket. The unheated room was freezing, but his skin was beaded with sweat and his hidden fingers clutched a gun.

The clock read three minutes until midnight. The plane would leave at 12:07. Allier's passport had been taken ten minutes ago and not returned. The man named Demars—who had all his luggage—was inexplicably missing from the aerodrome, and this was only one of the factors contributing to Allier's sweat. He hated to fly. When he'd undertaken this operation he'd asked for a submarine out of Brest. A destroyer from Tønsberg. He'd gotten an eight-seater with ice on its wings and no guns to speak of.

He was praying he'd be allowed to board, although Allier was one of those who could not believe in God. Not now.

He was a spare, bland-faced man in the good cloth coat and spectacles of a banker, mid-forties perhaps, clearly European but shockingly unmilitary for the times. His eyes drifted away from the damning clock—the man Demars was still missing—and roved indifferently over the faces of his fellow passengers. Two men arguing politics in Dutch. A gawky boy in his teens, his looks feverish and his hands drumming nervously against the arm of his chair, fingers spilling cigarette ash onto the linoleum floor. A gray-haired woman stolidly eating pickled herring from a waxed paper box furnished by an Oslo shop. None of them spoke. None made eye contact. Only the tall, burly blond fellow in the impeccable camel-hair coat was staring openly, a slight smile curving his lips, at the Italian girl with the sleeping child.

And who could blame him? Allier thought irritably. She was exquisite, with her fur collar grazing her faintly flushed cheek, her dark knot of hair shining beneath the arc of her hat. Her fingers were gloved in ostrich skin; the frail hunch of her shoulders might reflect the penetrating cold, or the solicitude that kept her bent, Madonna-like, over the face of her infant. Was she even twenty? Her passport and ticket lay on the hard wooden bench beside her; like Allier, she was bound for Amsterdam in the dead of night.

Turn back, he urged. *Go north. Go west. Go anywhere but home.* He had caught one glimpse of her mouth, curved like a G clef, and her eyes, disconcertingly blue in an olive-skinned face. The blond hero opposite had glimpsed them, too.

"Madam," the man said gently in Italian, "you look

chilled to the bone. Perhaps a cigarette? . . . If I were to light it for you . . . ?"

The girl ignored him, failing to so much as lift her head. Allier exulted in this, in the snub offered the blond hero who might from his looks have been Norwegian or even English but who Allier knew now was German—a broad-shouldered, perfect German in civilian dress lounging in the very aerodrome where he, Allier, had elected to escape. This could not be coincidence; this was part of a plan. The fact of the German presence meant that Allier was already a dead man. Demars and the luggage would not be coming.

He tossed the folded newspaper into a waste bin and moved casually toward the door leading out to the planes. One of them bound for Perth, the other for Amsterdam. The propellers whined in the cold, the pilots worried about ice. It was possible that they would all be told to go home—to try again tomorrow—and for Allier there would be the certainty of an armed escort at some point along his route back to the French legation, a sudden flurried movement into an enemy car, a bullet in the temple after how many agonizing hours of interrogation? He continued to stare through the waiting room window, his gloved hands clasped behind his back. Conscious of movement. Some kind of rank closing behind.

It was barely two weeks since he'd vaulted up the marble steps of the Armaments Ministry and accepted the fake passport in his mother's maiden name. *Freiss.* He was Michel Freiss of Salzburg, aged forty-one, a banker with no interest in this phony war between France and the Germans that had been going on for seven months now without a shot fired. That night he'd taken the last train across the border, bound for Amsterdam, and then by slow degrees traveled north to Stockholm and finally Oslo. There were five days of negotiation in a tiny snowbound town near the Telemark mountains, ponderous dinners and pledges of eternal friendship and risky flourishes of the French flag. Oblique counsels in the legation, none of the usual diplomats in on the secret, and the lights burning all night in the German intelligence pavilion across the garden wall.

"You're famous," the French ambassador assured him with a twisted smile. "Everybody wants to talk to you. Our people caught this the day you left Paris."

It was a decoded German radio transmission he carelessly handed Allier: *At any price intercept a suspect Frenchman traveling under the name of Freiss.* What the ambassador had not bothered to point out was that Allier had been betrayed before he'd boarded the night train to Amsterdam.

Who? he asked himself now. *A spy in Dautry's office? Somebody at the bank?*

The two-beat note of a police siren was audible, suddenly, in the distance; insistent, rising, certainly closer.

Perhaps it was the lab. One of Joliot's people. Or fucking Demars. He's probably sold the luggage.

"Mr. Freiss," said a voice at his elbow.

He turned, caught the untroubled face of Norwegian Border Control. A woman, neatly uniformed. Her clipped hair so fair it might almost be white. She was offering him a bunch of papers, but he ignored her extended hand. The police sirens had pulled up to the aerodrome door. The butt of his gun twisted in his fingers, slippery with sweat. In a matter of seconds the door would burst open, a clutch of men tripping over themselves in their haste to seize him. He might have time to take one of them down—the big German, perhaps—but there were these women, that child in the Madonna's arms...

"Your passport and ticket for Amsterdam," Border Control persisted. "Everything is in order. You may proceed to the tarmac."

He glanced over her head and met the German's eyes. The man was still smiling faintly, the same indulgent look he'd turned on the young Italian princess, who was rising now from her seat, magnificent and indifferent. *He's let me run all this way so he could follow my trail*, Allier thought. *I'll lead him no further.*

He took his passport and ticket from the woman's hand and without a word held the door wide. The Italian girl flicked him one glance from her arresting blue eyes as she passed; not even this, Allier thought, was comfort before dying. Then he and the blond hero followed her into the cold.

There was confusion about the planes: a huge black Daimler had driven straight onto the tarmac and thrust itself between them. A man was running distractedly beneath the wings, shouting inaudibly over the clatter of the engines and barely avoiding the propellers. His driver pulled an astonishing number of suitcases from the idling car. The police and their sirens were silent now, beyond the runway gates; it was the Daimler they had escorted through the streets of Oslo, wailing right up to the Amsterdam flight. Allier felt his face flush with heat and his hands clench: *This is what hope feels like. Terror and a clenched fist.* He recognized the dapper, black-haired figure pirouetting beneath the fuselage; he recognized the suitcases. Demars's driver was loading them even now into the belly of the Perth plane.

Allier counted them as best he could across the distance and darkness. *Thirteen,* he thought. *Please God let there be thirteen.*

Demars collided headlong with the German's camelhair coat; whiskey fumes and cigar smoke wafted through the frigid night air.

"Pardon, most esteemed sir." He spoke Norwegian and he clutched the German's sleeve like a spoiled child. "Which of these is the Amsterdam plane? Have I missed it? I must at all costs make the Amsterdam plane!"

They argued the destination of both flights, the Daimler's right to park in the middle of the tarmac, the abuse of police escort, the advisability of arriving on time. Allier kept walking. He did not look back. The Italian girl boarded the Amsterdam plane with a grimace on her face, the saintly infant now screaming in her arms. Allier's ticket fluttered to the ground. He pulled a second one—stamped for Perth—from his breast pocket.

As the Amsterdam pilot taxied toward his takeoff, Allier caught a glimpse of the blond German under the tarmac lights: hatless, his coat flying back like wings, running hopelessly after the wrong plane.

Fog diverted them. As was expected.

They landed near dawn in a town Allier had never heard of, somewhere on the east coast of Scotland. A small field, quite deserted, the waiting-room windows blacked out with painted canvas. The pilot gave him tea. From politeness he tried to drink it.

"Did you hear?" the man asked him. "The Germans shot down that plane. The one bound for Amsterdam last night."

Allier thought of the young Italian girl, the two men arguing in Dutch, the child that would have been wailing, certainly, as the flames bloomed in the cockpit and the frantic pilot beat them back. The long tight fall into the North Sea, implacable as a destroyer's hull.

He set down the tea.

"What have you got in all those suitcases?" the pilot asked curiously. "The crown jewels of Norway?"

Allier glanced at the man. The truth was a breach of security but the pilot would never believe him, anyway.

"Water," he replied.

AMERICAN BUSINESS

CHAPTER ONE

Later, they would remember that spring as one of the most glorious they'd ever known in Paris. The flowering of pleached fruit trees and the scent of lime blossom crushed underfoot, the chestnuts unfurling their leaves in ordered ranks along the Champs-Élysées, the women's silks rustling like wings as they hurried to dinner—all had a perilous sweetness, like absinthe. Sally King, who had lived in the city for nearly three years now and might be acknowledged as something of an expert, maintained that even when it rained Paris was ravishing. The streets shone in the sudden torrents regardless of grime or automobile petrol or the piss in the open urinals; they glistened with a brilliance that was consumptive and suicidal.

She was surging against the tide of people on the Pont Neuf that night, across the narrowest point of the little island that sat like a raft in the middle of the Seine, having already fought her way past the shuttered bookstalls of the Quai de la Tournelle. She did not move swiftly, because the French heels of her evening sandals caught in the cracks between the paving stones. It was dark, blackout dark, and she would have liked a taxi but there were none to be found. She could sense the panic in the hunched shoulders and too-rapid steps of the Parisians, some of whom turned despite their fear and stared at her openly: Sally King, tall and angular, all her beauty in the impossible length of her legs, the clarity of her frame beneath the candy-wrapper gown.

She had been living among them long enough now to perfect her schoolgirl French and she understood the spattering of rumor and fear. *They've broken through the line. The Boches are through at Sedan. The army is in retreat—*

The news from the Front had blown through the city like a boiling wind. A whisper on the northern outskirts. The report of a friend of a friend. The streets were blazing with half-truths and exaggeration under the deep blue dusk of the shaded lights, and most people were milling south. Sally pushed north, toward the Right Bank and the exquisite little flat fronting on the Louvre. Philip Stilwell's place.

He had left her waiting at a table with a splendid view of Notre-Dame, conspicuously alone at La Tour d'Argent, not her favorite restaurant in Paris but certainly the most expensive. It was unusual for a woman to arrive without an escort but Gaston Masson, La Tour's manager, was accustomed to the peculiarities of Americans. If the rest of his diners chose to speculate on the cost of Sally's dress, her probable immorality, her purpose in waiting nearly an hour for a man who never showed up—she was at least decorative, and hence valuable against the backdrop of the Seine. Her face, with its high cheekbones and too-wide smile, was said to be famous. She was freakishly tall. She carried a gas-mask case instead of a purse and wore last year's Schiaparelli—an economical gesture in time of war. Shocking-pink silk, embroidered with acid green bugs.

"Perhaps M. Stilwell is delayed," Masson observed

apologetically. "If the Germans have broken our line . . . if they have crossed the Meuse and even now are on the march through Belgium . . . a lawyer might have much to do . . ."

But not tonight, Sally thought as she picked her way across the ancient bridge. *Tonight he was going to ask me to marry him.*

The note had come at five o'clock, hand-delivered by one of Sullivan & Cromwell's messengers because she had no telephone in her flat in the Latin Quarter. *Sally dearest I might be a little late for dinner this evening as I've an appointment with a member of the firm . . . Ask Gaston to seat you and order up a bottle of champagne. . . .* A lawyer's wife, she'd thought, would have to adjust to such things. But Philip had never come; and rudeness was unlike him.

At the end of the bridge she hesitated. The darkened bulk of the Louvre loomed on her left. Without its usual blaze of light the city seemed forlorn and spectral, the people muttering through the streets like an army of the dead. Sally heard an air-raid siren shrill, and the high-pitched tinkle of breaking glass. A woman sobbed. Gooseflesh rose along her bare arms and she understood how solitary she was, how vulnerable. She ought to head for a bomb shelter, but nothing had fallen on Paris during the tedious eight months of phony war, so she squared her shoulders and walked toward Philip.

Another woman would have doubted herself. Assumed that he hadn't shown because he didn't love her. That simple thought never occurred to Sally. She had mapped Philip's soul quite thoroughly during the long months of the past winter, her job abruptly over, the whole question of her future hanging in the balance. She knew he'd been worried for weeks, and that it had something to do with S&C—with his work at the law firm of Sullivan & Cromwell.

They'd met the previous August, Philip new to Paris and losing his way on the Rue Cambon, searching for S&C's door and stumbling instead into the House of Chanel, which sat at number 31. Sally had been descending the famous staircase—Coco's preferred runway—to the admiration of the men and women seated expectantly below. It was Mademoiselle's fall collection, the last collection she would design for years, as it turned out. Sally had worn one of Coco's little black dresses, very chic and timeless in the usual manner; it was Chanel who'd made black fashionable when it had always been strictly for mourning. That August the color was disastrous, a presage of Poland's martyrdom, all diesel fumes and charred steel.

Philip watched the entire show from the doorway, and when approached by one of the *vendeuses,* stammered something about shopping for his mother. Sally'd agreed to have dinner with him, although she never really ate during the couture season. It was the beginning of an affair that had carried her headlong to this final night, the empty chair across the snowy linen, the curious gaze of the Paris streets. *A meeting with a member of the firm,* he'd said. And something had gone wrong.

Philip, she thought, fear knifing jaggedly through her. *Philip.*

She'd hung on all winter and spring in her apartment in the Latin Quarter, believing the news would change—hostilities would end—Hitler would go away. She rehearsed the truths Coco had taught her over the past three years, her inner voice less cultivated and more Western: *Raise the waist in front and a girl looks taller. Lower the back, and you hide a drooping ass. Dip the hemline in the rear because it'll hitch up along the hips. Everything's in the shoulders. A woman should cross her arms when her measurements are taken: that way she allows for enough give.*

He lived just off Rue de Rivoli where it met Rue St-Honoré. An old limestone pile arranged around a courtyard, a tall double doorway flung open all day. Some dead aristocrat's *hôtel particulier,* long since sliced into flats. Not a fashionable address, but Philip was too young and too foreign to know that. He wanted the heart of Paris: a view of the river from his salon, the cries of the knife-grinders beneath his window, church bells crashing into his bed at all hours of the night. Cracked boiserie and parquet that screamed underfoot. Mirrors so fogged they resembled pewter. Sally had lived in Paris longer but Philip loved the city better, loved the heartiness of her food and the guttural accents and the birdcages on the Ile Saint-Louis. Sunday mornings the two of them threw open the shutters and leaned on the windowsills, their shoulders suspended over the street, staring out at the world until their eyes ached.

She had four blocks still to walk when she saw the phalanx of cars from the *préfecture de police.* Philip's double-doored entry sprawled wide. Catching up her gas mask and silk dress, she began to run in the vicious sandals, straps cutting into her feet.

He was tied to the mahogany bedposts by his wrists and ankles, blood spattered the length of his nude body. She stood in the bedroom doorway swaying slightly, the police still unaware of her presence, and studied him: slack mouth, startled gray eyes, the latticework of ribs too embarrassingly white. The armpits monkeylike, the gourd of the hips and the knot of pubic hair at the groin, glistening with wetness. The erection still flagrant, even in death. Philip's penis, alert and red, something she'd touched once in a car. The whip forgotten on the rug beneath him. There was another man, also nude but a stranger to her, dangling from the chandelier. His toes were horribly callused, the joints blistered yellow.

Her mouth twisted and she must have gasped something in English—Philip's name, possibly—because one of the official French turned his head sharply and saw her, incongruous in her shocking-pink gown. He scowled and crossed the room in three strides, blocking her view.

"Out, mademoiselle."

"But I know him!"

"I'm sorry, mademoiselle. You cannot be here. Antoine! *Vite!*"

She was grasped by the arm not ungently and led from the apartment, past the divan on which they'd had quick suppers, past the shutters they'd thrown open, a pair of highball glasses half-filled with drink. The wastebasket had overturned, and a few shards of glass were scattered on the threadbare Aubusson. She was dragged beyond the obscene figure dangling from the chandelier and into the hallway, where she began to shudder uncontrollably and the young man, Antoine—he wore a regular gendarme's uniform, not a detective's khaki raincoat—stood uncertainly clutching her elbow.

"Sally."

The quiet voice was one she knew. Max Shoop, who ran S&C's Paris office, in his elegant French clothes, his eyes remote and expressionless. They would have called Max, of course. She turned to him as a small child turns its face into its mother's apron, whimpering, her eyes scrunched closed.

"Sally," Max said again, and put an awkward hand on her bare shoulder. "I'm—sorry. I wish you hadn't seen that."

"Philip—"

"He's dead, Sally. He's dead."

"But how...?" She pushed Shoop away, eyes open now and staring directly at him. "What in the world..."

"The police think it was a heart attack." He was uncomfortable with the words and all that had not been said: the meaning of the whip, the determined tumescence. Two men dead with a simultaneity that suggested climax. But Max Shoop was not the kind to admit discomfort: He maintained a perfect gravity, his face as expressionless as though he commented upon the weather.

"Who," she said with difficulty, "is hanging from the ceiling?"

Shoop's eyes slid away under their heavy lids. "I'm told he's from one of the clubs in Montmartre. Did you... *know* about Philip?"

"That he was... that he..." She stopped, uncertain of the words.

"My poor girl." Lips compressed, he led her away from the flat, toward the concierge's rooms one floor below. The good stiff shot of brandy that would be waiting there.

"It's not," she insisted clearly as he paused before the old woman's door, his hand raised to knock, "what you think, you know. It's not what you think."